2nd *hymn a*

Angel at the
Paradise Hotel

To
Gail,
with love e blessings,

Theaa x

Angel at the Paradise Hotel

Teresa O'Driscoll

ROUNDFIRE
BOOKS

Winchester, UK
Washington, USA

JOHN HUNT PUBLISHING

First published by Roundfire Books, 2023
Roundfire Books is an imprint of John Hunt Publishing Ltd., No. 3 East St., Alresford,
Hampshire SO24 9EE, UK
office@jhpbooks.com
www.johnhuntpublishing.com
www.roundfire-books.com

For distributor details and how to order please visit the 'Ordering' section on our website.

ISBN: 978 1 78904 885 8
978 1 78904 886 5 (ebook)
Library of Congress Control Number: 2021941987

A CIP catalogue record for this book is available from the British Library.

Design: Stuart Davies

UK: Printed and bound by CPI Group (UK) Ltd, Croydon, CR0 4YY
Printed in North America by CPI GPS partners

We operate a distinctive and ethical publishing philosophy in
all areas of our business, from our global network of authors to
production and worldwide distribution.

Previous books
Non-fiction

Pray Then Listen: A heart-to-heart with God
Published by Circle Books ISBN 9781789043693

Pray Then Listen: A heart-to-heart with God e-book
Published by Circle Books ISBN 9781789043709

9 Days to Heaven: How to make everlasting meaning of your life
Published by O Books ISBN 9781905047734

9 Days to Heaven: How to make everlasting meaning of your life
e-book
Published by O Books ISBN 9781780999364

For Mum and Dad – with the angels but always in my heart until we meet again...

Always welcome strangers, as by doing this some people have entertained angels without knowing it.
Hebrews 13:2

Prologue

June 2020

Bethany Griffiths sat immobile in the back garden of her Cardiff home, sun warming an upturned face framed by tousled blonde hair. But in her mind she was on the afternoon EasyJet flight winging its way from Bristol to Corfu. A journey so familiar she could almost feel the steady vibration of the engines, and hear her favourite tipple as tonic fizzed over ice into gin and lemon.

Her mouth watered.

This summer, though, there would be no gallivanting to that green and beautiful Greek island, nor anywhere else for that matter.

The whole of the UK was in lockdown. People confined to home for most of the time.

They were caught up in an event that smacked to Bethany of a John Wyndham sci-fi novel. But this was no fictitious *Day of the Triffids*. Neither had the UK become a police state. A tricky new coronavirus, labelled Covid-19 – rampaging around the globe infecting millions and leaving hundreds of thousands dead – had extended its reach to the UK.

The only way to curtail its progress was for people to stay apart. And Bethany was following the rules to the letter.

But on this sunny day, with holiday plans scuppered, she longed to be abroad. To escape as far away as possible the *dread* of being struck down by the terrifying virus.

She guided her thoughts towards Corfu's Korkyra resort, the place she had begun her own Greek Odyssey almost three decades ago.

"A simpler era before mobile phones and emails," she muttered, smiling at the memory of an admittedly stuffy phone booth in the Sunset taverna. "And when people found love by a look of attraction

1

across a crowded room not an internet chatroom!" Her tummy did a little flip at the memory of Aeron's blue gaze across the dance floor of the Candy Bar.

Wriggling into a more comfortable position on her padded wooden chair, bare slim legs stretched over manicured lawn, she was now eager to reminisce. To become, through imagination, a time traveller. And as the years rolled back she began to relive that fateful summer of 1992 which had changed her life, many lives, forever. Though not all for the better.

Yet, it was a summer of hope.

It was the summer she met an angel…!

Chapter 1

June 1992

Angel Gabriella arrowed headlong through the lemon brilliance of a June dawn towards deserted Korkyra beach. Nearing touchdown, with a beat of immense downy wings and agile backflip, she turned feet first. Applying a full-fan brake, her final seconds of descent were sedate.

This was her trademark landing.

Instantly, body, but not wings, became visible, long filmy white tunic billowing around a tall slender frame.

Though almost as old as time itself Gabriella the angel of Greece looked just like an unremarkable young woman in her early twenties, with olive skin, thin face and lips, and short nose.

As her gaze fixed on the small white hotel, self-importantly crowning the headland just above the beach, her large grey eyes brightened with curiosity. "Hmm…," she muttered thoughtfully. No movement yet. The damp sea breeze ruffled pale curls into a halo as she turned to inspect the former fishing hamlet.

In the handful of years since her last visit tourist villas, picked out by the pizazz of their pristine terracotta roofs and spacious balconies, now mingled amiably with weathered pastel homes. Viewed from the beach the buildings looked like tiny squares of rich cream, shell pink or soft ochre, scooped up and scattered haphazardly down green slopes and along the waterfront. The hotel, like a designer's finishing touch, transformed Korkyra into a low-key resort – presently shimmering in morning glory.

But beneath the apparent tranquillity the angel detected the undercurrent of malevolence.

Just then, the mortal, a young dark-haired local man, emerged from a side door of the hotel. A raging, hangover-driven thirst had woken him from a fitful sleep. The lackadaisically dressed Jason, faded navy shorts and T-shirt covering a stocky frame, manoeuvred through the car park, onto the road, and cautiously down the slipway.

The angel delicately sniffed at the air. Yes. She picked up the sulphurous stench of a stalker demon's recent presence, undetectable to humans, lingering around the approaching man like a dog's calling card on a tree.

With alcohol-sensitized light brown eyes squinting against the dazzling sunrise Jason stepped gingerly along the beach. When he stumbled, in a little indent of soft sand, a heavy lock of hair flopped over a broad forehead. Tan skin, lips with full lower and thin bow-shaped top, and a strong nose, all lined up into a boyishly handsome face, which caused many a female, of any age, to do a double-take. Raking the stray hair back with thick splayed fingers, pain stabbed sickeningly in his temples.

Heavy drinking was not his usual style. Last night, though, people lingered so late at his pool bar that he ended up sharing a bottle of Metaxa brandy with a new business contact. Tourists were very welcome for his bank balance. But often he wished they would go to bed earlier.

His mind flitted to that long business conversation. It could lead to a lucrative deal, so maybe the hangover was worth it.

Gabriella, with some distance between them, nonchalantly sank cross-legged onto the shore as if gazing at the gently swelling Ionian Sea. Actually, she was looking at Jason's guardian angel, suspended by spanned wings just above the water. His towering frame was topped with a large head of long wavy hair glowing blue-black against a snowy robe. Gabriella greeted him telepathically. The angels had worked together many times over millennia.

Jason dropped his towel onto night-cooled sand and clawed off shorts and shirt. Adjusting the waistband of skimpy trunks he sprinted, as he had done from childhood, straight into the shallows. He was relying on this dawn dip to clear his brain and set him up for the long stretch until siesta time. Thigh deep he sucked in a preparatory breath, launched through a wavelet and underwater, ignoring the

4

assaulting chill while racing ahead as far as lungs would allow.

Gasping, he sprang up through a silvery comber, arms reaching heavenwards, diver's timepiece winking at the sun.

While Jason purposefully streaked short distances back and forth parallel to the shoreline, Gabriella asked his guardian angel many probing questions.

Things were escalating.

Her arrival was not a moment too soon.

At length, refreshed, Jason waded languidly onto the beach with the unstudied grace of a man now at one with himself and the world. He checked his watch. He had an early meeting with the new contact from last night – who had been keen to set it up. When Jason thought of the potential profit a big smile split his face.

Money was the key to all his plans.

It would make his dreams come true!

With time to spare he sprawled backwards on the towel, stretching as luxuriously as any cat. Idly he grabbed a handful of sand and let the gritty grains trickle through parted fingers. Lulled by the familiar hiss of the incoming sea and its gurgling retreat, he sighed contentedly and slipped into a doze.

The guardian angel hovered above his ward.

A well-primed Gabriella, now eager to speak with the man, jumped up and strode silently towards the prone figure.

Standing over Jason she cast a shadow, and, using her supernatural powers, subtly electrified the atmosphere. The aim was to unsettle him, making him, hopefully, more amenable to her message – a method she often used for such occasions. As Jason's skin suddenly prickled a shiver of apprehension ran up his spine. *Dear God, what on earth is happening to me?*

There it was. He had spoken to God – in whom he did not believe – and that was her cue. "Hello," she said sweetly.

"Oh!" Startled, Jason's body jerked as eyes flew open. Quickly he recovered. "Hello," he echoed, rising onto elbows.

Gabriella slowly withdrew the electric influence.

As the weird feeling receded Jason stared at the girl with interest. *Hmm, nice shiny blonde curls, but plain face.* The girl regarded him steadily. *Good job she can't read my mind!*

But she could.

She was.

So was the guardian angel – who started to chuckle. His gigantic body shook in merriment, inky hair tumbling over thin shoulders.

Gabriella bit back a grin and focussed on her task. When her gaze turned frosty Jason sensed a problem. "What?" he blurted, sitting bolt upright, which reignited the pain in his head.

The angel came straight to the point. "You know, obsession with money can destroy lives." She spoke slowly and emphasized the last two words.

"Excuse me?" Under his deliberately blank expression he was thinking, as most people did, that she looked vaguely familiar, but couldn't quite place her.

"I know you heard me," she said evenly.

Jason nodded. "But I don't know why you're saying that to *me*."

His spine straightened with indignation, and like a politician under fire, as he deflected her real inference his response was suitably skewed.

"I'll have you know that I run the Paradise Hotel and work hard for every drachma!" Gabriella's gaze still accused him. "I don't think it's wrong to be successful," he snapped, defensively. "And when you're successful you make money."

"Yes, but at what cost to others?" she asked bluntly.

He didn't understand what she was talking about. "I charge reasonable prices."

"I am not talking about your prices. It is the human cost I am referring to."

"I don't know what you mean," he stubbornly insisted. Who was this person, this stranger, trying to throw him pearls of wisdom? She couldn't have been more than a couple of years older than him, so hardly in a position to lecture!

Gabriella watched as a scowl pinched his mouth and nose. To disturb his equilibrium she turned up the volume on her power again.

Jason shivered, goose bumps rising on arms and legs. Yet, despite the horrible creepy feeling, the words "human cost" grabbed at him.

His guardian angel whispered into his ear.

His father's face suddenly floated up to his mind's eye.

"Yes, your father is definitely paying for your greed," said Gabriella.

"My father? Why are you talking about my father?" *And why am thinking about him?* Then impatience flared. *My father paying for my greed? If it wasn't for me my father would be... destitute!*

"Destitute is a very strong word," Gabriella commented dryly.

"Destitute?" *What the...?* His frown of confusion was a single deep line between thick dark brows.

Baffled, he looked past the girl and up at the sky – now a flawless aquamarine. His insides felt wobbly. Did he have such a hangover that he didn't know when he was thinking or speaking? He shuddered.

"Whether you accept it or not, your heart has been overcome by greed." Gabriella was gently adamant. The guardian angel nodded vigorously. "And unless you turn from that greed," she paused, her eyes riveting into his, "its destructive poison will seep into *more* lives." Her prolonged steely stare added weight to the warning.

It was vital that he took her seriously.

Jason was finding this whole exchange bizarre.

And yet... And yet... As he looked into her intense grey eyes a part of him wanted to agree with her.

How odd!

The guardian angel was now joined by a second invisible creature. With a high-pitched howl Jason's stalker demon zipped in on fly-like wings and settled proprietorially on its quarry's shoulder. The grey, scaly creature – no bigger than a man's hand – thin tail lashing, red eyes glinting spitefully at the angels, was determined to neutralize Gabriella's warning.

If Jason took heed it would ruin the demon's plans.

There was a great deal at stake.

Everything hung on the man's avaricious nature.

As Jason, unaware, as always, of his invisible companions, continued to consider a new way of living, the demon pushed in on his thoughts.

Stalker demon: "You need to keep making money!"

Jason: *What am I thinking! I need all the money I can make!*

Guardian angel: "There are more important things in life than making money."

Jason: *Hmm... There are lots of things I would like to do in my life but squeezing extra profit from everything takes up so much time.*

Stalker demon: "Everything you want costs money!"

Jason: *But without money I can't do anything!*

Guardian angel: "Money will not bring you the most important things you are dreaming of. Often, when you put things off, thinking you will do them later, that chance is lost forever!"

Jason: *I know I've let lots of opportunities slip through my fingers. I wonder if it's worth it...*

Jason had plenty of work to do looking after the hotel guests and keeping them happy. After that it would be wonderful to have a little extra free time. He knew exactly who he would spend it with!

It was certainly a tantalising idea.

But as his stalker demon continued its diatribe, he inwardly shook himself.

At the age of twenty-two he was now a man, and at this stage in his life it was essential to make as much money as possible. That was definite!

He had another thought. The girl had mentioned destructive poison seeping into lives... Whatever that meant...

Oh well, that was clearly just fantasy on her part.

Everything fell back into place in his head.

No! The girl was mistaken.

He was *not* greedy. He was simply working hard and doing his best.

The triumphant stalker demon cackled loudly like a broody hen. It flicked a long forked tongue derisively in Gabriella's direction then shot away into the distance.

Gabriella ignored its jibe as she spoke to Jason, "You are deluding yourself." Her gaze softened to regret.

His denial could have *terrible* consequences.

Yet she could say no more.

Jason's brain felt fuzzy. He closed his eyes and sank back onto the damp towel.

She raised her left arm with forefinger pointed at his head. Under her power he fell into a deep sleep.

Gabriella instructed the guardian angel. He would orchestrate a vivid dream which they fervently hoped would make Jason more receptive to her warning.

Her work complete, for the moment, she faced the guardian angel, hands crossed briefly over her upper torso – a customary gesture the guardian reciprocated – and they nodded to each other.

Gracefully, she ambled towards the beach path leading to the minimarket. Hidden by a tall grey-green tongued cactus, she became invisible for her next encounter.

Chapter 2

Aeron Lehman peered curiously into the familiar gleaming window of Korkyra Minimarket.

Gabriella and his guardian angel stood side-by-side behind him.

Sporting twin grins the angels stared at the backs of a pair of long, bony legs dawdling below a bulging rucksack crowned by the black dome of a baseball cap. Gabriella pointed and chuckled. "Walking luggage," she quipped.

When the already-scorching sun, playing on those pale limbs, chased the man inside, Gabriella and the guardian angel swooped in over his head.

Jockeying his burden through the narrow entrance, the tinkling of the doorbell vied with hollow clunks as the acoustic guitar, slung in a leather bag over Aeron's front, struck the wall. Behind the checkout the owner glanced up from his newspaper.

"*Ya soo*. Hey there Spiro, how's it goin' man?" Aeron's casual greeting hid a pang of self-doubt. Suddenly desperate for the balm of being remembered, his light blue eyes searched the shopkeeper's face.

"*Ya soo.*" Spiros' thin smile held no recognition, though he knew the man's accent was American. His clothes were a bit of a giveaway too. He was wearing cargo pants. Did anyone really think those tiers of bulging pockets looked good?

Crushed, Aeron gulped. His New York home seemed very far away.

An astute Spiros sighed softly. Many people fell in love with Korkyra resort and came back again. But picking out individuals from the kaleidoscope of visitors was tough.

Other locals said the same thing.

It created a small problem that ran like a dark thread through the season.

A trio of angels watched intently.

All angels were known to each other, but Gabriella had not worked with Aeron's before. The shortest of the three of them, he stroked a dark bushy beard and looked concerned. He was, though, relieved to have the angel of Greece at his side.

As Spiros' guardian looked on, pale eyes wide with concentration, Gabriella spoke to him and he whispered into his ward's ear.

Spiros stared at the man's guitar and had a flashback.

He had seen this American singing at a friend's wedding last summer.

Grinning, a slight underbite marshalling a crowd of white teeth, Spiros rounded the checkout, paunch first, and vigorously pumped Aeron's hand. His firm grip, from many years of freight handling as a seaman, had a settling effect on Aeron.

Gabriella beamed at the angels. It had worked!

Aeron, touched by the now-warm welcome, returned the cordiality with a compliment on the shop's extra room, linked-in by a handsome red brick archway. Should he mention the new competition? He had noticed a second minimarket on the other side of the resort. *No, subject too loaded, man.*

Spiros recalled the visitor's family. "Where your wife and kids?"

Aeron's heart sank as his wife's angry tear-stained face sprang up from memory. In a flash he reminded himself that she had got over that. *Melanie was fine when I left! She understood it was the only way I could avoid going over the edge.* He took a deep breath and lifted his dimpled chin in defiance of his troubled conscience. "I'm taking a break alone," he answered. Huffing through parted lips he shook his head. "Too stressed out, man."

"*Katalaveno.* I understand." Spiros' small dark eyes closed briefly as he sighed with empathy.

Aeron was baffled. Surely, in this idyllic place no one suffered from stress. Did they? He had presumed not. But maybe that was naïve.

Meanwhile, Spiros wondered what Aeron's problem was. Definitely not money-worries like his, because everyone knew tourists were rich. How he wished he was rich!

He knew about stress all right. In his mid-fifties, with a wife and two teenage daughters to support, the shop takings were down. He was trying not to be bitter about the other – completely unexpected! – minimarket. But having gone into debt to expand the shop it now felt like he had looped his neck with the chain of a ship's anchor.

Stifling another sigh he dismissed his own problems. Rolling his Rs like a Scotsman he declared, "You in the correct place." He pointed a stubby finger, "Soon, you relax."

"Hope so." Aeron flexed long gaunt cheeks pulling lips into a smiley, which would have made his kids giggle. His stomach lurched, though, when he remembered that leaving his children had been even harder than leaving Melanie. He tried valiantly to reassure himself. *Don't worry, it'll be okay!* He had to believe that or he was sunk.

Determinedly he inspected the thinly stacked shelves of goods. His beloved Zabar's it wasn't, but the ambience of the shop spoke to him. His mind held up a card bearing the word SIMPLICITY; used to writing slogans for an advertising agency this happened a lot. Yes, simple was what he craved.

His tensed mouth relaxed as he sighed with relief. "It sure is great to be back!"

After a little polite chitchat Aeron explained he had come for the summer and wondered if Spiros' brother, Yiorgos, who owned rental apartments, had anything suitable.

"I think is no problem," Spiros said. "I call him now." Then he froze, remembering the hold his brother had over him at the moment. He was the last person he wanted to speak to! Manfully, though, he took a steadying breath. As he picked up the receiver from the big red Bakelite payphone, he glanced above it to the icon of Christ. Silently he prayed for help. After dialling the number he fed a silver ten drachma coin into a slot and pressed the Talk button.

Aeron hoped there *was* no problem. He didn't have a clue where to start looking next for a place to stay. The Paradise Hotel, his usual choice, was definitely beyond the budget this time. He began to feel jittery again, and hated himself for that.

The doorbell jangled and looking up at the newcomer, he came eye to eye with Jason. *Well would you look at that! I think of the Paradise and in walks the manager.* He smiled and they exchanged a few friendly words. Suddenly, his backpack seemed to weigh double and as he gratefully slipped the burden from his shoulders he missed the cool exchange between shopkeeper and customer.

Spiros used to have a great respect for Jason's father, a former sea captain. Now, though, he just felt sorry for him. He shook his head as the young man left. *Who would have thought that a son would treat his own father like that?* He still found it unbelievable.

Chapter 3

For the umpteenth time Katarina, Spiros' younger daughter, glanced surreptitiously beneath thick sooty lashes, at the clock on the dingy classroom wall. She liked the history teacher, an old man in his fifties like her father, so, though itching for the lesson to end, she tried to hide it.

Twenty more minutes!

Going on seventeen, with the end of her education only weeks away, her concentration was not good at the best of times now. She was clever, though, and determined to do well in her final exams. But this was just to prove to herself and her family that she could.

Her dream was to marry her boyfriend as soon as possible. He had recently proposed – though their engagement was a secret to all but her best friend, Maria. Their clandestine date, when she should be having the last lesson of the day, was the main reason for her restiveness.

In this heat would she still look presentable by then? Aware that her navy skirt was damp at the waistband she was thankful for the freshness of her best crisp white cotton blouse. As she wriggled on a rickety ladder-back wooden chair she dragged her long dark hair into a ponytail with a scrunchie. When a sudden breeze from a nearby open window found her hot neck it felt blissful.

The teacher held up a photograph. "These Early Neolithic pottery shards were found in northern Corfu." Twelve boys and girls wore uniformly blank faces. "I know they don't look very impressive," he admitted. "But can you imagine living about eight thousand years ago?"

One boy pouted and gave a single click of the tongue while raising his chin briefly: the Greek informal, non-verbal "no". Around him, others did the same. Katarina glanced over at Maria. They shared a smile of complicity and joined in, though it was a little impolite.

Abruptly the teacher turned his back and with chalk tapping

and scraping wrote 6000 BC on the blackboard. The class exchanged worried looks.

But when he turned back to them the teacher was grinning. "Me neither," he conceded, ineffectually brushing chalk dust from the front of his grey shirt. His pupils laughed, relieved he was amused not offended by the breach of etiquette. "But you see how long and important our island's heritage is?" The humoured class responded with much vigorous nodding.

The lesson continued and Katarina drifted off into a daydream about her secret fiancé. She remembered the day she had fallen in love.

She was twelve years old and it was the feast of Spiridon, patron saint of Corfu. It was a big celebration. Spiros, his modernized name, was the most popular for males on the island, including her father. She had been standing with friends watching the adolescents eyeing each other up. The seeds of attraction leading to marriage were often sown on these occasions.

At the heart of the square a small group of teenage girls formed a conspicuous whispering knot. The boys meanwhile milled around in a corner calling out to each other, jostling and laughing loudly on any pretext. Each fresh burst of merriment drew studiously haughty glances from the girls.

Katarina and her friends giggled about how gawky the boys looked. But one caught her attention as he stood slightly aloof from the horseplay. He was laughing, though, and it lit up his face. He was the most handsome boy she had ever seen.

Then it happened.

The scarf was torn from her shoulders by a gust of wind and as it streamed in a long pink silky line past the boy's shoulder he lunged and grabbed it.

Turning to find its owner he looked into her eyes and her heart leapt, while a fluttering in her chest felt like a hundred dancing butterflies. The green flecks in his twinkling light brown eyes mesmerized her. As he pressed the bunched-up trophy carefully into her hands she shyly smiled her thanks. He smiled back, brief and sweet, before returning to his friends.

Katarina was enchanted.

She understood that he would marry one of those older girls. Though without hope, she felt she would love him all her life.

But he had not married.

Somehow, miraculously, he had fallen in love with *her*. Even though he was a handful of years older she did not care. This age difference, and more, was common in the village. Becoming his wife would make her the happiest girl on earth!

Clang! Clang! Clang!

Katarina was jolted out of her daydream. Outside the door the handbell signalled the end of the lesson. She breathed a huge sigh of relief, whispered goodbye to Maria – who would cover for her if necessary, and slipped through the stream of pupils which flowed towards the playground. This was a short break before Geography, the last lesson today.

She made for the girls' cloakroom in the other direction. Pushing open the door she caught a light, clean, familiar waft of bleach and local olive oil soap. Hastily she splashed cool water from the old chipped basin over hot cheeks.

Applying just a touch of lipgloss in front of the speckled mirror, she took a moment to be thankful for inheriting her mother's narrow, sharp jawline instead of her father's underbite. And that she had her mother's petite figure too.

Her parents! How would they take the news of her engagement? They didn't even know she was dating someone. She winced in the mirror at the thought. "Gosh. I hope there won't be trouble..."

But she'd cross that bridge when she came to it.

Quickly she freed her hair from the scrunchie, noting with dismay its slightly lank appearance. Heat and humidity had dulled its morning shine. She fluffed it out with her fingers.

Better.

She left the room and held her breath as she crept along the deserted corridor.

A door slammed close by and her heart thumped. On tiptoe she tottered through the front entrance, made it unseen past the metal gate, and raced to the end of the short tree-lined road.

Jason waved at her from his car and her heart skipped a beat. *I'm so lucky! He's handsome and wonderful and we're in love!*

She slid into the passenger seat and they sped away from the edge of the village and disappeared round a tight bend.

Chapter 4

Spiros' brother, Yiorgos, arrived at the minimarket in a little open-backed truck. It reminded Aeron Lehman of his son's Meccano set as it looked like an ingenious assembly of spare parts. It was. Yiorgos wasted nothing. He was known for his frugality.

But it was also known in the community that he had, in his garage, a big black shiny Mercedes in which he drove his wife and children like royalty. This was the badge of his success.

Yiorgos, taller and thinner than his brother, nimbly hopped down from the cab. Wired by a diet of tobacco and endless tiny cups of strong syrupy Greek coffee he marched into the shop.

Fixing his cigarette between nicotine-browned teeth – arranged in the same underbite as Spiros' – Yiorgos squinted through a curl of smoke. His gaunt lined face showed he was the elder brother.

Vigorously he shook Aeron's hand and got straight down to business. "How long you stay?"

"Hopefully, the whole summer, if I can find a job." Scooping off his cap Aeron fingered a nape-full of damp fawn curls, glad, for once, of the shortness around the ears: his compromise to a business style. He often moaned to friends that for a family man in his late-thirties compromise was a way of life. Melanie used to roll her eyes if she caught him saying that and he'd turn it into a joke.

But it wasn't.

"No problem," Yiorgos announced, rolling his Rs like his brother. "I got just the right place for you. *Ela.* Come. I show you." He called over his shoulder, "Thanks brother."

Spiros nodded. He began to breathe a bit easier. It looked like nothing was going to be said.

But just before Yiorgos closed the door he turned back. "Oh, by the way," he began casually, lighting yet another cigarette. "I may need to talk to you in a few days."

His sharp look was at odds with his measured tone. As soon as he turned his back on his brother, though, that expression switched to a satisfied smirk.

Spiros' heart sank. Those were the words he had been dreading. His eyes flicked up to the icon above the till and he muttered yet another quick prayer for help.

Gabriella held a brief exchange with Spiros' guardian angel before following the other two with their wards.

Yiorgos hoisted the rucksack onto the back of his truck and leapt behind the wheel. When Aeron clambered into the cab cradling his bagged guitar a cloud of smoke, mingling with the brown odour of stale tobacco, hit the back of his throat. The vehicle laboriously scaled a steep track and came to a halt outside a pale pink single story block. Aaron grabbed the door handle, eager to discreetly breathe a lungful of fresh air.

As he followed Yiorgos up the path, a tall attractive blonde in a cream sundress left the first apartment, flung a gold beach bag over one shoulder, and locked the door.

"*Ya soo*, Bethany. *Ti kanis?*"

"*Kala,* Yiorgo. *Ti kanis*?"

"*Kala,*" Yiorgos replied with a cheerful wink and a click of his tongue.

They routinely said "hello, how are you?" and the answer was always "good". Bethany Griffiths was friendly but her Greek minimal – though she did know the rule of dropping the "s" off the end of a name when speaking to the person.

Yiorgos turned to Aeron and introduced him.

"Perhaps you be neighbours." He gave a brown grin.

"Ah. Hiya. Really nice to meet you." Her Welsh accent was a light singsong, which suited her pretty animated oval face, glossy red lips, and even white teeth.

As Aeron exchanged a smile with Bethany he felt the fizz of attraction. "Hey there." He raised his left hand in greeting. Was it his imagination that her dark blue eyes darted to his wedding ring?

Yiorgos addressed Bethany. "You stay here few times, yes? You like it here, yes?" His widened eyes asked for help.

She picked up the hint. "Oh, yeah, it's really great," she enthused. "So lovely and quiet. And you wait till you see the balcony view. A-*may*-zing!"

"Oh, okay. Thanks." Aeron thought the view right in front of him was pretty amazing.

"Right, better go then." Bethany sounded flustered as she fingered her fringe then tucked shoulder length locks behind her ears. "Really looking forward to a swim."

Aeron felt a pang of regret as bright eyes disappeared behind big square tortoiseshell sunglasses settled snugly on the bridge of her snub nose.

Mentally he berated himself. *Whoa, man!* But he couldn't resist a peek over his shoulder at her retreating figure as Yiorgos led the way along the block.

They stopped at the last door.

Aeron followed the man into the cool dark pine-scented interior. When the shutters outside the sliding floor-to-ceiling glass door were thrust open, a basic but pleasant apartment was revealed. *Nice one.*

They were standing in a good-sized room with twin beds and a wardrobe in the corner. Next door was a dining-kitchen separated from a lounge by tall shelving. The lounge had two couches which turned into single beds. The compact shower room was tiled in powder blue.

Aeron wanted the apartment. But would the price be reasonable? He had promised Melanie he wouldn't blow a chunk of their savings. Perhaps he should be looking at studios. As his stomach ulcer began to burn, he frantically searched through the numerous pockets of his cargo pants before finally unearthing a roll of antacid Tums. Popping a tablet into his mouth, he began sucking determinedly.

Gabriella conferred with the two guardian angels. Aeron, frangible in body and spirit, needed this apartment. But Yiorgos presumed, that because Aeron was older than the usual seasonal workers, and American, he could afford to pay more.

As Yiorgos put his hands on his hips his guardian was already whispering that it was better not to push it and lose this chance of renting the apartment for the whole summer.

Aeron crunched on the Tums.

Yiorgos, though, had listened to his angel and their haggling was good-natured. When they reached an agreement both men looked pleased.

Aeron handed over a small stack of ten thousand drachma notes for a month's advanced rent – which was much cheaper than anything in Manhattan. Then he hauled the hulking old backpack into the apartment. He remembered the last time he had used it at an obscure music festival. *When I was young, free and single!*

Smiling wistfully at the memory he propped the pack against the bedroom wall and went through the open sliding door to explore the communal balcony.

Bethany had not exaggerated the view. "Awesome!"

Ahead and to his right valleys ran and hills climbed in a green sweep. Down below, the shimmering expanse of sea was rimmed by a long pale strip of beach. Strategically placed at the centre of the sands were rows of sunbeds topped by bronzing bodies. The rest was unspoilt.

Aeron took a few deep slow breaths, nostrils picking up a faint but distinctive whiff of Corfu scent: a unique blend of warmed wild herbs, camomile and margarita daisies, delivered on a light breeze.

Suddenly, like someone flicking a switch he felt...

What?

Happy!

The sensation, so long absent from his life, was astonishing.

"Wow!" He chuckled. "Incredible!"

He went inside, grabbed his guitar, found a plectrum, and did a quick tune up. Strumming the instrument he absentmindedly picked up a love song he'd written years ago for Melanie.

Girl so fine with your hand in mine we'll walk the land.
With you beside me, here to guide me, I'll come to understand
That love is more than just a word that's written in the sand.

His hands stilled, and in the pause his mind threw up an image of Bethany gracefully walking up the path, flimsy cream dress billowing in the breeze over long shapely legs.

"Forget it!" Aeron roughly put the guitar aside. "I need to sort my head out, not mess it up more!"

Prompted by Gabriella his guardian suggested a swim and snooze on a sunbed. Aeron concurred.

Gabriella, satisfied that things were fine, for now, was ready to move on. She and the guardian angel with hands crossed over upper torsos nodded to each other in farewell. With a beat of huge wings she shot straight up into the air.

Her trademark take-off.

The guardian's brown eyes twinkled as she disappeared.

The twinkle faded, though, when he turned back to his ward.

Aeron had no inkling of the awful timing of his visit. His vulnerability would make him a target for the increasing local demonic presence. The angel would have his work cut out to protect him, even with the help of Gabriella.

* * *

Jason navigated a road bisecting a string of brooding olive groves. The gnarled trees clambered up steep banks at one side and fell away on the other. After a few minutes he spun the wheel hard right and the car slowly bumped over the rutted dirt track to his uncle's grove, long regarded as their place. The second he cut the engine Katarina flung herself into his arms.

Jason rigidly kept their relationship chaste, which filled him with pride.

After drinking his fill of sweet kisses he pulled away, absentmindedly finger-raking a stray lock of hair back from his face. He yawned widely and accepted a stick of gum from Katarina.

"You look very tired," she said. "What were you up to last night?"

"Up to!" The green flecks in Jason's brown eyes danced with mischief as he chewed. "What do you think I was up to?" He bunched his lips with mock pique. "Are you accusing me of something?"

"I only asked a simple question." She laughed lightly.

"Yes. But you're inferring I was up to no good." He feigned indignation.

"Jason, I'm only teasing you. I know you were working and probably had to keep the bar open late."

He nodded and smiled, his even teeth showing white against tan skin. His joke was a bit thin, she knew his work, but it came from the light-hearted happiness he felt in her company.

He drew a cigarette from a pack he had just bought from her father. Jason had no scruples about their secret engagement and looked him straight in the eye as always. He would do the honourable thing and ask for her hand in marriage but not until the end of the season. By that time he hoped to have sorted away quite a bit of extra money.

"Tell me about your day," he said, lighting up.

Katarina flicked heavy dark tresses over both shoulders and wrinkled her nose. "Mostly it was okay but the last lesson was history and so boring today. It was all about broken old pottery dug up on the island. I mean, honestly, who cares!"

Jason laughed thinly. "You forget I studied archaeology in

Athens."

"Well, you must have hated it like I do, because you didn't become an archaeologist."

"No, I didn't hate it. But, my father needed me here." They would be married soon so he could tell her little confidences.

"Oh, I didn't know that. I thought you dropped your course because you didn't like it."

Her words were prodding fingers on an old wound. He was passionately proud of his heritage. He and Katarina's history teacher had that in common. In studying archaeology he was chasing his dream of being the one to discover the tomb of Alexander the Great in Egypt. But that dream was over. His father had needed him, and here he was... For Jason, though, his country remained the centre of the universe.

"Always remember the influence Ancient Greece still has on the world, Katarina." He prodded her shoulder lightly. "After all," he reminded her, "wasn't Socrates the father of philosophy, Hippocrates the father of medicine, and Greece the cradle of civilization itself?"

Sensing his seriousness she nodded diplomatically.

He lifted a lock of her hair rubbing it thoughtfully between his fingers. *My lovely Katarina. I can't wait to make you my wife!* "But my career switch has worked out well," he said, carefully stubbing his cigarette out in the car ashtray. He smoothed the precious lock back into place and forced himself to keep his mind in the present. "Don't you think so, Miss Golden Eyes?" It was his pet name for her.

"Very well," she agreed.

Jason smiled at her fondly then checked his watch. "Damn! We should have left five minutes ago." He put Katarina aside and fired the engine. If she missed the bus it would cause trouble.

As they sped back into the village and saw a throng of pupils at the bus stop Jason breathed a sigh of relief. He swung the car up a narrow street and gave Katarina's hand a quick squeeze. "Go," he urged. "I'll phone you soon."

As always Katarina was torn. Leaving was a wrench, but missing the bus unthinkable. She sprang from the car.

Racing around the corner she found Maria and was pleased to learn that her absence had gone unnoticed.

She wasn't the only girl ducking lessons for the same reason. A couple of the other older girls with boyfriends were snatching the chance to see each other away from prying eyes. It was the custom. Few were caught and many married couples looked back at their courting days and smiled at their truancy for love.

The friends joined hands and scampered the length of the street.

Once on board the bus they put their heads together and whispered the entire half-hour journey to Korkyra. Their conversation was punctuated with frequent giggles as the girls confided secrets.

Jason, making his way in the opposite direction, headed for the bank in town. He thought about Sotiris, the supplier he should have met with this morning. He had missed the meeting when he fell asleep on the beach. But he was still sure they could do business together.

His guardian angel whispered into his ear.

Suddenly he remembered the scary dream he'd had during that snooze, filled with fire and screams and being overpowered by dark shapeless demons with glowing red eyes. He shuddered. *Forget it!*

His mind turned back to Sotiris. A deal with him would save the hotel a lot of money. He grinned at the thought of the percentage of that extra profit which would end up in his own bank account. He would buy more stocks and shares. His investments were doing well. At this rate he would soon be a rich man. Rich enough to make his new bride very happy.

His guardian angel reminded him about Gabriella.

The weird girl on the beach this morning popped into Jason's mind. For some reason she had accused him of being greedy but that was just crazy. *What planet did she come from?* He deserved every drachma he was piling up.

Changing down into second gear to chug up a long steep hill he began to whistle cheerfully.

Chapter 5

The next day Gabriella zoomed into Korkyra, tumbled backwards mid-air, and landed sedately, before furling great wings with a snap. She paused, invisible, beside an old rustic cottage – clearly part of the original fishing hamlet.

Built at the foot of a hill greened by olive trees and spiky cypress, its nearest three neighbours were a stone's throw away on either side and in front. Beyond these crouched similar bungalows, strung like pale beads of pink, cream, and ochre along the grey ribbon of road snaking the seashore.

Mature gardens, bursting with leggy crimson geraniums, pink and yellow roses rambling through lush foliage, and cascades of amethyst bougainvillea, lent charm to the simple traditional dwellings. The owners of the showy new villas, pushed randomly among them, found it strange that many visitors preferred these to theirs.

Just inside the open kitchen door a distressed old lady, grizzled hair secured in a tight bun, cradled a young man's taupe canvas shoe.

"Dear Lord, why does Nikos do it?" she prayed aloud. "It is so wrong!"

As Soula brandished the offending shoe tears spilled from dark eyes down seamed cheeks aged from smooth to shrivelled olive. Her grandson had been on the beach in the dark with a tourist. Again! Being a waiter at the hotel, he met too many young women for her liking.

"I beg him not to do it but he just smiles and says, 'Yaya, it's just a bit of fun. You worry too much.' But, Lord, how can I stop worrying? What if people find out that he's dating these visitors? The whole family will be disgraced!" Her voice caught on a sob. "Please help us, Lord," she pleaded.

Soula's guardian angel and Gabriella listened to the prayer for Nikos that she continued to speak aloud. Around the small resort, and nearby village of Hora – where most locals lived, other people fearful of changes in their culture sent up many similar prayers for help.

The guardian angel shook her head sadly. "I am sorry to see her so upset," she said.

Gabriella nodded. "It is not easy working with wards is it?"

The angel shrugged in resignation.

Gabriella and the guardian watched the old lady pick up the other shoe and walk outside to the small stone courtyard. There she turned the pair upside down and slapped the sole of each quite viciously against the low wall until the particles of sand had stopped sprinkling out.

With a final despairing shake of her head, Soula wiped her eyes on the snowy apron worn over widow's weeds of black cotton blouse and skirt.

With a heavy heart she went back into the house to make breakfast for her daughter, errant grandson, and her son-in-law, who would soon – God-willing – return from a night's fishing.

Gabriella moved with the guardian angel into the cramped kitchen, eyes skating over abraded grey carved marble sink and surfaces. When the old lady heated oil in a pan and added cakes of raisin-studded dough, the sizzling *tzaletia* – a recipe inherited from Venetian invaders – brought back memories. The four centuries of their rule in Corfu had been a very busy time for the angel. Invasions always caused huge problems. The latest one, this time by tourists, was, in its way, as problematic as the others.

When the cakes were cooked Soula lightly sprinkled them with orange flower water and granulated sugar. She set them beside a dish of plump olives glistening blackly against white cubes of feta cheese. Glancing at the clock beside the cooker she clicked her tongue in dismay.

Stepping into the narrow gloomy hallway she rapped on a door. "Niko, time to get up. The day is already half gone!" Hopefully that would wake her daughter, Eviania, too.

At the sound of her returning son-in-law dropping his boots outside the kitchen door she breathed her usual sigh of relief. She, like other villagers, had lost her beloved husband to the sea, and never took safety for granted. She smiled broadly. The transformation in her weathered face was striking. It was clear to see that she had been a beautiful woman, and still was in her way.

Hastening forwards she greeted him. "Here you are, Luka. Now we can get breakfast over with." She spoke brusquely, smothering her emotion.

Lukas was not fooled and leaned to kiss her cheek fondly.

Soula decided she would speak to him later about Nikos and the foreign girls. Maybe he could make his son see sense. If this behaviour didn't stop, people were sure to find out. No one would want him as a husband for their daughter and then what would happen? Would he be forced to marry someone from another village?

Unthinkable!

Then she had another thought. Greece had a policy of conscription. Nikos planned to go into the Army. Unlike his father, or his Uncle Spiros at the minimarket, he was not fond of sailing. Although she would miss Nikos, the Army would get him away from all this nonsense. Maybe she would start praying for his call-up papers to come through quickly.

Gabriella spoke a few words of counsel to the guardian angel and said a brief hello to the man's angel. Then, with crossed hands placed briefly over upper torsos the angels said goodbye, and she left.

* * *

Jason drove back from town in the late afternoon. He had been for coffee with friends and stayed longer than he should have. The Paradise Hotel was almost full and dinner would be hectic. He hoped the preparations were almost complete. His waiter Nikos would have all thirty tables organized. He knew he could trust him to do that without any instructions as the boy had worked well for him last summer.

He still regarded Nikos as a boy, but it now struck him that he was fast becoming a man. Jason knew Nikos looked up to him and he enjoyed the admiration. He smiled. Then he sighed wistfully. Oh to be eighteen again! No responsibilities and no heavy workload. Happy days!

Distracted by his thoughts he sped up the little hill at the far end of the resort, barely reduced speed as he swung sharp right, and tore up the hotel driveway. Nearing the top, two females stepped out of the square white building straight into his path. Stamping the brake pedal to the floor the tyres squealed as he brought the car to a jerky stop, just inches away from them.

The shock registered on both girls' faces was echoed on Jason's. It had been a near miss and as his hammering heartbeat slowed he berated himself for his stupidity.

Then he looked properly at the girls. The tall blonde, Bethany, he knew. But his mouth fell open at the sight of her friend. Shiny red curls tumbled over lightly tanned shoulders, a pale wispy dress hinting at a slim figure.

He leapt out of the car. "I'm very sorry," he shook his head and looked deeply apologetic. "My mind was somewhere else," he admitted. "I'm not usually so careless."

The redhead found her voice first. "Sure, you were driving much too fast!" Fright flipped to temper and hands flew to hips. "It was irresponsible." Her eyes blazed. "If you had hit a child at that speed you would have killed them."

A mother walked past with two small children in tow and underlined the truth in the girl's accusation.

"I promise you that I don't usually drive like that."

He looked into the angry girl's eyes and marvelled. They were the colour of emeralds. He didn't know eyes could be so green. He wondered where she was from. He thought she may be Irish. A sudden breeze blew a tendril of hair over her face and without thinking he reached up and brushed it away.

The girl jumped back as if he had struck her. *How dare he*? He had almost hit them with his car and now he was touching her hair.

Jason was now captivated by her mouth. He felt an urge to trace the bow shape of her lips with his finger. He resisted. But as their eyes locked – hers in anger, his in wonder – it seemed to him that everything just stopped for a few seconds.

"Aw, come on, Clare, let it go," Bethany Griffiths spoke quietly but firmly. "We're both alright." She turned to Jason whom she had known for a few years and liked. "Not to worry, Jason," she soothed. "No harm done."

"This time," Clare O'Hara hissed under her breath.

Jason grinned, enchanted by the feisty Clare. "Look, I'm the manager of this hotel. Why don't you come back in and have a drink on the house," he invited, gesturing towards the pool bar overlooking the sea.

"Oh, that would be lovely—" Bethany began.

"No, thank you." Clare cut her friend off. "Bethany, let's go."

Bethany looked at Jason regretfully.

"Maybe another time…" Jason tried again.

"Of course. Thank you." Bethany came here often anyway.

"Well…" He had no words.

"Well." Clare was terse. She refused to bend. Instead she turned on her heel and marched off down the driveway.

"Bye," said Bethany, and reluctantly followed her friend.

Jason thoughtfully watched their progress down the hill until they disappeared from sight. The resort was very small. He knew he would see the beautiful Clare again. No one was lost in Korkyra.

He was determined to make her like him.

* * *

Clare and Bethany strode along the narrow road in silence.

Clare, still feeling cross, was lost in thought. She had taken an instant dislike to Jason. *Too good looking and sure of himself! Just like Patrick!* Patrick, her childhood sweetheart in Dublin, had turned arrogant towards the end of their relationship – only a few short painful months ago. He dumped her the day after her twenty-first birthday, saying he'd met someone else.

To make matters worse he implied she should be grateful that he waited until after her party to drop the bombshell.

She wasn't.

She shuddered at the memory, then bristled remembering Jason touching her hair. She hoped she wouldn't see him again but in this small resort it was inevitable. "Thinks he's God's gift to women that one," she muttered to Bethany.

"I think he's very handsome, though I don't fancy him." Bethany glanced sideways at her friend. "Look, I'm not being funny or anything, but you were a bit rude to him weren't you."

"Sure, he was very careless."

"Hmm." Bethany pressed her lips together thoughtfully. "We all make mistakes, though, don't we?" She smiled to soften her words.

Clare didn't want to fall out with her new friend. "Ah, you're right, we do." As hot sunshine beat down on her head she slowed her pace and Bethany did too. But she continued to brood over Patrick. *Was it a mistake to go out with Patrick for all those years?* She had chanced upon him and his new love shopping in the centre of Dublin one Saturday afternoon. He was holding the pretty girl by the hand and they looked so happy together. Fortunately, he hadn't spotted her but that little scene continued to haunt her. Patrick's betrayal still scratched at her insides with sharp talons.

Huh, men! She shook her head.

She was in the middle of reading *Diana: Her True Story* written by Andrew Morton. Hot off the presses the book was an explosive exposé of the Princess of Wales' life and marriage.

She'd grabbed the controversial book at the airport. It made her feel a fraction better knowing she wasn't the only one who'd been betrayed.

Pushing away the pain she scooped her jumble of red curls into a crinkling top knot with a scrunchie. Composed, she turned the conversation back to the matter in hand. "Right now, let's go and ask around for some cheap accommodation. And if we don't find somewhere we can ask Manos tonight at the Candy Bar. Sure, he seems to know everyone."

"Okay." Bethany nodded her agreement. "So long as you understand that I'm not making any promises." She bit her lower lip thoughtfully and glanced across the beach at the sea: today like polished jade.

She was on a career break to fulfil a lifelong ambition of writing a novel. A short visit to Manhattan had drawn her in. The people there were so edgy and colourful and she thought it would be a great place to write about. She had already set plans in motion to go and live in the Big Apple for a while. She was having this pre-booked holiday first.

That was the plan anyway until she'd met up with Clare. Now she was wavering.

Clare's smile was open. "You haven't made any promises. And I accept that." She knew all about the New York plan. But knew too that Bethany loved Korkyra.

Clare and Bethany had hit it off immediately. Clare had no idea of the age gap between them. Bethany could easily pass for mid-twenties. Clare had a job lined up but the wage was low. There was no way she could afford to live alone. If Bethany stayed on at the resort they could rent together and split living expenses.

A little knot of worry rose in her chest. She definitely did not want to go back to Dublin right now.

Then an idea struck her. "Hey," she said. "We could ask the man in the car rental office if he knows of any vacant accommodation."

"Oh, that's a thought." The reply was polite but lacked enthusiasm.

"Look, we'll just give it a try." Clare was conciliatory.

"Sorry." Bethany looked sheepish. "Course we'll try. We'll scour the whole resort and then we'll see." She nodded. "I am interested. It's just..."

"I know. You'd other arrangements." She nudged Bethany and winked. "Look," she said, "if you decide to go with the flow and stay here you can always go back to 'Plan A' for the winter."

"That's true."

From nowhere a deep longing surfaced in Bethany, goading her. She hadn't taken time out from her job just for the novel. Perhaps, instead of trying to push herself to feel better, a summer of relaxation would help her to...

To what?

Accept? Move on?

She inwardly shook herself, squared her shoulders and tried to sound decisive. "Let's go and see the car man."

Chapter 6

Aeron Lehman sat on his bed and brooded.

After a day lazing in the sunshine he was physically rested but mentally wired. He felt hemmed in by the white walls. He needed some action.

Go get a job, man!

He was going to try for a bar job. He'd brushed up his skills at a friend's bar in Manhattan. With a routine based around work he expected to feel more grounded. Only then would he have a go at finding the cause of his stress. He shook his head. On the surface he had a great life: happy marriage, wonderful kids, and brilliant job. The lot!

How am I going to even start this soul searching stuff? I'm desperate! His heart began to hammer at the thought that maybe it was all hopeless.

This was the suggestion of his stalker demon, working away on Aeron's insecurities. To the malicious delight of the demon this idea of hopelessness was beginning to take root in the human.

Perched on the man's shoulder, grey, scaly and invisible, it silently whispered familiar hateful words guaranteed to deflate and discourage.

Aeron, like everyone else, had been shadowed by his personal stalker demon from birth. It took every chance to dart in and try to demolish anything good. Its success rate vacillated. But recently Aeron had begun to buckle under its negative force. And since their arrival at Korkyra, where the stalker demon had met up with bands of powerful rogue demons eager to assist, it was gaining more ground.

Stalker demon: "You'll never sort yourself out. There's nothing to sort. You're just selfish and hopeless!"

Aeron: *Am I just being selfish coming here without my family hoping against hope for peace of mind?*

Stalker demon: "Peace of mind? You'll never have peace of

mind because you just worry over nothing. You don't have any real problems you're just selfish and hopeless."

Aeron: *I know I don't have any real problems so why do I feel so stressed out all the time?*

Guardian angel: "You are usually well-balanced and practical. Something has gone wrong in your life and you need to sort yourself out."

Aeron: *I used to be so sure of myself. I don't know what's happening to me.*

Stalker demon: "You're just selfish and hopeless and that's all there is to it!"

The demon flicked out a forked grey tongue then squawked with delight. It was hell-bent on driving the man to despair.

"For God's sake get a grip, man!" Aeron yelled at himself.

The instant Gabriella appeared, the demon let out a high-pitched howl of rage and shot to the corner of the room. There it hovered on its fly-like wings shooting malevolent glares as she conferred with Aeron's guardian angel.

Aeron was much closer to despair than even *he* realized.

Reading his thoughts and gauging his overall mood, Gabriella judged that a little distraction would do for now. She asked his angel to remind him of his plans for the evening.

Aeron looked through the open balcony door at the fiery red sunset. It stirred him up. He should make himself a bite to eat then get cracking, he decided.

The demon was beaten; for now. With a screech of temper it vanished.

The angels breathed a sigh of relief. As Aeron headed for the kitchen Gabriella said goodbye to his guardian angel and left the two of them to it.

* * *

Within the hour a spruced-up Aeron, wearing loose faded denims and an open-neck blue shirt, stepped purposefully down the slope and at the minimarket turned right heading for the Candy Bar. A hubbub of music, voices and laughter floated out to greet him. His step faltered, though, when he recognized the record: *Please Don't Go*, by the K.W.S. band. It was one of Melanie's favourites this summer. She used to turn it up on the radio and look at him with pleading sad eyes. *Oh, heck! No! Just forget it!*

Taking a bracing breath he strode up the stone path, past the dancing fountain, through the courtyard, and into the low pink rectangular building. The spacious room was packed with tourists lounging on thickly cushioned bamboo armchairs around small glass-topped tables, enjoying a pre-dinner drink.

At the polished wooden bar a large knot of customers jostled amiably for service. A tottering stack of dirty glasses at one end of the counter bore witness to an earlier wave of drinks. Aeron noted with a smirk that this detritus was doubled by carelessly placing it beside a mirror.

The man behind the bar was red-faced above his white T-shirt, forehead slick. When he came to fill a glass with draft beer Aeron said in a low voice, "I'm an experienced barman. I need a job and I think you need some help." The man glanced up, dark eyes gleaming with interest but face impassive. Aeron persisted, "Try me free for a couple of hours then make your mind up."

The man finished serving the beer. After a final appraising look at Aeron, he nodded and raised the flap on the bar to admit the newcomer. While he mixed a shaker of shots he showed Aeron around the bar and how to keep a tab for each customer. Aeron turned his attention to the people waiting and smartly dispensed drinks. Between the two of them, they soon cleared the queue. Before the next onslaught the men shook hands and introduced themselves briefly.

"I am Manos and I own this bar."

"Hey man, I'm Aeron. I'm staying up at Yiorgos' apartments

on the hill, and I'm here for the season."

They both looked up as a striking, willowy brunette, dressed in loose black trousers and lacy top, swooped in, top-knot jiggling with each stride.

"Diana, why you are so late? We have many customers." Manos threw his arms wide to indicate the seated crowd and jumble of used glasses.

Diana Appleton's light brown eyes twinkled. "Really sorry, Mano." She spoke respectfully but without conviction. "My friend Kevin took me to Kassiopi and the blinking rental bike broke down." She bit back a giggle remembering how upset Kevin had been. He was working as a DJ at a nearby resort and took himself very seriously.

The man weighed that up. He didn't want to be too heavy-handed and lose her. She was a real asset to the bar. "Better start clearing up," he said. But Diana had already begun loading a tray with used tumblers.

Aeron nodded and smiled at her before turning to serve a customer.

After swiftly restoring order from chaos Diana sidled up to Clare and Bethany for an update on the apartment hunting. Careful not to draw more flak from her boss, she meticulously wiped their table as Clare reported they had found nothing so far. Cheap accommodation was limited in the small resort and everything seemed to have been snapped up already.

But there was hope!

Manos knew a lady who had an old villa to rent and they would view it in the morning. He had warned them that the place was spartan but hopefully that meant low rent.

Clare was animated with excitement but Diana noticed that Bethany seemed less enthusiastic about the whole thing. Ah well, it would soon be sorted out one way or another. "Best of luck with that," she said, but jumped as Manos appeared at her side. "Diana," he said. "You have another phone call today!"

"Oh, okay, thanks, Mano." As he bustled off she turned back to Clare and Bethany. They knew all about her tenacious ex. "Flipping heck!" she tutted. "Some people just won't take the hint!" But she gave them a cheerful wink before swanning off to dispose of the cigarette butts.

* * *

Tonight, Jason had been working on autopilot. As usual, though, he had threaded his way between tightly-packed-in tables taking orders and keeping dinner flowing smoothly. Generally, his aim was to keep everyone happy, but this evening he wanted only to please a certain absent redhead.

Now, when the night was drawing to a close and most diners had left, Jason stood behind the small counter at the restaurant's side entrance. He leaned on his elbows, cupped face in upturned hands, staring straight ahead at nothing.

Katarina's face superimposed itself over Clare's and her expression was accusing. He loved Katarina, of course he did. He planned to marry Katarina.

Jason's guardian angel, towering behind his chair, wings folded over narrow shoulders, kept reminding him about Katarina.

But red hair painted itself over brunette and green eyes over golden-brown in a delicious dilemma.

Meanwhile, his stalker demon lounged proprietarily on his shoulder. Its red eyes glinted dangerously at the angel and thin tail lashed as it suggested to Jason that until he and Katarina were formally engaged he was a free man.

After the formal engagement in the autumn he planned to marry next spring. The thought of marrying Katarina brought a smile to his lips. She would adore him and bear him children to carry his genes into another generation.

Though his family was religious Jason didn't believe in God.

When he died that would be it. Over. Done. But through his children he would, in a way, live on.

Two redheaded kids flashed into his mind.

Never!

He would definitely marry Katarina and make fully Greek-blooded babies.

"Jason, may I have a word please?" A plummy English voice broke into his thoughts. He looked up into the round eager face of Gavin Bellingham, the holiday rep. Standing tall and solid in front of him, clipboard pressed against his Oxford blue shirt, he bristled with efficiency.

The man had a droopy dark moustache and badly highlighted hair. But someone obviously found him attractive because Gavin had, most unexpectedly, turned up with a bride this summer.

The lovely Suzanna!

"Of course, Gavin," said Jason.

The man consulted his guest list. "All present and correct." Gavin Bellingham sounded more like a sergeant major than a holiday rep. "The welcome meeting will be at eleven o'clock sharp tomorrow morning." He then outlined the usual things he needed for his clients – which irked Jason. He wondered why Gavin insisted on repeating the familiar details.

A flash of light made Jason look up.

Flanked by two girls in miniskirts his head waiter's crisp white shirt, black trousers, and crimson sash glowed as his photograph was taken. Handsome Michalis, in an improvised Corfiot costume, featured in many holiday albums.

Jason raised his hand to attract Michalis' attention. "Sorry, Gavin, but I just remembered I need to sort something out with my father before the end of the evening. Can I pass you onto Michalis?"

"Oh." Gavin stopped mid-flow and looked a little flummoxed at the interruption. "Naturally, Jason, whatever you say."

Jason felt a twinge of guilt. Gavin was always respectful.

"Michali, Gavin is just running through what he needs for the welcome meeting tomorrow morning. Will you make sure there is nothing extra needed."

"Yes, of course, Jason." The two men exchanged a knowing look. Gavin and his repeated instructions was a weekly event in itself.

But Michalis was more receptive to Gavin's methods than Jason. He too was a stickler for detail. Planning avoided blunders – like that one yesterday. If Jason had involved him in the meeting with that man Sotiris – a supplier of what, he still didn't know – he could have soothed him when Jason was late. Instead, he had to watch him stride angrily away.

"Gavin, please come and sit down." Michalis indicated the table closest to the door, reserved for the family. "Would you like a beer?"

Gavin nodded and sank with a grateful sigh onto the hard wooden chair. It had been a long day.

Michalis gestured to Nikos the waiter to bring refreshments.

Jason walked away into the empty kitchen with a feeling of relief.

His guardian angel hovered overhead.

His stalker demon still lounged on his shoulder and directed its quarry's thoughts.

Jason's mind soon wandered back to the lovely Clare.

* * *

Aeron had noticed Diana's brief chat with Bethany and her friend. He had been pleasantly surprised when she walked in earlier. Bethany seemed pleased he had taken the apartment. He had no idea how much longer she was staying. When they took their drinks from him and found a table his eyes were glued to her every move.

It struck him as odd that he found Bethany more attractive

than Clare because redheads were more his type than blondes.

He had married a redhead.

An unsettling thought grabbed him: perhaps he was drawn to Bethany because she was the physical opposite of his wife, Melanie. But as his mind held up a flashcard bearing the accusatory word: DISLOYALTY, he quashed the thought.

Aeron's guardian angel glared at the sniggering chattering stalker demon.

Slightly shaken by feelings of temptation he slopped beer onto the bar as he set the glass down in front of his customer. "Sorry, man," he apologized politely. Hopefully Manos – who was keeping a sharp eye on him – had not noticed the gaffe.

The holidaymaker was affable. "Not to worry, mate." The man picked up his drink and went to join a crowded table of friends.

He had not fallen out of love with Melanie, Aeron firmly assured himself.

He was not looking for a summer fling to make himself feel better. *No way, man!*

He had been a faithful husband up till now and he planned for that to continue.

Aeron picked up a cloth and started to vigorously mop up the spilled beer as if trying to clean away all thoughts of infidelity. He was glad when his next customer asked for a big round of cocktails. It took his whole concentration to get each concoction right.

Beside him, Diana Appleton began washing yet another tray of glasses: soaping with hot water, rinsing under running water, then lining them upside down on a fresh towelling mat to drip-dry. Rubbing at a lipstick smear with the sponge she noticed the hot water had given her fingers the look of pink prunes.

She and Aeron introduced themselves. She told him she was here for the summer sharing a little house with a few friends, including Kevin. "I found myself between jobs so when they asked me to come here I jumped at the chance," she said brightly. "Beats London in the summertime. I love it here!" She didn't mention the ex. She glanced over at Bethany and Clare on the little dance floor in the corner of the room. Clare caught her look and waved. Bethany, a fan of the long disbanded band Abba – this year enjoying a revival of their music – had her eyes closed singing along to their *I Have a Dream*.

When it got to the line which spoke about believing in angels, her guardian angel smiled.

Her stalker demon whispered urgently into Bethany's brain.

She opened her eyes and her gaze strayed to Aeron. She couldn't help but notice that he looked cute in his sky-blue shirt with the sleeves rolled neatly to just below the elbows.

Her guardian angel reminded her that she never dated married men. It was her rule.

She closed her eyes and carried on singing and dancing unaware that Aeron was watching her surreptitiously.

Aeron's stalker demon made sure that he noticed her many charms.

Chapter 7

The shrieking alarm clock dragged a reluctant Gavin Bellingham up, up, up from a deep dark well of exhaustion. Fumbling for the snooze button he cradled the clock to his broad chest and flopped back onto the sweat-dampened pillow. Only mid-June, with most of the season still ahead and just a few hours off here and there, he was already drained.

A sliver of sunlight pierced the partly opened shutters and its sharp glare, over closed eyelids, kept him awake. Presently he squinted at the clock. Five minutes to seven. What was on today's agenda? Ah. First thing: go to the bank. He had to be there before opening time to avoid hours of queuing. These built up because Greek banking involved endless form filling. Galvanized, he sat up.

He gazed affectionately at his still-sleeping wife, gleaming golden hair spilling over the snowy pillow. What he would have given to kiss her awake. Regret nipped as he crept from the bed. *Being a holiday rep is not the easy job my clients think it is!*

Large pudgy feet slapped the lacquered boards of an open spiral staircase as he climbed down to grab a can of chilled cola from the fridge in the little dining-kitchen. The ancient villa, dilapidated when he bought it for a song a few years ago – with a sizeable fee from a meaty role in a television drama – was simply renovated. Hopes of other such roles hadn't yet materialized. Each summer, though, when he returned self-cast in the role of Dapper Holiday Rep, he congratulated himself on the wise investment.

Standing at the kitchen window glugging the fizzy drink he basked briefly in Suzanna's remembered praise of their stunning sea view. The neat cream-washed building crouched on a narrow shelf of land cut midway into the olive-clad hillside.

Showered, shaved and dressed he went to kiss Suzanna's cheek before leaving the house. "Sleep, my darling," he said, as she blinked a few times. "I'll see you later."

"Mmm, see you later," she parroted, eyelids drooping.

As Gavin left the house he took a swig of a fresh icy cola and bit into brittle refrigerated chocolate before pulling the door closed behind him. He stepped into blinding sunshine. "Frightfully hot," he told Suki the tenacious stray cat Suzanna fed.

"Meow," the Siamese agreed. Glad of his attention she raised her thin tail high and regally escorted him down the garden path to his car. When he got in she scooted back to the covered veranda, dropped down languidly, and closed her slanting blue eyes.

He wound down the windows on both sides of the car before swinging quickly out onto the narrow country road. Speeding along, cooled by a pleasant through-draft, he planned the finer details of the day.

He grinned and with a forefinger stroked his moustache with satisfaction.

Once up and about, he loved his job.

Naturally, he loved being an actor more, but this pattern of summer holiday rep then winter actor worked. Sort of.

He checked his watch. *Making good time.* With one hand on the steering wheel he twiddled with the radio dial. Nothing suited his mood and while he continued to change stations he overtook another car at speed, beeping his horn impatiently.

Finally he found some music he liked and loudly sang along with a love song. It reminded him of Suzanna.

My wife!

He sighed happily. He loved her so much.

They had met only months ago in Yorkshire when he was there playing a small role in a local production. They married after a whirlwind romance. Gavin had promised that though he was working here they would also have a long honeymoon in the sun.

She had been enjoying the sunshine for weeks but Gavin didn't have much spare time and she was getting impatient. She wanted to spend more time alone with him.

Naturally.

He chuckled, pleased with himself. His beautiful Suzanna was mad about him. And he was mad about her too; naturally. He'd have to try and squeeze more time off.

Savouring the moment alone at the wheel of his speeding car in the bright summer sunshine he beeped his horn a few times just for the heck of it. *That would have made Suzanna smile.*

His mind turned to money. The travel company paid him quite well but with a wife to support he definitely needed more income.

He thought about Jason and how successful he was at making money. He always seemed to have a new scheme on the go. And Gavin had seen him gloating over the stock market pages in the newspaper. "Keep focussed" was Jason's mantra about money.

Well, Gavin had got focussed. After mulling things over, just last night he had come up with a great idea for making cash on the side. Now he began to formulate a plan of action.

He had no inkling of the evil force driving him on.

A small band of rogue demons had been roped in by his stalker demon to facilitate the plan. Now the diminutive grey, scaly creatures were perched invisibly on his shoulders and head giving him suggestions.

Gavin was very pleased with the new details he was thinking up.

His guardian angel, when he could get a word in edgeways, suggested it would be better to drop the plan and concentrate on his job and his new wife.

Gavin batted those suggestions away with barely a thought. He was very pleased with the way his idea was developing and determined to make it work.

* * *

Spiros clumsily rattled and chinked bottles of soft drinks,

lining them up in the chill-cabinet. Stifling a yawn he rubbed a hand across gritty eyes, longing for his mid-afternoon siesta. Last night, and too many others, had remained sleepless while his mind twisted and knotted around money. Last winter his business was solid. Now things were shaky.

Beyond the salt-smudged window the blue water set his thoughts roving over happy years at sea. Sailing out of the island's port he used to leave troubles behind, and his income was good and regular.

Unlike now.

If anyone asked about the new shop affecting his shop he always laughed it off. There's plenty of business for us both, he would say, adding in a jokey voice behind the back of his hand that, of course, his shop was much better. Even those who knew him well failed to notice that the accompanying glint in his dark eyes was more manic than amused.

Spiros glanced down the side aisle at Katarina who was slouching on a chair at the checkout. Home from school, after a quick lunch she had taken over so her sister Eleni could have a break. Even at this distance her expression was clearly sullen. He shook his head.

Katarina sighed as she took the money for a carton of orange juice. Rebelliously she ignored the customer's outstretched hand and slapped the change onto the counter. Yes, it slowed things down when there was a queue, but she didn't care.

The man fumbled with the small drachma coins and sighed. He was on holiday recuperating from a heart attack. He didn't need the hassle. He wished the other minimarket was nearer so he didn't have to use this one.

As perspiration trickled down Katarina's back beneath a loose T-shirt she yearned for air-conditioning – so costly few people in the resort could afford it. Hot, bored and resentful, she counted the minutes until her sister's return.

She noticed her father making for the backdoor of the shop,

and knew he was going to the house for a snooze. Shoulders sagging, face drawn, he didn't say his usual goodbye. He looked unhappy. Katarina did not know why. Perhaps he was as bored as her. She sighed again and wished he had not opened the minimarket.

Sulkily she served the next customer. She longed for a swim.

I'll feel better when I get into the sea.

No. I won't feel better until I see Jason again.

For some reason she had a niggling feeling that all was not quite well between them. But he had been normal with her when they met the other day.

Jason loves me and I love him!

She would try not to worry.

* * *

The two friends were almost at the beach when Jason pulled up in his car.

"Afternoon ladies." He beamed at them. "Notice I stopped very slowly then?"

Clare O'Hara glowered.

"Hiya, Jason." Bethany Griffiths was friendly as always.

"How have you been? Are you enjoying your holidays?" He was determined to soften Clare towards him. His stomach was flipping at the sight of her.

"Yes. Having such a great time we've decided to stay for the whole summer." Bethany raised a palm towards Clare. "We've found a lovely little house to rent."

"Oh, you're both staying for the season!" The green flecks in his eyes danced with excitement. "We have to celebrate that good news," he said. "Why don't you come over to the hotel tonight for drinks?"

"Well, we..." Bethany glanced at her friend.

"We can't tonight." Clare was emphatic.

"Oh, what a pity." Jason was ogling Clare's tanned legs below a skimpy white sundress. "Of course, it's short notice. I understand." He didn't want to press them. Clare was here for the whole summer! "But I hope you'll take me up on my offer some night soon."

"Course we will. Thanks, Jason." Bethany was effusive. She was embarrassed by her friend's coolness and shot her a look.

"Yes, thank you," Clare said woodenly.

"Great." Jason started his car. "Enjoy your sunbathing, ladies." He waved and beeped his horn as he sped away.

"So much for his slow driving." Clare couldn't resist the jibe.

"Clare, he's a nice man."

"If you say so." She sounded unconvinced.

* * *

Nikos saw Jason talking to Clare and Bethany. As he watched him pull away from the curb with a little squeal of tyres, he wished he was driving a nice car instead of walking. He sighed. *Ah, well. I'll just get my army stint out of the way then concentrate on making some good money.* He was expecting the call-up any day now.

Then he had an idea: Jason was an inspiration when it came to money. Perhaps in the future he would help him make some sound investments.

One day I might be rich! That thought put a bounce in his footsteps.

* * *

Aeron Lehman walked to the Sunset beach taverna to make the metered long-distance call home. There were no phone boxes in the resort. Seated in a hot stuffy booth he dialled the number. After a few seconds delay came the steady beep-beep-beep of the busy signal. By the time he got the ringing sound his shirt was stuck to his back.

When his wife answered she sounded stiff.

He ploughed on regardless. After a brief exchange he asked after his children. He looked forward to a nicer chat with them.

Jamie was at home but Suzy had left for school. He swallowed his disappointment. He asked to speak to his son.

"Before I put him on I should warn you that he's upset with you. He doesn't understand why you're not here. And neither does Suzy."

A knife twisted somewhere near his heart. "Please try to make them understand, Melanie."

"That's a tall order, Aeron. It's difficult to help the kids understand something I don't understand myself." She sounded flat and sad.

"You told me you did understand." His voice crusted with impatience. She had been quite tender when they last spoke.

In the ensuing silence he knew she was weeping. Guilt rose as nausea from the pit of his stomach. "Melanie, please don't do this," he pleaded. "I just need time and space to work things through."

A searing pain began to gnaw at his stomach. His mind held up a white card bearing the words EMOTIONAL BLACKMAIL.

"Melanie, gimme me a break!" he gasped through a grimace of pain. "You're setting my ulcer off again!"

The crying ceased instantaneously, like a switch had been thrown. "Speak to your son," she muttered thickly.

He barely had time to switch emotional gears before his son said, "Hi, Dad, when are you coming home? I miss you."

"Hey, is that my Jamie?" Love washed through him.

"Yes, it's me, Dad. When are you coming home? Mommy cries all the time."

Aeron sighed. No let up. "I love you, Jamie, and I love Suzy and Mommy too. That's definite. Okay?"

After a pause the boy responded. "Okay."

"But I've been sick. You know I have an ulcer in my stomach that hurts me, don't you?"

"I know, Dad, but you take medication for the pain."

"Yes, I do, son, but the medication wasn't helping much because an ulcer is something you get with stress. You know what stress is, don't you?"

"Yes, Dad."

"Well, if you keep on being stressed an ulcer gets worse."

At the age of ten Jamie struggled to be manly but he was clearly on the verge of tears.

"Jamie, please try to be patient with me." Aeron had pleaded with his wife, and now begged his son for understanding. "I just need to do my own thing for a while." He paused and breathed deeply. "Jamie, please help your mom and Suzy," he asked. "And remember you'll be coming over to see me soon and we'll have a great time together. Okay?"

Silence.

"Okay, Jamie?"

"Okay, Dad."

Aeron heard their front doorbell peal. Then Melanie was talking to a man whom she appeared to have asked into the apartment.

"Hello, Mr Richards," Jamie called to the man.

"Say goodbye to Dad now, Jamie," his mother told him. She took the phone from her son.

"Uh, who just arrived, Melanie?" Aeron tried to sound casual.

"Jamie, take Mr Richards into the kitchen please." Melanie spoke to the man and said she would just be a few moments. "Aeron?"

"Yes, Melanie, I'm still here." He spoke through gritted teeth. "Who is that man?"

"Oh, it's David Richards. He's a new partner at the office."

"And how does Jamie know him?" He was holding his breath.

"Oh, he met him the other day. He had a dental check-up and afterwards he came back to the office for an hour until I finished work."

"And why is this man in our apartment?" His tone sounded churlish, even to his own ears.

"Oh, he's just come to fix the kitchen tap. I mentioned it was driving me nuts. Drip, drip, drip." She tut-tutted.

"Why didn't you get a plumber?" He thought that was a reasonable question.

Melanie spoke in a tense whisper. "He volunteered. He lives a block away. He won't charge me."

Aeron decided to let it drop.

"Talking about saving money, you'd better be going, Aeron, this call will be costing a fortune." Was it his imagination or was she being sarcastic?

"Okay, I'm off." He felt rattled but tried to end the call on a positive note. "I love you, Melanie." There was silence on the other end of the line so he continued his goodbyes, "Kiss Jamie and Suzy for me. I'll phone again soon."

When he hung up he pressed his fingers against his mouth fighting off panic. The pain in his stomach was equal to the pain of his mental turmoil. For the physical there was a soothing lozenge. But for the emotional pain...?

He was thousands of miles away from his wife and children but he felt the agony of guilt as strongly as a migraine.

And now there was a strange man in his home and there was nothing he could do about it.

Chapter 8

Exhilarated, Gavin Bellingham was doing a spot of research in the wholesalers in Corfu Town. He was excited by this first step towards implementing his sideline. He planned to make an appointment with a local businessman to persuade him to come on-board. It was, he decided, essential to have some facts at his fingertips for the meeting.

He was on the lookout for cheap alcohol. At the resort the bars prided themselves on serving the good brands. But for his purposes – make lots of money in a short time – the profit margin had to be as big as possible. Not that he would be supplying the stuff himself, naturally, but with some idea of its cost he could work out his cut more accurately.

Bottles holding all kinds of spirits glistened as he paced up and down the tall narrow aisles. He searched methodically. "Ah!" He honed in on a ridiculously low-priced gin. Now that was what he was after. Then he spotted some equally cheap, and presumably nasty, vodka. He laughed at the label which looked almost the same as the authentic one and the brand name had just one letter different.

Furtively he checked no one was watching before yanking pen and paper from the top pocket of his shirt to hastily scribble some notes.

He tried to ignore the fact that his proposal could well put his own job at risk. That was quite scary but it was crucial to make more money this season. He wanted to emulate Jason by buying a portfolio of stocks and shares. Jason had assured him yesterday that was the way to make real money. He had a wife to support and who knew when his next acting job would be. Although, with his talent, he felt he really should be acting full-time.

After a few more interesting discoveries he glanced at his watch. Enough research. He still had to get to the bank. He sighed at the thought of maybe a couple of hours wasted in a queue. This didn't seem to bother the locals, who used the time to socialize. But it annoyed the heck out of him.

* * *

Clare O'Hara had yet to be persuaded to make a return visit to the Paradise Hotel. But that afternoon when they left the beach hot and hungry, Bethany Griffiths pleaded for sandwiches and a cold drink by the hotel pool.

"Ah, let's go there then," Clare agreed. "Hopefully Jason won't even be around."

As they arrived a petite blonde stood up, threw a couple of limp beach towels over one arm, and handed a pair of yellow water-wings to her equally blonde little boy. Bethany moved towards them. "Hiya, Ingrid, long time no see."

"Bethany!" The women greeted Greek-style, with an air kiss on both cheeks.

"Pano, you are much taller than when I saw you last year!" Bethany stopped herself from stroking his shiny hair. The little boy's blue eyes gleamed with pleasure before he hid himself shyly behind the folds of his mother's long pink skirt.

Bethany made introductions. "Ingrid is married to Michalis," Bethany told Clare.

"Ah, right. He's such a nice man and so knowledgeable," Clare enthused. "I'm interested in hotel management and I've been asking him lots of questions." She sat on a sunbed and put down her beach bag.

Ingrid nodded and looked pleased. "Yes, he has worked in France and Switzerland, you know, as well as different parts of Greece." Her English was heavily accented with her native German.

A curious Panos came out of hiding and stared at them open-mouthed.

"Won't you stay and have coffee with us?" Bethany asked.

"I wish it was possible, you know." Ingrid was regretful. "But already I am running late. I have to make Michalis something to eat before he starts his evening shift."

"Aw, what a shame. I've been looking out for you."

"For how long have you been here?"

"For weeks, actually. I've lost count. But I'm staying the whole summer this time."

"The whole summer!"

"Yes." Bethany grinned. "I've taken a year off from my job to write a book." She put her hand to her throat and huffed through parted lips. Saying it out loud reminded her of how scary the whole plan was. But Ingrid looked delighted. Encouraged, Bethany went on, "I'd love to interview you for my novel."

"Me?" Ingrid's eyes widened in surprise.

"It's just that you know so much about living here and it would take me years to find these things out," Bethany explained.

"You should come to my house one morning and I will make you tea and we will discuss how I can help."

"Sounds great, thanks very much."

Bethany waved to Panos as he left with his mother. The little boy smiled shyly and waggled his hand back at her. She stood and watched until they walked down the hill and disappeared.

As Clare settled onto one of the sunbeds in the shade of a big white umbrella she glanced up at her friend. "Are you okay, Bethany," she asked, but got no reply. "Beth? Beth!"

"Oh!" Bethany looked sharply down at Clare. "Sorry, did you say something?"

Clare studied her. "I just asked if you were okay." Bethany's face was closed. "Only, you looked a bit... upset?" Clare wasn't sure that was the right word, but there was something...

"Oh, I'm fine, thanks."

Clare knew that she wasn't, but obviously Bethany was not going to say what was on her mind.

"I need to eat," said Bethany, dropping her gold beach bag onto the other bed. "I'll go to the bar and order. What do you want?"

Clare watched her friend weave between tables walking slowly as if carrying a heavy weight. When she reached the bar and gave the order she sat on a stool and looked down at her hands, clearly deep in thought. But when she came back she was determinedly cheerful.

Clare sipped orange juice through a straw. "Jason's not here I'm pleased to see."

"Hmm." Bethany was non-committal. "This is the life," she muttered, stretching her long legs towards the glinting oblong of turquoise water.

Clare adjusted the back of her sunbed to upright and dug the Princess Di book out of her beach bag. "It's grand," she agreed. "I just wish I didn't have to go to work tonight." She was a barmaid for Yiorgos in his club called Pandora's. "But I tell you, it's so quiet there I can't see him keeping me on much longer."

"Oh, really." Bethany jerked her head around to look at Clare. "You never said."

"Well, he hasn't stopped me yet but he has hinted."

"Maybe you should start looking for something else then."

"I think you could be right."

Nikos arrived bearing a tray which he held aloft on one hand. "Your food, ladies." This is what Jason said and he copied him. He set the plates of freshly cut cheese and tomato sandwiches out on the little table between the sunbeds.

As he walked away Bethany was already tucking into her food. "I just love this crusty village bread." She popped a crisp into her mouth and crunched it up with the sandwich.

Clare noticed her friend seemed back to normal. "Mmm, grand." She wolfed down half a sandwich. "Didn't realize I was so hungry till I started eating." With the other piece in her hand she turned back to the riveting book. A slow reader, she'd only got halfway.

Jason walked up to the bar. A small cry of alarm attracted his attention and when he saw Clare in a skimpy pink bikini ineffectually swatting a wasp away with a book, his jaw dropped. He moved in quickly. "Need any help?" He batted the wasp away gently with a tray. It took the hint and left.

"Oh, thank you! Sure, I hate wasps." Clare shuddered. "I've got a phobia about them."

"Phobia, that's a good Greek word," said Jason conversationally, wanting to keep her talking. He found her irresistible. As Clare picked up his appreciative look she frowned. "Don't blame me that I find you attractive," he muttered. His brown eyes sparked a question at her: don't you find me attractive too? Don't push your luck, her face replied. But then they simultaneously smiled and the ice was broken between them.

"So, how are you, ladies?" He turned to Bethany and smiled. "You haven't been to have that drink with me yet." He wagged his forefinger at them in reproach.

"Clare is working at Pandora's now."

"Oh, I didn't know that." He regarded Clare thoughtfully. "I heard not many people were going there."

"You heard right, unfortunately. So I don't know how much longer I'll have the job."

Jason didn't miss a beat. "You can come and work for me," he said. "I'll need another person to help in this bar soon."

"Oh, that's a very kind offer." Clare looked interested.

"Well, think about it and let me know." A customer called out to him. "Excuse me," he said to them both.

Bethany was intrigued. "Would you work for Jason?"

"Might do."

"So all he had to do to get into your good books was to scare a wasp away." Bethany smiled knowingly. Clare opened her book but her mind kept honing in on the look that she and Jason had exchanged. She took off her sunglasses and closed her eyes.

Soon Jason came back. "Look," he said, "I've got to leave in a few minutes but I wanted to say that on your next night off, Clare, I hope you lovely ladies will join me for that drink." Clare and Bethany smiled at him. "Oh, and Clare, don't forget to let me know if you want the job. I'll keep it open until you tell me. But please don't leave it too long." He was all business.

Clare stood up. "Thank you, Jason," she said, shading her eyes from the bright sunlight with one hand. "I really do appreciate your offer. Sure, I'll get back to you soon about that."

"I look forward to it." He was smiling again but not flirting. He walked away.

Clare wondered if she had imagined that Look. She played it over again in her mind. She didn't think so, but you never knew with men did you?

* * *

Ingrid walked home with a happy heart. It was the start of summer and she was living on this beautiful island with the man she loved and their wonderful son.

While she counted her blessings Panos ran ahead trotting as fast as his little legs could carry him, determined to keep in front. It was a game he and his mother played since he had turned six in the winter and become a schoolboy.

As they walked past the Candy Bar Panos looked over with fascination at the little fountain sparkling in the sunshine. He laughed and pointed.

They were turning up the lane towards their house when he noticed a huge yellow butterfly hovering in a field, over a row of fat purple aubergines, and stopped to watch. It was so close that he reached over to stroke its wing. But as he stretched out his arm it fluttered up into the air.

He chuckled. "Mama, look." He pointed at the butterfly.

"Beautiful." Panos continued to watch until the impressive insect flitted and fluttered from view. "Ice cream?" she asked.

His mother had dangled this reward for leaving the

swimming pool without a fuss. He gave her his full attention, grinned broadly and nodded deeply a few times.

He liked to nod and did it often.

Ingrid took his hand and together they headed for home. When they got there they made a joke of trying to go through the narrow gate side-by-side. Chuckling, she shepherded Panos indoors.

As she scooped ice cream into a small glass bowl and pulled a spoon out of the cutlery drawer she continued to smile contentedly.

"Pano!" She called her son from the lounge to come and get his ice cream.

His pale eyes went round with pleasure when he saw his mother drizzling chocolate sauce liberally over the top.

His very favourite.

Carefully, he took the bowl from her. "It's cold," he complained. Ingrid ruffled the top of his head. "Did you expect it to be hot?" she teased. He shot her a look of disgust. She twinkled at him and he smiled back.

A feeling of love sprang up from her heart.

Her darling boy.

She felt so happy. So very blessed. Her eyes misted with love for a few seconds.

"Mama?" Panos was staring at her.

She cleared her throat and became practical again.

"Go and eat that up before it does get hot. Your father will be home from town soon and I have to start his meal or he will have to eat..." She stopped and thought. "He'll have to eat grass like a donkey!" Ingrid pulled her mouth into a silent exaggerated "Ooh" then grinned.

Panos guffawed. "Baba will eat grass like a donkey! Grass like a donkey!" He giggled and repeated this a few times more as his mother laughed along. They enjoyed joking with each other.

When Ingrid looked pointedly at the ice cream, Panos nodded deeply a few times. Slowly he padded to the next room carrying his bowl carefully between both hands, his mouth watering with anticipation.

While Ingrid started peeling potatoes she continued to count her blessings. Her life was very sweet indeed.

Chapter 9

A dawdling Spiros steered the car to the edge of the narrow country road to let a van zip past. His arm resting on the lip of the open window baked to nut brown in the hot sun. In his misery he didn't notice. *It was almost a waste of fuel going all the way into town to buy stock.* He had not been able to afford even half the items on his daughter Eleni's list.

Approaching the resort he passed Pandora's, his brother's club, with a deep sigh and much head shaking. The low white building with a fancy sea-facing courtyard, which he knew had cost a lot of money, had proved a flop. Why he had branched out in that direction Spiros didn't know. He earned plenty from his construction work and apartment rentals but he never seemed satisfied with what he had. And now he had overstretched himself.

"And so have I!" Spiros' stomach contracted with dread.

As he reached the top of the hill he suddenly felt nauseous with fear. Braking sharply he spun the wheels onto the gravel shoulder of the hairpin bend, cut the engine, and flung open his door. Gulping fresh sea air, he passed a trembling hand over his clammy face.

What on earth was he going to do?

"Come on, come on!" he shouted at himself in exasperation. "It's not the end of the world!" But at that moment it felt like it. "Why, oh why, did I extend the shop?" He was in debt for the first time in his life. And to Yiorgos of all people!

Yiorgos, who had a way of insinuating that Spiros was inferior. That he, the elder son of the family, was also the one his parents loved best. He said this in many subtle ways.

Their mother did too.

Only yesterday in the shop she had pointed that out, yet again. "Look how well Yiorgos is doing," she said. "I'm so proud of him." He just smiled and nodded and felt inadequate, as usual.

Spiros stared glumly over the cliff, past the long pale stretch of shore speckled with people reduced by distance to ants, to fasten, as always, on the wide border of sea. As golden arrows of sunlight struck the shifting blue expanse, their dazzle triggered the memory of many happy voyages. He pined for the easy friendship of his shipmates and their tight-knit floating community.

Back on dry land his local community was being pulled apart by a groundswell of discontent. Some people hated tourism and the changes it brought. While others, like him, tried to make a living from it.

He thought of the paltry stock in the boot and sighed.

"Oh, this worry is making an old man of me." A friend had died last year of a heart attack brought on by stress over money. Lately, *he* sometimes got twinges of pain in his chest. Would that happen to him too? He felt afraid and automatically sketched three quick crosses over his heart. "Oh, God, please help me!" His voice cracked with despair.

Gabriella zoomed in and spoke with his guardian angel. "Encourage him to confide in his wife," she counselled.

Spiros listened and wondered if it would be the right thing to do. He had tried to shoulder the burden alone but perhaps together they could find a solution.

His stalker demon was furious at Gabriella's intervention. It had been goading Spiros for days, delighting at the man's distress.

Stalker demon: "Do not tell your wife about this problem she will be livid about the debt and because you didn't tell her about it!"

Spiros: *If I tell Anna, she'll be angry with me for going behind her back.*

Guardian angel: "You are a good husband. You tried to protect Anna from the worry of the debt, certain you could pay Yiorgos back."

Spiros: *I just tried to protect Anna. She worries about debt.*

Stalker demon: "Protect? You are just devious!"

Spiros: *Anna might think I have been devious. But it really wasn't that way at all.*

Guardian angel: "You have to tell Anna. She loves you and she respects you."

Spiros: *I have to tell Anna. She loves me and she respects me. She will understand.*

Stalker demon: "She will understand all right. She will understand that you are devious. She will never respect or trust you again!"

Spiros slumped over the wheel. The family was his responsibility and he couldn't stand to lose Anna's trust. But he couldn't take much more of this solitary pressure.

He pictured Anna's face angry. "Oh, I can't tell her!"

His heart thumped so wildly it scared him. "Oh, I don't know what to do!"

The demon tittered in delight and flicked its forked tongue rudely at the angels.

Gabriella and his guardian looked at each other in frustration as Spiros' thoughts twisted this way and that. Gabriella shrugged her shoulders. The seed of a solution had been planted and now it was up to Spiros to decide what to do with it.

The choice was his.

The two angels spoke a few more words. Then Gabriella, with a vertical take-off, flew off to another conflict.

Still dithering, Spiros glanced down at the resort and the familiar pattern of buildings jumped out of the greenery.

Right at the far end, on the headland, sat the Paradise Hotel. Even at this distance he could still see people on sunbeds clustered around the glittering turquoise pool.

Customers.

Profit.

Spiros felt a stab of envy.

With a sigh he turned the ignition key, steered the car over the clattering gravel back onto the road, and continued down the hill.

The narrow road leading to the hotel cut Z-shaped through the resort. Slowly he drove downwards to the base of the Z.

On the left side of this short stretch he glanced with a shudder at the new minimarket, the main cause of his reduced profits. The owner of an old villa had added a room on its front, and Spiros now grudgingly admitted that the new shop, with its orange awning, looked smart. Its windows flashed in the sunshine so he couldn't see inside. A tourist couple, dressed for the beach in matching denim shorts and white tops, opened the door and went inside. He sighed. They should have been *his* customers.

Beyond the new shop, a handful of sizeable tourist villas were spaced out along the narrow road between green hedges backed by field after field of vegetables. A few beach towels and bathing suits fluttered on clothes lines in backyards. A thin black cat walked slowly across a patch of yellowed grass.

Just before the sharp right-hand bend he saw Aeron standing outside the Candy Bar deep in conversation with a few visitors.

After the bend, the road went straight on for about another hundred yards with a taverna on the left, and on the right the sea view was obscured by fields, trees, and a few villas.

Approaching the sharp left-hand bend, where his minimarket sat on the right, beside a pathway running down to the beach, the sea was visible again.

After the bend and straight on for a further hundred yards, many of the buildings scattered along the left of the road formed the original fishing hamlet on the slopes of a green hill. He shook his head as he briefly longed for the simple past.

On the right his eyes lit on the prime seashore location where a dozen or so new villas had been built, mostly with tourist rooms above and either a little bar, or taverna underneath.

Scantily clad tourists went into or came out of these places.

No one seemed to be making for his shop.

A dejected Spiros sighed hugely as he swung behind the minimarket and parked the car next to the front door of his home. He took a deep breath and went in to face the dismay of his wife and daughter over the meagre new stock from town.

* * *

The sun was a red globe atop the inky rim of sea when guardian angels began to make their way to the shoreline. With a beating of mighty wings they swooped in over water and cliffs to congregate on the elbow of sand hidden from the main beach by a wall of rock.

The wards of the guardians lived in Korkyra or Hora – so interlinked in everyday activity that their angels always had their daily meeting together in this one place. Gabriella, the angel of Greece, was there with them.

Small clusters formed as angels most involved with each other's wards gathered to confer.

Then one large group began to form around a single tall guardian with long dark hair tumbling over thin shoulders. Gabriella fanned her wings and went to hover just above and to the right of him. Mainly she was here to listen and evaluate details relevant to her mission. As the angels began to recount the day's events in relation to the guardian's ward his large dark eyes widened with dismay.

"Jason is starting to draw Clare in," said her angel, head shaking in dismay as she looked up at the man's towering guardian. "I am concerned that he will succeed."

The smaller clusters of angels broke up: their conferring complete. Now they ringed the group – the outer circle hovering just above the water, wings spread and overlapping. Their uniformly pale faces and white robes turned rosy in the rays of the fiery orb which still sat on the horizon. It would remain there until the angel meeting ended.

"My ward is worried about her grandson. Nikos is very impressed by Jason and his moneymaking and wants to copy everything he does."

Gavin's angel spoke up next. "Jason has been bragging to Gavin about money – encouraging him to make investments that he clearly cannot afford." He glanced first up at Jason's guardian then round at the others before locking gazes with Gabriella. Her huge light grey eyes were filled with concern.

"Spiros was envious of Jason again today," his angel said. Many of the angels nodded with empathy. They too were dealing with the effects of jealousy in relation to Jason's apparent good fortune.

When all the angels whose wards had been affected that day by Jason had finished speaking the guardians lined up in orderly fashion. In straight rows standing twenty deep they filled the beach.

The angel of Greece then flew to hover over the sea in front of the guardians. As she turned away to face the setting sun a deep almost palpable silence fell over the throng.

With eyes closed and hands steepled in front of them they lifted their faces heavenwards. From high in the sky a freshet of golden light enveloped the angels. They became one with it so that in an instant only luminescence was visible. Then, as the light faded the angels reappeared – pale faces beaming with joy.

After a farewell to each other, hands crossing briefly over upper torsos, the angels dispersed swooping back to their wards over sea, beach and cliff.

The sun began to slowly sink below the horizon.

Chapter 10

Bethany Griffiths woke up and lay in the shutter-darkened room. Gosh, the last week of June! It was still hard to believe she was in Korkyra for the whole summer!

Stretching up her arms, she breathed deeply before swinging her feet down onto the cotton rug. After twisting a metal handle she pulled the double windows inwards. Then, unhooking the catch, she pushed open the wooden shutters and sighed with pleasure as sunlight flooded the room. It highlighted the big square of fuchsia silk laid over the bedcover and bright fan of scarves on a wall peg – her personal homely touch.

She padded into the dark kitchen. Clare was obviously still asleep – often working late, she didn't surface until noon. As she opened another set of windows and shutters and gazed at the sun-dappled olive grove she remembered a Cardiff window with net curtains and a cold pane of glass as the barrier between the rain and the house across the way.

Leisurely, she sat on one of the mismatched chairs at the big round table – the only furniture in the kitchen-dining-living room – drinking a mug of milky tea. To think that only a short time ago she would have rushed to shower, apply make-up, and don the power suit before dashing off for a day filled with other people's priorities.

In Wales, as an IT trainer, she had been part of the push to computerize daily tasks. One of the things she taught office managers was electronic mailing. It was a method, using part ASCII machine code and part programme, to send each other messages. A bit complicated, most people couldn't see the point of it. "If I want to get in touch with someone I just pick up the phone," said one manager and most agreed. On the face of it, it did seem a strange way to communicate.

But who knows. It may catch on.

Sipping tea she thought, as she often did, back to her decision to take a year's unpaid leave.

Coming up to her fortieth birthday she had begun to reappraise her life. Certainly there had been lots of good things along the way. But her situation had not panned out like she thought it would! She felt like a mouse going round and around on a little wheel and getting nowhere.

She had questions without answers, and no one to ask.

She began to feel restless.

Then she saw the film *Shirley Valentine* and when the heroine said something like, "Why do we get all these feelings, all this life if we don't use it?" it totally resonated with her.

A scribbler from childhood, tired of butting her head against the glass ceiling of sexism in the Civil Service, Bethany had wangled a career break, and cut free from the day job for a whole year to write a novel.

It was a gamble, though. Bethany had just one year to write the novel and she had pictured herself living in New York and basing it there. Plan A, Clare called it.

But she was happy in Korkyra and her novel, set instead in a fictitious resort on Corfu, was shaping up nicely.

But no matter what, her life just had to change!

Her stomach contracted with pain. No. She wouldn't think about that now.

But sometime soon it would have to be faced.

Accepted.

She determinedly pushed the painful subject to the back of her mind yet gain.

Looking at the sunny olive grove it was difficult to picture herself in an office. She rinsed her empty mug and left it out for a refill. First she wanted cereal.

Pulling a box of muesli from the cupboard, something clattered down onto the worktop. She picked up the little book of matches with the Candy Bar logo. Suddenly she got a clear mental picture of Aeron – kind pale blue eyes and chin with a film star dimple.

Her thoughts flashed back to the look of delight on his face when she told him she was staying the whole summer. A little tingle of pleasure ran up from the pit of her stomach to the back of her throat and blossomed to a huge grin. "Aeron. Aeron." It would be so nice to date him...

She sighed and shook her head regretfully. "If only you weren't married." But he was. And she didn't date married men.

Aeron is cute, but hey ho.

She pushed all thoughts of him deliberately from her mind – much to the anger of her stalker demon, and delight of her guardian angel – and shook cereal into a bowl. She needed to plan out some questions to put to Ingrid. She was going over to visit her later.

* * *

Katarina was staring out of the grimy classroom window daydreaming. Exams were next week and this was a period for revising. Having begun quite diligently she was now hot and hungry, and her attention wandered.

Her cousin Nikos had come into the shop yesterday afternoon, and, finding her alone, stayed for coffee and a chat. His father and her mother were brother and sister. She usually liked talking with him. She was going to miss him when he went into the army, which would be any day now. But he had started speaking about foreign girls and she didn't like what he said. At all.

"They're more sophisticated and knowledgeable than local girls," he insisted. "And they listen and empathize – which makes them very attractive and nice to be with."

"Don't tell me that you prefer these foreigners to the girls you grew up with," she demanded belligerently.

Her cousin faced her wrath squarely and thought about her

accusation. "You know, Katarina..." He stopped and looked serious. "Come to think about it, in many ways, I do."

There was an uneasy, electrically-charged silence between them. It was Nikos who broke it.

"Have you ever thought there may be more to life for you than just school, getting married, and having babies like all the other girls here?" He warmed to the idea. "Have you ever dreamed of travelling to other countries, of having a career, and making your own money?"

Katarina's tawny eyes went round and dark brows arched in shock. Nikos had just verbally ripped apart their whole way of life. She was momentarily thrown. But as she stared transfixed at her cousin she noticed his blue eyes were warm and encouraging. He appeared to be offering her something that, until now, had seemed unattainable, and therefore not worth considering.

For a few moments a vision of a very different kind of life tantalized her.

But she recognised it as a mirage and shook her head to clear it.

Eventually she responded in a flat voice, "Fancy dreams, Niko. How would that ever happen to me? How would I start this fantasy career you speak of and make enough money to do all this travelling?"

The reality of Katarina's situation was difficult and Nikos could only see one solution. He winked. "Perhaps you will meet a foreign boy to take you away to paradise."

But they both recognized that there was no way Katarina would ever have any kind of relationship with a foreigner. She would be automatically shunned by the community, and doubtless her family too.

Yet, remembering Nikos' words now made her smirk. If only he knew that soon she would be living in Paradise, the hotel that is, married to Jason.

First, though, there were exams to sit and she wanted to make Jason proud. Flicking dark hair back over her shoulders with both hands she returned to her notes. She was revising English Language. It was her top subject. She refused to speak it in the shop, though, but did enjoy listening in to conversations.

As she began to run over a list of vocabulary a sardonic smile crept over her face. The customers would have been shocked to know just how much of their conversations she understood.

* * *

As Ingrid led the way into the kitchen Bethany praised the immaculate little pale pink house which faced an open field. Pine cabinets lined one wall of the compact room. A grey marble sink overlooked a window onto the large back garden.

On a small dining table sat a tall vase of velvety scarlet roses. "Gorgeous!" said Bethany.

"From Michalis," said Ingrid. "Yesterday was our ninth wedding anniversary."

"You married a romantic man!"

"He is a wonderful man," she enthused. "A good husband and a great father. He just adores Panos, you know."

Ingrid's obvious happiness warmed Bethany. "I suppose Panos is at school?"

"Yes, so we can talk without interruption." Ingrid rolled her eyes. "He is a very good boy, you know, but has too much energy to keep still and quiet for very long."

"He's a lovely boy. You must be so proud of him."

Ingrid nodded. "Since he started school, I miss him very much," she confided, setting a pitcher of iced orange juice and glasses on a tray. Bethany had agreed it was too warm for tea.

The day was a real scorcher and the backdoor stood open to catch any breeze. Bethany had a notebook and pen at hand but mostly she just listened as Ingrid talked about her life.

"I was working in Athens as a chambermaid in a small hotel and Michalis was working in the famous Grande Bretagne Hotel opposite the Greek parliament. We met in an open-air café by the ancient Agora." She smiled broadly at the memory. "We fell in love almost from our first look."

The two women paused to silently ponder on love.

Bethany wondered what it was all about. For her, relationships were complicated. Yes, she had loved. But love was not always enough to keep things going. Her glance strayed to the bare third finger of her left hand.

One thing was certain: she was happy to take a break from love. Her mind skipped to Aeron. *Good job he's married!*

Ingrid thought only of Michalis.

Bethany quashed thoughts of the forbidden Aeron and learned that the couple had married quickly.

"Our wedding was in a tiny Byzantine church not far from Michalis' hotel."

"Lovely." Bethany imagined candles winking on shiny brass chandeliers and softly illuminating old icons, and vases filled with fragrant flowers.

"Yes, it was lovely."

Then Bethany reached the heart of the interview. "How did your families react to the mix of cultures?"

Ingrid had a lot to say about this. His family and her family shared a mutual disappointment about their marriage and suspicion of each other. It had clearly been a very painful experience.

Finally, though, Ingrid chuckled. "But they came round in the end because of Panos." *Talk about dismantling the Berlin Wall!*

"We decided to move to Corfu when Panos was still a baby. We wanted him to grow up in a peaceful environment."

"I understand completely." Bethany nodded. "Korkyra seems the perfect place to raise a child."

As Ingrid nodded a slow smile blossomed over her face and

fired up the blue of her eyes.

Bethany's eyes widened, momentarily taken aback. Then she understood. "Ah," she said, with a grin.

"Yes," Ingrid responded. "I am expecting another baby. But we have only just found out and we will not be telling people yet."

Spontaneously Bethany hugged her and offered congratulations and good wishes. And she promised to keep the news of an expected baby a secret. That done, it seemed a fitting end to the interview.

As Ingrid walked Bethany out onto the garden path their goodbyes were interrupted by an ear-splitting whining noise. Bethany spun round. The din came from an old red car gunning up the lane. "Going a bit fast isn't he?" she gasped. "Thinks he's on a racing track." She was shaking her head in disgust as the car reached them.

The driver, window rolled right down, turned to snarl under his breath, malevolent dark eyes glinting above a long sharp nose, incongruous in his small narrow bronzed face.

A cold shiver ran down Bethany's spine. She sensed the presence of evil.

Bethany was right about the evil presence. Takis was under attack from a small band of rogue demons led by his stalker demon. They buzzed around him feeding his prejudices, whispering the worst and darkest thoughts they could conjure up right into his receptive brain.

As the car disappeared Ingrid shook her head in exasperation.

Bethany didn't have a clue what to say. Goose pimples raised up on her legs as the very bad feeling persisted. At length she asked quietly, "Do you know that man?" Ingrid nodded. "Does he always drive that fast?"

Ingrid sighed deeply. "Always," she breathed.

"Dear God...!" breathed Bethany. Angel Gabriella zoomed in and advised her to wait in silence for more details.

Ingrid had no friends among the locals. The women who deigned to speak to her were polite but determinedly distant. Some shunned her when she was alone, only speaking when Michalis was present. And most never looked into her eyes.

She knew they acted like that because, in World War II when Hitler invaded Corfu, his soldiers had done bad things. She longed to tell people that she too hated what they had done.

What she found harder to bear was the coolness of her in-laws. Michalis' mother, father and both sisters, though they clearly adored Panos, only acted friendly to her in front of their son. She never told Michalis about this, as she knew her own parents were as unfriendly in their thoughts. They were careful, though, on visits, to keep this from Michalis for the sake of their grandson, whom they loved dearly.

All of this meant that Ingrid had no one to confide in. Gabriella hoped she would do so now to Bethany.

Ingrid's stalker demon was on full alert.

Ingrid's guardian angel advised her to open up.

Ingrid mentally shook herself. "That is Takis who lives up the road with his parents. He got that car in the winter and always he drives fast like that up and down the lane." She gave a small sigh. "You have seen how he looks at me, well it gives me the shivers, you know."

"It gave me the shivers too." Bethany shuddered. "If looks could kill I'd have been dead."

"I think that too but what worries me more is that he could hurt Panos, or another child, driving so recklessly."

Bethany had to agree that it was dangerous.

Ingrid said she was going to ask Michalis to speak to Takis.

Gabriella instructed Bethany's guardian angel to urge her to advise caution.

"I wonder if that's a good idea," said Bethany.

"What do you mean?" Ingrid had her own reservations but wanted Bethany's opinion.

"Well... it sounds like Takis might be a little... unbalanced." She didn't want to alarm Ingrid but she felt she had to warn her.

Gabriella whispered advice.

Bethany took a deep breath and spoke bluntly. "Look, he drives that car like it's a lethal weapon. Maybe it's better not to upset him. Perhaps Michalis could ask someone else to mention it."

Gabriella and the guardian angels nodded. "Well done, Bethany," said Gabriella.

Bethany felt like she had said the right thing.

The stalker demon told her that was not true.

Bethany then wondered if she should have kept quiet.

Ingrid shook her head as if to clear it. "I will think about what you have said, thank you. I appreciate your concern."

Bethany didn't know what else to say. She had tried to persuade Ingrid to reconsider. She could only hope that she would.

As the stalker demon screamed with hysterical laughter and vanished, Gabriella and the guardian angels shrugged at each other. They had done their best.

The choice was Ingrid's alone.

Chapter 11

Gavin Bellingham was driving through the village and saw Michalis climbing into his car. He slowed down and tooted his horn. Michalis waved. The men exchanged a few words of greeting and Gavin drove on. He liked Michalis. *A real professional like me.*

Then Gavin's conscience gave a twinge. Was his moneymaking scheme professional?

His guardian angel took the opportunity to remind Gavin that he prided himself on his integrity.

His stalker demon began its trickery.

Stalker demon: "Integrity! Don't make me laugh. When did integrity ever put money in your pocket?"

Gavin: *I've tried to have integrity in everything I do but where has it got me? I'm hardly a rich man am I?*

Guardian angel: "You are rich in many things, including love."

Gavin: *I know I'm very lucky to have Suzanna for a wife and love is a form of riches.*

Stalker demon: "Now you have a wife the riches need to be tangible. Make some real money! It's your responsibility."

Gavin: *I have added responsibilities now I'm married. I need to support the two of us so I have to make some extra money.*

Guardian angel: "Yes, but if you follow this plan, you could put your job at risk."

Gavin: *But what if I lose my holiday rep job? I'll be in trouble.*

Stalker demon: "You won't lose your job. You will mainly stay behind the scenes. Any involvement you have can be attributed to your interest in doing the best for your clients."

Gavin: *No one need know that this is my plan. I can make it seem like I am just doing my best for my clients.*

Guardian angel: "Is this really the best you can do for your clients? For one thing, you will not have as much time for them. Do you think that is being professional?"

The argument had come full circle. "Oh, what the heck!" Gavin felt exasperated. He needed to make more money to support his new wife and himself. And his idea was brilliant for this.

He glanced at his watch. Good. He would be at his appointment right on time. Now that was professional.

In his mind he ran over what he would say during the meeting. His plan was simplicity itself. He smiled and beeped the horn a couple of times in good humour. He liked the way he had worded that. He would use that line. Possibly as an opener.

He arrived at Pandora's at three o'clock precisely and found Yiorgos standing behind the bar in his empty club.

Yiorgos had no idea what Gavin wanted to see him about. Or why he wanted to meet him here. He hardly knew the man and he had a lot to sort out so he didn't need any timewasters today. He had been forced to let Clare go because there weren't enough customers to serve. And he had decided to cut his losses and try to rent the club out.

He wished he had not tried to run it himself.

He'd got the idea of building a club after watching Jason run his disco at the hotel. The tourists really seemed to enjoy themselves. The place was always crammed. It looked like a goldmine. And, of course, running a club would give him a bit more prestige in the community.

Well that was the plan anyway. But now he knew the fiasco made him look foolish.

The good thing was that financially his experiment had cost very little – though his brother presumed the opposite. He already owned the piece of land. And the building materials he'd used were mainly leftovers from other jobs. He was the busiest builder in the resort and with his team – on minimum wage but steady work, so they stayed loyal – he always had more than one project on the go. The furnishings he'd got by barter for a small extension to a shop in town.

Admittedly, the failed venture had left him temporarily a bit short of ready cash. And while he could easily have gone to the bank, and dipped into a fat pot of savings, he had no intention of doing that. Not when Spiros owed him money. Maybe he would go to see him this evening to ask him to start paying some back. Of course, he knew that Spiros's minimarket wasn't doing as well as before but, well, this was business.

In reality, it was much more than business to Yiorgos. It gave him real pleasure to have this power over his brother.

His baby brother who could do no wrong in their mother's eyes.

Well, let her see who the better businessman of the two really was.

"Ah, Yiorgo." Gavin pinned on a big confident smile. "Good to see you." The man looked sour but Gavin ploughed quickly onwards. "Thank you for agreeing to this appointment at such short notice. I think you will find it worth your while."

Yiorgos, cigarette clamped as usual between stained teeth, squinted through a haze of smoke as he motioned Gavin to a table and set down a couple of glasses of cold beer. Gavin took a large grateful swallow before making his pronouncement.

"I have a plan to make money for us both." He looked Yiorgos straight in the eye and delivered his choice line. "The plan is simplicity itself." He paused theatrically. Yiorgos ground his cigarette out in an overflowing ashtray and made no comment but Gavin knew he had grabbed his attention. He pressed on. "This place is very attractive." He looked around him in genuine appreciation.

Booths with tables and red velvet benches ringed a big dance floor with huge coloured spotlights trained on it. Tall palm trees in red pots were opulently dotted around. Outside, a deep balcony, edged with a waist-high whitewashed wall, overlooked the blue bowl of sea below the cliff. "You've obviously spent a lot of money on it, and so far, I believe, you haven't seen a return on your investment."

Yiorgos looked stern. He wondered if he should deny it, if only to keep his pride. Then he pulled himself up sharply. Gavin had mentioned making money and he was open to that. "I am listening," he growled. Gavin accordingly outlined his idea to an attentive Yiorgos.

Their two stalker demons whispered enticing words about quick profits. The two guardian angels tried to counteract this, advising caution instead.

Gabriella joined the guardians in the tussle. All three angels tried their best – putting forward suggestions to show that the plan was a bad idea.

But they could only advise.

Finally, Yiorgos said he would think about it. But this had nothing to do with his conscience getting the better of him. He had already decided to go with Gavin's idea. All he had to do now was think the details through, especially what financial agreement he would make with Gavin.

When Yiorgos made a firm appointment to meet Gavin again in a couple of days the stalker demons, who felt their battle was won, began shrieking wildly and mocking the angels.

The angels looked at each other and sorrowfully shook their heads. But they were not allowed to stop Gavin and Yiorgos from doing what they chose.

* * *

Around ten o'clock Jason glanced up and there was Clare, looking like a lovely apparition in a gauzy lemon dress. His heart missed a beat. Yet, wanting to cover his eagerness, he inwardly shook himself. "Hi," he said deliberately casual. "Nice to see you both again."

"Hi." Clare's voice was low and uncertain. Her eyes slid coyly away from his gaze.

"Table for two please, Jason," said Bethany.

"Of course." The restaurant was full. He led them to the family table. "So, you got a night off then?" He put his head on one side and studied Clare.

"Umm, not exactly." Clare gave a little embarrassed giggle. "I got the sack."

"Oh."

"Last night was so quiet that Yiorgos said he couldn't afford to keep me on. But it was all very friendly," she assured him.

"So is Pandora's loss my gain then?" He was direct.

"Can I come and talk to you about it tomorrow?"

"Of course." He handed them menus and took their order for drinks.

Bethany watched his retreating back. "I think you fancy him." She smirked at her friend.

"I do quite like him." Clare admitted that much.

"Hmm." Bethany grinned. "As I recall, missy, you thought he was arrogant before." She could not resist teasing her friend.

"I know." Something had shifted inside.

"But if you work for him won't that make it awkward?"

"There isn't a thing between us. I'm not presuming there will be. And I do need a job, as soon as possible."

Bethany nodded and turned to her menu. "I'm starving," she said.

"Sure, you're always starving." Clare couldn't believe how much her friend ate and that she stayed so slim. "Must be the sea air." Her appetite had vanished the moment she saw Jason so she asked if they could share a meal.

When Jason came to take their order he continued to act businesslike.

Nikos brought a basket of fresh-cut bread, bottled water and carafe of local red wine, smiled broadly and left.

Clare poured tumblers of water, Bethany poured wine. They lifted their wine and chinked the small thick glasses. "Cheers," they said together.

Soon a second waiter arrived with a large tray of food. Bethany stacked her plate with golden fried courgettes and spooned up giant butterbeans simmered in a rich tomato sauce. Clare helped herself to thick slices of cucumber and tomato and some cubes of crumbly feta.

Bethany spread a potato dip called *scordalia* onto a morsel of bread. "Oh, wow! That's fantastic." She chewed with relish. "I'm going to try making this at home." She ate more and guessed at the ingredients. "Very garlicky, though," she added. "Maybe you shouldn't eat it, Clare." She grinned wonkily through closed lips and a full mouth.

Clare looked up sharply. "Don't know what you mean," she said airily.

Bethany swallowed and chuckled. "Yeah, right." She noticed Clare didn't touch the dip but made no further comment. The simple food was so tasty that Clare managed to eat more than she thought she would.

When the table was cleared Jason brought a platter of lush red triangles of watermelon glistening with black seeds. "Can I offer you ladies a cocktail?"

They looked at each other and nodded. "Lovely," they said in unison.

"Would you like to see the list?"

"Why don't you surprise us?" Bethany asked and Clare agreed.

"Okay." He grinned broadly.

He was gone a full ten minutes. He returned bearing two tall overdressed cocktails held aloft on a small tray. Mellon vied with strawberries, and tiny paper umbrellas sheltered the pale foaming liquid from the golden stars of fizzing sparklers.

Clare clapped her hands with excitement. "For us?"

He nodded placing them down with a flourish. When the sparklers ran out he removed them.

Clare smiled at Jason shyly then took a sip and pronounced it delicious. "What's it called?"

"Jason's Special." He grinned.

"I hope you're not trying to get us tipsy. Because, I have to tell you..." she paused and looked him straight in the eye, "I'm not that sort of girl." Her meaning was clear.

Suddenly serious he took her chin in his hand and tilted it upwards. A long moment passed before he said in a low, hoarse voice, "You know better than that." Slowly she nodded.

He definitely did not plan to seduce Clare. Instead, he found he wanted to know everything about her.

A man strode up to the table and Jason pulled his hand away. Clare glanced up sharply as the man barked out a sentence in Greek. "There are customers waiting!" The man's face twisted into a snarl.

Jason's jaw clenched but his expression remained impassive. He replied in English, "Yes, Vasili, I'll be right there." The man strode away.

He turned back to Clare and Bethany. "My father," he explained. "Acts like he owns the place. And actually..." he smirked and theatrically raised one thick dark eyebrow, "he does!" They smiled back at him and the slight chill in the atmosphere lifted as he had intended. "Look," he added quickly, "I finish here in a few minutes." This would be news to his father. "Can I take you both for a drink?"

"Oh, that would very nice, thank you." Bethany accepted his invitation for them both.

"Great." Jason grinned happily, but this slid into a grimace as he followed his father into the kitchen and closed the door behind them. It did not block out the raised voices. Greek, spoken in fast staccato like machine gun fire was exchanged between father and son.

As this began Jason's mother, Margarita, crept, unnoticed, into a corner and began to silently weep.

When he'd had a lot to drink Vasilis tried to boss Jason around. Usually, Jason, feeling superior, let him rant for a while. But tonight, as his father accused him of keeping customers waiting by spending time with those girls, Jason couldn't be bothered to, as he thought, try to keep his father's ego intact. Instead he shouted back which made his father even angrier.

As Vasilis reached with trembling hands into the fridge for a bottle of beer Jason felt sickened. Margarita felt equally sickened by the way her husband used alcohol as a crutch.

Abruptly, Jason turned away and went back to the girls.

Bethany's chair was empty. "She decided to have an early night." Clare looked embarrassed.

Jason made no comment. He took Clare's hand as he walked her to his car. Then everything seemed to go into slow motion as if they had all the time in the world.

They were together and alone at last.

The road out of the village was unlit but their eyes grew accustomed to the dark, and soft moonlight enabled them to see each other with quick glances.

"I'm taking you to a really nice bar in the next resort."

"Sounds grand." Wherever they ended up would be nice. She smiled. He saw it and squeezed her hand. His brain zinged with happiness.

Katarina?

Guilt caused a sharp intake of breath.

I refuse to think about Katarina right now. It will work itself out.

He felt the hand of fate in his encounter with Clare and he put his trust in it.

Chapter 12

Soula moved slowly through her kitchen just after dawn and picked up one of Nikos' shoes which, as usual, he had kicked off just inside the front door. No sand. "Good boy," she muttered automatically, cradling the shoe. There hadn't been sand in his shoes for weeks but she couldn't stop herself checking.

As she put the shoe back beside its partner she thought about how excited Nikos was about going into the army. His call-up papers had arrived quickly after she prayed about it. And even without him actually leaving home, the problem of him dating foreign girls seemed to have been solved.

"Good," she muttered, then chided herself for standing daydreaming. "That will never get the breakfast made!" The *tzaletia* cakes were already keeping warm in the oven. She spooned coffee powder and sugar into the *briki* – a small metal pot with a long handle – then filled it with water and assembled four tiny white cups and saucers.

Glancing at the clock she clicked her tongue in dismay. Almost seven. She needed to call her grandson to get up. And her son-on-law would be home soon from a night of fishing. The usual frisson of fear for his safety ran through her, but she breathed deeply and pushed it away.

She had lots to do today. She wanted to strip the beds and wash the bedding. She hoped her daughter would go out with her friends and let her get on with it. Sometimes she moaned about the lack of help but Soula preferred to be mistress of her own home – the home she and her husband, Nikos, had lived in from the day of their marriage.

When her daughter, Eviania, married – a marriage arranged by Nikos before his untimely death one stormy night – her new husband simply moved into Soula's house. It was a common enough arrangement which suited them all.

Soula thought of her dead husband, as she so often did. He would have worried about Nikos – named after him. She sighed softly, then gave a little mirthless chuckle. She had yet another worry about her grandson. For years he had planned to train as a mechanic when he'd finished with the army. But now, instead of looking forward to a steady job, he was talking about different ways he could make lots of money. Some of his ideas seemed crazy.

He kept mentioning how Jason had made money through investments. Soula never commented but she had her own ideas about Jason. Mainly they were scathing. In her eyes he was a bad influence on her grandson. The sooner he was away from him the better.

But she would miss the boy so much...

And oh, how she missed her husband. She sighed and sniffed back a tear as she went to wake her grandson.

* * *

Spiros walked into the wholesalers in Corfu Town with a new lightness in his step. He was more cheerful and optimistic than he had been for weeks. The other night when he got into bed his wife Anna had said softly, "Spiro, I know you have a problem please, please, tell me what it is." So finally, worn down with worry, it all spilled out.

Anna's reaction had shocked him.

First she threw her arms around him, buried her face in his chest and sobbed, and he wished he hadn't told her. But then she blurted out that she'd feared he was seriously ill and keeping it from her. And she grabbed him by the arms as she hiccupped and laughed saying, "This is nothing! This is money only! These are family troubles and we will deal with them together!"

He thought he would float right up to the ceiling in that moment of deepest relief. He started chuckling along with Anna. But moments later he slumped forwards, face in hands, and began to quietly weep. Anna, his wonderful Anna, held him tight, and consoled him like she was consoling one their girls, until he was calm again.

After that they had lain in their marriage bed, holding hands like teenagers, whispering to each other and talking things through until the early hours. Anna had pleaded with him to tell their daughters over breakfast in the morning and ask for their help.

And, over coffee, after a shaky few minutes when an embarrassed Spiros confessed his secret to the stunned girls, Anna compassionately took over. She told them they were intelligent young adults and asked for ideas to help turn the business around. Eleni especially, the elder by a year, who worked full-time in the shop, would surely know some useful things.

Spiros was surprised by how many good suggestions Eleni began to come up with. He had listened intently, watching his daughter's dark eyes flash with enthusiasm.

Then Eleni had gone to her bedroom and brought back a thick stack of drachmas. "My savings," she said handing the banknotes over to her father. "The first thing we need to do is stock the shelves as normal." They all knew she liked to save instead of spending pocket money and birthday gifts, and her sacrifice was great. But she spoke in a low and respectful voice urging him to take the money. "Please, Baba, go and buy the rest of the things that were on the stock list."

Spiros hung his head, ashamed of his fabrication. "I'm sorry," he said lamely. "I brought you up not to tell lies…"

"Baba, I understand. You were trying to protect us from worry." Eleni smiled. Spiros patted her hand gratefully.

"I'll pay you back every single drachma as soon as possible," he promised.

Katarina had sat stunned and slack-mouthed while all this was happening, devastated at seeing her father so humbled. Then the words started spilling out. She was furious with her uncle for pressurizing his brother like that, and said so vociferously.

But then she went quiet.

She sat up straighter in her chair.

And for the first time Spiros could remember, she showed a

real interest in the shop and its success. Her tawny eyes flashed with excitement as she started throwing out ideas, good ideas, on new things they could try.

Thoughtfully, Katarina reached up with both hands and flicked her thick mane over her shoulders. "Oh, oh, I know what we can do," she said, jabbing the air with an index finger. Her family had rarely seen her so animated as she suggested speaking to Nikos, almost casually, to ask him to take a look at their rival's shop and see what they could do better in theirs. She was sure he would do it for her without asking too many questions.

Nikos was bright, she pointed out, and also very loyal. So what if he was their relative? There was no law against him being a customer at the other shop and as he was leaving in a day or so, to go to the army base on Crete, it would be quite natural for him to call in and say goodbye. He was doing the rounds and saying goodbye to everyone wasn't he?

When the whole family agreed it was a good plan Katarina blushed with pleasure. Then she worried that her idea wouldn't help, so before they opened the shop, together they all stood in front of the icon which hung above the cash register and prayed for help.

Their guardian angels were very happy about that.

Nikos had reported their rival was selling a small range of souvenirs such as miniatures of ouzo in fancy bottles, boxes of honey-coated almonds, and also postcards. With this in mind the family had put their heads together and come up with some other suggestions including a few strings of worry beads, inexpensive leather belts, and key rings.

The subject of selling newspapers and magazines had also been broached and a rep from the Hellenic Distribution Agency was calling into the shop tomorrow. Spiros wasn't totally convinced tourists would want to know about things that were going on back home while they were on holiday, but he was keeping an open mind these days.

Though nothing had changed yet financially, Spiros felt renewed confidence that things would soon get better. Actually, because of the mega relief of bringing everything out into the open, they already had. Also, seeing how his wife and daughters supported him instead of condemning him had been a lesson. Privately he had promised Anna that from now on they would make all major decisions together. It had warmed up the love between them.

Spiros already had a trolley-load of goods when he got to the alcohol section. They needed more Corfiot wines, some souvenir ouzos, and also some miniatures of liqueur made from locally grown kumquats. He was debating over a variety of bottles when he looked up and saw Gavin the holiday rep. He was a good customer and sent him customers too. "Hello," he said with a big friendly smile.

The whole family had promised to practise their friendly smiles and use them as often as possible. (Katarina had pulled a face when her mother suggested this, but had reluctantly agreed to do it.)

"Hello, Spiro." Gavin smiled back. He had no need to be convinced of the friendly smile; he had long been a convert. "Just checking prices," he volunteered, then thought better of it and clammed up. He and Yiorgos had been discussing costs and the man disagreed with his estimates. He was back to get more details.

Coincidently, Spiros' mind darted to his brother Yiorgos. He hoped, when business picked up, to pay him back as soon as possible. The whole family agreed that should be the priority. Gavin's thoughts about Yiorgos concerned how much money they could make together. He would be helping by bringing in customers to make his new club a success at last. In return Gavin would make some real money too.

Spiros carefully placed a selection of bottles into his already stacked trolley and said goodbye to Gavin.

Gavin waited until Spiros was out of sight before pulling paper and pen from a shirt pocket to jot down as much information as he could.

He needed to come to an agreement with Yiorgos as soon as possible. Every day that passed was a moneymaking opportunity wasted. Hmm, he liked that line. He would use it on Yiorgos when he saw him later.

* * *

After the meeting Gavin climbed into his car whistling softly. *That went well.* He and Yiorgos had reached an agreement that was good for them both.

Yiorgos had told him initially he wasn't really very interested in going ahead but supposed they could give it a try. Then he named a ridiculously low sum that he was prepared to give Gavin. Gavin had told him to just leave it and turned to walk out. But Yiorgos called him back and they discussed the whole thing properly.

Gavin thought they were pretty standard negotiating tactics.

But the thing was done now and a verbal agreement made. If he had thought there was any point in it he'd have got Yiorgos to sign something. But they both knew it would not have been worth the paper it was written on. He could never take him to a court if things went wrong.

No. They were in agreement. And while the plan worked, Gavin was sure it would stand.

Now Yiorgos was going to put together his side of things – including hiring a better, more experienced DJ. He wished him luck with that. Surely, though, this far into the season, the best would be working?

Anyway, that was Yiorgos' problem. Gavin was already making his own plans. The two men would meet again in a few days to talk about their progress.

They had decided they would try to get started as soon as possible.

Gavin tooted his horn a couple of times. He couldn't wait to get home to Suzanna. He hadn't told her anything about his plan so far. He had kept it as a surprise. He wanted to tell her when he was certain it was going to happen.

Ah, his lovely wife, Suzanna. She would be so pleased with him.

Well, he hoped she would be anyway. He hoped she wouldn't start saying he had put his job in jeopardy or anything like that. She had been a little bit cool with him for a few days and he wasn't sure why.

But when she knew there was some nice money for them in the offing she was sure to cheer up.

Hopefully.

Chapter 13

Clare O'Hara lay stretched out on a towel beside the pool, one hand dabbling at the tepid blue water. The tiles beneath her back were pleasantly warm. It was mid-morning so the sun had not yet reached its zenith.

Already the second week of July, she had been on the island for a couple of months but still never took the sunshine for granted. Suddenly, aware of being watched, she opened her eyes to see Jason hovering with a tumbler of orange juice. They shared a smile as he got down on his hunkers to hand over the drink and snatch a quick kiss.

They had been dating for some weeks now and at the start, though she found him more and more attractive, she had been wary of getting too involved. After all, she was here, in part, getting over Patrick. But he had been so persistent and persuasive that she fell under his spell. When he declared his love she found herself doing the same.

A summer romance in a gorgeous place.

Maybe it was just what she needed.

Grand!

Clare sipped her iced drink and chatted with Jason. Then he glanced up and swore softly under his breath. Without another word he marched back to the bar.

Katarina was seated on a tall stool in an obviously studied pose: one elbow on the counter, chin propped against hand, glossy lips pouting and eyes cool. Her ankle length cream T-shirt dress though demure nonetheless revealed her lean neat figure.

Jason was thrown. Not least because he found her magnificent, reminding him of why she was his fiancée. But he was as wary as a bird beside a hungry cat.

Katarina rarely came to the hotel. She certainly wouldn't be here if her cousin Nikos hadn't gone off to the army.

Though her expression was inscrutable he was clearly in trouble. It was really bad that Clare was here now. He scuttled behind the barrier of the bar before even saying hello. Her reply was a mere arch of shapely dark brows.

Playing for time he added a fistful of ice cubes to a tall glass, and slowly filled it with cola in a trickle from the dispenser while trying to gather his wits. Having not been in touch with her recently, he realized it was almost inevitable that she would come to find him.

He silently acknowledged his mistake. *Careless!* He planned to marry Katarina so he must be more careful to keep her sweet.

Meticulously he cut a slice of lemon, added a straw to the glass and took a deep calming breath. Finally he faced her and placed the drink squarely on a coaster.

She ignored it.

Instead her eyes raked his face searching for clues to the reason for his absence. She didn't understand it because during their last clandestine meeting in the olive grove a couple of weeks ago he had been his usual loving self. Happy, upbeat and affectionate he also seemed thrilled by her excellent exam results, saying that he was very proud of her.

Admittedly, he issued the warning before they kissed goodbye that she would need to be patient with him for the summer while they both worked. But he promised to call as often as possible. Since that day, though, to her dismay, he had phoned just once.

She had been thoroughly miserable. This had pushed her to take the risk of setting tongues wagging if she was seen coming here. She had made sure there were no locals around when she walked in.

She had hoped that he had just been distracted by work and that her visit would be a happy reminder of their love. She had prayed that she would see that love clearly shining in his eyes.

But no.

Her antennae were out and feeling the way. Oh, yes, he was smiling, and she picked up the hint of tenderness about his lips.

But she was not convinced by it. A terrible thought punched her heart. *He's hiding something! Definitely. Definitely!*

He decided to let her have the first word so he waited as her glare accused him.

At last, the girl spoke up spiritedly, "Where have you been, Jason? I haven't heard from you for ages!"

"I've been busy, Katarina, as I warned you I was going to be." His excuse sounded reasonable to his own ears. "The hotel is full, the restaurant is full, and the bar is busy. I haven't had a moment to myself."

On full alert she picked up a note of smugness. He was really saying: "I warned you about this and you can't come here blaming me!" Her nose wrinkled with disbelief. She didn't swallow it. "You could have made enough time to see me even for an hour now and then, or at least to pick up the phone and call me!" Her tone was flinty. Impatiently she flicked dark glossy locks over her shoulders with the backs of her hands, contempt sparking from yellow-brown eyes.

"You can see how it is." Jason waved an arm airily in the direction of the pool. As her hostile stare intensified he blustered, "Look around you, look at all the tourists. You can see for yourself how busy I am."

"Not too busy to talk to girls though are you?" she retorted hotly.

The claws were out. But the last thing he wanted was a fight in front of Clare. "What do you mean?" he asked warily, wondering what she had seen.

"I saw you talking to that girl when I arrived! You seemed to be very happy doing that!" she yelled.

"I don't know what girl you're talking about," he smoothly countered. "There are many girls here. They are customers and I talk to them."

He sounded almost pious, she noted. It stung. "That girl over there, the one on her own, the one who is working for my uncle at Pandora's," she persisted flinging a hand in the direction of Clare.

"She works for *me* actually."

"What!" Katarina was stopped in her tracks. "Since when?"

"Since a few weeks ago. Pandora's had no customers so your uncle fired her." He let that information sink in then tried to justify his friendliness with Clare. "I do talk to my staff you know." He bunched his lips petulantly.

The two now glared at each other. He affected injustice while she was clearly infuriated by his high-handed attitude.

Long moments passed while the tension built between them.

Katarina had come to the Paradise hoping for reassurance of Jason's love but she had not got it. Instead, he was twisting things around and seemed to be treating her like a small child.

Disappointment fuelled her temper. She wanted to lash out.

Looking down at the bar she caught sight of the full glass and without thinking picked it up and flung the contents in his face.

His anger was real now. "Oh, very clever and very mature!" His lips curled with sarcasm, but she was already striding away. He grabbed a towel and began to wipe off the sticky liquid. The ice had stung his face but his main concern in that moment was Clare. One glance at her pinched expression and glare told him she had seen everything. *Not good!* What story could he tell her?

His mind was a panic-ridden blank.

It would have to be convincing. He was nowhere near ready to end their relationship. He loved her, though he knew it was wrong and only for the season.

My last summer of freedom!

He didn't want anything to jeopardize that.

* * *

Michalis, cool, slim and handsome in crisp white shirt and black chinos attracted many admiring glances from females, young and old alike, as he strolled along the single high street of Hora.

The crumbling village, dating back well over a hundred years, still prospered, though in a modest way. Plain pale-grey stone buildings, housing a handful of dusty shops, a couple of tavernas, and one *zakaroplasteio* – a patisserie doubling as a café for the village ladies, families, couples and youths. There was also a *kafeneion* – the typical male-only café-bar found in every village and town in Greece. All were fronted by a thin ribbon of pavement.

Across the narrow road a metal railing guarded a sheer drop down to a green valley. Cars, vans or farm vehicles either manoeuvred past each other in both directions, or snarled when someone parked and blocked one lane.

Michalis, returning to his car parked just around the corner, looked up and saw Takis coming out of the greengrocer's. A faded denim shirt lay pale against the fisherman's bronzed forearms, neck and face topped by a thatch of sun-streaked hair.

He and Ingrid had discussed speaking to the young man about his fast driving. Tactfully, not mentioning Bethany, Ingrid put forward her suggestion about enlisting a third party, someone else with children who lived along the lane.

Michalis' guardian angel whispered that it would indeed be better if someone else spoke to Takis. His stalker demon whispered the opposite, urging him to be a man and fight his own battles.

As Takis got close, Michalis noticed the man's long sharp nose was red and peeling and looked like it belonged in another face. He suppressed a grin and made a decision. "*Kalimera*," he said, stopping in front of him.

Takis could not go by without stepping into the passing traffic but he did not reply to the greeting, just stared blankly at Michalis with flinty dark eyes.

When Michalis voiced his concerns for his young son and other children on the lane and asked him politely to slow down a bit in future, Takis went berserk. "No one tells me what to do!" he screamed.

"No one tells me that! No one!" His thin face turned puce with anger, fists bunching menacingly at the ends of wiry arms.

Michalis clenched his own fists, not thrown by the display of temper. He knew the man was volatile. His own blood was rising. As a father protecting his offspring, he was ready to do battle if necessary.

His stalker demon urged him to punch Takis into silence.

Michalis itched to crunch that sharp red nose. Go on, his face said to Takis, just try it and see what you get from me!

Heads turned at the sound of yelling. Takis' father, Petros, scurried from the baker's, a long crusty loaf jammed under one arm. Father and son were similar in build and looks, but Petros' hair was white. "What's the matter, son?" he asked gruffly. Takis stopped raving like someone had flicked an "off switch". Though his bronzed face was still ruddy with anger, his expression was blank and glassy eyed.

Michalis found the instant calm more shocking than the hysterical outburst. Takis appeared to be really unbalanced. Was the man mentally ill?

Michalis' guardian angel urged compassion.

Michalis' anger drained away and was replaced by concern. "Look, I'm not telling you what to do, really I'm not." He spoke kindly. "It's just that I'm sure you wouldn't want to hurt a child, so I'm asking you to drive a little slower along our lane." Michalis looked at Petros. "That's all I'm asking." Appealing to the father, he noted the knot of curious men now surrounding them, but whose side they were on was unclear.

Petros now understood what had happened. He shot an icy glare at Michalis, put a firm gnarled hand on his son's arm and led him away.

Michalis' eyes canvassed the audience for their support but not one of them looked to be in agreement with him. An old man wearing a faded red cloth cap took a pipe from his mouth, hawked loudly then spat on the ground beside Michalis' foot. His insult was plain. "*Xenos*," he muttered.

Michalis turned on his heel and marched away. "I'm no foreigner," he mumbled to himself. But the truth was that, since bringing home his German bride and their child, he had often felt an outsider in his own village.

Chapter 14

Head down, a stony-faced Katarina charged out of the resort desperate to put a distance between herself and Jason. Up past the tiny village church as the ground changed from tarmac to sharp pebbles in dried mud, she stumbled once or twice.

Pushing on past the old harbour – still very much in use with fishing craft bobbing in a groundswell – the road suddenly widened and freshly bulldozed earth rose steeply to her left, still topped with tenacious scrub. She hurried forwards, the exposed sun-dried ground now smooth beneath her feet. Down the slope she strode and onwards until the seashore brought her to a halt. The newly constructed harbour, as yet unused, stretched out before her.

Unconcerned about her pale dress she sank onto the pebbles facing the sea. The navy-blue horizon lightened to turquoise as the sea swept in wavelets towards her. She saw in her mind's eye the drink, straw and ice cubes hitting Jason full in the face.

Oh, no! Oh, no!

What had made her do that?

She was wracked with regret over her impulsive action.

"Stupid! Stupid!" She shouted at herself.

She loved him. Had she lost him?

Tears flowed at last, as hot as the sun that scorched her bent head. They tapped into the misery of the last week's waiting.

She knew Jason was busy. Of course she did. She was busy too. But last year he had been in touch often and they'd snatched sweet brief interludes whenever they could. That's why it hurt so much when he hadn't even phoned. But now everything had gone sour in the space of a few minutes.

Why, oh why, had she gone to the hotel? With her face pressed into her palms she sobbed and sobbed in anguish.

But she'd had to confront him.

Something was wrong.

Then a sobering thought stemmed her tears. She sat bolt upright and wiped her wet face with trembling fingers. She remembered thinking he was hiding something from her!

What was it?

She had accused him of chatting to tourists.

Was he dating a tourist?

She did not want to believe it but a lot of the local boys did this in the summer months, even her cousin Nikos. She shivered despite the heat.

Jason had only recently proposed and she presumed their future was together, but maybe he had found a stranger more attractive than her.

Her mind threw up an image of Jason holding a stereotypical blonde girl in his arms and gazing into her eyes. No! No! He wouldn't do that!

Would he?

"Oh damn the tourist industry!" she yelled over the sea, scrambling up and starting to pace up and down the pebbled beach, sandaled feet crunching and slithering. Her heart hammered with such anguish that her head spun. She sank back onto the ground before she fell. She had loved Jason since she was twelve. She couldn't imagine life without him.

"He loves me! I know he does!" He had told her often enough. She refused to accept he would betray her.

"No, no, oh please, God, no!"

She tried to calm the rising fear and hysteria that were gathering like choking smoke in her chest. What if her dreams of a lifetime of happiness with Jason never came true? There was no one else on earth like Jason. Great shuddering sobs tore from a throat-constricting panic. "Jason! Oh, Jason!" She sobbed his name over and over, her voice getting quieter and quieter until it was only a soundless movement on her lips. And the tears petered out too, drying on her hot cheeks while her brain rejected the unhappiness.

Eventually she became aware of the sound of the sea bubbling and sucking into the small caves, formed by thousands of years of erosion, in the cliffs beside her. It caught and held her attention for a few minutes and soothed her, just a little.

Perhaps everything would be all right after all. Maybe she had overreacted. Stiffly she eased herself up from the stones onto her feet and began to retrace her steps for home.

But when she came to the old harbour, the familiar spot drew her to a halt. She still had a little more time left of her break. She needed to be absolutely calm to face the family. They knew nothing about her and Jason and they must not see her upset or the questions would start.

* * *

Clare was doing laps in the pool trying to stay calm. Why had Katarina thrown a drink over Jason? The two had shouted at each other in Greek so she didn't understand a word, but alarm bells were sounding in her head.

Could Katarina be a former girlfriend of Jason's?

Jason knew about Patrick, her childhood sweetheart until a few months ago, but now she realized *his* past had remained a closed book. While her limbs moved rhythmically in the water, she waited for Jason's explanation.

After a few minutes he came to speak to her. Without hesitation she hauled herself out of the pool and scrambled to her feet. She was trembling inside with nerves but tried not to show it.

"You saw that." There was no question about it. She nodded slowly a few times. The usually feisty Clare was subdued and unreadable. "I can explain everything," he said in low flat tones. *I hope I can anyway.* "But not here." He made a snap decision. "Let's take a drive into town."

Clare pointed to her wet hair and bikini. "I'll need to shower and change my clothes."

Smiling, he pointed at his own wet hair and damp shirt. "I'll go and organize some cover for the bar and get ready. Then I'll take you home so you can do the same."

Soon they were heading out of the resort.

After winding around the hairpin bend in a slow steep climb the road levelled out. Clare glanced to her left at Pandora's. She was glad she didn't work there anymore though she had got quite fit climbing that hill every day.

Jason glanced at Clare. Her damp hair was loose about her bare tanned shoulders and as she teased it with her fingers in the breeze from the open window, Jason had a problem keeping his eyes on the road. He wanted to bury his face in the silky rose-scented red curls.

The atmosphere between them was companionable and Clare realized he would not speak about the fight with Katarina until they were sitting in a café. Little did she know he was wracking his brains about how to explain.

The bright sunlight was suddenly blocked out by thick overhanging olive branches as they sped along. At the old stone-built olive oil factory the road twisted sharply to the left. Then they were out into the sunshine again and soon had a glimpse of the green valley that stretched as far as the blue summit of Pantokrator mountain in the distance.

"When things quieten down I'll take you on a trip and show you my favourite places on the island," he promised.

"Great," she said, privately wondering if they would still be together in a couple of months.

The road snaked steeply downwards and once in the valley they motored past fields of vegetables, some with rows of carefully staked tomatoes and green beans. In the foothills tall thin cypress pines stood like ever-watchful sentinels.

Even through her fog of upset Clare was moved by the beauty

around her. She loved this island almost as much as she loved her own Emerald Isle. Whatever happened with her and Jason she must try to be philosophical. She had come to this beautiful place to get over Patrick, spend the summer doing a different job, and to meet new people. She hadn't intended to fall in love.

Jason had told her not to worry and that he loved her but something was badly wrong and her chest felt tight with nerves.

Approaching the town they passed the Port where ships were disgorging visitors and cargo, which Jason said came from Athens, Alexandria, and many other places.

He sighed as they stopped in a queue of cars at a red traffic light. "Corfu Town is always busy." Clare peered at the pedestrians streaming past them on the narrow pavement. "Spot the tourists," she giggled. It was easy. Clad in shorts and T-shirts, skimpy skirts and cutaway tops, they stood out among the more formally dressed-for-town locals. She glanced down at her simple, modest dress of black cotton splashed with golden roses which said: smart, summer.

"Same the world over." Jason looked amused.

"I can see it's mainly locals here."

"Yes." Jason agreed. "About forty per cent of the island's population of over a hundred thousand people live in and around the town." The light changed to green and the leading car moved forwards. Jason slid into gear and moved off. Turning hard right he drove up a side road parallel to the tall boundary wall of the New Venetian Fortress. Jason smiled when a car pulled out of a line of parked vehicles. He claimed the vacated space.

Holding Clare's hand Jason led her up the wide cobbled street lined with shops towards the popular café strip. "This is called the Liston because originally only families on an elite list could use it," Jason said.

The back of the arched walkway was lined with cafés and restaurants. "Most people think this is Venetian but it was built by the French when Napoleon ruled the island."

Each establishment had a few tables and chairs outside their door under the arches. While across a broad path of cream marble further tables and chairs were set out in the open air.

"We have arrived," Jason announced, as they reached his favourite café about halfway along. He moved towards an empty table set at right-angles to a wide green swathe. "That cricket pitch was built by the British," he volunteered.

Jason held up a hand and a waiter hurried over from the café to take their order. Waiting for their drinks, Clare looked around. An old grey fort jutting out into the sea dated back a thousand years, according to Jason.

The waiter arrived with their drinks and tumblers of iced water. A thirsty Clare drank half her water straight down. Jason took a deep breath and changed gear. "I'm very sorry for what happened today," he began. "Katarina is very young and has clearly misunderstood the way things are between us." *We are not yet formally engaged and she shouldn't be putting this pressure on me!*

Clare watched him briskly stirring the creamy foam of his iced coffee with the straw as if his life depended on it. "And how *are* things between you, Jason?" She spoke with quiet deliberation.

"We were friends. That's all. And now there is nothing between us." He spoke boldly but Clare sensed he was nervous.

"And how long were you... *friends?*" She reached over the table to hold his hand, willing him to look at her.

"For over a year," he said quietly, looking hard at his coffee.

A year. She and Jason had only known each other weeks. "And when did you stop being... *friends?*"

"When I met you." As the lie tripped off his tongue his mouth ran dry.

"Ah." This was complicated. He had been seeing the girl until she came on the scene. Clare glanced at Jason. *And for all I know, after I came on the scene too.* She took her hand away and sank back in the chair. Sipping absentmindedly at her orange juice, she looked to her right over the grass towards the shimmering blue sea.

Silence lengthened between them.

Finally Jason cleared his throat. "Clare, I love you," he said truthfully. "You do believe that don't you?"

She gave no answer. Then, turning her head she looked him in the eye. "So, why did Katarina throw the drink over you today?"

He realized he couldn't fudge things any longer so he answered honestly. "She was angry because I hadn't been in contact with her."

"If it was over between you why did she expect you to contact her?" Anger edged her voice. She knew he was wriggling around the truth.

"She doesn't want to accept that it's over."

Hmm. Clare considered this. "Does she know about me?"

"No, I didn't want to hurt her, so I didn't tell her."

"I understand." She understood only too well. Patrick had given her details about his new love and she wished he had not. "Is it completely over between you two?"

Jason gazed intently into the sparkling green eyes he loved so much. "Yes, it's completely over for me," he lied emphatically.

She had to ask. "But is it over for her after today?"

"I hope so." *I hope not!*

"Maybe you should talk to her again and make her understand."

"Maybe," he sounded uncertain. He reached for her hand and raised it to his lips. "My Clare," he whispered. "I love you, please trust me." He had such strong feelings for Clare. He would fight for their summer together.

He also loved Katarina and she was his future. He needed to tread very carefully from now on to keep the two females happy.

Clare had not known Jason long which made it difficult enough to second guess him. Was he stringing her along? She really didn't know.

But she did love him.

She wanted to trust him.

* * *

Bethany was taking a break from writing. Wearing a long gauzy pink sundress and a wide-brimmed straw hat above her huge sunglasses she set off down the lane past the vegetable fields.

The last field before the top of the road was home to a solitary donkey which stood in the shade of a tree nibbling at stubbly grass. As she called a friendly greeting it raised its head to look her speculatively in the eye.

Down the hill and past the olive groves she paused at the sharp bend in the road. "*Orea thea,* nice view," she extolled, practising the new Greek words while drinking in the tall clear blue sky falling into a vast cobalt sea. "*Prohora,* onwards."

The locals were pleased when foreigners made even the smallest stab at the admittedly difficult language. Those fluent in English joked that since Greek had been updated about a decade before, even Greeks found it hard. This certainly applied to the written word and spelling had apparently become a bit of a guessing game at school, even for teachers.

She had been studying her phrasebook and was determined to go beyond the likes of "please" and "thank you". After all she was not a tourist.

"*Prohora.*" She repeated the word in a theatrical way but it sounded quite good. She hoped she was saying it right.

Nearing the seafront she nodded and smiled at the passing tourists. At the minimarket, Spiros' dog, Hygeia, trotted out from her kennel to, unexpectedly, walk along beside her. Sizable and solid as a Labrador, but of indeterminate breed, her short brown-banded coat was glossy. Bethany reached down and fondled the dog's long silky ears. "Hello girl." Nikos at the hotel had told her his uncle's dog was named after the goddess of health, and apparently it was where the word "hygiene" came from.

Bethany was heading for the old harbour up the hill, past the Paradise. Each time a car approached she was nervous of the dog getting hit and tried to shepherd her into the roadside out of harm's way.

Hygeia idled for a while behind Bethany. Then she passed her and led the way. Bethany wondered how long the dog would stay with her. She had never had a dog and didn't know much about them. She preferred cats. But when Hygeia stuck with her, Bethany smiled and realized the word "dogged" was a good one.

They soon reached the old harbour, formed by a long grey concrete arm. Tethered along its leeward side a dozen or so little fishing boats called caiques, and motorboats gently bobbed. Walking down the slipway she stepped with a crunch onto the narrow shoulder of shingle to her right.

A girl was sitting on a large flat rock staring out to sea and Hygeia bounded up to her, barking in greeting. "*Ya soo,* Hygeia," said the girl. She affectionately rubbed the top of the dog's broad head then swivelled to look at Bethany – who recognized her immediately.

"Katarina! *Ya soo.*" Then Bethany saw the girl had been crying. "Are you okay," she asked with automatic concern, before remembering that this was Katarina, the Unfriendly One, as she and Clare referred to her.

"What do you care?" Katarina spoke bitterly in clear good English.

Bethany was shocked. In the shop the girl only spoke Greek and if asked a question in English just shrugged like she didn't understand. Now Bethany realized that was a sham.

Although her instinct was to move away, and leave well

alone, she hesitated. The wide-brimmed hat now felt like an obstacle and she removed it. "I don't like to see anyone upset," she murmured, ruffling her damp fringe in the soft cooling sea breeze. The girl's bottom lip wobbled at the unexpected kindness. "Is it a boy?" Bethany asked. The startled look in Katarina's swimming tawny eyes confirmed her intuition, though the girl's tightly pressed lips said she was determined not to confide.

But the usually haughty Katarina looked so dejected it touched Bethany's heart. She sat down on the rock a few feet away from her and stared at the swelling sea seeking inspiration.

She turned her face towards the girl. "I think it must be very difficult for you, and for everyone in a way, to have us foreigners living among you." She set her hat down on the rock between them and anchored the brim with a large brown pebble plucked from the beach. The girl's eyes held a spark of interest but her mouth remained obstinately clamped shut.

"You have your culture and we have ours," Bethany continued, wondering just how much the girl understood her English, and wishing she could think of a way to break through the barrier between them. Idly she looked down at her long pink dress. *Ah!* "Some girls wear very short clothes, which you may not like," she ventured. Watching Katarina's scowl, she sought a rudimentary explanation. "It's just the fashion. Summers in Britain are usually much cooler than here so they enjoy dressing like that in the heat." She fiddled with the pebble on the hat brim turning its smooth surface around and over.

"Yes, but they take it too far," Katarina responded fiercely. "They go half-naked on the beach in front of grandmothers and grandfathers, and everyone."

Bethany nodded, pleased the girl was perking up. She wanted to compliment her English but thought better of it. Instead she stuck with the subject. "I agree with you," she said. Katarina's glower switched to surprise. Bethany nodded for emphasis. As she remembered something she'd read about bathing in Britain in Victorian times, she grinned. "Oh, how times have changed," she said, and went on to explain. "Over a hundred years ago British women were completely covered up when they swam." She mimed dressed to the neck, down to the ankles and wrists.

"Oh." Katarina looked interested.

She considered how to explain a bathing machine to her. She continued with her mime alongside the words. "They had to change into this swimming costume in a little house on wheels which was then pulled into the sea. They stepped from that into the water for their swim." She paused and chuckled. "And afterwards, they got back into the house, which was pulled out of the sea. They changed back into their clothes before leaving the house." She mimed long dresses, gloves and hats too.

Katarina's amusement showed clearly that even though she didn't understand all the words she had got the picture! As Bethany started to giggle at the stark contrast between the historical women and the modern, Katarina spluttered, her reserve cracking. Her loud chuckles joined Bethany's and they laughed and laughed; the sound rippling over the dancing blue waters.

Eventually, wiping tears of laughter from her eyes, Katarina glanced at her watch. "Oh, I have to get back to the shop." She stood to leave.

Bethany groped for some final words. "I hope everything turns out okay for you." She smiled at Katarina but was dismayed to see the girl's face close up again. "Thanks," she muttered, adding, "goodbye," before turning to slowly crunch her way up the pebble beach.

Chapter 15

Yiorgos looked at the mock-up of the promotional cards Gavin handed him. "Good. I like them."

Gavin was pleased. In just a few days he had organized a group of pretty girls to hand the cards out in this and nearby resorts. He hoped to attract customers from all over the island when the word got round. There were also small posters which would be printed and put up in strategic places.

Yiorgos was hiring bar staff with the promise of good wages if things took off as he hoped. He just wished he had kept Clare on. She was great at her job and very lovely too. He had tried to get her back but she told him she was already working at the Paradise Hotel. Ah well. He admitted he was no competition for Jason.

Well, not yet anyway, but who knew what could happen.

Yiorgos was very pleased with a new development. He was congratulating himself for his good luck.

"I have hired a new DJ," he told Gavin importantly.

"Oh." Gavin was interested. "I hope he's a professional. Remember a lot of our success hangs on him."

"He is a real professional." Yiorgos preened and lit a cigarette, blowing smoke in the direction of the ceiling in a long steady thoughtful grey stream. He *had* worried that he wouldn't be able to find a really good DJ. Then the young man had turned up today, right out of the blue, asking for a job. He'd explained he had a big collection of records and bags of experience in top London clubs. He said he had been working in another resort but the place was too quiet.

Yiorgos knew all about that.

He'd tried him out and hired him on the spot. He was fantastic. Yiorgos cringed when he mentally compared him to his current DJ. He had paid him a small retainer until next week when they opened Pandora's with the new formula.

Yiorgos, still looking proud said, "So you can put his name and experience on the cards and posters."

Gavin picked up his pen and looked expectantly at Yiorgos.

"Write this," Yiorgos said, reading off a notepad, "Famous London DJ, Kevin, of Hippodrome and Stringfellow's, now live at Pandora's, Korkyra."

It was not true of course. Kevin had been a punter in both famous clubs but not worked in either. But who in Korkyra would know that? And he knew his stuff. He was a great DJ.

Gavin gasped and laughed with delight. "What a find! Congratulations." He reached out and shook the man's hand enthusiastically. He thought of all the money that would soon start rolling into his bank account.

"You bring your wife to the opening night?" Yiorgos wouldn't bring his wife but that was not the point. Foreigners, they took their wives everywhere didn't they?

"Oh, yes." Gavin beamed, acting up a storm. "She's really looking forward to it," he lied. Suzanna was furious with him. She said it was a terrible idea and wondered what on earth he had been thinking of to get involved in this sort of tacky thing.

"Money, my dear," he had said, trying to keep his dignity in the face of her unanticipated wrath.

"This is a risky scheme, Gavin, and could cost you your rep's job which is definite money." Her bright blue eyes had flashed in anger. Despite quaking in the face of her temper, a new and unexpected facet of her character, Gavin had been awed by her beauty in that moment. Just thinking of it made him feel hot under the collar.

It was a hot day, though.

He thought of his car parked in the shade of a big tree and longed to be speeding along with all the windows open pulling in cooling sea breezes. "See you in a day or two, Yiorgo," he said. "We have lots to do before then." The men nodded at each other, both mentally running over their lists of tasks.

After driving to the printer's to finalize the promotional copy, Suzanna was next on Gavin's list. He had to go and try to smooth things over with her. She was hardly talking to him now. He was finding it very difficult to juggle work with pleasing his wife.

He sighed and felt hard done by.

As he drove home he suddenly found the sun was too hot, the sea too dazzling, and the tourists too many.

Being a holiday rep is a very difficult job!

* * *

Katarina argued with her sister, the man who delivered the vegetables, and the electrician who came to mend a broken fridge, and, finally, after exchanging heated words with her father over something trivial, stormed from the shop into the house.

This was out of character and a nonplussed Spiros started to go after her, but Anna put a staying hand on his arm. "I'd just leave her alone for a while if I were you." When her husband looked surprised she explained. "She's been in a bad mood all morning and shouting at everyone!"

He stared at the back door through which Katarina had just made a dramatic exit. He felt torn. He was in the middle of unloading new stock. Things had turned around and the shop was very busy now. He decided to leave her. If there was something wrong with the girl it was best tackled when he had more time.

The disgruntled Katarina reached the safety of the room she shared with Eleni and flung open the door. Her startled sister leapt up from bed as Katarina flounced in and slammed the door setting a couple of silver framed prints of flowers juddering on the wall either side of it.

"What on earth is the matter?" Eleni demanded, recovering from her fright. She had showered after a swim and wore only underwear. The thin pink rose-patterned curtains were drawn against the sun's glare but only filtered the light. "I'm trying to relax before I start work again!" she shouted irritably.

At her sister's angry words Katarina suddenly had no more fight left in her, so instead of answering anger with anger as she had done all morning, she lunged for her own bed, and dropping face-down burst into noisy sobs instead.

In the cramped, though neat and pretty room, the twin beds were separated only by a little table and Eleni was beside Katarina in a second hugging her shoulders and stroking her hair, all vexation at being disturbed instantly dissolved. Though only one year senior sometimes, like now, she felt much older and wiser. She muttered soothing words but asked no questions as the bout of weeping reached its crescendo, then died away quickly like a summer squall.

When Katarina finally took a few gulping breaths, Eleni stood and padded over the white fluffy rug to the little dressing table. She came back holding a wad of tissues. "Here," she said.

Katarina rolled on her back and took them, mopped her face then struggled up and blew her nose hard. "Thank you," she said meekly to her big sister.

"You don't have to tell me," Eleni said kindly, though she was burning with curiosity. "But if you want to, I'll listen." Surreptitiously checking her watch she saw her break was almost over. Opening the pale wood wardrobe she shunted wire coat hangers. She chose a long white T-shirt bearing the testimony: I love Corfu. It had been her idea to stock these in the shop and she wore it as promotion. They were selling very well. She pulled it over her head and settled it on her petite body with a secret self-satisfied smile.

Katarina had not spoken so she went to sit on the pink velvet stool at the dressing table. Brushing her long wavy hair she watched her sister's reflection through the big oval mirror.

The vulnerable Katarina hesitated only a few seconds more before blurting out, "I've been seeing Jason and he doesn't seem to want me anymore."

Eleni's dark eyes went as round as saucers. "What!" she gasped to the mirror. This was news to her. She spun round and gawped at her sister.

Grief was making Katarina more open than usual with Eleni. "Don't tell Mama and Baba but we are unofficially engaged."

"Engaged!" Eleni exploded with shock. But if she wanted information she needed to stay quiet. With great effort she pulled herself together. "Go on," she said quietly.

"But now he has no time for me and I don't know what to do about it."

"You haven't done anything silly with him have you?" Eleni's question was sharp.

"No, of course I haven't!" Katarina retorted hotly, "I respect myself and he respects me."

"Okay, okay. I was just asking." Eleni folded her arms and looked peeved.

"Sorry."

"And no, I won't tell on you. You should know by now that I am trustworthy." *Though you clearly don't trust me or you would have told me about this before.*

"Yes, I'm sorry."

Eleni sighed. "It's okay," she said grudgingly, choosing to ignore the many secrets she kept from Katarina. "Anyway, did you two have a row or something?"

"Yes, a stupid row." Cringing at the thought of the incident at the Paradise, she gave no details. "And he hasn't called me since."

"For how long?"

"A few days."

"That long, eh?" Eleni's mouth twisted sarcastically up at

one corner.

Katerina blushed. "I know it doesn't sound long."

"You're right, it doesn't."

"But the row was mainly about him not being in touch with me and not getting together with me," Katarina hurriedly explained. "So, you see, I hoped he would phone straight away."

"Ah, now I understand." Satisfied her sister was not a complete idiot she turned back to the mirror and began to brush her thick locks straight back from her face into a high ponytail. "When you tackled him what did he say?"

"He just said he was very busy at the moment and hadn't got time to see me."

"Well, it is a busy time for him, and for all of us, so perhaps that's all there is to it." She secured her hair with a white cotton scrunchie and put silver hoops into her ears. The earrings, Katarina's idea, were also stocked in the shop. The profit was good and their father was pleased.

"I want to believe that." Katarina had tried desperately hard to believe that. "But I know he's more than just busy with business." The corners of her mouth drooped in misery. She had to tell Eleni all of it now she had started. "He's changed towards me," she admitted dejectedly. "He's still friendly but it's like he's closed himself off." There, she had said it out loud for the first time. She had not dared to speak this even to Maria, who knew the minutiae of the row.

"Do you have any idea why that is?" Eleni checked her watch. Almost time to go back to the shop. She stepped into cut-off denims and pulled up the zip.

"Well, I could be wrong, but I think he might be going out with a tourist."

"Hmm!" Eleni sniffed. "Well, he wouldn't be the first would he?" The dark pools of her eyes clouded.

"Yes, but Jason is my fiancé!" Katarina yelled.

"Keep your voice down if you want to *keep* this secret." Eleni hissed urgently.

A subdued Katarina whispered back. "You're right, sorry."

The sisters were silent as they thought about the way village life had changed so much since the tourist industry began only a handful of years ago.

Katarina felt a sudden flash of resentment against Jason.

The emotion died away as quickly as it had come. She loved him. They had shared a precious happy year but now she was so miserable... As a heavy gloom descended over her whole body she felt ancient instead of young.

When Eleni left for work Katarina lay on her bed feeling hot but lighter in spirit for having unburdened herself.

Then she began to wonder again what, if anything, she could do to get over this impasse with Jason.

Finally a light bulb lit up in her head and she started to smile.

She knew exactly what to do!

* * *

Clare had no idea what she was going to do about Jason. She had spent the afternoon mooning around the house. Now she sat at the big round kitchen table hunched over a mug of cooling coffee.

Jason had been so loving and kind with her since that day in Corfu Town. Despite her reservations this had made her fall even more in love with him than before.

But the depth of her love for Jason had shattered all peace of mind, and that was scary.

Logic told her she was a fool. Having gone into this relationship with open eyes knowing it was only a summer romance she now desperately wanted...

What?

She shook her head and gazed through the open window as a pair of big blue butterflies fluttered around each other in a circle then flitted among wildflowers under sunlit olive trees. "Life is so simple for you two," she muttered.

So what did she really want from the relationship with Jason?

Permanence?

Marriage?

Could she commit to living in Korkyra away from her family and home for the rest of her life?

Is he The One?

That was a very big question. And she did not know the answer.

All I know is that I love him and want to be with him.

She shook her head to clear it. "Huh," she said. "This is ridiculous. I need to lighten up." She would get ready and go to join Bethany at the beach.

Chapter 16

Shortly after dawn Jason's mother, Margarita, slipped unseen through the side door of the hotel. After passing right through the sleeping resort she began to climb. Though the hill was high, the road wound gradually around it, lessening the gradient. She made this journey, this pilgrimage, regularly and always for the same reason. The bonus, was that this regular climb kept her fit. Hard work played its part too. The sun rose higher and hotter and when the road passed through one of several olive groves the dappled shade was welcome.

She walked past a number of old bungalows haphazardly dotted along the narrow road. At the top of the hill she turned and glanced briefly at the view of her village. The resort was revealed at its most picturesque. The wide dark-blue border of sea at its front, the ring of green hills at its back, and a china-blue dome of sky above created the perfect foil for the prettily scattered buildings.

Born in Hora, Margarita had moved here when she and Vasilis married. In their little seaside bungalow they had raised their son in a happy and relaxed atmosphere. Though her husband was away at sea a lot she was content to be a mother and wife. She also enjoyed the status that his captaincy gave her. When he retired at aged fifty and decided to open the hotel it was with her blessing. And they worked well alongside each other. But now. She shook her head sadly as she made her way into the little ancient church.

Pushing the door open a shaft of sunlight peppered with dancing dust pierced the shadowy interior, while rose-infused incense auspiciously perfumed the air.

Just inside the door, on a stand, was a shallow round gilded container filled with sand. It held a single lit mustard-coloured taper. She fished in her purse for a few small yellow twenty drachma coins. Dropping them into a moneybox she took up a candle touching wick to flame before pushing it into the sand beside the other.

She began moving around the small church kissing icons and murmuring prayers as she went from one silver-framed picture to another. Margarita was praying for her son. She came as often as she could for this purpose. As she walked she kept sketching three crosses swiftly over her heart with the bunched fingers of her right hand.

All the while arrows of sunshine pierced the high narrow windows, striking silver icons and brasses holding ruby flickering oil lamps. They barely illuminated the old fading wall frescoes.

It was so very difficult for Margarita to watch her husband sink deeper each day into a crippling malaise. And to watch her son grow steadily more arrogant and greedy.

She sighed deeply.

Jason had been such a good boy, always polite and loving. He was also a very good student. She and Vasilis were filled with pride when he went to the university in Athens to become an archaeologist. But then, when the hotel's profits began to go down, instead of coming up with advice he had thrown up his studies and come home, and put himself in charge.

The take-over hadn't been immediate. But Jason belittled Vasilis – whose experience as a sea captain had not served so well in business. Jason soon annihilated the last of her husband's shaky confidence. One of the hardest things to accept was that Vasilis turned to alcohol for consolation and not to her. He had up till then been an upright sober man. She still could hardly believe the evidence of her own eyes when his were bloodshot and his words slurred.

It was devastating.

And now, to make matters worse, just when Jason had hinted he had met a local girl whom he would marry, there was this foreign girl whom he seemed besotted with.

She shook her head sadly.

She wanted Jason to work with his father instead of ignoring him. And she wanted him to marry a nice Korkyran girl and give her lots of grandchildren. She shook her head again, wiped a tear from her eye and kissed more icons while whispering prayers with increasing fervour.

Unseen the angel Gabriella was giving advice to the woman's guardian. Silently, words of encouragement were passed on to her, which gradually sank deep into her spirit – where they brought comfort.

Still, though, living alongside this unfolding scenario, Margarita watched and worried, and continued to pray almost against hope.

* * *

Sleeping, waking, sleeping, waking, Bethany finally threw back the coverlet and tiptoed into the kitchen to make a mug of strong tea. She drank this at the open window and the brooding early morning shadows in the olive grove reflected her own painful thoughts. She shook her head, sighed deeply, and began to pace like a caged tiger.

"I've got to get out of here," she whispered, sounding desperate.

Swiftly, she dressed.

She scribbled a note for the sleeping Clare, set it on the table, and left.

As she reached the beach the rising sun was chasing away shadows and throwing surrealistic colours around: purple into the sea and apricot onto the sand.

Bethany kicked off her shoes and savoured the cool grittiness beneath her feet. With slow deliberate steps, each one held back by the sinking, shifting softness of millions of tiny grains, she covered the short distance to the shoreline.

The gently bubbling shallows reminded her of Parfait Amour liqueur. The tepid water felt like silk rippling past her ankles. She deliberately blanked off her tumbling, painful thoughts. A little further on, though, she stepped back onto the beach knowing the dreaded time had arrived.

She sank down onto cool dry sand, took a bracing breath, and reached into her pocket. Her fingers grasped the edge of a thin airmail envelope, and with some crackling resistance she extricated it from its hiding place.

She knew the contents but still delayed pulling out the letter by studying the familiar handwriting on the envelope. During their courtship they had written to each other frequently. They'd had so much to say. But in the end, after eight years of marriage, there was so very little that was said, which she still found incredibly sad.

Now, though, in the space of a couple of pages, too much had been said.

A bombshell, or two, or three, or four had been dropped.

She put her hand to her heart and took another fortifying breath. Then she pulled out the thin sheets of lined blue paper and began to read them slowly word for word. Sentence building upon sentence which caused a crescendo of pain.

Dear Bethany,

I hope that you are well and happy and enjoying living on the island. I am writing with some bad news I'm afraid. I am so sorry to tell you that my mother passed away a short time ago. It was very sudden and it has been a very sad time. Her funeral was small but it all went off as well as these things can.

Now that I am writing I think it is time to let you know what has been happening in my life. I have not done so before because I did not want to hurt you. But I need to tell you that I remarried last year. We have a one-year-old daughter and there is another baby on the way.

A cataract of tears obscured the rest of the words. Bethany wrapped her arms around her body and rocked back and forth while sobs tore from her throat as the numbness, following the shock of reading the letter yesterday, finally exploded into grief.

Hot tears ran down her face and dropped from the edge of her chin. The first tears were for the death of her lovely mother-in-law. She was sorry, so sorry, she had gone. Her ex-husband, Nigel, would be in a state over his mother's death, though his letter was controlled. They had been very close.

Then, though she felt guilty for the thoughts, her own problem raised its head and got mixed up with her grief. The letter had opened up a window onto a hopeless situation in her own life. She had not been able to give her husband a child. And to be a woman and not to be able to bear a child was anathema to her.

Her childless state was something that she struggled to accept – no matter where she was. From time to time on the island it had leapt out and caught her up in an unexpected knot of pain. There had been the day at the Paradise when she met up with Ingrid and her son, Panos, again. When they were leaving she had suddenly, right out of the blue, been flooded with regret that she would never have her own son. Never be a mother like Ingrid.

"I'll never be a mother! Never!" She shouted at the gilded dawn sky and sobbed and rocked.

As she continued to rock within the circle of her own arms she was unaware that she was going through the motions of comforting the child that she herself would never have.

At length, a delicate little cough announced the arrival of another person on the beach. Surreptitiously she wiped her eyes with her fingers, fished a tissue from up her sleeve and blew her nose. Smoothing the crumpled pages of the letter she pushed them back into the envelope and stuffed it in her pocket.

Mentally nudging away the melancholy she turned her head to face the newcomer. Stepping lithely towards her was a tall slim blonde girl who looked vaguely familiar. Between them some pigeons spread out like a quivering mottled cloak breakfasting on scraps left by yesterday's visitors.

"Hello." Gabriella greeted Bethany as she got close, while the living cloak of birds swirled upwards, hovered in mid-air, then, obviously reassured, fell back down to finish eating.

"Hiya," Bethany replied, and stood up.

The girl stood beside her on the shoreline and together they gazed appreciatively at the shifting lilac sea. "I love it here," said Bethany, feeling much calmer.

"Me too," said the girl.

Bethany introduced herself. When the girl reciprocated Bethany said she thought Gabriella was a very pretty name. She knew then, though, that they hadn't met before.

"Are you staying here?" Bethany asked.

"No. But I am not too far away so I come here a lot."

"You here for a visit or the summer?" Bethany had a feeling the girl was not a tourist. She seemed to sort of belong, though she clearly wasn't Greek.

"The summer." And all the summers, autumns, winters and springs. "I like it when it gets busy." Gabriella, whose work had begun in prehistoric times, thrived on busyness. "You?" She feigned ignorance.

"I've taken a career break to write a novel."

"That sounds interesting," the girl said lightly, with a smile that lit her face and brightened the clear grey hue of her large oval eyes.

Bethany, feeling a little mesmerized blurted out, "I was just thinking about my life."

"Oh?" Gabriella's smile broadened encouragingly. Bethany's guardian angel had just been telling her all about it.

She didn't want to go into detail. As much as anything she was feeling quite exhausted with emotion. "Let's just say that it hasn't panned out as I hoped it would." She smiled thinly. "And I've just found out that someone else is living my dream." She glanced down at the sand then stooped to pick up a translucent white shell – the size and shape of her thumbnail. As she ran a finger over its ridges she tried hard not to cry.

"I am very sorry to hear that, Bethany."

Bethany looked at the shell and blinked away the tears. "Thanks," she muttered.

After a pause Gabriella spoke up. "Look, I understand this must be very difficult for you to accept." Bethany nodded. "But life does not always go according to plan."

"Yes, I know that."

"The thing about dreams, though," Gabriella continued, "is that you can choose a different one. And, who knows, it might turn out even better than the original."

Bethany's head shot up and she looked into the girl's face. There was something about Gabriella that she found compelling. It wasn't so much what she said, but the authority she said it with.

"I can see that you are hurting right now," Gabriella continued. "But this will pass. And, actually, you have already chosen a new dream and you are working to make it come true."

Bethany looked puzzled.

"Well, you organized the career break and here you are writing your novel. That is a huge first step in a new direction."

Bethany conceded this with a nod.

"And, as this is such a new step, you have not yet realized just how important it could become. Because, writing," Gabriella explained, "can be very powerful." She paused as Bethany's mouth opened and closed, but no words were forthcoming. "Write thoughtfully," she advised. "Have clear objectives. Strive for meaning. And above all, try to help mankind in some way."

"Um..." Bethany's thoughts were whirring, but she still couldn't speak.

"Oh, and most of all..." Gabriella paused and looked straight into Bethany's eyes. "Do not give up! Keep on writing, no matter what." Bethany felt momentarily spellbound.

As the silence deepened between them their eyes turned towards the glinting lilac water.

Bethany began to feel joyful. Yes, Gabriella was right. She *had* already taken the first step to change her life. She had made a huge decision and was heading in a new direction. And the fact that she didn't know where she would end up now began to feel exciting. She smiled broadly. "Thank you, Gabriella," she said. "I'm so glad we met today!"

"Me too." Gabriella's echoing smile was warm.

"Strange, isn't it, that sometimes we can't see what is right in front of us," Bethany observed. "It's like pain and fear puts a screen up hiding the obvious, and it takes someone else to point things out." When Gabriella smiled right into her eyes she had the strongest feeling that she was trying to tell her something more. But perhaps she was wrong about that.

Gabriella had, though, said all she was allowed to, but she did hope that Bethany would heed her advice.

After a few more moments Gabriella said she had to go. She nodded when Bethany said she hoped they would meet again soon.

As Gabriella walked away Bethany sank to the ground. Lost in thought, the time ticked on. She made herself a promise. "I'll try harder to accept my new life. I'll work on my book and make sure it has meaning as well as being, hopefully, entertaining. And I'll try to take each day as it comes."

It sounded good in theory. She just hoped she could stick to that plan.

Chapter 17

Clare was meeting Bethany at the Paradise, but as she strode in she stopped, and gasped. Katarina was there and appeared to be sharing a huge joke with Jason.

He was on his side of the bar, head back, mouth open with laughter. Katarina was opposite him, sitting on the stool she had sat on the other day, but this time grinning happily. As Clare drew nearer she watched the girl raise her hand to rake thick shining dark hair away from her forehead only to have it fall cascading around her face again. The gesture was sensual and calculated. She wondered what affect it was having on Jason.

Her stomach was churning as she perched on a stool at the other end of the bar to the laughing pair. Jason saw her. "Hi," he said, then excused himself from Katarina.

"What can I get you to drink?" he asked politely, as if she was just another customer.

"Orange juice, please," she replied, wondering what to say next. She wanted to shout questions at him, but, after all, it was she who had suggested he talk to Katarina. But she hadn't expected to be confronted with this camaraderie.

When he gave her the drink his eyes flicked towards Katarina. "Tell you later," he mouthed, then added loudly, "Bethany is over there, are you joining her?" Clare looked over and waved at her friend. "Yes, of course. I came here to meet her." *Not to see you with that girl!*

"Good. Have a nice afternoon and I'll see you for work this evening." He turned his attention back to Katarina.

Clare was stung by his obvious dismissal. *Don't be silly.* Tears prickled her eyelids. *It's circumstantial evidence.* So what if he was laughing with her? It didn't mean he wanted to be with her again, only that they'd shared a joke.

Bethany stood up as Clare walked over. She didn't know exactly what was going on but she had been surreptitiously watching Jason and Katarina with some suspicion before Clare arrived. "Don't show him you're upset," Bethany smiled broadly. "Smile," she instructed her obviously worried friend. "They're both watching us."

Clare copied her friend and smiled as if she was very happy. In truth she felt utterly miserable.

"You sip your orange juice and after a little while we'll leave. We'll go to the beach and talk about it." Bethany was anxious for Clare not to show her feelings to Jason and Katarina.

Was Jason Katarina's boyfriend?

Oh dear. Oh, no. Clare would be devastated.

* * *

Gavin was at Pandora's. He didn't have a thing to do there but was excited about the opening tonight and decided to pop in. A huge banner hung at the entrance announcing the changes and the "new vibe" as they had decided to call it.

He had persuaded Suzanna to come with him tonight. She still wasn't happy about his involvement but had unbent a little. "I'll see it for myself and then give you my feedback," she said. That was yesterday. Fair enough.

"You got nothing to do?" Yiorgos seemed frazzled, a cigarette clamped as usual between his teeth he squinted through a wisp of smoke.

"My side is all organized for tonight."

"Okay, good." He nodded and ash fell from the cigarette onto the bar. "But me, I got lots to do." He picked up four bottles of spirits by their necks and added them to the line already marshalled along the back of the bar.

"Don't let me stop you. I'm just going." He gave Yiorgos a little wave, glanced up at one of the potted palm trees with appreciation, and strode out to his car. The windows were open. The heat was terrific today.

Gavin drove down the hill, through the resort, and up to the

Paradise Hotel. Michalis came rushing up to him in reception. "Where have you been, Gavin?" He was clearly agitated. "Your London office has been trying to reach you on the phone for hours." The phone calls had disturbed his routine. "They kept insisting you were here," he added. "I kept telling them you were out dealing with clients." He threw up his hands in exasperation. "I did not know what else to say."

"Thank you." He knew the man had tried to cover for him. "I appreciate it," he said humbly. Michalis nodded and went back into the restaurant. Gavin felt uncomfortable. He should have been here. He had been busy with the publicity for Pandora's.

The phone rang as Jason came in from the pool bar and he picked it up. "Gavin, it's your London office, *again*," he said, giving the man a piercing look. When Gavin reddened Jason took pity on him and warned him in a low voice, "The woman sounds quite angry."

"Thank you, Jason." *Oh heck.* He walked slowly to the phone running an excuse over in his head. He was thankful when Jason walked into the restaurant. He was going to tell a lie about a client difficulty and didn't want him to hear.

* * *

When Gavin arrived at Pandora's with Suzanna and saw the queue outside he was delighted. "What a great start, my darling. Don't you think so?" He beamed at his lovely wife, looking toothsome in a simple turquoise shift and low silver sandals, hoping for some encouragement.

"Mmm," she said, determinedly noncommittal. She didn't like his involvement one little bit.

Together they scrutinized the crowd which was almost exclusively younger tourists who had flocked in from other resorts. Most of the girls wore very short skirts, skimpy tops over dark tans, lots of make-up, and tottered on high-heeled strappy sandals. The boys were in blue or black jeans and pale shirts with the long sleeves rolled up to the elbow. The girls giggled, nudged each other and fiddled with their hair, while the boys tried to look cool.

Gavin forgot himself and openly ogled the girls. Suzanna caught him in the act and threw him a blank knowing look. He looked abashed and putting his arm around her, moved towards the entrance.

The doorman recognized Gavin and ushered them in. As the door opened a wave of music broke over their heads. Kevin was hard at work "creating an atmosphere with sound" as he told Yiorgos. As Gavin passed the ticket table he watched in satisfaction as each person paid over the quite substantial entrance fee. They were given a slip of paper which entitled them to drink as much as they liked for the whole evening at no extra charge.

When Gavin went to the bar he and Suzanna got a beer from a happy Yiorgos and stood watching the crowd. Suzanna commented on the candles in red glass holders on each table and said it looked romantic. Gavin was delighted by her positive remark.

The dance floor was already filled with gyrating people. Suzanna's silver-clad foot was soon tapping. "Shall we?" Gavin took her hand and led her to the floor. As she relaxed into the music she gave him one of her big smiles. Gavin was pleased to see her look happy. He'd been nervous to bring her after all the negativity.

They stayed for a while. Had another beer and a few more dances. For the punters the night was in full swing. Gavin smiled with satisfaction at the party atmosphere. Kevin was doing a great job. The place was full and everyone seemed to be enjoying themselves.

Gavin congratulated himself, looked at his watch, and decided it was time for him and Suzanna to call it a night. It

was changeover day tomorrow and he had to be at the airport
at daybreak.

They said goodbye to a jovial Yiorgos.

* * *

A few hours later a speeding Takis slammed on his brakes
as ahead of him a pair of drunken girls staggered out of
the darkness into the beam of his headlights. He came to a
screeching, skidding halt and only narrowly missed them. They
screamed with laughter and waved at him before weaving their
way back, arm-in-arm, to the roadside. He swore softly before
driving off.

A little further on his headlights picked up two young
couples staggering and lurching along. Then a lone boy turned
and vomited into a bush. As he continued the short drive
through the resort he saw many other young drunks.

It puzzled him.

Used, as he was, to tourists taking a little too much alcohol,
and the odd drunken one, he had never seen anything like this
before.

Maybe they had all been to a party.

Some party!

Those young people had degraded themselves. It was
something he never wanted to see again.

Ever!

* * *

By mid-morning the next day reports of the drunken antics of the
youngsters had ignited the indignation of the local community.
This had spread like a forest fire around the resort, to Hora, and
soon reached the furthest corners of the island. The report of the
events became wilder as the torch was passed along.

The *kafeneion* in Hora, where local men had gathered to socialize and drink coffee, buzzed with nothing else. The playing cards and backgammon boards were set out but ignored, and newspapers tossed aside. The men crowded around the rustic tables. They talked together then broke off to speak to friends. But the topic remained the same.

Takis, his deep fisherman's tan drained by the eerie pale greenish-yellow light – which typically lit *kafeneions* around the country – waved his tiny white cup of strong coffee at his father and seethed. "If I hadn't been able to stop in time I'm the one who would have been blamed!" He took a sip of coffee. The room fell silent, except for the rhythmic clicking of numerous swung worry beads, as everyone tuned in to a first-hand experience. "The drunken foreign girls stumbled right in front of my car. I almost had heart failure!" Takis lit a cigarette and sat back in his chair to let his audience assimilate that statement.

Petros and many others nodded, tutted, and muttered, *po, po* while with a cupped right hand circled clockwise a few times as if scooping air towards them: the classic words for "well, well" linked with the non-verbal sign for "unbelievable".

Takis blew a long thin stream of smoke up at the peeling yellowed ceiling. "Well, I managed to stop, no thanks to them. And guess what they did?" He looked wild-eyed at his father, then around the room. Curiosity froze the company. "They laughed!" Jaws dropped in unified shock. "Yes, I almost killed them and they were so drunk they thought it was hilarious!" He shook his head, long sharp nose twitching in disbelief.

There was more muttering of *po, po*, more hand waving, and comments like "crazy foreigners", "stupid foreign girls", and other derogatory things which bounced from table to table.

Though many had links, in some way, to local tourism the general consensus in the *kafeneion* was that its influence was bad. They wished the visitors would go home and never come back.

This latest happening fuelled this wish.

Foreigners were trouble, they all agreed.

Takis and his father continued to speak about this when the others had gone back to their own discussions. When Takis drove his father home from Hora they passed Panos playing with a little friend on the grass verge alongside his house. Takis' temper rose when he remembered Michalis trying to tell him what to do and how to drive.

Petros muttered something bitter about foreigners and mixed blood.

Takis mumbled his agreement. "You know that Jason is dating an Irish girl?"

"Yes, of course," said Petros. Like many men here he knew most things that went on in the community.

"Well it seems as if he is really smitten with her." Takis paused before he dropped the bombshell. "Rumour has it that he may even marry her…" He didn't take his eyes off the road but felt his father's shock.

"That's very bad news! Are you sure?"

"That's what some of the men are saying."

"Well, we've got to hope that doesn't happen because look how the men copy Jason." Petros curled his lip. "One marriage to a foreigner is bad enough." The local community had never really got over the shock of Michalis' marriage. "But any more… Well…" He found the possibility too awful to verbalize.

They arrived at their home in silence. Father and son were deep in thought mulling over the probable implications of Jason's marriage to an outsider.

"Nightmare," muttered Takis as he switched off the engine.

"Yes," agreed Petros.

Chapter 18

It was past four when Bethany Griffiths left her house. The book was building nicely and now she was taking a well-earned break. What she needed was a good walk. The air was still baking hot so she headed for the beach, hoping for a cooling sea breeze.

As often happened, her mind jumped over the fourteen hundred or so miles to Cardiff, and what she would have been doing at that time at work. With the time difference of two hours behind she would have been in class leading a group of managers through their new micro computer system, which was about to become part of their daily life.

She remembered experts said these computers would lead to a paper-free society, saving millions of trees over time. But with all of the new printouts it seemed to Bethany that computers generated more paper use not less. Ah well. Maybe in time the trees would be safe.

She had only gone a few steps up the beach path when Hygeia came bounding out from her kennel beside the minimarket. Bethany noted the dog's large mouth was all smiley and grinned back. As they reached the beach Bethany spotted paw prints in the wet sand and knew Hygeia was in for some good tracking.

Bethany was happy to have Hygeia with her again. She had started to really enjoy her company. She kept glancing back at the dog; not so much to see if she was still with her – now used to her tenacity – but just to share the joy of the walk in the late afternoon sunshine. From time to time when Hygeia was close behind her she reached down and affectionately ruffled the back of the dog's neck. Hygeia seemed to like it.

Bethany waded carefree through the shallows past the rows of occupied sunbeds. She was oblivious of the admiring glances she attracted with her long tanned legs, blonde hair held in a high pony tail, and gleaming gold beach bag slung over one shoulder.

Half-way along the beach she stopped to speak to a couple of tourists. Judy, a tall brunette, wearing a short voluminous turquoise wrap which emphasized her thinness, stood by a sunbed smoking and watching the world go by. As they exchanged greetings her husband gave her a brief distracted wave. Engrossed in a novel, Colin lay, role of fat spilling over khaki shorts, balding head protected from sunburn by a baseball cap, and nose protected by a piece of white card held in place with sunglasses.

They visited the resort a few times each year and Bethany had met them last year.

She liked the couple.

As she resumed her stroll, this time on the wet sand at the water's edge, Hygeia lagged behind, intent on worrying at a little bundle of rope and seaweed. She called her and encouraged her to follow. The dog happily bounded forwards.

Together they finally rounded the cliff, stepped up over the rocky lip onto the next part of the beach and continued to walk. There were only a few people on this bit of beach. Enjoying the solitude Bethany's thoughts turned to Aeron. They'd had a bit of a banter last night at the Candy Bar but of course, it was only light-hearted and innocent. She did really like him, though. And she thought he liked her.

Ah well. There was no way anything at all could happen between them, him being married and all... "Not blinking likely, eh, Hygeia!" The dog gave two small barks as if in agreement. "That's right girl!"

They approached the beach's tapered dead-end of sheer rock and water. Bethany turned, saying, "That's it. Let's go back." Hygeia lifted her front paws and head in a little leap, did a few scampering on-the-spot circles, then with tail wagging exuberantly led the way back along the beach.

Wading through the shallows, someone called her name. Aeron was waving from a sunbed. *He's all tanned and sun-blonde and gorgeous.* Her heart beat faster.

He was collecting his gear together.

"I'm meeting friends at the Sunset," he said, "would you like to join us?"

"Great," she said. *He's only being friendly. And so am I.*

With Hygeia still leading the way they walked up the beach chatting casually.

At the head of the beach path she and Aeron were going on further to the taverna while the dog was clearly going home. Bethany leaned down and stroked Hygeia's neck fur. "Thank you for your company," she told her. "See you soon." The dog gave a short bark and trotted back to her kennel.

At the Sunset Bethany knew all the friends Aeron was meeting. As well as the summer workers she was pleased to see Judy and Colin there. It seemed that from their previous visits they knew most of the people at the table.

"It's that sort of place, isn't it," said Bethany without surprise as she sat down beside Judy. Aeron said that he and Melanie and the children had gone for dinner a few times with Judy and Colin and their children last year.

Sipping cool lemonade while the others drank cola or beers, Aeron mostly sat back and listened to the easy chatter. A couple of the guys were talking about the new opening of Pandora's last night.

"Know the doorman," reported Gary, a man in his mid-twenties from Birmingham working at the pizzeria for the summer. "He let me take a look inside." He ran a hand back and forth over the top of his short sandy hair. "You never saw anything like it. The place was packed out and every single punter was drunk as a skunk."

"What, every one of them?" Aeron was sceptical.

"Looked like it to me, anyway." His piercing blue eyes twinkled with amusement. "It was like they were celebrating Christmas, New Year, and everybody's birthday in the place. And most of them only teenagers by the looks of it."

Around the table there was much head shaking and tutting.

Colin sipped the last of his beer and put his arm around his wife.

Judy smiled at her husband and looked over his shoulder at the beach bathed in sunshine. She was so happy to be back in Korkyra. It was pouring down with rain in Manchester. *Two whole weeks of lazing around.* "We'll be over at the Candy Bar tonight, Aeron," she said. "No Pandora's for us." Everyone around the table laughed.

Colin and Judy went back to their sunbeds and their children. Gary and the others went for a game of snooker in the room next door.

Left alone, it was Bethany and Aeron's first chance to speak properly. Aeron knew Bethany was taking time out to write a book but he mostly wanted to know why she was here alone.

Bethany told him she was divorced.

"Oh, sorry to hear that." He found it hard to believe that anyone would leave Bethany.

Bethany looked over the golden sand to the blue dancing water edged with white foam. It seemed like another lifetime. "We wanted to start a family and it didn't happen and when we grew apart I left him."

Ah, she left him.

A shadow crept over Bethany's face, and was gone. "Actually, I've had a letter from him saying he's remarried, has a baby, and another is on the way." Aeron looked at her sharply. Her eyes met his and spoke of shock.

She paused and pondered. "Marriage, children, and convention was how I saw my life unfolding. But obviously, my being a mother just wasn't meant to be." She gave a small regretful laugh.

"I'm very sorry to hear that, Bethany." Aeron looked sympathetic.

She swirled her cola in the tumbler. The last thing she wanted was to pass on her worries. "Ah, well. Part of life's rich pattern, and all that."

Understatement of her life. "Actually, let me tell you something that you'll probably find really funny." He looked interested so she went on. "Have you heard of the film *Shirley Valentine*?"

"Of course. But I haven't seen it."

"Well, I saw the stage play, and then the film, and they had a huge impact. A line from the script really struck me. Shirley says something like, "Why do we have all these feelings and dreams, all this life if we don't use it?" And I thought: Exactly! Why am I just stewing in my disappointment?

"Anyway, I decided to have a change for a while." For some reason she didn't mention Plan A and New York. "And, apart from writing, I'm having a go at, you know, finding myself."

She grinned suddenly. "I don't think I'm the only one trying to find myself here, am I?" Aeron raised his glass in a toast of agreement.

"Well, that's my excuse for being here in a nutshell. What's yours?" she asked playfully.

"Ah, I have a good excuse too." His tone was bantering. "Just couldn't stand the wife and kids anymore so I left them." He pulled his lips into a smiley.

"Really?" Did he mean it? Was he separated?

"No, not really." He dropped the smiley. "Far too simplistic explanation," he continued lightly. Then in a serious tone said, "Actually, I love my wife and kids very much."

"But?" Bethany prompted, sensing pain.

"But," he paused and considered his reply. He was stretched almost to his limit. The need to share overcame his natural reticence. "Just had to get away and think about myself for once." A big tense silence filled the small space between them. He looked down at the wooden table covered in red checked plastic and felt Bethany's eyes on him. "Thought I was going mad," he muttered into his glass of lemonade. Much to his chagrin, emotion clogged his throat.

Bethany reached out and gave his forearm a quick squeeze of understanding. "Sorry. Didn't mean to pry."

"You didn't." He swallowed hard. "Anyway, that's *my* excuse." He didn't raise his head but glanced up quickly and their eyes met briefly.

"It's a good one." Her reply was light.

Aeron turned the topic away from himself. "Why did you decide to write a novel? Seems like a lot of work to me."

"Yes, it is a lot of work but I love it. It's my dream." Remembering Gabriella's advice she smiled to herself. Then she saw that Aeron was frowning. It made her curious. "What about you, Aeron, do you have a dream?"

"Huh, dreams!" he chuckled bitterly. "I remember them."

Bethany waited for an explanation but Aeron had clammed up. She wanted to help him so she sent up a quick prayer for guidance. She was doing this a lot now.

The angel Gabriella winged in swiftly and joined the two guardians. This was a crucial moment in Aeron's life. The trio would help as much as allowed.

Gabriella, looking very serious, took charge and made a suggestion.

"Aeron," Bethany began, posing this important question as casually as possible. "If you could do anything at all in your life what would it be?"

"Well done, Bethany." Gabriella smiled at her guardian angel, who looked pleased. "Now wait," she advised.

Bethany sat back and sipped her drink.

Aeron looked down at his hands as if for inspiration. "Dear God, what in heaven's name is wrong with me?" he muttered, shaking his head.

His guardian angel threw up his hands in delight. "Finally, he has asked the right person the right question!" Gabriella nodded. What a breakthrough.

Bethany had no inkling of how deeply Aeron had buried his dreams. They were consigned right to the very back of his brain bearing a label: "Never look at these again!" Yet his subconscious visited them regularly which created a general air of dissatisfaction – whose source he did not recognize.

Aeron raised his head and gazed with sightless eyes at the

sea. He took a deep breath. "I love to sing and play my guitar and write songs." He pulled his smiley face unconsciously. "And if I could have continued to do that, even if I didn't make a whole stack of money, just enough to get by... that would have been my dream come true." He exhaled noisily. *There. I've finally said it out loud after all these years.*

"Ah, interesting. So, why didn't you do that?"

"Wife, kids, commitment: classic stuff," he said ruefully.

"You fell in love." Bethany nodded sagely.

"Yes, but love wasn't the obstacle. My wife fell pregnant with our daughter."

"Oh, unplanned was it?"

"You can say that again! Just as I was about to give up my day job." Aeron's mouth pursed as if he could taste the bitterness and it sickened him. On the brink of his band turning pro, Melanie had suddenly announced her pregnancy. Since she was on the pill at the time the shock had rocked his world. He hadn't wanted to accuse her of doing so deliberately but he suspected it. *If Suzy hadn't come along so soon in our marriage I would be living my dreams. Melanie and Suzy have ruined my life!*

WHAT?

Where had that thought come from?

Gabriella, who had received the answer to Aeron's prayer, silently prompted Bethany.

"Do you ever feel resentful about that?" Bethany gently asked.

That's the problem! Aeron gasped in shock. *My problem in my life, in my marriage, is that I am being eaten up with resentment! My stomach is being eaten away by resentment.* This self-knowledge wrapped itself like a tight band around his chest and his breathing turned ragged.

"Aeron, are you ill?" Bethany put a concerned hand on his arm.

"Bethany! Aeron! Well, well, well." Like lightning, Bethany pulled her hand from Aeron's arm to the table top. They looked up at Donna, a woman they had both met before and disliked.

Though fashionably attired in dark leggings under a long scarlet sleeveless top warn loose over her bulky figure, the colour was an unfortunate match for her round perspiring face. "I heard you were here for the season, Aeron. No wife and kids with you apparently."

"Hi, Donna," Aeron said softly. As he politely got to his feet a white card popped up in his mind saying SPITEFUL TROUBLEMAKER.

"Donna, how are you?" Bethany forced a smile.

Aeron sat back down.

"Oh, don't let me interrupt." Donna's puce face outlined by flat, damp, mousy hair was all smiles and sarcasm.

"Why don't you join us for a drink?" Bethany tried to be welcoming.

"No thanks, Bethany. I just came in for a beer for my husband." She made it sound like a saintly act.

"How is your husband?" Bethany liked the man, whose name she couldn't remember.

"He's very well, thank you." Donna's tone told Bethany to mind her own business. She ordered beer. "Well, enjoy yourselves." Her voice was heavy with innuendo.

Afterwards they sat in silence. Bethany felt like they'd been caught out doing something bad.

Donna was a gossip.

It wasn't great timing. Aeron's wife and children were arriving in a few days. An uneasy Bethany sipped the last of her cola and put the glass aside. "I'll leave you to your thoughts." She gave him a brief encouraging smile.

"What?" Aeron looked vague. "Oh, yeah, right." He stood up courteously as Bethany rose from the table to leave. "Thanks for the company and the talk," he said. "It was..." He searched for the right word: "Illuminating." He smiled. "I think that's how you writers would put it."

As Bethany slowly walked home her stomach knotted at the thought of Donna-the-gossip seeing her with Aeron. The woman was a meddler.

But everyone knew she and Aeron were just friends.

Didn't they?

Chapter 19

Sitting behind the cash register, Spiros looked up sharply when his brother entered the minimarket, and slipped the little calculator into his pocket. Yiorgos, he noted, was all but swaggering with self-importance.

And he had arrived in his big black shiny Mercedes.

Spiros had heard nothing but complaints from the locals about his brother all day. Some had gone so far as to tell him that bad liquor was being served at Pandora's. The cheap brands were supposed to be the same strength as the good ones but he'd once tried a knock-off gin and found it far more potent.

But Spiros angrily defended Yiorgos against that allegation. He would never do that, he had repeatedly insisted. He's a decent man trying to earn a living to keep his family, like we all are, and I'm telling you that he would not stoop to that. Secretly, he hoped his brother would not. At the start of the season Yiorgos had condemned such practice and said he sold only the best brands at Pandora's.

When pressed, though, Spiros had agreed with his customers that the drunkenness was a bad thing.

He looked keenly at Yiorgos, eager to find out what exactly had happened at Pandora's.

Yiorgos looked around the shop and saw they were alone. "Spiro," he began solemnly, as if about to deliver a lecture, "we both know there was a risk that I would need the money you owe me before the end of the season..." He paused, and Spiros' heart skipped a beat in panic. Things had definitely picked up in the shop. The newspapers had brought in many more customers, who bought other things at the same time. The souvenirs too were selling very well, and the silver jewellery. But he could not yet afford to repay his debt in full.

He couldn't read Yiorgos' face to learn what he wanted.

But Yiorgos read Spiros' face. "Don't panic, brother," he reassured him. "I've come to tell you that I have found a solution to fill Pandora's and I am hopeful that it will put me financially back on track."

Relief flooded Spiros' face. "Ah." He exhaled softly through half-closed lips.

"Yes," Yiorgos went on, relishing the feeling of magnanimity towards his little brother, "the new way of doing things was very successful last night." He preened, waiting for congratulations.

"I'm glad for you, Yiorgo." Spiros said the words, but with reservation.

"I thought you would be more glad, actually, Spiro." Yiorgos twisted his mouth with distaste. His brother was clearly jealous of his success.

Spiros didn't want to upset Yiorgos, especially as he was in his debt and had just been given a reprieve. But he felt he had to say something. After all, he reasoned, his own livelihood depended, in part, on keeping good relations with the villagers.

But how to broach it?

"Yiorgo," he began tentatively. "There has been a lot of talk among the locals today."

"Talk?" Yiorgos snapped. "*What* talk?"

"So many drunken youngsters, Yiorgo." Spiros sighed and shook his head. "Lurching about the resort, and falling in front of cars, and things like that."

"Was anyone hurt?" Yiorgos bridled.

"Not that I know of," Spiros admitted.

"Well then. What is there to talk about?" Yiorgos raised his lips flat against his underbite and rolled his eyes. Inadvertently, Spiros facially mimicked his brother and thought deeply. Should he say it? Yes.

"There is talk of you serving bad liquor at Pandora's."

Guilt flitted across Yiorgos' face.

"I told everyone who mentioned it – and there were quite a

few – that you would never sell such liquor."

Yiorgos' thick straight lips worked over his stained teeth and his nostrils flared in temper. "Tell those busybodies to mind their own business."

"Oh, Yiorgo." Spiros couldn't mask his disappointment in his brother. "That stuff is so unpredictable—"

"And you mind your own business too," Yiorgos flung at him, as he stormed out almost knocking over a young female tourist.

Spiros watched his brother jump into his flashy car and zoom away. He shook his head and sighed deeply. He had a very bad feeling about all this. He just knew no good would come of it.

* * *

Clare O'Hara was doing her evening shift at the Paradise and feeling so miserable it was difficult to concentrate on the customers. She had been mixing up orders much to her dismay.

Last night a group of visitors stayed until gone four in the morning and Jason had quickly dropped her home then went back to finish closing up. Now, she wanted to hear words of love and comfort from him. But it was impossible to talk with all these people around.

At her side, Jason spoke. "Are you all right?" It seemed that her misery was at last apparent to him. "You don't look very happy."

"Sure, I'm fine," she answered, the words sounding unconvincing even to her. "Good," he said, instead of pressing for an explanation. He continued serving customers.

Eventually, she got her rhythm back and they worked together in harmony.

Clare loved working with people. She found it much more stimulating than working in a small office all day as she had done back in Dublin. So instead of remaining in her problem she was lifted up by jokes and friendly banter and even began to enjoy herself.

She went into the hotel to fill the ice bucket but when she came back she almost dropped the container, because there, perched elegantly on bar stools, were two girls, one of whom was Katarina. Jason was standing between the two and Katarina was saying something to him.

As she approached, unseen, Katarina put her hand on Jason's arm in a way that spelled possession to Clare. They both laughed loudly. *I don't believe this.* Clare was furious. *Well, Jason certainly looks amused by Katarina.* She took the ice behind the bar and turned away from the distasteful tableau to serve a customer.

Fortunately, they wanted a complicated cocktail and during the minutes it took for her to create the foamy concoction, she achieved a small measure of calm by breathing deeply and concentrating hard. Jason came back behind the bar and everyone seemed to finish their drinks simultaneously and needed replenishment so once again the two worked together, though this time Clare did not feel any harmony. Instead she studiously avoided his eyes and any contact with him.

Once, their hands brushed as they reached for a bottle at the same time. Clare recoiled as if burned and surprise registered on Jason's face but she turned away from him before any comment could be made. All the time she was aware of the two girls staring at her. Did they know that she and Jason were together? Suddenly she felt embarrassed at the thought that they probably did.

But why feel like this? I didn't know he had a girlfriend. I thought he was free to love me.

In a lull she thought of the day they had met and how they had later fallen for each other. It was not planned, it had just happened. It had been wonderful but now things were becoming so painful and confusing that she began to think their love might be one sided, or maybe, even, too-hot-not-to-cool-down as that old love song said.

Jason stood beside her, and started to stack beer glasses into the fridge. They liked to do this so that when the liquid was poured into the chilled glass it immediately frosted white and looked cool and inviting. Clare was acutely aware of his gaze but couldn't meet it. Finally, he said softly, "Don't worry, baby, trust me. I know this must be difficult for you but I can't stop her from coming here if she wants to."

Clare made no reply. Don't worry, trust me, he had said. Well she was trying to trust him but the obvious ease of communication between him and the girl was telling her she was a fool.

Eventually Katarina and her friend made moves to leave and called Jason over to speak to them. Clare couldn't hear what was said but Katarina's sudden scowl showed she wasn't pleased.

Jason turned away to serve a customer and the girl stared at him with open hostility. *Oh no, not again! No more drinks over his head, please!* Suddenly Clare was completely on Jason's side. Just leave him alone and go away quietly, she pleaded silently to the girl. After a few moments her plea was answered as the girls stood and without another word, left the bar.

Jason and Clare continued to serve drinks but after a few minutes he found the opportunity to squeeze her hand and wink at her. This time she met his gaze, relief bringing a beaming grin to her face which he echoed. Suddenly the mood around them both lightened.

* * *

Not everyone thought the new set-up at Pandora's was bad. The visiting youth around the island found it enticing. They wanted some of that action. The queue outside the club that night was even longer than last night. Yiorgos and his staff were delighted.

Yiorgos had calmed down from his run-in with Spiros after

talking things through with his wife. He knew there was some very bad alcohol out there but he was not serving it. Such stuff could kill. He wouldn't touch it. But as only he and Gavin knew exactly what he was serving, he supposed it was natural for people to speculate.

Admittedly, though, the cheap stuff they were serving was more intoxicating than regular drinks, but these foreign kids loved to get drunk, didn't they? And a hangover wasn't such a terrible thing. Look at the fun they were having dancing the night away to Kevin's music.

He looked at the heaving dance floor. Then a young girl heaved up over the dance floor. He sighed and signalled to his barman to fetch a mop and bucket.

That was a downside.

He wished they would go outside to do that.

Very many youngsters did oblige him that way much later in the evening.

The locals and tourists making their way back from a night out at different venues wished the youngsters could either hold their drink better, or not drink so much. It put a damper on their own evening having to witness these public displays of over-indulgence.

* * *

Aeron was washing the last few dirty glasses. The Candy Bar was almost empty and he hoped the stragglers would leave soon so he could too. He looked up from the sink as Bethany arrived. "You're a late bird," he said cheerily. "And all alone."

He looked closely. *Hmm, she seems upset.* He dried the glasses wondering what the problem was when she blurted out, "I've come from the Paradise and Judy was there, remember her, we had a drink with her and her husband, Colin, at the Sunset the other afternoon?"

Aeron nodded. "Yeah, nice lady. She and Melanie got along like a house on fire."

"Yes, well," Bethany pursed her lips in dismay. "Judy just lectured me for going out with a married man!"

"Uh..." Aeron looked shocked. "I didn't know you were seeing anyone, Bethany." He leaned towards her and grinned. "You're a dark horse." He was acting cool but feeling jealous, though he knew he had no right.

"I'm not." Bethany's tone was flat. "It's you and me she's talking about!"

Aeron's jaw dropped. White card, message: BAD NEWS, MAN!

"I tried to tell her it was a load of rubbish but she clearly didn't believe me. Said everyone knows we're involved with each other."

Aeron shook his head. "Man, I don't believe this."

"Well, I'm not being funny or anything, but you'd better believe it." Bethany sighed deeply. This was a nightmare. "Judy said she knows your wife and likes her so she was making it her business to – as she put it – make me see Melanie's side of things."

Aeron gasped with distress. "Oh heck, I hope she doesn't tell my wife *her* side of things!" His stomach began to knot. With an automatic reflex he began hunting through his pockets for some Tums. He didn't find any. Carelessly he had left them in the apartment. He tried to breathe deeply and tell himself that everything would be fine.

Eventually he found his voice, "I'm embarrassed that you've been upset like this, Bethany." He shook his head slowly. "I am very sorry. I feel like I've compromised you somehow."

"Actually, you haven't, if you think about it. All we've ever done is talk in public. We've only had one private conversation, and that was in public too, now I come to think about it." Bethany bit her lip and looked worried. "What are we going to do?" She was devastated. "I'm really not happy about this. I'm here writing my book and trying to find peace of mind, and I haven't got a boyfriend because I don't want one. Everybody knows that. Or, so I thought, until now."

He looked up at the ceiling and considered the matter. With a sigh he switched his gaze back to Bethany. "I don't think there's much we can do, realistically," he said dejectedly. "If we stop speaking to each other they'll probably say, 'Oh, they've split up now' and it may make things worse."

Bethany rolled her eyes in frustration. "Okay, I agree. We'll try to speak normally to each other when we meet, but..." Her voice trailed away. "What a mess." She sighed again and shook her head.

"Oh, boy, this could get difficult and complicated, couldn't it?" he remarked with a wry grin.

"Ah, well." Bethany tried to feel philosophical. She looked appraisingly at Aeron. *Yes, still attractive!* But she had never so much as flirted with him. Instead she had kept reminding herself that for her married men were taboo.

He sensed the appraising look and he found himself doing the same. They gazed at each other with the most intimate look since their meeting two months before. Light blue eyes met dark blue eyes and twinkled.

"You're lovely, Aeron," Bethany said softly at length. "And I'm not saying it wouldn't be nice. But we both know it's not on the cards, and never was."

"Oh, now I'm a wounded man." He put both hands over his heart in mock seriousness.

As they both chuckled a woman sitting in the corner with her husband looked over at them sharply with interest.

"Better go now," Bethany muttered.

"Hmm." Aeron couldn't help but agree. "Sorry, Bethany." He pulled his lips into a rueful smiley and sighed. "Life's not always fun, is it?"

She looked at the ever-so-cute dimple in his chin. Felt her attraction for him. Pushed it away. "No, it's not."

Chapter 20

Gavin Bellingham's alarm clock began shrieking beside his left ear. Groggily he fumbled for the snooze button. As his brain registered the time the day's agenda opened out in his mind: Must be at the hotel in an hour to transfer two clients. Better get up. Now!

Suzanna tried to sleep again but lay listening to Gavin's movements. The bedsprings creaked relieved of his bulk, his feet padded across the bare polished bedroom floor, then went pat, pat, pat going down the open staircase to the kitchen below. From there came the sound of the downstairs loo flushing, bottles clanking in the fridge door, and the frequent ring of the telephone. Suzanna was still awake when Gavin padded back up the stairs heading for the shower.

The day was already hot and the solar panels had heated the water to tepid so he emerged feeling refreshed. Standing in front of the mirror he quickly checked for a receding hairline then smoothed a blob of mousse onto his striped hair and brushed it flat and back at the sides and top. Got to get a hair-cut, he told himself for the umpteenth time.

As he emerged from the bathroom Suzanna stretched her arms languidly over the pillow. "Are you going to take me out for lunch today?" she wheedled. "You've been promising all week."

Lunch with his lovely wife. Gavin smiled at her tenderly. "Actually, I *can* take you to lunch my darling."

"Oh, goody!" A change of scenery and a nice meal too. She flashed him one of her broad smiles which she had been rationing lately.

Gavin savoured the moment. "I've got to be at the hotel in about half an hour to transfer some people to the next resort, then I'll be back to work for a while at home," he outlined. There was a marvellous little taverna at Gouvia on the way into town. "I know just the place for lunch, right beside the sea."

He needed to plan more things for Pandora's but didn't mention this. Last night, the fourth since the new venture, had been the busiest so far. He thought of the big pile of money he would be getting from Yiorgos in a couple of days. First share of the profits in the new venture, as he liked to think of it. *It's all going frightfully well.*

Mentally he dismissed the complaints from around the resort. Michalis, up at the Paradise, had told him the locals were up in arms about the drunkenness. The man had no inkling of Gavin's involvement. People knew he was recommending Pandora's to his younger clients but that was all. Yiorgos wanted to take all the credit for the idea so that was no problem.

"I'm looking forward to lunch already," said Suzanna turning over and tucking one hand under the pillow beneath her chin.

Gavin went to the next room and selected a shirt and trousers from the pile of crisp sun-dried washing, plugged in the iron and manfully attacked both. Suzanna hated ironing but he didn't mind it. He'd told her that his mother showed him how to do it. "I still haven't mastered the shirts though, they never turn out quite right. But that's okay." It was perfectly okay with Suzanna. Practice would make perfect. She said she had no intention of running around after him like a second mother.

Snuggling back into a doze Suzanna was startled awake when Gavin kissed her cheek. She opened her eyes and drank in his fresh and dapper morning look and smiled with appreciation.

"Back soon," he promised.

Wouldn't be a holiday rep for anything. Suzanna soon drifted back to sleep.

* * *

The sun flashed off the windscreen of Aeron Lehman's little white hire car as it rounded the sharp bend of the steep hill. Below, after a last glimpse of pastel buildings over a grey shoulder of rock, the resort vanished from view. "Oh, heck," he murmured, feeling vulnerable. It was like leaving behind a security blanket.

After reaching the hilltop soon the vehicle ducked under overhanging olive branches and their brooding shadows matched his gloomy mood.

Driving to pick up Melanie and the kids from the airport Aeron's complaining ulcer showed their visit was premature for his health. He crunched on a chalky Tums and tried to calm his agitation by concentrating on getting there safely. He was almost glad to have to navigate over the many deep ruts on the narrow twisting road.

His family had broken up their trip, as they usually did, with a few days in London. He had phoned them there.

"See you Friday, Dad!" Jamie had sounded so excited. Despite his reservations a grin blossomed on his lips.

Jamie and Suzy. *Awesome!*

They would have such fun together.

But the thought of seeing Melanie threw him back into a panic.

One part of him couldn't wait to hold her in his arms. But the other part... Well... Their phone calls had got cooler and cooler.

"Oh, heck!"

When he arrived at the small airport he parked beside the perimeter fence, not far from the entrance. He checked his watch. They should have just landed. He walked inside and studied the Arrivals board. Yes, the Olympic Airways flight was on time. All he had to do now was wait for his family to claim their bags.

He stood with a small knot of people opposite the automatic double doors. *Everything will be great!* He crossed his fingers and hoped.

After a few minutes the twin doors swished open and passengers began to stream through. Melanie laboured with the trolley piled with teetering luggage. As she spotted Aeron she smiled. Even at a distance of yards he could see the smile didn't reach her eyes. His heart sank. *Oh, man, here we go!*

Beside her Suzy looked shy but pleased to see him. Jamie carried a football in a string bag which bumped against his leg as he ran into his father's arms. Aeron swung him high then swooped him low to kiss his forehead enthusiastically. He set his son down and hugged his daughter.

Melanie, he noticed immediately, was glowing. Her auburn hair swung in a glossy bob and light blue jeans and pink top moulded over her trim figure. "You look fantastic." His compliment was sincere.

His wife looked, with obvious distaste, at the way Aeron's thick sun-bleached hair fell over his collar and ears. She turned her face from his kiss and presented a cool cheek.

For the children's sake Aeron forced himself to be jovial. "Come on everybody let's get you to Korkyra and onto the beach."

"Ye-e-e-s!" Suzy and Jamie chorused with excitement.

"Great." Even Melanie looked pleased about that. Once again Aeron hoped all would go well.

* * *

As Aeron got busy making a sandcastle with Jamie he felt contented for the first time in ages. *This is awesome!* The boy filled his new red bucket with seawater again and again until the fine white sand was wet enough to mould.

Working side-by-side father and son built a long, low structure close to the shoreline, and people were kind enough to step around it when they passed.

From time to time Aeron looked over at Melanie lying on a sunbed, in the shade of an umbrella, slowly turning the pages of a magazine. He noted with a heavy heart that she never looked at him.

It was like he wasn't there.

But then again, I haven't been there for months, so maybe this is payback time. He hoped not.

Suzy had already made friends with two sisters who'd been on their plane. A few yards away from Melanie they had pulled a sunbed to the water's edge, and the three of them sat on it. When Melanie glanced at her daughter a big smile lit her face. Covered in a baggy pink top and slathered in suntan lotion Suzy swung her legs, and her face was animated as she chatted with the girls.

When the castle was finished the girls were nice enough to crowd around it with compliments.

Aeron grabbed the camera and starting shooting lots of photos of the children. Melanie's reluctance to come into shot was a surprise. Even if she was mad at him she usually put the kids first.

"Aw, come on, Mom," Suzy cajoled.

Slowly, Melanie peeled herself off the bed and walked over to Jamie. She kept the sunglasses on so no one knew that her big smile was a fake.

When the kids went along the beach to Korkyra Minimarket to buy ice cream Aeron confronted Melanie. "Is this how it's gonna to be the whole time?"

"What do you mean?" She stubbornly pursed her lips. She knew exactly what he meant but wanted him to verbalize it.

But Aeron wouldn't play along. "Have it your way, Melanie. I hope you enjoy your vacation." Abruptly he stood, and for a second she thought he was going to leave her on the beach. He was considering it. Instead, he headed into the water and swam a long way out trying to control his anger, and his disappointment.

He wished Melanie had not come here if she was going to remain so aloof. It wouldn't be long before the kids noticed, and then they were sure to be upset too.

What a mess. Aeron felt very sorry for himself.

Chapter 21

Newcomer Evan Lewis savoured the warmth of the night air as he left the Paradise Hotel and ambled along the narrow coast road. Pale T-shirt and jeans hugged his meaty, rugby-formed frame, holiday garb perfectly suiting the sounds of trilling cicadas and whooshing waves rushing onto the shore.

Something dark darted overhead and looking up he saw a few small creatures circling a dim street light. "Bats not only in the belfry," he muttered cheerfully, running a hand over unkempt fair hair.

He was off to join his mates. The pair had gone on ahead of him to start some serious drinking in a nearby bar. Evan was not a heavy drinker – though he enjoyed a pint of good Welsh ale to unwind.

The holiday had come right out of the blue. A poor medical student at Cardiff University, Evan Lewis had not planned a trip this summer but had taken the place of a friend who dropped out at the last minute. His parents had willingly paid his share. From a former coalmining village in a little Welsh valley they were so proud of him, and glad he would have a rest from his studies.

Tonight he and his mates planned to go to Pandora's. They wanted to dance. And they hoped they would meet some pretty girls too.

A tall slender girl walked down the short driveway of a villa.

"Hello." Evan threw the girl a friendly smile. She looked a bit familiar, somehow.

"Hello." She smiled back.

Heading in the same direction it seemed natural for them to walk together. Evan was taller than the girl but didn't tower over her. He liked that.

As the row of villas ended the pale stretch of beach opened out to their left, overhung by a sharp crescent moon glinting in the inky sky. The impact of its beauty stopped Evan in his tracks. He pointed to its faint reflection on the dark sea and the red and blue facets of the single star winking beside it. The girl agreed it was indeed a beautiful sight.

As they walked on they introduced themselves. "Gabriella, what a nice name," said Evan. "I've never met anyone called that before." That familiarity? She probably resembled someone he used to know.

"Where are you going?" Gabriella asked, though she knew exactly where he was going. He told her about the club his mates were keen to try. They were drinkers, he explained, and were drawn by the entrance fee including as much alcohol as they could down. *He* was more interested in dancing, he assured her. She knew he spoke the truth.

"Do you know the place?" He hoped to invite her. Gabriella had turned up her inner radiance and Evan found her very attractive indeed.

"I have heard of it," she said. "But if you like to dance why do you not go to the Candy Bar?" Many people, including Bethany and Clare, loved to dance there. "They play great music."

"I've heard it mentioned but haven't been yet." He sounded interested.

"It is good fun." She wished she could say more, but there was a limit to her suggestions.

Evan wondered if that's where Gabriella was going. She said she might pass by there later. He said he might see her there then. Gabriella was non-committal, but spoke of the Candy Bar even more warmly, and said it was a place you could even go on your own, and fit right in.

Evan liked the sound of the bar and thought he might well go there later, even if he couldn't get his mates to join him. "But if they persuade me to go to Pandora's instead I'll definitely go there tomorrow." He and Gabriella parted with smiles at the little road junction and went in different directions.

Evan's guardian angel would keep trying to persuade him to go to the Candy Bar *tonight*.

* * *

Clare was in the restaurant of the Paradise Hotel as Aeron arrived with his wife and children. Manos had given him the night off. "So that's Melanie," Clare commented to Jason, "and Jamie and Suzy. What a lovely looking family they make."

"What? Oh, yes." Jason was distracted. The restaurant was filling up quickly. He glanced over at the outside bar. "Clare, you have new customers."

"Right, boss." Clare smiled broadly at Jason and hurried outside with the replenished ice bucket.

Michalis handed around the tall menus to Aeron and his whole family. Jamie looked proud when he got his. The dishes were written in Greek on one side and English on the other. His father helped him choose. The meal was made fun by everyone sharing bits of their food so they all got a taste. Even Melanie seemed to enjoy it.

After eating they went outside to the pool bar for dessert and Aeron introduced Melanie to Clare. While Clare scooped chocolate ice creams for the kids into little steel dishes she felt the woman's eyes boring into her back. She thought it was quite natural for Melanie to be a little suspicious. After all, Aeron had been alone here for ages. But she would soon find out he had been faithful.

Busy though she was Clare couldn't help but notice that the couple didn't have much to say to each other.

Oh, dear. Clare hoped things would warm up between them. She felt sorry for them.

Mind you, who am I to feel sorry for another couple? Sure, my own love life is so uncertain.

Clare desperately wanted to trust Jason but it was very difficult. Katarina had been to the hotel again today with her friend. They'd swum in the pool and then sat at the bar to drink cola and flirt with Jason.

Well, Katarina had flirted.

Definitely.

Clare had watched her as carefully as she could without being obvious.

Whether Jason had flirted back was less certain. Perhaps, as he said, he was just trying to keep the peace in front of the customers.

* * *

Evan Lewis and his mates were singing at the top of their voices as they staggered home from Pandora's. Evan had tried his best to get his friends to go to the Candy Bar instead. He had felt the place pulling him very strongly. But when they promised to go tomorrow he gave in. They were giving an emotional rendition of *Cwm Rhondda*, regarded, by many, as the unofficial Welsh national anthem, and Evan's rich baritone dominated the other two.

> *Guide me, O Thou great Redeemer,*
> *Pilgrim through this barren land.*
> *I am weak, but Thou art mighty;*
> *Hold me with Thy powerful hand.*
> *Bread of heaven, bread of heaven,*
> *Feed me till I want no more...*

The villagers whose sleep they had disturbed were surprised at the melodious beauty of the drunken chorus.

Evan halted in the middle of road, shoulders back and diaphragm flattened, he threw his arms out palm upwards to make a dramatic finish.

> *Feed me till I want no more!*

Unfortunately, he closed his eyes too, and, overcome by

dizziness, promptly keeled over landing limp and unhurt on the flat of his back.

"Evan, get up, will you, boyo." His friend Morgan swayed towards him with a helping hand extended. As Evan reached up to grasp his hand Morgan overbalanced and spread-eagled on top of him.

While Evan and Morgan tried to untangle themselves their mate Dai doubled over with laughter. "Evan Lewis I've never seen you so drunk." As great chuckles rippled through him he grabbed his stomach and almost fell over too. "There's proud of you I am, boyo."

Pinned to the ground by his pot-bellied beer swilling friend Evan looked up at the stars, which appeared to be dancing in the sky, and hiccupped. "Not wrong there, Dai," he readily owned up. "Get off me, Morgan there's a good lad." But Morgan was now helpless with laughter and incapable of standing up. "Can't," he tittered, after trying to push himself away.

"Dai, get him off me will you, boyo, we'll be here all night." Evan was still in good humour but feeling winded by his friend's substantial bulk.

"Right you are." Dai leaned over and grabbed Morgan by the waistband of his jeans and tried to heave him up. But he was too heavy to budge and he almost toppled over with effort which made him and Morgan laugh even harder. Their laughter was infectious and a sense of the ridiculous gripped Evan and set him giggling. This hurt his trapped stomach and he gave Morgan a hefty push which sent the man rolling onto his back screeching with laughter.

When the released Evan tried to get up he still felt dizzy with alcohol and he kept collapsing back. Finally he hit on the idea to roll onto all fours, and from there getting into standing position was not easy, but eventually not impossible.

The three friends continued weaving their way back to the hotel.

* * *

Gavin stretched out on the sofa and drew Suzanna towards him.

He kissed her soundly before telling her the good news. "I spoke to Yiorgos today and if business keeps up I'll make a killing."

Suzanna shuddered. "I don't like the way you've phrased that."

"Sorry, my darling. I'll make us a lot of lovely money." He smiled at her. "There, is that a better way to say it?"

"Much," she kissed him back.

When she married Gavin she thought he was loaded. It was definitely part of his charm. Disappointment at the reality had not really gone away. It had taken a lot of the shine off the marriage for her.

Still, things seemed to be looking up a bit.

Although not keen on Pandora's – it struck her as somewhat seedy – she did like the sound of the money rolling in. Perhaps she wouldn't have to get a job in the winter. She was trying not to think too far ahead but it wasn't always easy.

Chapter 22

Driving on the edge of the resort Takis' mind was filled with anger and hatred against all foreigners. Talk at the *kafeneion* tonight had centred again on the drunken tourists spilling out of Pandora's. Everyone agreed their behaviour was disgusting.

Takis had already manoeuvred his car around knots of youngsters staggering up the road. Slowly rounding a blind bend he came to the short stretch of road that was lit. He saw another little group ahead. Even at a distance he recognized minimarket-Spiros' daughter Eleni and her friend. They were standing with a couple of tourist youths. What was this?

Fraternizing!

He scrutinized them closer. The girls looked angry. They turned and made to walk away. As a team the two boys lunged at them and grabbed a girl each. The girls screamed in fright.

Takis put his foot down and sped towards the group.

All looked startled as he jammed his breaks on and came to a squealing stop beside them.

Without a thought of "two-against-one" he leapt from the car. "Problem, Eleni?" His tone was a challenge.

"Taki, thank goodness!" Eleni clutched his arm with relief.

The two boys had moved a few feet back from the girls. Takis could see the tourists were drunk. "Only a bit of fun, mate," the taller one who had grabbed Eleni muttered.

"Didn't look like you intended much fun for my friends." Takis' thin face was tight with fury.

"Sorry, love." Tall apologized to Eleni.

"Get in the car." Takis spoke coldly to the girls who instantly obeyed.

His hands itched to lash out at the young men to teach them a lesson. He was Navy trained and felt powerful enough to do that. But he let it go. He suspected he would be the one to get into trouble if he hurt them. Nothing had actually happened to the girls, he had seen that.

He committed the two guys to memory. "I'll be watching you. You're a long way from home."

"Won't happen again, mate," Tall promised. His friend smirked – he was making no such promise. He'd made a mistake. Takis lunged and knocked him to the floor with one punch. With balled fists at the ready he waited for the boy to rise.

Eleni jumped out of the car and pulled him away. "*Pame,* let's go," she hissed. "Mustn't upset the tourist police." He allowed her to push him towards the car. *These damn foreigners!*

He was shaking with temper as he fired the engine. "What the hell are you doing out at this time of night?"

"We've been to a friend's name-day celebration." Eleni spoke for them both. "And Taki, we've walked here at this time of night for years. It's always with a friend and it's never been a problem."

Takis knew this was the truth. Korkyra was a safe place. "Yes, well things have changed since your uncle started that fool's nonsense at Pandora's."

Eleni sighed deeply, realizing the truth of Takis' words. She had been very scared. Her Uncle Yiorgos had a lot to answer for. He had been the talk of the village for days.

She would not dare to tell her father what had happened tonight. Then again, the jungle drums in the village would make sure he soon found out. Perhaps she had better tell him first.

* * *

Evan Lewis and his two mates had made it back to the Paradise and were now fooling around on the balcony. Evan had got it into his head that he could dive from there right into the floodlit swimming pool.

Three invisible angels stood watching as Evan clambered

onto the narrow concrete ledge. Gabriella landed right beside them.

As Evan reached the end he spun round quite neatly, seemingly oblivious of the fact that he was on the fourth floor with a drop of nearly fifty feet below him. As he made his way back towards the angels his mates were clapping and cheering him on.

"Evan, you are a wonder, boyo," Morgan shouted.

Dai whistled with his two little fingers in the sides of his mouth.

Gabriella kept her eyes trained on Evan. She shook her head as he shouted, "Look at me, I should be in the circus!"

"To be fair, it is not really his fault," said his guardian angel reaching out and holding Evan's arm as he missed his footing, and almost took the plunge. "Evan is moderate in everything he does, including drinking. He had a few drinks that is all. But the alcohol was unusually potent."

Gabriella's thoughts flew to Gavin and the deal he had made with Yiorgos – against angelic promptings – as another angel came winging in and landed beside her.

Evan reached the end of the ledge and jumped down onto the balcony. But his ankle turned as he landed. Unbalanced he fell heavily backwards and his head struck the sharp corner of the little square marble table.

Evan Lewis looked at the group of smiling angels and hastily stood up.

A piercing scream made him tear his eyes away from theirs.

As he looked at Morgan and Dai his lips formed a circle of shock and disbelief.

He was lying on the floor with blood seeping from his cracked scull.

But he was also standing up! *What the...?*

One of the angels stepped forward and put a calming hand on Evan's shoulder. "Do not be afraid, I am your guardian angel," he said quietly.

Evan's eyes flicked to the angel's face then back to his friends' frantic efforts to revive him. Morgan yelled for towels to try to stop the bleeding.

Evan made an attempt at levity. "You can try that, boys," he told his mates. "But by the looks of the extra company you're not going to have much luck." He might as well not have spoken for all the notice his friends took.

Another angel spoke to Evan. "They cannot hear you." Evan looked into her face. "Gabriella!" He was startled; confused. "Have you died too?"

The angel shook her head. "No, Evan."

His eyes became like saucers as he noticed her folded wings. "You're an angel!"

She nodded. "I am Gabriella, the angel of Greece." She paused to make introductions. "As he just told you, this is your guardian angel, and these are your friends' guardian angels." Evan looked curiously at the fourth. "Ah, yes. Meet Ruth, the angel who has come to take you home."

A light dawned in Evan's dark brown eyes. "Oh, Gabriella, you tried to warn me." He pressed his lips together, shook his head, and ran a hand over his unruly thick fair hair. "I had the strongest feeling that I should go to the Candy Bar. But I let myself be persuaded to go to Pandora's instead. I should have followed my instinct." Gabriella nodded. They shared a long look of regret. "Thanks for trying anyway."

There was a pause while he attempted to digest the whole situation. An urgent thought struck him. "Hang on a minute." He spoke to his guardian angel. "Why didn't you save me?"

"That is a good question," his guardian said, and the other three angels nodded agreement. "The answer is this: I have protected you on numerous occasions, including when you slipped and almost fell over the balcony tonight."

"What!" Evan was incredulous. "You protected me from

plunging over the balcony, but thirty seconds later, if that, you let me hit my head? Is that what you are telling me?" He wanted to be clear.

His guardian angel nodded. Evan looked at Gabriella for confirmation and she nodded too.

His angel explained, "Today, I was only permitted to guard your life on earth until your time to leave arrived. This time and date was one of those written before your birth."

"*One* of the times?" Evan was further puzzled. "I can only die once, why are there more than one?"

His angel spoke up. "If you had gone to the Candy Bar you would still be alive. Today's recorded time and date would have been passed over." He smiled wryly. "As other dates have been before today."

"Like when?" Evan thought he might as well get all the information. It was so very odd. He felt absolutely fine and cheerful. His normal self in fact.

"Do you remember, one summer when you were six years old, walking in the woods with your elder brother following the path of a stream, and a young man tried to persuade you to cross over for some sweets?" His angel paused to let him think.

Evan's mind spun backwards.

As he remembered that day his brown eyes went wide.

The stream, though small, had steep earth banks, and he could still picture the young man standing on the opposite side. "I wanted to go over to get the sweets," he said. "But my brother wouldn't let me, and I wasn't happy. Then my brother shouted at me to run. I wasn't going to stay there without him so we both ran. And we ran and ran until we got right out of the woods and half way home."

But where was this story leading? Evan shrugged his shoulders, and put up a hand for the angel to continue.

"Well, that man meant you harm," his guardian angel said. "That was the first potential time and date of your death recorded before you were born."

Evan suspected he was running out of time, so he cut to the chase. He desperately wanted an answer to the ultimate question that now burned within him. "If I had gone to the Candy Bar tonight... If I had listened to Gabriella, and followed my strong instinct... How much more time would I have had?" He braced himself for the answer. He wasn't sure, even now, that he wanted to hear it.

Yet, he did.

"You would have lived until you were ninety-three years old."

Evan dropped his head forwards and covered his eyes with his hand. There was utter respectful silence until he recovered his composure. Lifting his head Evan dragged his fingers slowly down his face until they cradled his chin.

Gabriella, filled with compassion, put her hand onto Evan's shoulder and looked deep into his eyes. "I am very sorry," she told him softly.

Evan, though, was surprised that his feelings of regret were already diminishing. Something like joy was starting to bubble up inside him. "*I* made the choice, though, didn't I?"

"Yes," Gabriella nodded. "The choice was *yours*. *All* the choices in your life have been yours."

The angel Ruth spoke to Evan's guardian angel. "Time to go," she murmured. The angel nodded then turned to Evan with a question in his huge oval brown eyes.

Evan's eyes raked his distraught friends one last time and glanced at his prone and lifeless body then he nodded decisively at his angel.

Ruth spoke directly to Evan for the first time. "Do not be afraid," she said. "I am taking you to a place more wonderful than you could ever dream of."

A tunnel of brilliant white light opened up in the sky above the hotel's swimming pool. The angel Ruth steadied Evan with a touch to his shoulder, as his guardian angel held his hand. Evan smiled happily and stood tall. Together the three of them stepped towards the light.

Gabriella called out, "Goodbye, Evan." She watched as the trio walked into the tunnel.

Evan was amazed to find his grandmother waiting there for him. "Nan!" he yelled in excitement and pleasure. "You look thirty years younger than when I last saw you, but you're still my Nan!"

"Hello, Evan, boyo. We've all come to meet you." Behind her were an equally rejuvenated group of relatives including his great-grandmother and great-grandfather, an aunt and uncle, a cousin, and lots of other people who looked familiar to him, though he couldn't quite place them. She took her grandson's hand and as she kissed his cheek the tunnel became a vividly coloured vortex and disappeared from Gabriella's sight.

Gabriella spoke to the two remaining guardian angels standing sombrely next to the two distraught friends. It would be a tough time for all now. The angels would be working hard as a team to strengthen their wards.

After a quick conference with them Gabriella flew onto her next task.

Chapter 23

Bethany was startled awake by long, sharp whistles, and the demented rattling of shutters. Hands shaking, heart thudding, she listened for a few seconds then chuckled loudly with relief. The strong, dry, northerly wind, the Greeks called Meltemi, had arrived, and was scouring the walls of the bungalow and tearing through the olive grove.

The smile faded from her lips, though, as the eerie sounds continued. They matched the gloomy mood of Korkyra. For the last couple of days a pall of sadness had hung over the resort. The death of the young Welshman had shocked everyone. His name was spoken in hushed tones everywhere. Evan Lewis had been a university student in Cardiff, Bethany's home city – so she felt an affinity with him and his grieving family.

Clare said Jason had been summoned in the middle of the night by Evan's distraught friends. The police and an ambulance had arrived quite quickly but the man was dead before the calls had even been made. His parents arrived yesterday and were staying at the hotel. They wanted to take their son's body back to Wales as soon as possible but an inquest had to be held first.

His two friends, Morgan and Dai, were in a mess. They wanted to go home but they had to be witnesses at the inquest.

What a tragedy.

Police closed Pandora's down and took away bottles of alcohol to test. Staff were questioned. No one in the resort had seen Yiorgos since the death. Rumour had it that he was in police custody. Clare was relieved not to be part of that. But she said it wasn't easy working at the Paradise right now either.

Clare's bedroom door was closed so Bethany crept into the kitchen. She drank a mug of coffee and felt restless. She would dress quickly and go down to the sea to write about the Meltemi. It would be perfect to put into her novel. Also, she wanted to keep busy.

When she reached the beach she was not surprised there weren't many people about. Sitting down cross-legged on a folded towel the wind whipped at her hair, clothes, and notebook as she gazed around.

The Meltemi changed the whole look of the place.

She wrote that the cloudless sky was overlaid with a gauzy mist which tinted the china-blue to a deep hyacinth. She saw and wrote that the wind swept back and forth over the sea, so that one minute it was flat polished jade, and the next ruffled into an expanse of white feathers, which reached towards the horizon and breached its straight dark blue line.

Further up the beach her attention turned to the tourists who, despite the extreme conditions, were determined to sunbathe. The owners of the sunbeds had positioned pairs of umbrellas behind them, with poles thrust almost horizontally into the sand. Acting as a windbreak the umbrellas quivered under duress but held. But then a cheeky gust would send the umbrellas whirling across the beach, necessitating a frantic dash to recover them. Meanwhile the exposed people were assaulted by the Meltemi ripping at hair, wrestling sunglasses off noses, and blasting sand over bodies leaving a fine coating firmly stuck to suntan lotion.

As Bethany watched and wrote, amused by the scene, one by one people gave up the battle and headed for the sheltered poolside at the Paradise and a drink to wash the grit from their mouths. The Meltemi had won.

But a few stalwarts stayed. They fixed brave grins on their faces and vowed they would not be driven off, not while the sun was shining on them. So wind and man fought on.

After a while, she too decided to head for the Paradise.

She hadn't run into Aeron and his family yet but the Meltemi seemed to be chasing everyone there today so they would probably be there too.

On one hand, she would like to meet them – especially the children. But on the other, she was nervous that an erroneous rumour about her and Aeron may have reached his wife's ears.

* * *

"Melanie!"

Melanie stopped in her tracks. Everyone wanted ice cream so she volunteered to bring it from Korkyra Minimarket. She needed the break. The vacation was not going well. The strong winds had driven the family off the beach and back up to the apartment.

She studied the plain face of the woman in an ornately embroidered white dress crossing purposefully on short heavy legs over to her side of the road. With a sinking heart she recognized her from previous visits. "Donna, how are you?" Trying for a note of bonhomie she was just about to compliment the woman on her pretty dress but Donna seemed eager to speak.

"I heard you were here." Donna had been thrilled when she learned that.

"Yes, here I am." She smiled automatically. This woman was a busybody.

"Aeron's been here the whole summer, though." Her tone was commiserating.

"Yes, the whole summer. He's convalescing." She didn't know why she felt a need to explain. She hardly knew the woman and didn't like her.

"You're very trusting." She felt rattled by the coolness of Melanie's welcome. "I wouldn't let my husband stay in a holiday resort on his own for a week, never mind a summer."

"Yes, well..." *I had no choice but I'm not telling you.* "Look, I have to go, my family are waiting for this ice cream." She held up a little carrier bag.

The woman felt dismissed. *Right, she's asked for it.* "I don't suppose the rumours are true anyway." She affected an innocent smile as she threw the barb.

"Rumours?" Melanie bridled.

"There's probably not a grain of truth in them."

"So why are you bringing it up?" Melanie snapped. What had Aeron been doing?

"I just thought you should know what people are saying." The woman attempted to look offended. "Hey, don't shoot the messenger."

"Hmm." Melanie tried to look unconcerned. "Tell me all."

Donna couldn't resist the invitation. "Just ask him about Bethany."

"Is that it? No juicy details to pass on?"

"Well, you're a cool one, I must say."

"Not really, Donna." *I won't give you the satisfaction of knowing I'm upset.* "But I don't believe Aeron has been unfaithful to me."

"I'm sure you're right. But you know how people like to gossip."

"Sure do." With her eyes Melanie told Donna that she was one of them. "Thank you, Donna. Must go."

"Well, have a nice day, as you Americans say." Donna grinned, clearly elated by her meddling.

* * *

When Bethany arrived at the Paradise she spotted Clare standing by the pool, pad in hand jotting down an order from a table of four. Bethany waved at her friend and sat on a tall stool at the bar.

Jason looked distracted. "Bethany, hi."

"How are you doing?" Bethany was all concern.

"It's a bad business." He shook his head and looked solemn. "The boy, Evan, he seemed very nice: polite, quiet." He bit his lip. "It's unbelievable that he died."

"I'm very sorry for Evan's family." Bethany pressed her fingertips briefly to her forehead. "What a terrible thing. Only twenty-three."

"I hardly knew what to say to his parents." Jason sighed deeply. "Nightmare."

Clare walked behind the bar and placed a soothing hand on the small of Jason's back. She looked at Bethany. "Doesn't this sort of thing shake your faith?" Clare couldn't make any sense of it all.

"A lot of things in life don't seem to make any sense but we just have to keep on going." Bethany didn't want to say too much. The situation was very delicate. A young life had been lost.

"It's all right for you, Bethany." Jason poured pineapple juice over ice in two tall glasses, added straws and put them on a small tray for Clare to serve poolside. The high fence was holding back much of the Meltemi but Bethany shivered in the wind-cooled shade.

"What do you mean it's all right for me?" Bethany looked puzzled.

"Well, you believe in God, right?" His lips twisted in cynicism.

Bethany and Jason's angels were joined by Gabriella.

"Yes, I do." Bethany nodded.

"Don't you ever wonder what it's all about?"

"Now, that's a big question," chuckled Bethany.

"And?" he prompted. Bethany pondered. Did he really want to know or was he winding her up? "Don't you ever have doubts at all?" he persisted, leaning his elbows on the counter waiting for an answer.

"Course I do," Bethany freely admitted.

"You do?" His thick dark brows arched in surprise.

The guardians, standing tall and still, looked intently at

Gabriella, awaiting her instructions. She spoke urgently.

Bethany's angel advised her to trust that Jason's question was genuine.

Bethany decided to open up and tell him a little of her path of faith. "I lost my cousin Catherine when she was the same age as Evan. It was so bad. She was killed in a car crash." Bethany paused, remembering. "It was late at night and they think the driver fell asleep at the wheel." She shook her head. "Drove into a tree." She still missed Catherine, even after many years.

"I'm very sorry," Jason muttered.

"I love trees. Couldn't believe a tree was instrumental in killing my lovely cousin." Her angel advised her to be as brief as possible. "Anyway, it was difficult to handle and I lost my faith for a while."

"Oh, I see." He didn't have a clue what she was talking about.

"It wasn't that I stopped believing in God. He is as real to me as you are. But I turned my back on Him." A little catch in her voice betrayed emotion.

Her guardian shot a meaningful look at the other two angels, remembering the testing time well.

"After months I remembered that God is Love and I decided to trust Him again."

Gabriella smiled broadly at Bethany's guardian, who nodded and smiled back with emotion-misted eyes. The interim time had been dismal for both Bethany and guardian. The angel had been hugely relieved when her ward had finally listened to her entreaties about love.

Jason's eyes narrowed. Obviously he didn't understand what she was saying.

Bethany ploughed on. "Now, I believe that everything is for a reason. So Catherine's death must have been for a reason. But I have no idea what the reason was. It's way beyond my human comprehension, as so many things are. And since then I try not to ask "Why?" about things, I just trust God. And He helps me through everything."

"I don't really understand what you're saying but I respect your right to your opinion." Jason was unconvinced. *There is no God, everybody knows that. Well, everybody except Bethany.* He smirked.

Bethany gave him an open smile. She had spoken her truth because he asked her to.

* * *

A reporter from a big UK tabloid stood beside Gavin Bellingham's desk at the Paradise, pressing for any information at all about Evan Lewis and his family. "Look, guv, you're in a position to get me some'ink good. Know what I mean?"

Gavin knew exactly what the man meant, despite his strong cockney accent, which was starting to grate on his, already frayed, nerves. He had enough to think about without being pestered by journalists. One of his clients was dead. He had the parents to deal with. *And* the authorities. And now the insurance company said they wouldn't pay to have the coffin flown back to the UK because the deceased was drunk when he fell. Apparently that negated the contract. Evan's death was a holiday rep's nightmare.

On top of that Yiorgos was threatening to tell the police it was all his idea to run Pandora's that way. And while that was true, what was there to be gained from making that public knowledge?

He had tried to make Yiorgos see sense. He told him they were not responsible for the young man's death. He drank too much and fell in his room. Any drunk could do the same. Keep calm, he told him over and over. *You* haven't done anything wrong. *I* haven't done anything wrong.

Suzanna was furious with him. Threatening to leave him if his name was linked in the press with the boy's death.

"It's not my fault he died," he repeated every time she mentioned it. Which was a lot. "It really isn't."

"You're fooling yourself, Gavin." She wouldn't listen to what *he* thought was the voice of reason.

The reporter was still speaking. "I can make it worth your while." The man moved closer and spoke quietly and tapped the side of his nose as a signal. "Know what I mean?"

Gavin's ears pricked up. He knew exactly what the man meant. Money was now talking and Gavin was listening hard. "I'll see what I can do. How can I reach you?"

He wouldn't tell Suzanna about this. Best not to upset her further. She might call it profiting by the lad's death. But it wasn't that at all. People were interested in the sad story. He would be doing a public service if he could add some intimate details.

Jason walked past and threw Gavin a questioning look as he saw him take the reporter's business card. He spoke brusquely to the reporter. "Thought I told you to leave my hotel!"

"Just going, guv." The man sidled towards the door. A Greek friend had tipped him off about the death. He already had a good story building on drunken debauchery encouraged by a local club owner. The owner had given him exclusive rights in exchange for a fat fee. Suppose he needed it. They'd closed the guy down.

Gavin watched the reporter leave. He wondered what he could dig up for him and how much it would net. Maybe even more than he and Yiorgos would have earned with their new way of running Pandora's.

He rubbed his hands together. *Every cloud has a silver lining.*

He must remember not to say *that* to Suzanna either. She might find it offensive.

Women!

Chapter 24

Melanie's face was grim as she strode into the Candy Bar. Manos' teenage daughter was sitting with the kids for a couple of hours. The arrangement had been made yesterday, but after Donna's revelation she wished to be anywhere but here. She had not had chance to tackle Aeron about Bethany.

Yet.

The dance floor was packed. Apparently they had a new DJ called Kevin, who had taken over when the local one got called up to the Navy. She loved this song, *"Rhythm Is a Dancer"* by Snap! She had plenty of rhythm and under other circumstances she would have happily danced to it.

She spotted her husband behind the bar chatting with two pretty females sitting on bar stools in front of him.

She recognized the redheaded Clare from the Paradise Hotel. She knew she was with Jason.

Aeron looked up and saw Melanie. "My wife," he said. He had been expecting her. He smiled. "Hi there."

"Hi." Melanie didn't smile back.

Bethany regarded her with interest, taking in her shiny red bob, and trim figure in tight white jeans and halter-neck top.

"Melanie, you've met Clare." He nodded towards her. "And this is Bethany." Melanie sized up the blonde, noting her outfit, black leggings and long top, was casual not dressy. She didn't look like she was dressed to impress. But appearances could be deceptive. "Bethany, my wife, Melanie."

Bethany and Clare gave her a warm greeting.

"Hello," Melanie said coldly.

"Honey, what can I get you to drink?" asked Aeron.

"Sorry, are you speaking to me?" Melanie's question was a poison-tipped barb.

"Who else?" His eyes narrowed with surprise.

"Who else indeed?" She aimed a flinty glance at Bethany.

"Oh." Aeron sighed deeply. "Apparently not innocent until proven guilty here," he muttered.

Clare was swift to act. "Actually, we were just leaving." Almost knocking over her half-full wineglass she snatched her handbag from the bar. "Very nice to see you again, Melanie." As she placed a hand on the woman's arm her eyes pleaded with her not to believe any rumours. Bethany had filled her in.

Bethany downed the last of her gin and tonic. "Lovely to meet you," she said. Nervously she braved Melanie's anger and stared innocent and unblinking for a few seconds into her eyes. "Hope to see you again soon."

Momentarily this disarmed Melanie.

After she had watched the two women leave she turned back to the bar and perched on the stool vacated by Clare. Thoughtfully she sipped the drink Aeron put in front of her. She avoided looking at her husband while she thought things through.

* * *

Jason was getting nervous about Katarina. Trying to juggle two relationships wasn't easy.

He had hoped she would keep away for a while after throwing that drink over him at the pool bar, but to his dismay only a few days later she had turned up at the bar again. She was all smiles and apologies. He had gone out of his way to be nice to her, to keep the peace. But when she asked him to walk her home and he refused he feared she was going to start throwing things again.

Now she regularly visited the Paradise.

It was a tightrope situation.

He needed to make time to see her alone occasionally. If they had planned meetings perhaps she wouldn't feel the need to visit the hotel. She came at different times of the day so he had to be very careful to check around before showing affection to Clare. That was annoying. He was starting to feel a stronger pull towards Clare than Katarina.

That had never been his intention. He couldn't help falling for Clare, though, could he? Perhaps in light of his imminent formal marriage proposal to Katarina he should stop seeing Clare. But he loved her.

It was becoming complicated.

His head took over. He needed to see Katarina as soon as possible and get his heart back on track. He looked at his watch. She should be in the shop now. With mixed feelings he picked up the telephone. When she eagerly agreed to meet up he felt bad.

* * *

Back home in the apartment Aeron was having it out with Melanie. He was furious she would not listen to reason.

"What can you expect?" Melanie hissed at him, attempting to yell in a whisper so the kids next door wouldn't wake. They sat in their pushed together single beds feeling miles apart. Melanie's sloppy pink cotton nightdress, Aeron noticed, was not inviting. She clearly hadn't packed it for a romantic interlude. "You're here alone surrounded by nubile young women and you expect me to believe that you're living like a monk!" She crumpled the corner of the white sheet between her fingers in temper. They had talked about Bethany and he denied there was anything between them other than friendship.

In the end she begrudgingly believed him, but by then Aeron was irritated. "Melanie, you live in New York surrounded by hunky young guys and I believe that you've been living like a nun, not because you haven't had offers, I'm sure, but because you love me and stick to your marriage vows." Aeron was tired but clearly sleep was not on the agenda. He sat up in bed, pulled on a T-shirt, and propped a pillow between his back and the wall.

Melanie pounced on his words. "Have you had offers, Aeron? Has there been more than just this Bethany for company!"

"Melanie, look what is this?" Aeron was exasperated. *Attack is the best form of defence!* As the words popped into his head Aeron's heart jolted. *Surely not.*

"Melanie?"

He would know the truth by her eyes. Those beautiful hazel eyes that he loved so much couldn't hide a thing from him.

"What?" she snapped.

"Look at me, Melanie." She looked up from the sheet and met his gaze. Her face was flinty. "David Richards?" he asked softly. A definite shadow flitted over her eyes.

Guilt?

Fear?

What?

The look was so fleeting that he couldn't precisely define it. But there was certainly something. Somewhere in his being a bright light was extinguished; permanently. He joined his hands, pressing straight forefingers over his mouth as if to physically prevent speech, while his brain went into overdrive.

Every cell in his body sensed danger. His mind threw up a warning card: BE VERY CAREFUL! He knew he could lose everything that he held dear.

Looking back on it later, he was surprised that anger or hurt had not been the most dominant emotions at Melanie's betrayal. But, even in that moment of revelation, he acknowledged his culpability.

He was the one who had left his wife and kids alone for months.

Melanie had repeatedly begged him not to go.

The silence stretched like a yawning chasm between them.

The longer she waited to speak the wider the breach became.

"Tell me." Aeron could wait no longer.

"Tell you what?" Melanie was trying to be flippant but her voice was thin and forced.

"Tell me about you and David Richards." His ulcer was starting to stab and he almost welcomed the pain as a distraction from the emotional torment that was welling up in his heart.

"What's to tell?"

"Melanie, it's no use pretending." His voice was soft but adamant. "Tell me."

"Well, we…" her voice petered out.

"Are you having an affair?"

"Aeron, I…"

"Are you? Are you having an affair?" He heard his voice but it sounded like it came from beside him, as if he had stepped away from his body somehow. He felt weird.

Lying went against her nature. "I didn't mean for it to happen."

Aeron collapsed forwards as if from a physical punch. He shook his head to clear it.

This could not be happening.

Just a minute ago his wife had been accusing him of going with other women and now she was admitting that it was she who had been unfaithful. A white-hot flicker of self-righteous anger flashed through him. It pulled him bolt upright. "I don't believe this!" His fists bunched and itched to violently express his fury.

Melanie's expression was a cross between defiant and wary. "Don't blame this all on me." Her tone was accusatory. She mirrored his angry glare.

Melanie's words hit home.

Since the conversation with Bethany about his dreams he had begun to see things more clearly. *Don't blame this all on you, eh?*

Aeron swallowed the bitter pill of acceptance. Yes, he had

brought this on himself.

The anger drained away leaving him shaky and nauseous. He exhaled raggedly through pursed lips as if he had just run a marathon.

The question now forming in his brain was terrifying.

But he knew it had to be asked. He had to know what she now intended. "Do you want... a *divorce*?" His voice broke.

"If I'm going to be perfectly honest, I'm not sure." Melanie sounded like she didn't care one way or the other.

When Aeron's shoulders started shaking with quiet controlled sobs which pushed themselves through the fingers shielding his face, Melanie's composure was dented. Clearly his heart was breaking but she felt powerless to help him.

After all, hadn't he broken *her* heart?

Hadn't she cried night after night missing him and not understanding why he had left her and the children to come here on his own?

Wasn't he just getting a taste of his own medicine?

Hardened, Melanie turned away from her husband's pain. She wished herself back home in New York. With David.

Chapter 25

Jason drove, with the snail's pace of reluctance, over the sun-baked rutted mud track into the privacy of his uncle's olive grove.

He cut the engine and fiddled with the ignition key as he said, "It's been a long time, Katarina, but it's a busy time, as you have seen."

He looked up and saw her eyes were shining with happiness and his heart sank. Maybe this was going to make things worse, not better.

Suddenly he wondered if he should stick with Clare instead. He could marry her. He loved her. They worked very well together. "Look," he began, "if you want to stop seeing me I'll understand..."

"Of course I don't want to stop seeing you!' She broke in hotly. "I thought you wanted to stop seeing me." Her golden eyes were huge and dewy with vulnerability.

"Of course I don't." He swallowed hard, suffused with a feeling of discomfort which he recognized as guilt. "I've just been..."

"Yes, I know... busy." She finished the sentence for him.

He now studied the steering wheel as if seeing it for the first time.

"Jason," Katarina said at last, "will you please kiss me?"

He drew her into his arms and placed his mouth on hers. The once familiar lips now felt strange to him. Without appearing cool he brought their embrace to an end as subtly as possible and pointedly consulted his watch.

"Surely, we haven't got to go already." Tears of disappointment brimmed.

"No, I can stay a few more minutes, but I must go soon. I've got a lot to do to prepare for tonight." He added lamely, "I'm sorry, but you know how it is."

Katarina turned to look out of the side window, but not before Jason had seen her sulky pout.

Impulsively he grabbed her hand. *I don't think I can do this anymore.* "Katarina, this is how it's going to be for the whole summer. I don't have much spare time and neither do you. So I really think we should consider not seeing each other until the winter. Then we can be together as usual."

"It wasn't like this last summer." Her hand lay unresponsive in his.

"I didn't have so many responsibilities for the hotel last summer, that's why we could spend more time together." That wasn't strictly true but sounded a plausible excuse.

"Why has your father given you all this work to do? It isn't fair." She was petulant now.

"You speak like a child, Katarina." He dropped her hand and banged the steering wheel in a flash of temper. "I would have thought that with your father having the minimarket you would have understood how things are. We have a few short months in the summer to make money and we have to make the most of them. I want to make *lots* of money."

His mind flashed to the meeting he'd had with Sotiris yesterday. The meeting he should have had ages ago but had messed up by falling asleep on the beach with a hangover. They had struck a brilliant deal. He would be getting his fish much cheaper.

Now, all he had to do was tell his local supplier that he no longer needed his catch. He had no qualms about letting him down. Fresh fish was always in demand, he told himself. He was sure to find another customer.

"The downside is that I don't have time for myself because there are always so many things to do. But in the long run it will be worth it. I'm going to be *rich* Katarina."

"Is it so important for you to be rich, Jason? Aren't there more important things in life than money?"

"Tell me what you can do without money."

"You can be in love and be happy."

"Yes, but how long will you be happy when you have children and you can't give them what they need because you haven't any money? Everything comes down to money in the end, and if you grow up a bit you will realize that I'm right. You can't do anything without money, not in the long run. I'm thinking about the future and planning for that." He spoke in the abstract. It reflected his confusion between the two girls.

"And what about the here and now, Jason, doesn't that count for anything?" she demanded.

"Yes, of course it does, but summer is the time to work hard and make money. That's the way it is. I have to make the most of this time."

"Jason, are you seeing someone else?" The words were blurted out before she had a chance to stop them. They hung like a threatening storm cloud between them.

Jason's face was stony as he hid his surprise.

He decided to act indignant. "Katarina, have you heard a word I've said or have I just been talking to myself?" His voice was icy.

She swallowed nervously, not knowing what to say in the face of his disapproval.

"Well," he persisted, "are you going to answer my question?"

"I'm sorry," she managed at last. "I didn't mean to make you angry. It's just that I miss you, that's all."

"I miss you too," he lied. "But I've told you exactly what I'm doing and why, so can't you please be patient?"

The girl felt in the wrong. Dejection was in the slump of her shoulders as she looked away. Jason relented and reached for her hand. "Katarina, Katarina, when will you understand me? How long will it take, I wonder?" He turned the ignition key and fired up the engine. "Come on, smile for me, Miss Golden Eyes," he cajoled. She smiled tentatively to please him. "That's better," he said, kissing her lips softly. "Let's try and keep it that way, shall we?"

Chapter 26

Aeron sat in the sweltering airless booth at the Sunset taverna and stared at the telephone. His stomach churned and acid bit painfully into his ulcer. Melanie had asked him to give her some time to think things over. He had tried his best to be patient. But with the Sword of Damocles hanging over his head he couldn't wait another moment. He had to know her intentions. Was their marriage over or would she give him another chance?

He had offered to go back home with her immediately. But she refused to let him. "If you force my hand I will definitely leave you," she threatened. Powerless, he drove her and the children to the airport as planned. He had parked beside the perimeter fence and sat watching the plane taxi down the short runway and take off dramatically just as the seashore loomed. As the tiny cylinder was swallowed by the blue vastness tears had rained down his face and his body was wracked with huge anguished sobs.

That plane was holding the people he most loved in the world. It was taking them away from him and he had a terrible feeling that his life would never be the same again.

This afternoon he had swum until his arms ached. He was trying to calm down. Desperate to get some perspective. Lying on a sunbed letting the hot sun warm up his sea-cooled skin he had a tussle with himself.

If I push her she'll leave me. He remembered her threat.

If I don't speak to her and find out what she plans to do I'll go crazy! He was having to force himself to eat a little food to keep from keeling over at work, and his nights were long and sleepless.

He checked his watch yet again. He'd been letting the minutes tick by. It was Sunday and Melanie would have taken the kids to visit her parents.

Okay. It was time. His family should be home by now.

He took a huge fortifying breath and lifted the receiver. Listening to the long single repeated note of the ringing tone his heart was in his mouth.

"Melanie." He spoke his wife's name softly.

"Oh, it's you, Aeron." She spoke as if she was telling someone else that he was on the line.

"He's there isn't he?" Aeron felt sickened.

"Yes." Melanie was direct as always.

He forced himself to frame the question. The million dollar question. "You've decided haven't you?"

"Yes. Yes, I have, Aeron."

"Tell me."

Melanie hesitated, then spoke up clearly. "I'm leaving you, Aeron."

"Melanie, please don't do this. Please!"

"I don't want hear it, Aeron. You brought this on yourself; on us." Bitterness flooded her voice.

"So, what's going to happen?" He wondered why he was asking details but he just wanted to keep on talking. Talking to his wife. His wife who was in their home with another man.

"I don't think we need to talk about that now. You're there in another country. We'll sort things out nearer the time," she said with cold practicality. "Anyway, I have company so I need to go now."

"Melanie, please don't do this. Please don't leave me," he begged, his voice breaking with anguish.

"Actually, technically, you left me, Aeron." Her voice was brittle.

"Melanie, please…"

"Goodbye, Aeron." She replaced the receiver before he could say anything more. And though he knew it would have been pointless he did wish she had let him speak. But, he reasoned, with David Richards beside her what could he have said anyway that would have made a difference?

Strangely, as he left the booth he felt nothing.

He didn't feel the sun baking the skin on his exposed arms.

He didn't feel the pain gnawing at his stomach.

Numbed he walked up the steep hill to his apartment and closed the door firmly behind him. Sliding open his balcony door he stepped outside and slumped into the nearest chair. He would sit there immobile for the next few hours... not feeling anything at all.

* * *

A nervous Jason was planning to take Clare for a late lunch at the pizzeria on the seafront. She liked the place and he needed her to be in a happy mood. He needed to speak to her about Katarina and he was justifiably nervous.

"Thanks, Gary," they chorused as the waiter handed them a couple of menus. Gary fixed them with a grin which sparked into his very-blue eyes. He often came into the pool bar for a drink and a chat after work. Clare liked his Brummie accent and he said he liked her Irish one.

They ordered pizzas. Then Jason took the plunge and told Clare the news that, to keep the peace, he would carry on seeing Katarina.

Naturally, Clare was livid. "Why don't you just tell her it's over and ask her to keep away?" she demanded.

"I would but she won't keep away, that's the problem. And she'll cause trouble. You saw for yourself the sort of thing she'll do."

"Well, I don't like it, Jason, not at all." Her pretty face was pinched, green eyes bright with vexation.

"I'll only see her very occasionally and very briefly," he said, trying to pacify her. He picked up her hand and kissed it. "Trust me on this, you know I love you."

Clare was perplexed. She loved Jason. She wanted to trust

him. But her dreams about a future with him seemed madness.

She stared past the sharp blue horizon and wished their relationship was clear-cut. When a cheerful Gary brought their meal, though, his banter lightened the atmosphere. As he walked away Clare told herself that it did seem wrong to end the relationship today over a pizza. Decision made, she attacked her food with gusto.

Replete, Clare carefully lined up knife and fork, and sat back in her seat with a contented sigh. "That was grand," she said. Jason nodded in agreement. As he swigged water from a tumbler he looked around. *What the heck?*

Clare swivelled, looking over her shoulder to find what had shocked him.

"There's a fire!" Clare's eyes followed his pointing finger to a streak of grey smoke in the distance.

He jumped up and stepped down onto the beach to see where it was coming from. He located it easily on a green hill a couple of miles above the resort. He called out, "I'm going to make sure it's been reported." He clambered smartly up the slipway to the Paradise.

He was back in a few minutes. "They're onto it," he told a worried-looking Clare. "But it's going to take them a while to get some fire-fighters here." Hurriedly he paid their bill and they went to stand on the beach to watch developments.

"Fire is bad news at any time," he told Clare as they looked on. "But because there hasn't been rain for months the sun has dried the vegetation to a crisp, and the wind will fan the flames." He was thinking of how quickly it could spread, and how far, destroying everything in its path: homes, animals, and birds, as well as all the trees and undergrowth as they fuelled its progress. And lives were in danger.

People gathered together in worried knots on the beach.

"Unless that's put out quickly," Jason told one of the hotel guests who'd stopped alongside to look, "it could take out the whole hillside."

From that distance the flickering red flames appeared about two inches high and three inches wide as they danced on the greenery devouring it voraciously leaving only black smoke in its wake. The smoke rose up in a pall, and some drifted over the sea where it accumulated in a huge grey cloud of destroyed matter.

As they watched, the conflagration got taller and longer. A shared dismay was written over everyone's faces. The pizza felt heavy in Clare's stomach. A guest from the hotel stopped to speak to them. "Why don't they do something?"

"It *has* been reported," Jason assured him.

People started muttering that they were glad the fire was at a distance and not threatening them. But Jason knew they weren't as safe as they thought. "Let's hope the wind doesn't change direction, and that the fire is put out quickly," he said ominously. He didn't want to upset anyone but they had to be prepared.

His comments drew some troubled glances.

Bethany came walking towards them. "How long has this been going on?"

"At least twenty minutes apparently." Clare shook her head. "Terrible isn't it?"

"Oh, no! It looks like it's right behind the church," said Bethany, biting her lip and frowning. "I went there a few weeks ago. It's filled with gorgeous icons and ancient frescos. It's so special. And it looks as if it might be destroyed now if someone doesn't put this out soon!"

"It is a special place," Jason agreed. "My mother likes to go there sometimes and light candles for the family."

"Can you have a word with the Man Upstairs, Bethany?" said Clare.

"What? Oh, yes, of course! Why am I standing here worrying when I should be praying?"

Jason shook his head. He muttered, "Don't bother with that, Bethany. Waste of time." Clare gave him a little warning-off nudge.

Bethany walked away from the others to stand alone facing the sea. In a minute or so she turned and walked back to her friends.

Gabriella winged in and spoke with the guardian angels. She had been given permission to take charge of events.

A loud noise caused everyone on the beach look up. They spotted a helicopter whirring into sight from behind the hill. It crossed the bay, turned to face inland, and hovered to lower a big red receptacle by a stout cable. After scooping up seawater the chopper flew laboriously up, up, up and forwards. As it passed overhead, with blades thwacking the air, some of the swinging load spilt out and was whisked by the wind to a trailing foam.

The fire fighting machine crept towards its blazing target, but overshot and disappeared behind the hill. "Where's it going?" Clare gasped.

Then, thankfully, back it came, this time facing seaward and when perfectly in position it finally dropped the water-bomb in a white whoosh over the roaring red flames. "Oh, it's a technique," she muttered.

Onwards it came again, in preparation to refill its bucket for another saving loop.

Clare looked at Bethany and thought it was such a coincidence that Bethany had just finished her prayer and then the helicopter arrived.

A really amazing coincidence.

Clare's guardian angel silently intoned the word "miracle" into her mind, but she pushed it away. Coincidence was the only acceptable explanation.

The fire continued to rage.

When a second helicopter flew in from another direction the watching crowd sent up a ragged cheer. In a short while it was joined by a third and the sky team carried out repetitions of filling, looping, and dousing in a valiant attempt to quell the voracious flames.

Jason saw Gavin arrive with the lovely Suzanna in tow.

Suzanna was still being rather cool with her husband, which was starting to annoy him. He had told her, repeatedly, that he hadn't been trying to make money for himself at Pandora's, he was doing it for *them* and for their *future*. She did admit that he was now focussing on his holiday clients. He hadn't got anywhere trying to dig up news about the dead boy, Evan Lewis, for the journalist so that avenue of extra cash had been blocked off, much to his disappointment.

The couple stood beside Jason's little group and watched the fire. Gavin tutted. "The burning question is, no pun intended, how did the fire start I wonder?" He looked at Jason as if he may have an answer.

"A number of things can spark a fire right now, with the vegetation being so dried out at this time in summer," Jason explained. "It could have been a cigarette end, or a piece of broken bottle acting as a magnifying glass. Even a plastic bottle with some water in it can do the same."

"Gosh," said Clare. "I'd never have thought of a plastic bottle starting a fire, but it does make sense."

Jason's opining was interrupted by the blaring of a siren and a few seconds later a fire-engine whizzed past, a danger to holidaymakers dawdling on the, usually, sleepy roadside. "Better late than never I suppose," someone in the crowd commented, and everyone agreed.

* * *

Bethany arrived at the pool bar after dinner was over and told Clare and Jason the news. "The fire is out! No one was hurt and not too much damage done."

"I'm really happy about that," said Clare. "But think of the poor animals and trees."

The Greek television channels were making much of the fact that the fire-fighter helicopters had been in the area only by a fluke.

Bethany laughed when she heard that. "Probability factor?" she teased Jason, thinking of the talking computer in the *Hitchhiker's Guide to the Galaxy*, which Douglas Adams was rumoured to have written on the island. "Million to one?" She knew her prayer had been answered and thanked God for it.

Chapter 27

Clare had slept only fitfully. She had a bad dream about the fire yesterday. When she woke in the early hours she remembered too the unsettling conversation with Jason about Katarina.

Last night at the Paradise she had tried hard to act natural around Jason. Fortunately the bar had been very busy, which helped things along.

But sitting alone drinking a mug of coffee, while Bethany slept on, she stared at the olive grove dimly lit by the first pale rays of dawn, and felt as gloomy as the thick carpet of shadow beneath the trees.

Puzzling it through, she couldn't really understand the situation between Katarina and Jason. She brooded over what he had said trying to see what, if anything, lay behind the words. But she couldn't come up with a satisfactory answer.

Either Jason was a liar or Katarina was deluded.

In the end, Clare reasoned that only what he had told her really fitted the situation, because she knew that he definitely loved her. She could not be wrong about that.

Rinsing her mug under the tap she thought again that she just had to trust Jason, for now, and try not to torment herself with the thought of him with Katarina. She knew it would be difficult not to be jealous, especially if the girl came to the bar as she had before and she was forced to witness Jason talking and laughing with her. She would try to restrain herself from shouting, "Leave him alone, he's mine!" But then, he had been Katarina's before, so even that didn't seem right.

Clare had told Jason not to tell her when he met with Katarina. Now, though, she knew she would start to watch his moves.

She dried the mug and replaced it on its hook beside the others, and vacillated. Was it all worth it? Should she just finish with him and maybe go home? It was already a week into August and she had been here a long time.

It was strange to think of life outside the resort. Some people talked about the Olympics going on in Barcelona right now, but that seemed so far removed from them.

Inevitably, she thought about Dublin and her family and felt a strong pang of homesickness. But then the faces of Patrick and his new girl popped into her mind. She wasn't keen to see them again any time soon. Then she thought of Jason's handsome face and her heart gave a lurch.

Clare had not felt so strongly about Patrick. In fact, their relationship was like a phantom in comparison.

Jason seemed to be every bit as smitten as she was, forever telling her she was beautiful and how much he loved her.

She slipped into her room and lay back down on the bed. She would not run away home, she decided again. But she would work at putting a little distance between Jason and her heart. Perhaps a little self-protection would help to bring some order into this muddle.

She closed her eyes and fatigue overcame the caffeine.

Clare dozed.

* * *

Bethany had been writing for hours. Her characters were shaping up and becoming familiar, and the plot was building nicely. And, following Gabriella's advice, she was layering in some deeper meaning too.

She found the whole process exhilarating. Creating a new resort on the island, peopled with interesting lives and dilemmas, was an incredible experience in many ways.

Now, though, she suddenly felt an urgent need to walk.

Her guardian angel was silently whispering the suggestion into her mind.

Bethany stood and moved to the open kitchen window. Looking out at the little shadowy olive grove she debated. "I don't know... but for some reason, though I want to carry on writing, I think I should go out." Hmm.

She decided to follow her instinct.

It was early-afternoon and hot so she hurriedly covered up and stepped into the sunshine.

As she passed Korkyra Minimarket, Hygeia trotted out of the shade looking pleased to see her. "Hello, girl." Bethany affectionately ruffled her fur. The beach was crowded so together they headed for the other side of the resort.

As they rounded the corner by the Candy Bar Bethany spied Aeron.

"Hi, Bethany," his voice was flat and dejected. "See you've got company."

"Meet Hygeia," she pointed at the dog. "She belongs to Spiros at Korkyra Minimarket and often comes walking with me."

"I like dogs." Aeron sighed. "Never had one, though."

"I like all animals." Bethany smiled. "Which is why I'm a vegetarian. But I've never had a dog either. Cats are my favourite."

No sooner were the words out of her mouth when the dog spotted a cat and bounded towards it. "No! Hygeia!" Bethany yelled. But thankfully the cat shot through a breach in a wall and escaped.

While the thwarted dog barked and sniffed at the gap Aeron ran a hand across his brow. "Phew!"

"Dear me, I thought she was going to attack the poor thing." Bethany put her hand over her racing heart and chuckled with relief as Hygeia came back.

"Where are you going now?" Aeron asked.

"Nowhere really, just needed a walk. Been working on the book."

"Can I tag along? I could do with a leg-stretch myself. Been busy setting up new stock and cleaning things up." The industrious few hours had not stopped him brooding about Melanie, though. He had told no one she had asked for a divorce.

"Yes, join us. We're just wandering for a while."

"Cool." He was in great need of company.

They walked side-by-side chatting about the fire and how glad they were it had been extinguished without loss of life.

The road branched right and they followed the deserted country lane. Bethany turned to smile at Aeron but caught him looking at the ground. She voiced her concern over his dark mood.

"Wouldn't make a good actor then?" Aeron tried to keep things light.

"You don't need to tell me, Aeron." Bethany was not prying. "But if you need to talk I can be discreet."

All at once Aeron's courage deserted him and his face crumpled. "I just can't go on," he sobbed, and hung his head into his hands, doubling over as if in physical pain.

"Oh, Aeron!" Bethany gasped in shock. He was clearly in a bad way.

When she put a tentative hand on his arm he grabbed it like a lifeline. Bethany was appalled that, despite his sobs, she felt electrified by this, their first physical contact. But she willed the tingling away.

Finally, Aeron took one huge shuddering breath, held it in for a few long moments, exhaled with a deep sigh and relinquished her hand. Wiping his eyes with his fingers he looked shamefaced. "Oh, heck," he said. "Not very manly, huh?"

"On the contrary, Aeron, I think it's a real man who isn't afraid to show his emotions now and then."

"Well, thank you for that, Bethany. Seems like you're trying to let me off the hook."

Bethany felt afraid for him and sent up a quick prayer for guidance.

Her guardian angel smiled at Aeron's guardian. Gabriella made a trio in a flash.

Aeron was almost beyond constructive thought. Instead,

negative emotions were rising like a spring tide to flood his spirit. His stalker demon was whispering dark ideas at him. The demon was keeping its distance from the trio but they were not allowed to silence it.

Bethany's angel locked eyes with Gabriella, awaiting instruction.

Gabriella spoke to Bethany's guardian angel. The angel whispered "simplicity" into her ward's ear.

Bethany took a deep breath. "Aeron," she began tentatively, "what about your dream of music? Why don't you go for it?"

"Too old now." Aeron was defeatist.

"Hmm. Thirty-something is too old?"

"Yep. In the music business it's all boy bands and teenage heart throbs."

"There's always room for good stuff," she pointed out. "And I have this theory about age."

"Okay, Bethany, let's hear it," he said.

"Well, I think that we don't fully start to live until we're about thirty." She pinned him with a gaze and he nodded in agreement. "Life expectancy is rising all the time so we can, hopefully, live to a hundred."

"Maybe."

"Well, half-way between thirty and one hundred is sixty-five, so I reckon that middle-age starts then, and, if you're fit, old age starts at eighty-five or even ninety." She paused for effect. "So, Aeron, you're still a kid. Go for it!"

"Hmm. Nice theory." He nodded. "But. Not in the music business." Aeron doggedly refused to take that on board.

"Well, you know best." She wouldn't push it.

Bethany's angel again conferred with Gabriella before whispering a suggestion.

"But, hey, what about focussing on songwriting?" Bethany thought her question was reasonable. "I can't think there's an upper age-limit for that. And look how much I was influenced by the writer of *Shirley Valentine*, I think it was Willie Russell. Well, songs can be even more powerful. Very inspiring."

But Aeron was having none of it. He was just too down to see even a glimmer of hope for his dream.

Bethany began to feel very upset seeing Aeron so low. It was like he was in despair. *This is horrible! I wish I could help him but I feel powerless.*

Gabriella judged it was time to make an appearance. She warned the guardian angels, moved away to beyond the last bend in the lane, and became visible. Rounding the bend she sauntered towards them.

Bethany recognized, with a measure of relief, the girl she had met on the beach some time ago. "Gabriella," she called, waving eagerly.

"Oh, Bethany, hello there." Gabriella raised a hand in greeting.

Bethany said how happy she was to see her again. "This is Aeron," she said. "He works at the Candy Bar."

Gabriella said, "Hello."

Aeron greeted the stranger and as she gave him an appraising look he reddened. His unhappiness must still be written all over his face. It was. She lightly touched his arm. "Aeron," she said. "Please excuse me for mentioning this but you are clearly downhearted."

Her clear grey gaze blocked his attempt to lie. Instead, he gave her the briefest of nods.

Gabriella smiled encouragingly. "You believe in God, right?"

His bloodshot eyes went round with surprise. But he looked into her warm smile and once again felt obliged to be open. "Yeah, I do believe in God." He paused. He felt compelled to tell the whole truth. "But I don't know much about the whole thing." He glanced at her, then down at his feet.

Gabriella knew this subject was difficult for him but she had to deliver the message she had been given in answer to

Bethany's prayer for guidance. "Well, I want to tell you that, if you ever feel overcome by despair, just say, 'Dear God, please help me through this' and He will."

When Aeron hung his head an anxious Bethany thought he was going to cry again.

Gabriella continued. "I promise you, Aeron, I absolutely promise you, that God will help you through the pain. You only have to ask Him."

Aeron still didn't lift his head.

A silence grew between them.

Then Aeron sighed deeply. "Okay," he muttered towards the ground. "Thanks for trying to help." He sounded aloof.

Gabriella was being dismissed. She could say nothing more.

Turning to Bethany she gave her a broad warm smile. "So good to see you again, Bethany."

"Good to see you too, Gabriella."

"Aeron, I was glad to meet you. I wish you all the very best."

He muttered a brief, "Thanks, again."

As soon as Gabriella disappeared from sight he rounded on Bethany. "Who on earth is that?" he demanded.

"Oh, just a girl I met on the beach one day."

"Doesn't pull her punches, does she?"

"She *is* direct," Bethany admitted with a wry smile. "But I like her very much."

"Oh, I didn't say I didn't like her." He thought that under other circumstances the three of them could have had an enjoyable coffee together. "I just felt a bit stupid, really."

"Aeron, I understand, but I just want to say that I one hundred per cent agree with what she told you." Though his face was closing up she pressed on. "I couldn't have said it better myself." She nodded. "When the chips are down turn it over to God!"

She prayed he was listening.

Then they gasped as a big ginger cat leapt out of a wheelie bin, tottered on its narrow edge, spotted Hygeia, and lunged through the adjacent hedge. Hygeia sprang right over the bin, through the hedge, and vanished.

After a short hiatus, though, she was back.

Bethany and Aaron stood open-mouthed. "Clearly," chuckled Bethany, "the cats here can look after themselves!"

Their laughter broke the ice.

They started to walk again.

When they came to Bethany's road she patted Hygeia's head and the dog left them and walked home to the minimarket.

"See you later." Bethany and Aeron spoke together, and laughed.

"Thanks for your company." Bethany smiled at Aeron.

"Yeah, right." Aeron was cryptic.

Bethany planted a quick sisterly kiss on his cheek. "Remember what Gabriella said," she urged, prepared to risk a further rebuff.

"Will do." He was polite.

Bethany walked up the hill towards home feeling shaken.

She had stared straight into the face of despair.

She didn't know if either she or Gabriella had been any help whatsoever to Aeron.

Dread gnawed at her stomach.

Chapter 28

Takis gunned his car through the resort on his way back from the *kafeneion*. The place had been in uproar about the fire, with everybody convinced it had been started by a careless tourist. The outraged men vented their anger yelling similar things at the same time louder and louder trying to be heard above the rest.

The fire had threatened homes and lives, they angrily pointed out. Their friend Stavros, who had very little money, had had his olive grove destroyed. Yes, it was insured, but not for much. What would he do without the income from his olive oil? The church with the priceless frescoes had almost gone up in smoke too.

"Panagia moo!" An incensed backgammon player shouted the Virgin Mary's name. Everyone quickly crossed their hearts three times at the thought of the church being destroyed.

The consensus was that something should be done about this negligence. They all agreed that tourism was a curse on their community.

It was the usual wild talk but Takis was in a terrible mood anyway. Jason had cancelled his fish order for the hotel.

And Takis knew exactly why he'd done that!

His lip curled at the thought.

Michalis had obviously told him about their argument in the village and lost them the business!

And although his father had told him that there was already someone in the next resort interested in buying their fish, that wasn't the point!

Michalis was trouble!

Michalis was married to a foreigner!

As he drove home his mind was buzzing with rage.

His mind was being buzzed by a whole group of rogue demons assisting the stalker. The grey, scaly infestation crawled around his face and head and screamed at Takis. Led by the stalker demon they employed the words of hatred and prejudice that were so familiar to Takis.

Stalker demon: "Foreigners are the cause of all the troubles on this island."

Takis: *Everything that is wrong on this island has been caused by foreigners.*

Rogue demon: "Every foreigner who comes to this beautiful island destroys something. Yesterday they destroyed Stavros' olive grove."

Takis: *Foreigners are destructive. Stavros is ruined. Ruined!*

Guardian angel: "Foreigners are just people like you."

Rogue demon: "Greeks are wonderful people and foreigners are awful!"

Takis: *Greeks are the best people on earth! Everyone else is inferior!*

Stalker demon: "People should stay in their own countries and not come over here messing things up!"

Takis: *Why don't people just stay in their own country? They are making a real mess of Korkyra!*

As Takis turned the car into the narrow lane he saw the blonde-haired little Panos playing on the grass verge. Suddenly, a football shot across the road and the boy ran after it.

The demons went wild! This was the moment they had been planning for. Working for.

Stalker demon: "Look! There is the offspring of Michalis and that German woman you despise."

Rogue demon: "You hate Michalis. You hate his wife. You hate all Germans!"

Takis: *There's Panos. How could Michalis have married a German after what they did on this island?*

Stalker demon: "You hate Panos! You hate him for what

he is!"

Takis: *I hate Panos! I hate him for the German that he is!*

Gabriella was in the car with Takis' guardian angel. They bowed down on either side of him, their wings spread wide and overlapping to encircle him tenderly, though the closeness of the demons was abhorrent to them. Gabriella was advising the guardian angel to whisper the loving calming words which were most familiar to Takis.

The demons were screaming furiously.

Guardian angel: "Panos is just an innocent child."

Stalker demon: "Panos' grandfather probably shot your grandfather himself!"

Guardian angel: "Panos is just a small boy who never did anyone any harm in his short life."

Takis: *It could well have been Panos' grandfather who took my grandfather out to Pontikonisi Island and shot him in cold blood!*

Stalker demon: "You hate Panos! You have hated him since the first day you set eyes on him!"

Takis: *I hate Panos!*

Guardian angel: "What is there to hate about this small innocent boy? Nothing."

Stalker demon: "Panos' grandfather took your grandfather out onto Pontikonisi Island and shot him dead in cold blood!"

Rogue demon: "You should avenge that murder!"

Stalker demon: "Avenge that cold-blooded murder now!"

Rogue demon: "Do it now!"

Guardian angel: "Panos is a small innocent child!"

For Takis everything suddenly seemed to go into slow motion.

Gabriella and Takis' guardian angel continued to encircle him. Milliseconds passed and the car travelled nearer to the boy as the guardian angel urgently repeated that Panos was just an innocent child.

Another millisecond and another foot nearer the angel urged him towards forgiveness and compassion.

Stalker demon: "Avenge your grandfather. Do it now!"

A few more milliseconds and a few more feet nearer the angel desperately tried to draw Takis' attention back to love so that the power of the demons would be neutralized.

Guardian angel: "Do not do this. Panos is a small innocent child."

Stalker demon: "Do it now!"

Another few milliseconds and a few feet nearer the angel still whispered loving words, praying Takis would listen to him and the imminent abominable action would be cancelled.

The angel Gabriella had been present when Takis' grandfather was murdered. She recalled the appalling moment of execution. The way the sunshine glinted sharply on the sea and upon the rifles held in the trembling hands of callow frightened soldiers.

She had been impressed by the bravery of all the condemned. All had prayed fervently for eternal life. All their prayers were answered.

During his time on earth Takis' grandfather had been a kindly man. She knew that he would not approve of his grandson's hatred. She whispered this information urgently into Takis' brain.

Another few milliseconds and a few feet nearer to the boy, though Gabriella's words ran through the man's mind, something snapped inside him. The demons possessed Takis, shrinking in size and pushing themselves one after the other up his nostrils. The angels, repelled by the evil force now within the man, instantly leapt backwards away from him. And though, at a distance, they continued to speak of love, this was almost inaudible while their ward was under satanic control.

Once inside Takis' body the demons rushed down into his belly where they ran amok in abandoned possession. They punched the walls of his stomach with their tiny fists. They cackled hysterically and gave off the sulphureous stink of triumph.

Takis believed that the opportunity he had long craved had been presented to him.

Excitement gripped his belly as he pressed his foot harder on the accelerator. His heart was pounding in his chest. The car was picking up speed but everything was, strangely, still in slow motion. Closer and closer he came to the little boy.

Panos had reached his ball and bent his legs to retrieve it from the middle of the road. He heard the engine-whine of the approaching vehicle, and, looking up, recognized the driver. His blue eyes went wide like saucers when he saw the car hurtling straight at him. Terror twisted his angelic face as he turned to run.

Takis, fuelled by the evil presence inside him became one with it and laughed demonically at that terror. He felt the thrill of diabolical power. The demons screeched the monstrous lie: "You are the avenging force righting a wrong!"

"I avenge my grandfather," he screamed.

At the last minute, though, he slammed on his brakes and steered the wheel away from the boy.

* * *

Aeron had showered, forced himself to eat a sandwich, and was thinking it was time to be getting ready for work. Manos had told him to come in a little later than usual to make up for the extra time he had put in today. He glanced at his watch. Suddenly he felt exhausted. He would just sit out on the balcony for a few minutes.

He turned off the lights in the bedroom to prevent mosquitoes being attracted in. Pushing open the sliding glass door he ventured onto the communal balcony clasping a mug of hot tea. There was no one else out there. The white plastic chair and table loomed in the darkness and he sank down gratefully.

He gazed up at the blaze of stars. At first their beauty dazzled him. But after a few minutes they seemed to draw back and instead he saw the empty spaces around them.

All that dreadful emptiness.

He felt its weight pressing him down, down.

The inky sky mingled with the dark night air and flooded over him, then streamed into his mind.

His stalker demon now came rushing back and he had brought reinforcements. The band of rogue demons led by the stalker was preparing for a battle.

Stalker demon: "What a wasted life you've led!"

Rogue demon: "You've done nothing at all with your talents! What a wasted life."

Aeron: *I've just wasted my life. Wasted my time and my talents.*

Stalker demon: "You had such big ideas when you were young. But that was a long time ago. You're far too old to make anything of yourself now. What a wasted life."

Rogue demon: "What a loser you are."

Aeron: *I used to have such plans for my musical career. Musical career, huh! What a joke! I'm such a loser.*

Stalker demon: "Your wife thinks you're a loser too."

Rogue demon: "Her boyfriend is a real achiever. No wonder she fell into his arms the minute you turned your back."

Aeron: *I bet Melanie's lover boy is really rich and successful. No wonder she left me: I'm such a loser!*

Stalker demon: "You've lost your wife and kids and you've wasted your talents. It's all over for you."

Rogue demon: "You should kill yourself and give everyone

a break."

Guardian angel: "Your life has not been wasted. You have two great kids who love you. They are growing up and they need you."

Aeron: *I can't say my life has been totally wasted because I have two wonderful kids who love me.*

Stalker demon: "Your kids won't love you for much longer. They'll soon have a new father and forget all about you."

Guardian angel: "Your kids will always love you."

Rogue demon: "Your kids will soon forget all about you, loser!"

The evil band swarmed over Aeron's head, clambered around his face and jostled with each other for the prime position near his nose in readiness to be the first to rush inside and take possession. There was nothing quite so exciting for the demons than to persuade some poor vulnerable person to commit suicide.

For them, personal destruction was the ultimate triumph.

The pinnacle of their evil work.

At their prompting Aeron's thoughts became darker and darker.

Stalker demon: "Kill yourself. You know it's the right thing to do."

Aeron: *I might as well kill myself. It's the best thing I can do for my family.*

Rogue demon: "Okay, that's the decision made, now get on with it!"

Guardian angel: "Don't do this. You are feeling low but it will soon pass."

Aeron had fought this depression for a long time. He could not remember when he had last been completely free of it. He had known that coming to Korkyra had been his last chance of overcoming the wretchedness which, for too long, threatened to overwhelm him.

Well, it had not worked. At this moment he could not think of one reason to go on living. His mind held up a card: HOPELESS.

Tears spilled unheeded down Aeron's cheeks. His marriage was over, his kids annexed, his dreams dead. He might as well be dead too...

Chapter 29

Ingrid lay as still as a corpse on her bed, swollen face turned to the wall. Panos her darling son was dead and she too wanted to die.

Her anguished screams, loud wailing, and monsoon of tears had drained the strength from her body. Now she had withdrawn from the world. Wearing a vacant expression her eyes stared blankly at the white wall.

She was oblivious to the family members crowding the downstairs rooms. Michalis had just been to ask her if she wanted them all to leave. She didn't bother to answer him. It was of no importance who stayed or who went. Panos was dead.

Michalis had also begged her to eat a little food, or at least to sip some juice, if only for the sake of the baby she was carrying. But even to that she made no response. The baby? She had no thoughts in her head about any baby other than her baby boy, Panos.

Her face was immobile but her mind was acting like a cinema screen showing her over and over the broken body of her beloved Panos. She heard again and again the squeal of brakes, the soft thud and terrifying metallic scraping, and she was opening the front door and looking to see what had caused the noise.

She saw a red car buckled against the stone wall with a man standing beside it. He had his back to her and was looking downwards. She could not see Panos and her heart pounded with fear. She tore down her garden path and out of the wooden gate and immediately saw her son lying motionless and in a strange crumpled heap in the middle of the road.

She ran to him and threw herself onto her knees beside him. It was then she began to scream. Because one look into his open sightless blue eyes had told her that her son was dead, and that no medical treatment on earth would be able to bring him back to her.

For some reason, though, when the ambulance arrived this did not stop the paramedic from trying desperately to revive him all the way to the hospital, while Ingrid, moaned softly as tears rained unchecked. This was his job. He was bound to try. Paramedics always lived in hope and sometimes it was rewarded.

He used injections, heart massage and finally electric panels applied to the boy's chest. All the while Ingrid watched on and knew with certainty that it was all hopeless.

Panos was gone.

Some part of Ingrid had also gone.

Click went her brain and she started to run over the whole horrific scene again.

But no matter how many times she reran the scene it always came back to one thing: Panos, her beloved, beautiful boy, her child, her happiness, was dead. Gone. And she asked herself repeatedly at that point in the reruns why she was still alive. Why was this annihilating pain not killing her too?

Once she asked herself why Takis was still alive. His car crashed why didn't he die too? But as fury started to bubble up and her hands tensed into the avenging claws of a tigress robbed of her cub, the blue sightless eyes of the dead Panos filled her whirling brain and the anger ceased.

Panos was dead and gone. Nothing would bring him back. Nothing else mattered beyond a yawning chasm of despair that was threatening to swallow her up. Nothing. Not even the new life in her womb. Teetering on the brink of insanity, from the pain of loss, Ingrid was unable to take any comfort from its presence.

As for Takis, she knew that he would suffer, and if she was not overwhelmed with loss she may even have felt some pity for him. He would have the death of her son on his conscience for the rest of his life.

* * *

At the police headquarters in Corfu Town a sombre officer was hunched over a small stack of forms. Three metal cabinets, their grey paint chipped by many years of use, stood at his back, drawers bulging open with dog-eared files. The underarms of his short-sleeved, once-white shirt were ringed with sweat. A pool of light from a small lamp illuminated an overfull ashtray which sat on the desk between him and Takis, the driver whom he was questioning about a serious accident. While overhead the single naked bulb dangling from a short cable was moved by a tentative breeze throwing white light about the small scruffy room.

Takis calmly sipped water from a white plastic cup, took a deep drag of his cigarette, and looked off into the middle-distance through a blue wreath of exhaled smoke.

Gabriella had just arrived and was conferring with the guardians of Takis and the policeman. Sombre-faced the three hovered on spread wings over the heads of the two men.

The station had just got the call. The little boy was dead. Takis could have told them that. Though the police marched him off just as the ambulance arrived he was certain he had killed the boy.

The officer felt sorry for Takis as well as the boy and his poor parents. A life had been lost because of a ball which the little boy had chased into the road.

When he had been brought in Takis yelled the same two sentences over and over. "He ran into the road! He ran right in front of my car!" He was given a cigarette and some water and gradually his shaking stopped, the colour came back into his face, and as he calmed down he became silent. From then on he only spoke to answer direct questions.

His statement to the officer in front of him had mainly been about what he'd been doing before he drove up the lane. He'd been drinking coffee at the *kafeneion* with friends. He was on his way home to eat with his family. About the accident he had little else to say other than what he had yelled when brought in.

He remembered he had pressed down hard on the brake and turned the wheel to try to avoid the boy, but after that his mind, he said, was blank.

His father, Petros, had come to the station bringing the family lawyer. The lawyer had spoken to father and son in private before Takis made his formal statement. The lawyer said it was an open-and-shut case of accidental death. A horrific accident created by a poor boy running in front of a car chasing a ball. What a terrible tragedy. But still, an accident. The policeman finished writing up the report and read it over to Takis. It didn't take long. As he passed over a biro and asked him to sign Gabriella was instructing the policeman's guardian.

"He is too cool and collected," whispered his angel.

The officer noticed that Takis' hand was remarkably steady as he signed the statement. Covertly he watched the young man. For someone who had just taken a life, even though by accident, he thought him strangely calm.

Counselled by Gabriella the angel spoke again. "He has not expressed remorse."

It occurred to the policeman that Takis had not uttered a single word of regret.

A long time in the job the officer had seen it all; so he thought. But he had never seen someone so composed under such dreadful circumstances. It didn't seem natural. It was almost as if he didn't care that he had killed an innocent little boy.

The officer didn't exactly feel suspicious. But he did find Takis' attitude puzzling.

The officer's stalker demon zipped in. "It is obvious that the man is in shock. Shock does this to many people." He shot a malicious glance at the three angels and flicked out his grey forked tongue towards them.

The officer glanced at Takis. *Perhaps he's just in shock.*

The stalker demon squawked excitedly.

The policeman's angel spoke again. "Have you ever seen a

shocked person so cool and collected?"

Thoughtfully the policeman reached for his pack of cigarettes and drew one out. Placing it between his lips he clicked his plastic lighter and applied the flame. Exhaling a stream of smoke towards the ceiling he pondered. *Something is not right here.* Decisively he took up his pen and scribbled a few pertinent comments on a form.

With an angry screech the defeated demon vanished.

Gabriella counselled the two guardian angels then flew off.

The officer had recommended a little background investigation of Takis.

Meanwhile the man would spend the night in the cells.

* * *

Bethany was at the Paradise sitting at a table by the pool bar sipping orange juice. She was jumpy. She couldn't get the upset Aeron out of her thoughts.

Clare arrived for work and saw immediately that her friend was troubled. "What's wrong?" she asked quickly.

Bethany didn't know whether to tell her or not. But her whole body was clenched with nerves. "I'm worried about Aeron," she blurted.

"Oh, and why's that then?"

"I met him on my walk yesterday and he seemed a bit depressed." *Understatement but protecting his privacy.* "Then I saw Diana on the beach earlier and she said he didn't turn up for work last night." She hesitated but decided to press on. "So I walked up and knocked on his door and he didn't answer."

She pictured Aeron depressed and sobbing; Aeron not turning up for work; no Aeron on the beach; and no Aeron at home. She was stringing these facts together and trying not to think the worst.

No! Aeron was fine.

No! Aeron would not do anything stupid because he was depressed.

Clare narrowed her eyes. "You don't think he's done something stupid do you?" A friend-of-a-friend of hers in Dublin had committed suicide last year.

Bethany tried to stay rational. "He's probably fine and I'm just being silly. But..."

"Try not to worry. Sure, he'll be fine altogether. He seems a well-balanced kind of guy to me." She was determinedly cheerful.

But just then the church bell began to toll. A single thin and sombre note repeated at intervals of some seconds. The sound was so unexpected, yet so relevant, that Bethany jumped up out of her chair clutching her throat in distress.

"What?" Clare put her hand on Bethany's arm as her friend blanched. "What it is it?"

"The bell, it's tolling."

Clare shook her head. She didn't understand.

Bethany explained in tortured tones, "It's tolling because someone has died." The hand she put to her mouth was trembling. "I've never heard it toll in all the times I've been in Korkyra." As Bethany's eyes filled with tears Clare's filled too in sympathy with her friend's obvious distress. They stared at each other but neither could voice Bethany's fear.

"Clare!" Jason arrived and called her over.

Into Bethany's mind came the words from a John Dunne poem:

Do not ask for whom the bell tolls, it tolls for thee.

She shuddered.

"Bethany." Clare came back to the table and put her arm around her. "Please sit down." She spoke softly and with sympathy and her friend sank heavily into the chair as her legs went weak.

"Oh, Clare, it *is* him isn't it?" Bethany groaned.

"No, no, it's not Aeron." She firmly reassured her friend but continued to look solemn.

Bethany's head shot up. "It's not? Oh, thank You, God!"

Clare chewed her lip. She didn't know how to say the words; the awful words. Bethany realized that her friend couldn't speak. She stared at her for a few long moments before she dared to ask the question. "Clare, who's died? Who is it?"

Clare took a deep breath. "It's Ingrid's little boy, Panos."

"*Panos?*"

"Someone was driving up the lane and the little boy ran into the road chasing his ball. The driver couldn't stop. Killed him instantly."

"No! No! No!" Overcome with shock Bethany buried her blanched face in cupped hands.

Chapter 30

Aeron jauntily rounded the corner at the foot of his hill. Dressed in his cargo pants, and a bright blue T-shirt, he was headed for the beach. He caught sight of Bethany walking towards him.

"Bethany, I'm so glad to see you," he called cheerily. As she reached him he noticed she wore the same cream sundress he'd first seen her in. It was a happy memory. "I wanted to apologize for being so gloomy yesterday," he said without preamble.

"I was worried about you, Aeron," Bethany admitted, fiddling with the strap of her gold bag to stop herself from throwing her arms around him in relief.

A glint of sunlight on the sea over Bethany's shoulder dazzled Aeron briefly. Shading his eyes he gazed with appreciation at the sapphire waters. The glorious colours of this day compared to the darkness of last night, which had almost overwhelmed him, lifted his heart. He felt as light as the breeze which ruffled his curly mop of sun-bleached hair.

He felt blissfully happy to be alive.

Bethany thought that the beach gear sat well on his tall, tanned, slim body. He looked like he didn't have a care in the world. What a difference from yesterday!

"Bethany," he began, casting around for the right words. "I want to thank you," he said finally, his light blue eyes intense with gratitude.

"Thank me, for what?" Bethany was puzzled.

"You saved my life," he said simply.

"Well, hardly." Bethany smiled broadly. "I was just there at the right time to listen, that's all."

"No," he persisted. "It was much more than that. You really did save my life." He tensed his lips into a thin flat line and the dimple on his chin became more pronounced as he reflected.

Bethany was curious because Aeron sounded so solemn.

"What do you mean?"

"I almost topped myself last night," he blurted out.

"Aeron, I know you don't mean that." *I hope you don't, anyway.*

"Oh, but I do. I was so down that I started to think of ways to kill myself. I was determined to do it."

For the second time that day Bethany's face paled under her suntan. "But... you sound so good today." She found it hard to take his words seriously.

"If it hadn't been for you I would have done it." He was insistent.

Surely he wasn't being romantic? He didn't sound romantic but she didn't know what else he could mean.

There was no way she would have a relationship with him. Him being married. No matter what she felt for him.

She waited.

"It was like I had gone mad. All I could think was that I could not go on living. But then, right in the middle of all that, I heard your words."

"My words. What words?"

"Don't you remember what you said to me yesterday?"

"I said quite a few things, I think." She laughed lightly.

"Well, let me tell you what happened so you can understand that I'm not exaggerating your help."

Bethany clasped her hands in front of her waist and listened intently.

"I was so bad." With closed eyes he shook his head at the memory. He opened his eyes, sighed, and continued. "I was like a man possessed. That's the only way to describe it. I was so close," he put up his hand with finger and thumb only a whisker apart, "this close to taking my life."

Goose bumps ran over Bethany's legs in horror. "Oh, Aeron," she breathed in sympathy.

"Then, in the middle of this madness, this possession if you will, I faintly, very faintly, heard your words: "When the chips are down turn it over to God." It was like listening to a crackling radio and just being able to make out what was being said. But I got the message and I screamed in my head 'Dear God, please help me!' exactly like Gabriella told me to."

Bethany was transfixed with the drama of it all.

Aeron was gripped with the memory. "Well, the next thing I knew, I was taking off my shoes and getting into bed fully dressed, and feeling absolutely calm I fell asleep *immediately*. I slept a solid twelve hours."

"Oh, Aeron." Her knees were trembling. He had almost done what she had been dreading all day.

"Yep, isn't that incredible? One minute I'm crazy and about to top myself, the next I pray for help and I'm instantly calm and go to sleep." He inhaled deeply and breathed out slowly. "I don't mind telling you that when I woke up, I got out of bed and straight onto my knees to pray." His pale blue eyes were bright with emotion. "And I'm sorry to say that I haven't done that since I was a kid."

Bethany was happy to hear him put the credit where it was really due.

They exchanged a long look where his gratitude for a fresh start hit her eyes and was reciprocated.

"So," he said eventually, "I want to thank you for giving me the right words." He bobbed his head in emphasis. "If you hadn't told me what to do... Well, you and Gabriella. Fact is... I would be dead now." He bobbed his head again. It was the terrifying truth.

"Oh, Aeron." Bethany put her hand to her mouth. She didn't know what to say.

"I know," he said. "And there aren't really the words to fully explain, or thank... And I still don't really understand any of what happened last night... not from start to finish. But you know..." he paused. "I think this has been building for a long, long time. This crisis, I mean. And it was like you were sent to me yesterday... and Gabriella was sent to me... so you could... save my life..." His voice trailed off and he bowed his head.

Bethany was stunned. She would need to think hard about what he had told her. But she knew one thing for certain. "You know what, Aeron," she said, "I don't believe in coincidence." He raised his head sharply and looked deep into her eyes. "I think you're right about us being sent to you." It was amazing to feel instrumental in preventing a suicide.

But what if she hadn't taken a break when she did? Would Gabriella have spoken with Aeron like she did? Who knows? It didn't bear thinking about.

She looked up at Aeron's thin tanned face which had become so dear to her. "And now?" Her fear lingered. Would he go down that road again?

"Now, I already feel better than I have in a *very* long time. I feel sort of... transformed!"

"Oh, Aeron." She wanted to hug him in relief. But no. "I'm so very glad to hear that." Her smile was warm as the tension of the day left her body.

Then she remembered Panos and a wave of sadness washed over her.

She didn't have the heart to tell Aeron about Panos. He probably didn't know the family anyway.

* * *

Katarina sat behind the cash register deep in thought about poor Panos. The shop had been busy all day with locals dropping in to talk about the boy's death on the pretext of buying a few groceries. Mainly women, but some older men, they congregated at the back of the shop speaking in hushed tones to Anna.

They lingered.

Spiros began to offer them sweet Greek coffee in tiny plastic cups and they drank it gratefully.

Everyone was in shock. They all loved children.

Visitors often commented on this love. It was especially obvious when they brought their own offspring along for an evening meal in a taverna – mainly for lack of a babysitter. When these kids joined the troop of local juniors creating mayhem among the diners the waiters just smiled. Their tolerance was appreciated but not quite understood by the foreign parents, who often found other people's noisy youngsters quite irritating.

Katarina accepted a coffee from her father and went to stand beside her mother in the little mournful group. Everybody, even those who didn't hold with marriages with foreigners – Katarina included – had nothing but heartfelt sympathy for Ingrid and Michalis. It was reported that the bereaved couple were broken. Friends, family and neighbours were surrounding them with love but nothing was penetrating their stupor of grief.

Holding their coffee in their left hand they called on Christ for help and with their right hand made the sign of the cross over their chest three times in a swift fluid pattern. They prayed He would help the family through this tragedy.

Katarina remembered that Ingrid had always been nice to her. She felt bad now that she had never been friendly back. She had, though, been friendly to Panos, and was grateful to remember that. She also remembered her conversation with Bethany at the old harbour which had begun to soften her general view of foreigners. From that day she had spoken more to Bethany, widening her knowledge of her culture.

"That beautiful little boy," said an old lady, wiping rheumy eyes with her snowy apron. "Mown down by a motorcar? I still can't believe it."

"Yes, he was playing right outside his front gate!" Anna said. "In daylight, in summertime, on a quiet lane: he should have been safe!"

"How on earth could that happen?" Spiros, the experienced driver, couldn't understand it at all. Another local woman arrived to join the group. He moved slowly into the backroom to make more coffee.

* * *

In the *kafeneion* the atmosphere was heavy and subdued by the death of the little boy. The men sat nursing coffee or little thick glasses of local red wine that the owner had begun to pass around the place. It was a sad day for the poor bereaved parents and family. It was a sad day for the village. They hardly knew what to make of it all.

No one spoke against foreigners or tourists today. It was one of their friends who had killed Panos.

Takis had been in their company for years. A dour young man, not much liked, if they admitted it.

They admitted it now as neither he nor his father was there to hear them.

What they did not speak of was their personal bitter condemnation of Michalis for marrying the German girl, Ingrid. No one at this moment felt proud of their prejudice. The thought of the dead boy, that angelic blonde-haired, blue-eyed little boy, prodded their hearts. *Angelos*, they began to call him. Angel.

Their guardian angels stood among them tall and sombre with wings folded at their backs. In complete silence they cast glances around the room and at each other. Their guidance was not needed. The terrible event had stirred up the consciences of their wards.

Love had pulverized prejudice.

But at what cost!

In low rasping voices, through clouds of cigarette smoke, men verbalized their shock – like many in the community – that the boy had been killed in broad daylight on a clear stretch of road. Someone brought up the argument between Takis and Michalis. "Takis was warned by Michalis to slow down when driving up that lane," said one man, a fisherman like the father and son. "But did he listen? No, he did not!" Murmurs of agreement ricocheted around the dingy walls of the room. "Michalis said he was afraid for Panos and for other children living along the lane. Told him straight out."

The men shook their heads sadly and looked into their coffee or wine. A couple of them had been there that day, including the pipe-smoking old man in the faded red cap who had spat beside Michalis' foot. But they were too ashamed to tell that they had taken Takis' side against Michalis.

They all agreed it was a very, very bad business.

* * *

On the beach little knots of men and women from Korkyra and Hora who had come to swim stood and talked about the death. Visitors began to pick up on the bad atmosphere, then, they too, were collecting together to discuss the tragic accident that had claimed the life of a small innocent boy.

Soon the sad news ran like a wave along the whole long length of the beach. Parents cuddled their children and felt grateful to have them safe. There were more ice creams bought for their youngsters in the short time after the bad news was heard than in the rest of the day. They just wanted to spoil them and please them. They had learned that the boy had been an only child. Many women shed a tear of sympathy for the mother they did not know, and dreaded the same ever happening to them.

Fathers put away their newspapers and began to help their children build sandcastles or kick a ball around the edge of the water. Suddenly, no parent was taking their child for granted. No child was a nuisance. Families at the beach that day were pulled together by an invisible thread of love and appreciation. Mothers and fathers looked at their kids fondly and then threw each other small tight smiles. "We're the lucky ones," they said with their eyes.

It was a day that would stay for a lifetime in their memories. The smell of coconut suntan lotion, the sun bright on the water, the laughter of their children, and the sadness on the faces – echoed by their own – of the local people as they stood together and talked of the death of a small boy.

Chapter 31

Angels were milling around the seashore as the others flew in swiftly over sea and cliff to join them. A light breeze set robes billowing and ruffled hair and feathers. Soon they were all assembled. Gabriella, the angel of Greece, was with them.

In the rosy glow of the setting sun poised on the horizon they moved into small clusters to confer with those most involved with each other's wards.

Almost immediately, though, a large group formed around a trio of angels: the guardians of Takis, and his mother and father. All looked forlorn.

Directly in front of them stood the sombre guardians of Ingrid and Michalis, and beside them the guardians of Michalis' parents. With them were the guardians of the rest of Michalis' family and friends, and Bethany's guardian.

The small clusters broke up and soon every one of the angels was gathered around the trio of guardians. That evening there was not one angel present whose ward had not been deeply upset by Takis' murderous action. Gabriella flew up to hover above and just to the right of the trio.

"Ingrid is a broken woman," said her angel, tears rolling down pale cheeks and mingling with her long dark wavy locks. "And Michalis is a broken man," said his angel, embracing her in his wings. Every other angel present put their whole focus on sending the two grieving angels comforting love.

"I tried to stop him," blurted Takis' angel. "I tried so hard," He looked up at Gabriella. "We tried so hard…"

All eyes fixed on Gabriella who nodded. "We did. We tried so very hard to dissuade him from his heinous deed. But he would not listen to anything we said."

"He just would not listen," Takis' angel agreed.

Ingrid's angel reached for his hand. "I understand. I know you will have tried your very best to stop him." She looked up at Gabriella. "Thank you for trying so very hard," she said. "If anyone could have prevented this it was you." She shook her head. "But clearly evil had already rooted too deeply in his soul."

One by one the angels spoke up telling how their wards had been upset. With some, it had brought back bad memories of their own losses. Others, felt a strong sense of guilt for a number of reasons, starting with xenophobia. There was much nodding and empathy as each angel shared the effect of the murder on their ward.

When everyone had finished sharing the day's ramifications of Takis' actions the atmosphere became charged with waves of soothing love.

One of the angels who had been present with their ward in the *kafeneion* spoke up. "What Takis did has changed my ward for the better," he reported. "Before today he was very critical of every foreigner, but now he feels bad about that," he explained. "He thinks about the mother of the dead little boy and instead of hatred he feels only compassion for her." A number of guardians spoke one after another reporting that exactly the same change had come upon their ward.

Gabriella listened intently. When the angels finished their reports she spoke up with some excitement. "It is clear that this murder, this evil act, has had the opposite effect on the community than the one which Satan desired. Clearly he meant to fracture it further. Instead, though, it has stirred up the conscience of many.

"Love is flooding out of the people in a tide of compassion. This compassion is beginning to heal the community!"

The whole throng became wreathed in great smiles. This healing of the community was something they had long been working for. The news was marvellous indeed.

Then Gabriella said she had something that she wanted to share with them. She asked Bethany's angel and Aeron's angel to fly up and join her. "I want Aeron's angel to tell you some more good news." Keen interest buzzed through the throng.

Gabriella looked at Aeron's angel and smiled. "Please share with us what happened to your ward last night."

He swept the angels with an eager look. "As most of you know," he began, "Aeron has been very depressed for a long time." There were many nods. Only the newest arrivals, the angels of some holidaymakers, were unfamiliar with Aeron's story. "And I told you yesterday that he was reaching rock-bottom." He paused and sighed. "Well, last night he almost took his own life."

There were mutters of consternation among the throng. "Suicide is the greatest triumph for Satan," Gabriella reminded them. "This Father of all lies uses his biggest lie on poor vulnerable wards: Your life is not worth living so end it now!" She shook her head sadly. "Unfortunately too many believe him!"

"But," said Aeron's angel, "though he was seriously tempted to believe that lie, he did not go through with the suicide." He looked over at Gabriella and Bethany's angel and grinned. "And that was thanks to Gabriella and Bethany!" Spontaneous applause broke out among the throng. Good news! Great news!

Gabriella put up her hand in an appeal for silence. "Thank you for that, but as you know, I was just doing my work. It is Bethany and her angel whom I want to thank." Bethany's angel crossed both hands below her smiling face and bowed her head. Gabriella led the new round of applause herself.

"What happened?" Takis' angel asked. "I want to hear all the lovely details," he said. He was desperate to hear of triumph over evil.

Bethany's angel was happy to oblige. She began by recounting how, the afternoon before, she had urged her ward to stop work and go for a walk. Aeron's angel had asked for help with his ward. "The thing is that Bethany's writing was going very well and she didn't really want to stop at that point. But I urged her to do so and she listened to me." The angel looked pleased. "Yes, she listened to me," she reiterated happily.

"Anyway," she continued, "she met up with Aeron as we engineered, and when she realized his despair she sent up a prayer for guidance." The angels began to applaud again. This time their appreciation went on for quite a while. Her angel's bright blue eyes sparkled with delight.

As the clapping died down Takis' angel begged her to continue with the happy story. "Well," she said, "Gabriella arrived and gave Bethany some advice to encourage Aeron with his dreams. She tried to do that but he was not listening. So Gabriella made herself visible for a few minutes and encouraged him to pray. Later, Bethany tried again to bring up his mood. She left him with the words, 'When the chips are down turn it over to God' and in his deepest despair Gabriella reminded him of those words and he grabbed onto them and it saved him!

"And then this morning when he awoke he understood how his life had been saved and he got on his knees and prayed and thanked God for a new start." The angel's face was wreathed in a smile. "I plan to keep reminding him to pray about using this gift of a new start wisely."

The throng was thrilled to hear this story. It was the perfect note to bring their meeting to its most important conclusion. Beaming they marshalled into their lines and the angel of Greece flew out ahead of them to hover just above the sea facing the red globe of sun on the horizon.

In perfect silence, eyes closed, hands joined in front of them, they lifted their faces towards heaven disappearing momentarily into the golden flood of light. When this ebbed the reappearing angels were alight with joy.

They bid farewell to each other – hands crossing over upper torsos – before flying back to their wards over sea, beach and cliff.

Slowly the fiery orb of sun began to sink below the horizon.

Chapter 32

Takis was being led in handcuffs back to the tiny hot airless cell in which he'd spent the night. He had stood expressionless in front of the District Attorney, while his lawyer asked for his client's immediate release. The lawyer had been reminded that procedures had to be followed, and that he knew the rules as well as any of them.

Takis had already been told the rules by his lawyer. He knew that this afternoon he would be taken to the Criminal Court and charged with manslaughter. The hearing would be a quick formality and his lawyer would ask the judge for a period of forty-eight hours in which to prepare a defence against the crime for his client.

His lawyer had assured him that, at that point, Takis would be released on bail.

The lawyer had already heard, through the court grapevine, that the report from the scene of the crash revealed that every fact pointed to an accident. The tyre burns on the road showed the car had braked hard. The wheel had been turned away from the boy at the point of impact, so that he was hit with a glancing blow, not full on. The damage to the car showed it was travelling at a low speed when it struck the wall.

The evidence showed the truth of the statement his client had given the police.

After another quick appearance in court, the day after tomorrow, the lawyer would ask for a further postponement of the hearing.

During this time Takis would, his lawyer assured him, be a free man. The lawyer hoped that if he could delay the case coming to court for as long as possible he could persuade the judge that his client had suffered enough, no matter what the verdict, and that he should remain a free man.

Takis was hoping this would be the outcome of the case

against him. So he was calm and confident, even though he did not enjoy being held in custody. For one thing, he was longing for a decent coffee at the *kafeneion* where he would surely be treated as a hero for ridding the community of the son of a German.

* * *

Bethany left a little posy of wildflowers and a short note of condolence on Ingrid's doorstep. It was a heartfelt gesture. She wanted her to know how sorry she was for her loss. The funeral took place mid-morning but she didn't attend. Not knowing Ingrid that well it felt intrusive to be a witness to such grief that could only be guessed at.

At the time the service was taking place in the tiny church overlooking the sea Bethany sat at home praying for the little family now torn so cruelly apart.

Inevitably, her mind wandered back to the day of her interview with Ingrid, when she had seen Takis driving with such reckless speed up the narrow lane. The cold feeling running down her spine, and the sense of evil came flooding back, as did her warning for Michalis not to approach the man and complain but to enlist someone else to do it.

She knew, though, that Michalis had talked to Takis about it. His simple request for him to drive more slowly had caused quite a stir in the village, apparently. But Takis had taken no notice of the plea.

And he had killed Panos.

Driving more slowly perhaps he would have been able to stop in time when the little boy chased his ball into the road. Bethany shuddered at the thought of the terrible accident. Then the glittering malice of the man's eyes jumped into her memory and she gasped aloud. Had he done it deliberately?

She sat open-mouthed and her brain whirled with the

thought.

Was it possible that a young man would kill an innocent boy for no reason?

She realized that she was now seriously considering if a murder had been committed.

She jumped up and began to pace the kitchen. Horrible thoughts were crowding in her brain, one after another. *Got to get out of here!*

Hastily she got ready and left the house and by habit headed towards the sea. At the minimarket Hygeia bounded out of the shade and joined her. Bethany gave the dog's large flat brown head a perfunctory little pat and together they walked towards the old harbour.

The thought that Panos had been deliberately killed would not take root in Bethany's brain. Quickening the pace, as if to put distance between herself and the abhorrent idea, they soon reached the water's edge.

Standing on the scrappy pebble beach she shouted the word "No" as she tossed stone after stone into the shallows. Long minutes passed in this activity of denial. At first Hygeia ran in an out of the water thinking it a game, but soon gave up. One vigorous shake later she went to sniff interesting smells in some long course grass instead.

Finally, Bethany sank down cross-legged onto the beach and folded her arms. She had read enough Agatha Christie novels to know that a motive was the thing to search for in a murder case.

She shook her head. No one would murder a small boy because their father asked them to drive slower.

No!

And Ingrid had said nothing about a previous altercation. Bethany felt if there had been anything of substance Ingrid would have mentioned it that time when they spoke about Takis.

No!

No. Bethany decided to dismiss the very idea of murder. To

put it out of her mind and never mention her suspicion of it to anyone. Imagine if that idea came to the ears of Ingrid and Michalis.

No!

Bethany was certain no one else had even considered murder as the vaguest possibility.

* * *

The policeman slowly read over the statement Takis had made and signed. His eyes blurred with deep thought. He no longer saw the words, he saw instead – in his memory – the utter lack of compassion on the face of the young man who had sat in front of his desk that day.

The strange attitude had been duly noted. It had been passed along to the station inspector. Discreet enquiries had been made.

It didn't take long to discover the xenophobia of Takis, and his father too. The row between Michalis and Takis was easily uncovered. They now also knew, from a variety of sources, that Takis regularly drove recklessly up and down that lane.

The policeman sat back in his hard wooden chair and rubbed a weary hand over his perspiring face. He played with his pack of cigarettes, lifting and dropping them onto the desk. He was trying to cut down. It was making him nervous. He'd have one to help him think. *Any excuse.* He gave a short bitter laugh.

He picked up the statement again. On the face of it the accident was text book. Driving up the lane, little boy runs in front of car, Takis brakes hard and swerves to avoid the boy but it all happens so suddenly that he catches Panos with a glancing blow. It is enough to kill the six-year-old.

One witness saw Takis enter the lane. No one witnessed the accident. Takis stayed at the scene of the incident and willingly came to the station for questioning.

The policeman drew deeply on the fourth cigarette of the

day, and, exhaling, watched the stream of smoke fill the air.

No remorse.

And there was a motive for murder: xenophobia.

Placing the cigarette carefully on the edge of the ashtray he headed for the inspector's office. The cigarette would burn out long before he came back to it.

Chapter 33

Jason was asleep, dreaming that he was snug and safe on a big white fluffy cloud, floating in an endless blue sky. As he awoke, feeling blissfully relaxed, his eyes flicked open and shut. Still night. He tried to recapture the dream but it was already fading. The sense of peace, though, such as he had never known before, remained.

Jason's guardian angel had orchestrated his ward's dream.

Jason smiled broadly, revelling in the serenity, until a bright light disturbed him. His eyes flew open and as he sat upright his heart pounded in shock. Something inhuman was sitting on his old bedroom chair.

He gawped, transfixed.

A dazzling bluish-white light glowed from the being and surrounded it. After a few seconds he gulped a breath down and peered harder. It seemed to be a woman, transparent as pure crystal in sunlight, with great wings furled at her back.

This was the angel Gabriella in her most awesome manifestation.

Moments passed and when the apparition did not appear threatening Jason's breathing steadied, even as his thoughts ran on wildly. Jason, the non-believer in anything supernatural, was finding it extremely difficult to accept the evidence of his own eyes: that this being was, in fact, an angel!

But that was not possible because there were no angels. Angels, like fairies, like God, did not exist.

Then one thought flew apart from the others: "I must be dreaming!" He began to chuckle with relief.

"No, you are not dreaming." The angel spoke softly.

Jason, stunned to silence, sat rigid with fright. But as the adrenaline pumping around his body reached his brain he began to think more clearly. He stared at the being and became convinced that it was, definitely was, an angel. Wings. Ethereal. What else could it be? The wings were the clincher.

Okay, he now knew for certain that angels were real. But even more pressing was the other matter.

Angels, he had read, were messengers of… God! *Hmm.*

A question swam up from his core: angels, he now knew, were real, so, was God real?

"Of course God is real."

The angel was reading his thoughts.

"Yes, I am," she agreed.

Swift intake of breath from Jason. He hardly dared think anything else. As he tried to focus on not thinking he got the impression that the angel was amused.

What did it want? He thought that question as strongly as if taking part in a telepathy test. But the angel ignored that projected burning question and remained silent.

After long minutes passed the light surrounding Gabriella warmed to pale amber and her appearance solidified from ethereal to mortal-looking with wings. Her large oval grey eyes bored into Jason's, but not unkindly.

Something clicked in his memory and he gasped. "I know you! We spoke on the beach that day when I had an awful hangover."

Gabriella nodded.

"But… you're an angel!"

"As you see." Gabriella looked amused.

"But, you looked like an ordinary girl." Oh, this was getting too much to take in. An instinct made him pinch his arm. Hard. It hurt. Yes, he was definitely awake.

"You are awake. You know you are awake."

"You did this that day on the beach." He remembered the weird early morning meeting.

"Did what?" She couldn't resist teasing him.

"You were reading my mind." Of that he was now certain.

"Oh, that," she said airily. "Yes, I was."

Then something told him – his guardian angel, actually – that he should speak up. With a voice brimming with curiosity he asked, "Why are you here?"

Gabriella pierced him with her gaze. "Do you remember what I told you the day we met?"

"Um, what specifically?" He couldn't think straight with her looking at him like that.

"That your heart was overcome by greed."

"Ah, that," he blustered, "yes, I do remember, but I still don't agree with you, though." He stubbornly still refused to accept it.

"Whether you agree or not it remains the truth."

Jason's gaze shifted uneasily.

"And I warned you, that, unless you turned away from that greed, its destructive poison would seep into the lives of others."

Jason blinked a few times as a single line of puzzlement appeared between dark brows.

"Well, you did not. And it did!" She was not permitted to give him specifics.

He looked at her blankly. It seemed she was accusing him of something. He had no idea what she was talking about and began to protest. But Gabriella turned her head away and held up one hand palm forward, clearly signalling him to stop speaking.

He instantly obeyed.

She stood, drew herself up straight, and placed crossed hands below her neck. The downy feathers on her wings quivered while she adjusted them at her back. Jason watched in awe as she was surrounded again by the brilliant blue-white light.

Jason's guardian angel, still invisible to the man, stood straight and still beside her.

"I am Gabriella, the angel of Greece." She began her formal and solemn announcement. "I have been sent by God, Who loves you, to tell you that people are praying fervently and

235

repeatedly for your soul; which is in mortal danger."

Her intense gaze reached right inside him. He was transfixed with reverence.

"You are being overtaken by evil," she continued. She caught the faintest whiff of sulphur, but the demon was not allowed to interfere with *this* communication. She folded her hands together in front of her waist and waited.

"Evil!" he blurted in astonishment. What on earth was this creature talking about? "Look," he began. "I think you've got me mixed up with someone else. This must be a mistake." It was the only explanation he could come up with for this unfounded accusation.

Gabriella shook her head, and sparks of rainbow colour danced around her brow. "Jason, this is no mistake."

Jason watched the flickering lights in wonder. "I don't understand." He was flummoxed afresh.

"Jason, as you read in the Bible – the contents of which you decided not to accept – Jesus stated clearly that there is a war raging between heaven and hell."

Jason, a conscientious student, had read the Bible from cover-to-cover, but didn't remember that bit, nor much else.

Gabriella continued. "Every person upon the earth is part of that war: the fight for the supremacy of love or evil; God or Satan. Each human being is taking part in this war, whether you realize it or not." She paused to let her words sink in.

Finally she pronounced, "Everyone chooses to fight on one side or the other."

Jason slowly nodded. "Okay, I'm beginning to understand what you mean now, but I have to tell you that, I have *definitely not* chosen to fight for Satan." He was sincere.

"That is where you are wrong." Gabriella was emphatic. "You denied God and that automatically put you on Satan's side."

Jason inwardly shuddered. That was horrendous.

He had no idea just how horrendous it really was: how many times he had been overpowered and under the will of that devil. He would have gone insane if he had known.

The angel had one final message. "Jason, if you open your heart to Jesus Christ you will live with Him forever when your short human sojourn is ended."

Jason's mother believed that – as most Greeks still did – and had tried, unsuccessfully, to persuade him of it. But he had regarded his non-belief as sophisticated and modern. Now, though, he felt all of the angel's words like a physical weight upon his shoulders. He struggled to understand them, casting around in his mind to apply them to himself and his own actions.

Gabriella interrupted his introspection. "Yes, you have much to think about. And God will give you a little time to do that."

A little time...! "H-h-how much time?"

Gabriella gazed at Jason and a silence lengthened between them until the man's head lowered. Fear now gripped him and threatened to crush him to dust.

A sound of rustling brought his head jerking back up. The angel had moved and was now standing right in front of him – tall and majestic with wings half unfurled. "Jason, I urge you to think over every word I have said and you will discover that I have given you all the necessary information."

He closed his eyes and started to run over the entire conversation. "Can I just ask you..." he began, opening his eyes. But Gabriella had vanished.

"I have given you all the necessary information." Gabriella's words echoed loudly in his brain.

* * *

Further sleep was impossible. With a sense of urgency Jason pulled on jeans and T-shirt, and crept out of the silent hotel into the cool night air to prowl and ruminate.

Lagging behind was his invisible stalker demon, incensed by the turn of events. But once an angel had stepped like that, right into the equation, it was extremely difficult to neutralize the positive effect. It would never give up, though. Not until Jason drew his last breath.

On the other hand, his jubilant guardian angel was at his side.

Jason glanced at the moon and saw it was on the wane. Soon it would be daylight. Heading down to the sea's edge the sand slowed his pace to a steady plod beside the dark gently swelling waters. The deserted beach was a calm backdrop to the chaos of his thoughts.

He could scarcely believe what had just happened.

An angel! A real angel had come into his bedroom and spoken to him! And not only that she had come to him once before, in broad daylight, on this very beach, disguised as an ordinary girl!

The whole thing was incredible. "Incredible," he kept muttering. Then it struck him that the word was wrong because it meant something that was not believable. But the angel Gabriella, and not just any old angel but the angel of Greece, really had come to him, twice, and he could not deny that.

So now he knew for a fact that angels did exist. And the angel had spoken about God and now he knew that God did exist. No, he hadn't seen Him, but knew he could no longer deny Him. And, he didn't want to deny Him.

While walking the length of the beach he looked back over his life. Now, he could not understand why he had not believed in God before. He shook his head. "Why did I waste so much time and energy in rebelling against something so magical, so wonderful?"

He remembered Bethany, the day after Evan had died, saying something like: "God is as real to me as you. God is Love and I decided to trust Him. I don't ask 'Why?' now."

Jason watched the lowering moon shining on the calm sea like a silver rod whose tip was broken into shimmering shards by wavelets rushing towards the shore. Suddenly, he felt the presence of God and it humbled him.

The angel's accusations began pulsing through his brain. Under God's scrutiny he felt miniscule. A sense of worthlessness shattered his own proud illusions of himself to date. He bowed his head in shame. *I have to change, I want to change. I want to be a better person!*

After a short period of telling himself this over and over he raised his head, and, looking up into the vast star-studded sky he made a decision. With splayed fingers he pushed a lock of hair back from his forehead then made his request. "God, please help me to get on the right track in my life."

Two names jumped straight into his mind: Katarina and Clare.

"Okay. Thank You. I'll start there." He paused and pondered. "I don't know what I'm going to do but I need to clear things up with both of them."

Decision made, a feeling of peace washed through him. Then he felt drowsy. His bed beckoned again.

Within minutes he was back in the hotel, in his room, and asleep.

When he woke a couple of hours later he would feel refreshed and energized. Ready to start a new way of living.

Chapter 34

"Uh, Bethany, can I have a word with you please?" Jason double-checked no one else was in hearing distance. A few people, absorbed in books, sat under the shade of umbrellas at the far end of the pool. The mid-afternoon lull, when most guests were either snoozing on the beach or taking siestas indoors, gave him the chance he'd been seeking.

"Of course." Bethany was hot and desperate to swim but too kind to refuse. Jason looked rather serious, she thought, and wondered what he wanted to speak about.

She perched on a tall stool beside the bar as he placed a tumbler of fresh orange juice on a coaster in front of her. "Ah, a straw," he said, choosing a pink one and pushing it into her drink. She murmured her thanks, sipped and waited.

Jason took a deep breath. This was not going to be easy. "Umm, I want to tell you something. See what you think."

"Oh, yes?" she muttered, and sipped more cool sweet juice.

"Yes." He hesitated.

"Tell me." She wondered where this was going.

He watched her expression form into a question mark. *Might as well just say it.* He didn't know anyone else he could speak to about this. "Look," he began, "something really strange happened to me last night."

"Oh, yes?" What?

"It was the early hours of the morning, I was sleeping, and then I woke up." He hesitated again. "And then I saw her..."

"Saw whom?" Who was in his room in the early hours of the morning?

"An angel!" Eyes wide he slowly nodded. Quickly he looked around the pool to make sure no one else heard. "An angel was in my room," he whispered excitedly.

Bethany's jaw dropped in shock. It wasn't that she didn't

believe in angels. Of course she did. The Bible was full of them. But *Jason* and an angel? She sipped her drink and reflected. *I need more information.* "So, what happened?" she asked, deliberately nonchalant.

"Do you believe me?" He would not have believed him.

"I don't disbelieve you," she said cautiously. "But I would like to hear more." She hoped she had hit the right note of diplomacy. This could be a wind-up.

"She told me she is the angel of Greece."

"Oh, I've heard of the angel of Portugal."

"Yes?" It was more than he had.

"Yes, in Fatima, Portugal in 1916. The angel, looking like a young boy, appeared to three children, and afterwards the Virgin Mary appeared to them too, a few times. The last time, on the 13 October, 1917, she miraculously made the sun dance in front of a crowd of some seventy-thousand, including many top journalists."

"Oh, I've never heard of that." The new Jason looked impressed.

"It was written about in newspapers all over the globe. The facts are still there to find."

She turned her mind back to Jason's revelation. "So, what did the angel want?"

"She told me off." He was shamefaced. "Said greed was poisoning my heart and I was a bad influence on Korkyra; or something like that." He twisted his lips up to one side. "Said I was on my way to hell if I didn't change." His voice was low and sombre.

Bethany noticed Jason's hands shook as he picked up a cloth and began to rub the already shiny chrome body of the coffee machine. She didn't know what to say.

"Look," he said, "I know I didn't believe in God but I did think that if there was a God He would see that I am basically a good person." He was clearly upset. "I didn't think for one minute that if God did exist He would send me to hell! Everyone knows that's for really bad people, like murderers and tyrants and...and... Hitler," he improvised, indignant anew.

Bethany wanted still more information. "So, what else did the angel say?"

"She said that you are either *for* God or you are *against* Him." Bethany nodded. Jason told her about the ongoing war between heaven and hell, and their personal role. "Without realizing we choose sides." His voice, to his own ears, was unexpectedly forceful. He realized, in that moment, that he was choosing to commit himself to God.

Bethany was stunned by Jason's words. She now knew for certain he was speaking the truth. Cynic that he was, or had been, he simply could not have made that up.

"Say you believe me, Bethany, please."

"I do believe you." Jason looked thrilled. An angel had appeared to Jason. *Gosh! Amazing! Jason the atheist has been amazingly graced!* She inwardly chuckled at that sentence and wanted to write it down to remember.

Next she was fleetingly wistful. What would it take, she wondered, to get an angel to visit her? But of course, she was happy for Jason. "So, why are telling *me* this?" She smiled broadly. "I mean, I'm glad that you are, but I'm thinking... why me? Why not Clare?"

"Well," he took a deep breath, "I know that you are a strong believer and I needed to tell someone who... well... who wouldn't laugh at me." He sheepishly hung his head.

"I don't think Clare would have laughed at you."

"I'd have laughed at me."

Bethany put her hand on his forearm. "Jason, *I'm* definitely not laughing."

Jason raised his head and smiled. "Thank you, Bethany. Thank you very much." He already felt lighter in his heart. "You know," he went on chattily, "I saw the angel once before on the beach a couple of months ago. I had no idea then she was an angel. I mean, she looked like an ordinary girl."

Bethany was suddenly alert. For some reason she thought of Gabriella. "Um, what did she look like?" She held her breath. Could it be...?

"Tall, slim, big grey eyes, short curly blonde hair." Bethany gasped in shock as she recognized the description of the Gabriella. "What?" Jason asked sharply. "You've met her too?" He felt a flicker of disappointment. Bethany nodded vigorously. "Be-tha-ny." He drew out her name and imbued it with innuendo. "What have you been up to?" He sniggered to cover his pique. Why wasn't he the only one the angel had visited? "You're a dark horse."

Bethany looked at him blankly. Then the penny dropped. "Oh, I see where you're going with that." She chuckled. "No, she didn't tell me off, she said some encouraging things." She smiled at the memory. "Oh, and she told me her name was Gabriella."

"Yes, Gabriella, that was it." Jason looked impressed. The disappointment left. He was glad for her. "So, Bethany, you're going to get your wings someday."

"Oh, Jason, I don't think so." Bethany knew that could not happen to her. "I'm no Goody Two Shoes I can tell you right now." She giggled.

"Goody Two Shoes?" Jason's brow furrowed. "Look, my English is good but not that good."

Bethany laughed. "Oh, I can't actually tell you where the expression comes from, but it means that I'm no saint. I make lots of mistakes."

"Me too!" They laughed in empathy.

The gate from the beach path squeaked as a small group of people arrived. "Right, you have customers and I need a swim." Bethany gave Jason a huge encouraging smile.

"Thanks again, you're a true friend." Jason gave her a peck

on the cheek before turning his attention to the tourists.

Bethany looked at her watch. She was very hot. She'd have a quick dip in the pool.

Later she was meeting Clare on the beach. She wouldn't, though, be mentioning any angels...

Chapter 35

"Race you there and back," shouted Clare, jumping up and wading swiftly into the tepid turquoise water.

"You're on," yelled Bethany. Quickly overtaking her friend with a chuckle.

In seconds they were both waist deep, threw themselves into the water, and side-by-side began a fast crawl. Then Clare disappeared under the surface and soon reappeared a short way ahead. "Ha, Ha," she chortled, and took up the crawl again.

They had swum out quite a way and were now almost neck and neck when Clare suddenly shouted, "Turn, now!" Bethany was ready for her, though, and they both streaked, quick and sure, cutting through the smooth clear sea. Their strokes were noisy as they neared the shore again. As they finished, absolutely level, Bethany called out, "After a good clean race it's a draw." They giggled.

In the shallows they crawled playfully along the sandy floor on their elbows. "We're like crocodiles," said Clare. They stayed lying face down at the water's edge, just deep enough for the wavelets to wash over them and keep cooling their sun-warmed skin, chins cupped in hands away from the water.

After a couple of minutes of semi-floating Bethany said with deep satisfaction, "Oh, this is the life, isn't it!" She glanced over in surprise as Clare unexpectedly sighed.

"Yes, it's grand. But it's a pity that even in paradise I can feel hurt." Jason had been distracted today and distant with her. She felt insecure. Again.

Bethany didn't ask for details. She guessed that Jason was at the heart of her friend's observation.

Clare looked up at the beach and spied Jason making his way towards them, his hand raised in greeting. "Talking of which, here comes the man himself," she said softly to Bethany, before fixing on a big welcoming grin and giving him a wave.

As he reached the edge he called out, "Hello there, you beautiful mermaids!"

Clare noted Jason's mood was considerably lighter than earlier and felt her tension dissolve. She slowly drew herself out of the water and Jason bent to kiss her.

"Mmm, yummy and salty," he said, smacking his lips together.

Playfully she slapped him on the arm and he made to trip her up but failed. The next thing they were grappling with each other and inevitably ended up sprawled laughing in the hot sand. Sitting up Clare complained. "Look what you've done to me, Jason. I'm coated!"

"Come on then," he said, shaking the sand from his shorts as he stepped out of them, "let's get into that water and wash you off." He grabbed her hand and raced her into the sea. "Let's go out to lunch later," he suggested casually, as he rubbed at a patch of sand on her arm that stubbornly clung to her suntan lotion.

"Oh, lovely!"

"Lovely lunch or lovely me?" he teased.

Clare giggled. "Lovely both," she said, splashing water over him with her free arm.

"Oh, that's your game is it?" He grinned. "Well, two can play at that," he challenged. Grabbing her around the waist he dunked her briefly in the sea.

She surfaced, spluttering, and using the element of surprise succeeded in pushing him over.

Bethany laughed as she watched their antics. They seemed to be getting on fine. She just hoped it wouldn't all end in tears. She had the feeling that Clare wasn't nearly as tough as she projected.

Bethany looked absentmindedly up the beach. An approaching Katarina came into her line of vision and she waved at her. The girl was a bit friendlier now and even put the change straight into her hand at the minimarket. Bethany noticed the girl didn't do that to many other customers and she felt quite honoured.

Katarina waved back. This wasn't her usual time for swimming but her sister had asked to change breaks and Maria was coming to join her. She was thrilled to see Jason swimming. Dropping her towel she quickly stripped off her pretty sarong down to a utilitarian black bikini – which nevertheless displayed her tanned lithe teenage figure to perfection – and dived under the water heading straight for him. As she came up behind him she playfully pulled his foot. She surfaced with a laugh. She didn't notice Clare swimming away.

"*Ya soo,* Katarina."

"*Ti kanis,* Jason?" He didn't look happy. "What's the matter? Aren't you pleased to see me?"

Jason had seen Clare's hurt expression just before she left. He felt bad.

Suddenly he knew with clarity that his double-game was wrong. And, actually, came under the banner of "greed" – which had not occurred to him before. He was unaware that this insight was a pivotal moment in his life.

He thought of his choice to change and took a deep breath. "Are you sure you want to carry on going out with me?" Not the strongest overture to a closure, but a start.

Katarina looked confused. "What are you saying, Jason?"

He himself was confused, not by what he wanted, but by his apparent cowardice to speak the words.

Jason's stalker demon was going crazy as it shouted that he was mad to believe all that God and angel stuff, and its thin tail lashed in fury.

For a few seconds Jason wavered.

His demon yelled silently into his ear that he should continue to string both girls along.

Jason felt himself slipping back into his old disbelief. Then he pulled out the memory of the angel sitting in his bedroom.

His demon shrieked that it was only a dream.

But Jason knew the angel Gabriella was real. He took a deep breath and tried again with Katarina. "We see each other so little, it's not fair on you. You should be seeing someone else."

He paused again.

Why was it so difficult to say this?

Why was he being such a coward?

But he treaded water for a full minute, his hands pushing away at the sparkling sea, while he screwed up the courage to say what he knew he must. "Look, Katarina..." he began.

"I don't want to hear it, Jason!" Katarina broke in, sensing impending doom. With animal instinct she streaked away towards the shore, arms slicing desperately through water.

Thwarted, he followed. He had to tell her and get it over with.

She was a fast swimmer, and had a head start on him, so he didn't catch her up until she was standing to leave the water.

He caught her hand and turned her to face him. It was now or never. "Katarina, I have to tell you this. I'm very sorry but I can't see you again. I've met someone else."

Nothing could have prepared him for her fury. She yelled abuse, completely forgetting they were in a public place.

A couple lounging under umbrellas a few feet away heard the shouting and smiled at each other knowingly. They were used to flamboyantly loud Greeks. If you didn't know better you thought they were arguing.

Then the girl's voice became a scream of words and the man instinctively jumped to his feet. That was definitely a fight. He immediately saw the warring couple. He could see the girl didn't need his help. She was lashing at the man with her fists, and when he held her wrists to defend himself, she kicked at his shins. "It's Jason being attacked by some local girl," he reported with a wry smile.

Katarina's friend Maria was just arriving on the beach coming to look for her, and couldn't believe her eyes and ears. She rushed over and caught her friend by the arm. "Katarina! Katarina!" she hissed urgently. "Stop it, now. Everyone is staring."

The command acted like a bucket of icy water on Katarina's hot anger. In a heartbeat, acutely aware of being the centre of attention, anger was replaced by excruciating embarrassment that made her want to disappear. Wordlessly she snatched up her sarong, wrapped it around her dripping body, and, grateful for Maria's steadying hand on her elbow as countless gimlet eyes pried, quit the beach.

A few local men sniggered between themselves. In the community some were jealous of Jason's success and disliked him on principle. While many disliked him specifically because he paid his suppliers the lowest possible rates – which sometimes caused them real hardship. All were secretly glad to see Jason so publicly humiliated. The story would travel fast and create glee in many.

Feeling nauseous, Jason swam away from the beach towards the horizon. Katarina's reaction had been every bit as bad as he had anticipated, and he wasn't feeling proud of himself.

Clare left the water on trembling legs and sank down weakly onto the sunbed beside Bethany. Jason had finally ended it with the girl. But instead of feeling better, she felt worse.

Chapter 36

Michalis went back to work at the Paradise Hotel. He explained to Jason that it was the only way to keep his sanity, and Ingrid had agreed it was for the best. This was one of the busiest weeks of the season and he was greatly needed at the hotel. He didn't seem to do much good for Ingrid at home.

When Clare came in he asked her to ask Bethany to visit Ingrid. "She would have come you know." Clare spoke softly. "But she didn't like to intrude."

"I understand." Michalis nodded. He understood completely. The most considerate people had stayed away from him and Ingrid when they wished they would have visited in place of some who came out of macabre curiosity. "But she left us a nice message."

"Yes." Clare had read the note at Bethany's request. "Such a delicate matter," she had said. She had wanted a second opinion on the wording.

Bethany went the next morning when she knew Michalis would be gone to work. Feeling awkward she walked to the front door of the couple's home. Already a little shrine on a stand had been erected on the roadside, marking the place close to where Panos had met his death. Light flickered from the tiny oil lamp over the posy of fresh flowers and icons housed within the glass box. Briefly she prayed beside it for Panos' soul, and also for guidance when speaking to Ingrid. She was so afraid of saying the wrong thing to the grieving mother. What could anyone say really? Nothing could soften the pain.

Bethany knocked on the door and waited.

Nothing.

The door was slightly ajar. She pushed it open and called out to Ingrid.

"I am in here, Bethany." Ingrid sounded weary. Bethany stepped forward with trepidation, afraid of witnessing the woman's grief.

Through the doorway of the sitting room Bethany saw the

back of Ingrid's head above the chair and came to stand in front of her. Bethany bit her lip to hold back her threatening tears in the face of such raw pain. But pity screwed up Bethany's features and a sob tore from her throat. "Oh, Ingrid," she stuttered, "I'm so sorry, so very, very sorry that you have lost your lovely Panos!"

Ingrid's mouth puckered as she nodded to acknowledge the words of condolence. Her face, puffy from the river of tears she had cried since Panos had left her, remained dry. She did not feel she had another tear within her to shed.

The hand Bethany held was skin and bone and cold, despite the heat of the day. Bethany desperately tried to compose herself. She hadn't planned to cry like this. "Shall I make us some tea," she volunteered.

"Thank you." Ingrid nodded.

Bethany escaped gratefully to the kitchen and mopped herself up while making a brew.

Ingrid was sitting like a statue when Bethany returned with mugs of tea. "I'm sorry I didn't come before," she began, "but I didn't like to..."

"I understand." Bethany felt she did. The two women sipped their tea in silence. A clock ticked away seconds of their own remaining lives. It was a lonely sound. The stark contrast between the happy family atmosphere, when she was last in this house, caused Bethany to inwardly shudder.

Ingrid suddenly sighed then inhaled deeply like she was taking in oxygen with which to say something. Bethany looked up expectantly.

"I am not sure why I asked you to come to see me, you know. But your name kept jumping into my mind." Ingrid's speech was stilted and obviously difficult, but she fixed her reddened eyes to Bethany's like a drowning woman pleading for help.

"Uh, okay." What would Ingrid say?

"You know, I have been thinking and thinking and thinking..."

Ingrid's voice faltered, her lips frozen into the shape of the start of the next word that wouldn't come out. Bethany stared at Ingrid's mouth and knew what the word would eventually be.

It was the one most people asked in times of great pain.

Ingrid breathed deeply and tried again. "Why?" The word was breathy and elongated by the emotional constriction of her throat. But she persisted. "*Why* did God do this to me?" Anger, mingled with despair, made it more of an accusation than a heart-wrenching question.

Oh, no. Oh, no. I'm in this hot seat because Ingrid knows I'm such a strong believer. Though Bethany was gripped with sympathy, she was out of her depth with no answer to give. *I am not a theologian!* She would not mouth platitudes. Experience of life had taught her that much at least, so, shaking her head at Ingrid, she kept quiet.

Finally Ingrid cleared her throat and spoke up. "I have loved God, you know, for all of my life." She made a plain statement of fact. "And yet..." She faltered, shaking her head in fresh disbelief. "And yet! He has punished me in this way." Her voice wobbled and she pressed her lips together to stop their trembling. "He has taken away my child!" she accused. "My wonderful Panos who never hurt anyone in his short life." Her quivering voice was rising. "And I want to know why! *Why did He do that?*" She was shouting now leaning forward from the edge of the chair.

Anguish convulsed across the bereaved mother's face.

It tore at Bethany's heart. She waited.

She waited.

But Ingrid had slumped to the back of the chair and was gazing expectantly at Bethany.

Oh, no! She really expects an answer from me. But this is a conundrum. Also, she felt a little afraid for the baby in Ingrid's womb. Would all this distress harm it in some way? A heavily burdened Bethany sent up a silent prayer. *Dear Lord, I beg you, please give me an answer. Please give me some words to help this poor broken mother.*

Gabriella arrived to help Bethany's guardian angel. Ingrid's angel smiled hello. It was she who had advised Ingrid to send for Bethany.

As Gabriella gave directions the process began.

"I really don't know what to say to you," Bethany spoke haltingly. "But I do know that I don't believe in accidental death." She paused and breathed deeply, all of her senses tuning into Ingrid's reaction. Bethany was desperate to avoid hurting her. She gauged the woman was listening hard. *Oh dear.* She decided to plough on. "I believe that we are born when we're supposed to be, and that we die when we're supposed to." She exhaled and paused.

"I agree," Ingrid said in a whisper.

Silence stretched between them and Ingrid seemed to be waiting for more, but Bethany was floundering again. Then something came into her mind that seemed pertinent. "I've thought a lot about life recently," she began. "And though I have no real evidence, I know that God has given us free will so I think that we might have chosen our parents and our tests before we were born." She paused. "And if that is the reality, which I won't find out until I die, then it's a strong possibility..." Could she say it? Dare she say it? She decided to press on, "It's a strong possibility that you agreed to this test." Bethany cringed inside after she spoke and clamped her lips together waiting for Ingrid's response.

When Ingrid nodded Bethany felt she had walked another step through the minefield. But she had no idea what to say next. "Oh, Ingrid," Bethany blurted. "I don't want to make things worse for you. I don't really know why I'm saying these things."

"What could be worse?" Ingrid whispered.

Bethany was pensive. A question burned into her.

Dare she ask it?

Yes. It seemed too important not to.

"Ingrid, if you could choose again, and you knew you would only have Panos in your life for these few short years, would you choose to have him or not?"

Ingrid answered instantly. "I would choose to have him!" She threw up her head and looked Bethany straight in the eye. "Despite the pain, I would choose immediately to have him," she reiterated emphatically.

Bethany and Ingrid sat and regarded each other thoughtfully for a few minutes. Ingrid, weak with emotion and lack of food, used the arms of the chair to push herself upright. She put her hand on Bethany's shoulder. "Thank you," she said, simply. "I am going to think about the things you said."

She already felt herself moving a fraction, just a fraction, away from despair. And her hands, seemingly of their own volition, moved to rest on her slightly rounded abdomen.

Bethany noted the gesture and felt a little, just a little, comforted.

As she walked slowly back home she had a sudden moment of clarity: much of the pain in her life had come from not being able to see the whole picture. She remembered the words of St Paul: "Now we see through a glass darkly". Only when we saw God face-to-face would we get all the answers.

She prayed Ingrid would not turn away from God when she needed Him most. The Devil would be thrilled if that happened.

She shivered involuntarily despite the heat.

* * *

The angels winged in over sea and cliff for their evening meeting on the shoulder of sand at the far end of the beach. The angel Gabriella was with them.

As they arrived they moved into small clusters to speak with the angels of the wards most connected today. Katarina's, Jason's and Clare's angels made up one of these clusters. They spoke to each other earnestly. Katarina was very upset, her angel said. "But finally Jason is being honest with her," his angel pointed out, and she agreed. Clare's angel said that her ward did not know what to make of the public argument.

When the clusters had finished reporting to each other Gabriella flew up above them. They looked up at her expectantly. "I have an announcement to make," she said with a huge grin. "I visited Jason last night as a visible angel." The guardians looked impressed. This was a rare boon. "We had a talk," she continued, "and he now knows that God does exist." The angels could not understand how humans could deny this. "I know," said Gabriella. "But let us remember that we commune with Him daily." There was much nodding of agreement.

Gabriella called Jason's guardian to fly up beside her. "Please tell them what has now happened. "Gladly," said his angel. "Jason has begun to pray. He has prayed for help to put his life onto a loving path." His dark eyes flashed with joy as he spoke the words he had longed to speak. The whole throng, led by Gabriella, began to loudly applaud this soul-change.

When the applause died down Katarina's angel spoke up. "Ah, so that is why he has ended their relationship." Jason's angel agreed. "Yes," he said. "He has chosen Clare over Katarina and told her so."

Gabriella spoke again. "I have a great hope that Jason's soul-change will be the watershed that so many of you have been working towards." Her eyes ran over the throng. "I know that so very many of your wards will, hopefully, be positively affected by this change."

Jason's angel spoke again. "Jason has told Bethany about Gabriella's visitation." He looked down at Bethany's angel. She nodded. "Oh, and Bethany now knows too that you are an angel," he said to Gabriella.

"That is fine," said Gabriella breezily.

Chapter 37

"Really, Aeron's a fantastic singer." Bethany was enthusiastic. She smiled and almost clapped her hands as she spoke. She shook them instead for emphasis. She had thought about her conversation with Ingrid, and, though the woman had thanked her, she didn't really know if she had helped her at all. But she wanted to help Aeron, who had almost died too. "Yes, a really fantastic singer."

"I didn't know that." Diana Appleton wasn't entirely convinced. She knew he had a guitar but had never heard him play it. "How do you know?"

"When he first arrived I was staying a few doors away from him and I heard him a few times."

"Oh, disturbing the neighbours was he?" Diana chuckled.

"No, no. It was always early evening, and like I said, he's great and we all loved hearing him." She smiled at her friend. "So," she wheedled, "do you think you could put in a good word with Manos? Get him playing in public again."

"Don't see why not." Diana was happy to go along with it. She liked Aeron. And if Bethany had heard him and thought he was good, that was good enough for her. "One thing though." Something had just struck her as odd. "Why doesn't he ask Manos himself if he can play for him?"

Bethany sighed and shook her head. "I don't really know." She wanted to explain without being indiscreet. "Actually," she began, "between me and you I think he's a bit down since his family left, and I'm hoping this will cheer him up a bit." She bit her lip. "Please don't tell anyone I said that though, will you?" She made big round pleading eyes at her friend and smiled.

"Course I won't tell."

"Knew you wouldn't. That's why I'm asking you this favour."

"But what about Manos? How will he have heard about Aeron's

talents?"

"Someone told me that Spiros at the minimarket heard him perform at a wedding in the village last year and says he's great."

"Oh, fancy." Diana looked impressed.

"Yes, apparently it's common knowledge with the locals. So maybe Manos knows already but never thought to ask him."

"Right, so now we have a cover story no one need know that *you* wanted him to sing at the Candy Bar. I can just tell Manos that I heard that Aeron is great. And then I'll be telling the whole truth." She knew Bethany was hot on the truth.

"Fantastic!" Bethany beamed from ear to ear. "Manos could ask him to sing a few songs, early evening, to the pre-dinner crowd, and see how it goes."

"Can't see any problem with that." Diana looked pleased.

"Unless of course..." Bethany paused.

"What? Unless what?"

"I suppose there's always the chance Aeron will refuse."

"Ah, right. Like you said, he could be depressed."

"Hmm."

"Well, if there's a chance he won't do it maybe I shouldn't bother. You know how touchy Manos can be sometimes." She giggled.

He'd been furious the other day when her ex phoned – yet again! – and she refused to speak to him. In the end she'd picked up the phone and given him an earful. After all, the long and considerate explanations had done no good.

"Aw, go on, Di! Just mention it to Manos and let's see how it goes."

* * *

The row on the beach between Jason and Katarina ran around the village like wildfire. When Jason walked through Hora men openly smirked at him, while the women threw him vicious glances. In the *kafeneion* the fight had been discussed at length. Many men admitted it gave them pleasure to see Jason brought down a peg or two.

Jason was glad Nikos had already left for his National Service. He wouldn't have liked to face the young man, who was very close to his cousin Katarina.

Jason thought he understood the men's reaction. It was stupid to openly argue with a girl. But he couldn't fathom the women. Why were they so hostile?

He soon found out.

A few minutes after returning to the Paradise Spiros arrived, dragging a reluctant Katarina, by the arm, into the hotel's reception area.

Vasilis, taking in the scene, immediately ushered them into their private quarters and summoned Jason.

"So, you've got her pregnant and now you won't marry her," Spiros shouted, waving a fist in Jason's face. "Well, we'll see about that!" Never mind that he loathed the boy. He would not have his daughter disgraced.

Jason was astounded, "Pregnant! If she's pregnant, it's not my child. I've never touched her!"

"Everyone says you've touched her and she's pregnant," Spiros repeated. He lunged at Jason and started shaking him by the shoulders. Jason was too shocked to resist.

This was too much for Vasilis and he grabbed the man's arms saying, "Come on, Spiro, let's talk about this in a civilized way. My boy won't see Katarina have a baby on her own. He'll marry her. Calm down, it happens!"

A furious Jason found his voice. "I'm not going to marry her. It's not my baby!"

The three men continued to bicker, and Spiros to threaten, until the ignored Katarina could stand it no longer.

"Will no one listen to me?" she screeched at the top of her lungs. "I'm not pregnant! I'm not pregnant! I. Am. Not.

Pregnant!" She crumpled onto the nearest chair, with a paroxysm of weeping, just as Margarita arrived on the scene.

"What on earth is all this about?" she asked, speaking to the men as if they were naughty children. Spiros was first to find his tongue and flung the words at her, "Your son has got my Katarina pregnant and now he's saying he won't marry her!"

"But didn't I just hear Katarina shouting that she's not pregnant?" She turned to the stricken girl. "Have you lost the baby, Katarina?"

Katarina wanted to scream. *Oh, God, it's all too much!*

Gabriella arrived and spoke to the guardians.

Katarina jumped up in frustration and anger, "I'm not pregnant! I never was pregnant!" Her voice was loud and exasperated. "I have never slept with Jason! I have never slept with anyone! I am a good girl!" By now she was flushed with fury. "Have you all got that now?" They were idiots, the lot of them, and people in the village had nothing better to do than make up lies about innocent people!

Father, father, mother and the accused, were stopped in their tracks by the obvious honesty of the girl's words.

The mother took the girl by the hand and said, "Sit down, Katarina. Spiro, some Metaxa I think."

Seated at a small round table Spiros took a small fortifying sip of brandy. "Everyone is saying that Katarina is pregnant," he explained.

Jason's father interjected. "I'd like to know why they started this silly talk in the first place."

"Who knows?" Katarina was not willing to disclose their relationship. "The only thing I can think is that Jason was messing around on the beach the other day and tried to kiss me, and I got very angry and shouted at him."

"I was only teasing." Jason backed her up immediately. "But I went too far and really upset her." Then he added, "Sorry, Katarina."

"I hate you," the girl hissed at him. "And I wouldn't go out with you if you were the last boy in the world!"

Spiros was standing now. "You stay away from my daughter, do you hear me?"

"I hear you, sir," said Jason politely, relief flooding his every fibre as the man led away the glowering Katarina.

Vasilis watched until the door closed behind them before he spoke. "Don't go bringing disgrace to this family," he warned darkly.

Jason's gaze slipped to the floor in humiliation. "No, Baba," he muttered. He roused himself and checked his watch. "Please excuse me," he said politely. "I need to organize lunch."

Jason shuddered as he made his way to the kitchen. His thoughts had turned from his father to Katarina. When Spiros said Katarina was pregnant it was like a body blow.

He took a moment to analyse his gut reaction.

He didn't like what he discovered: jealousy!

Chapter 38

The caique rocked gently and Takis flicked his cigarette butt at the small passing wave. The nets had been set and they had only to wait for some unsuspecting fish to swim in. It was not yet dawn and in the darkness he sensed, rather than saw, his father's stare.

In the couple of weeks since Panos' death he had often caught his father watching him. Takis wondered if he guessed the truth. He was itching to confess. To brag. He knew his father would be proud of him. But unless his father broached the subject he planned to keep quiet.

He felt no remorse at taking a life. The boy should never have been born. Michalis should have known better than to marry one of the enemy and bring her here to upset the community.

Strangely, though, the community seemed saddened by the boy's death. At the *kafeneion* even the most outspoken against foreigners had expressed regret for the boy's passing. Many had spoken sympathetic words for the pain of Michalis and Ingrid. Takis had been shocked by the obvious sincerity of their words. And they were cool with him. So cool that he stopped going there. His father continued to go, though.

As Petros sat in the boat, and under cover of darkness watched his son, he wondered. He wondered why Takis had shown no remorse whatsoever at killing Panos. It was almost as if he was glad of it. He had begun to be suspicious of what had happened that day on the road.

At the *kafeneion*, when his lifelong friends told him what he should have said to Takis about fast driving that may have prevented the tragedy, he listened hard and nodded solemnly. He genuinely agreed with them. How he wished he had taken Michalis' side that day in Hora when he asked Takis, very politely, to please drive more slowly up the lane.

But no, he had sided with his son.

Petros' regret was fathomless.

When his closest friends expressed surprise that he had not visited the grieving couple he knew they were right. He must do it. He asked Takis to go with him but the boy refused point-blank, saying they wouldn't want to see him. So he went alone – though his wife had volunteered to accompany him.

It was one of the hardest things he had ever done in his life, he told his wife later. It was something he would remember for the rest of his days. Michalis and Ingrid sat hollow-eyed and mute as he spoke a few words of condolence. The words sounded empty, even to his own ears. Their pain was a knife in his soul and his speech stopped short.

After gazing at the ground for a few long moments he slowly shook his head. "I am so very, very sorry," he said again. His throat felt strangled with emotion. He knew he was doing the couple no good. With leaden feet he turned to leave.

"Thank you for coming, Petro." Ingrid spoke up clearly. "We appreciate it more than you can know."

His head jerked back towards her and their eyes locked. The tormented woman nodded to reaffirm her words.

He told his wife that he felt they wanted Takis to go and see them too. He had told this to his son, but he would not go. He was adamant that it would only make things worse.

"What could be worse?" Petros sadly asked his wife when they were alone.

A light breeze rattled the halyards and drew father and son back from their private thoughts.

"I'll get some hot coffee, Baba." Takis stood and stretched his cramped limbs, reaching for the flask.

"I don't want coffee." Suddenly Petros could not hold his tongue. "I want the truth!" The need to know was suddenly stronger than the need to protect Takis.

"The truth about what, Baba?" Takis, on the brink of revealing his heroic act, wanted to draw out his moment of glory.

"Panos!" Petros could say no more. He held his breath and

prayed his suspicions were unfounded.

Takis stood to attention as if he was a soldier. "I avenged your father; my grandfather." His father heard the pride in his son's voice, and as the bitter bile of revulsion rose in his throat he dashed to vomit over the side of the boat.

Takis looked puzzled. Why had his father done that? Why didn't he congratulate him for his brave action?

He watched as his father turned back from the rail wiping his chin with the back of his hand. Petros tried to stand, but his legs were weak with shock. Disgust, shame, and anger jumbled together in his mind like assorted fish shaken in a basket. Then a question began to formulate.

"When Panos chased the ball across the road you did try to stop, didn't you? It was an accident wasn't it?" Once more he held his breath and prayed. *Blessed Virgin, please let it have been an accident. Please don't let my only son be as lost to me as those poor wretches have had theirs taken from them.*

Takis still stood to attention as if on a parade ground. "*Accident?*" Takis shook his head. "I just told you that I have avenged the murder of your father; my grandfather." He sounded petulant.

The dawn was breaking and Petros could see the gleam of madness in his son's eyes. A shudder of repugnance tore through him. "You call driving into an innocent child an execution?"

"Yes, Baba, I do." Takis was emphatic. "A German killed one of our family and I have avenged that death."

"Do you know what you are saying?" Petros peered at his son as if seeing him for the first time.

"What do you mean?" Why wasn't his father congratulating him?

"Taki, I am asking you if you killed Panos *deliberately*." He still didn't want to believe it.

"Yes, Baba, how many times do you want me to say it? Shall I spell it out for you?"

Petros nodded. He needed to know exactly what had happened and then he would know what to do.

"Very well," said Takis. Bristling with pride he took a deep preparatory breath. "I was driving home from the *kafeneion* feeling very angry about all these foreigners messing up our lives. I thought of some things you said about the damage to the island by tourism, and before that by other invaders, like the Germans." He paused to make his point. His father said nothing, but he kept a steady gaze on him.

"Anyway, as luck would have it, when I drove up the lane Panos was playing on the grass verge, and when his ball rolled across the road he chased after it. So I speeded up and drove straight at him." He smiled at the memory. "And as I drove at him I shouted, 'This is for my grandfather!' And then at the last minute I slammed on my brakes and turned the wheel away so it would look like an accident." He smirked at his own cunning.

"Dear God, I raised a murderer." Petros slumped forwards, face in his hands.

"But, Baba, aren't you going to congratulate me?" Takis was incredulous. Where was the praise due to him?

"Congratulate you?" The words tore out of Petros' throat.

"Yes, congratulate me for avenging our family!" Takis yelled back.

"You murdered a poor innocent boy." His breath was ragged with shock and horror. "Left a mother and father childless and broken. And you expect my congratulations?" He shook his head in bewilderment.

"It was an execution," Takis screamed. "Why aren't you listening to me?" He lunged at his father and grabbed the front of his jersey.

As the sun rose over the horizon its rays threw a golden light into the face of Petros. "Am I to be your next victim, Taki?" His lip curled with contempt.

"No, of course not." Takis dropped his hands away from his

father as if scalded.

Petros saw the little gutting knife glint in the dawn rays. He looked at it thoughtfully.

* * *

"Baba, I'm thinking of making some changes to the lunch menu, do you have any suggestions?" Jason stood impassive as his father's bushy grey brows shot up in astonishment.

"Uh, well," Vasilis began, trying to formulate an answer to the totally unexpected question. He cleared his throat and tried to be businesslike. "I'll put together some ideas." He needed time to think. It had been years since Jason had consulted him on dishes. On anything.

"Thank you, Baba. I would be very grateful for a fresh eye on that." Jason smiled kindly and walked away.

Vasilis swivelled his head to stare thoughtfully at his retreating son. There was something very different about him. For the last couple of weeks Jason had been quiet around the place. And respectful towards him in a way he had not been since before he left the University of Athens to come back to Korkyra. Vasilis presumed it had something to do with the ruckus with Katarina and her family.

Finally, his son had been publicly humiliated.

It had punctured his inflated ego.

Vasilis did not like it that Jason was being gossiped about by the locals but the change in him was welcome.

His hand reached automatically towards the chill cabinet. Then he pulled back. "I don't need beer, I need to think of the menu," he softly told himself. He lifted his shoulders and took a deep breath. He would go and discuss it with Margarita. Standing tall, he strode into the kitchen.

Since the encounter with the angel Gabriella Jason had been doing some soul-searching. Trying to build up an image of his life so far he had begun by picturing the small boy he had been, and then, year by year, he had tried examining his relationship with his parents, especially his father.

It had thrown up some amazing insights.

He remembered, for instance, that his father had been his hero: strong, proud and successful. Starting the hotel had been the pinnacle. At that point Jason had seen his father as Superman.

In the little fishing village, which was transforming into a tourist resort, his father was the undisputed king. Jason thought he was well named: Vasilis meaning king. Then Jason fast-forwarded his memories a few years and he was at university and his father was drowning in responsibilities. Instead of helping his father out with some clever suggestions Jason had come home like a rescuer riding in on a huge white horse. Jason's face burned with shame when he remembered how he had dethroned the king and assumed power himself.

At the time he had considered it his right. If he was to give up his own dream of becoming an archaeologist then he must head up the business. He must be king in place of his father.

He had considered his change of path as a sacrifice. He had been lofty and arrogant. But in hindsight, he saw that he had actually been weary of studying, and took up the practical duties of running the hotel with barely a backward glance at his course.

He saw clearly that the better way would have been to support his father and become his right-hand man. *It was highhanded. I took over the business and the responsibility of the family. I was wrong!* Now he realized that this greed for power must have been one of the things the angel Gabriella had accused him of. *She was right.*

He knew, too, that he had made a lot of money since he took over, and presumed that was also part of her accusation. But he had shared everything with his parents, they all had benefitted, so he perhaps the greed for power was his biggest wrong. The greatest poison to his soul.

He didn't really know.

Life was not clear cut so maybe he never would.

What he did know, though, was that he desperately wanted to put things right between his father and himself. He had already started trying to do that.

His angel whispered into his ear.

"Oh!" His mouth gaped with surprise. Something had just occurred to him. He was probably hurting his suppliers by always demanding they sell their goods and services to him at the lowest possible rates.

He had told himself that was sound business. That by paying the least he could keep his own prices down and attract more customers.

But now, for some reason, he felt ashamed of what he had done. The locals, like him, needed to earn enough money over the summer to get through the winter.

His angel whispered again.

He winced thinking about the man who sold him tomatoes. He had three small children as well as a wife to feed, and yet, he had paid him less this year than last for his produce.

And he wasn't the only supplier he had done that to.

His conscience was now shouting loud and clear.

It shouted the names Takis and Petros above the other names of suppliers. He knew that he had spoken the truth to them when he said they would soon find other buyers for their catch. But to switch part-way through the season like that was... well... well it was bad.

His guardian angel was not allowed to tell him just how bad it really was. How it had influenced Takis into taking the life of an innocent boy.

"I *was* being greedy," he murmured. Guilt lay like a heavy cloak on his shoulders.

What could he do to turn things around?

"I know!" As the idea struck him he felt instinctively that it was the right thing to do.

"I'm going to sit down with my father and talk the whole thing through. There must be a way to be fair to our suppliers and customers alike and still make enough profit for a healthy business." And that, he saw, would be another way to draw his father back into his rightful place in running the hotel.

He felt lighter in heart as he began to unpick the whole supply issue and rethink things. *I hope angel Gabriella will be pleased with me.*

Chapter 39

Petros, though barely sixty, walked like a bowed old man to open the front door which was being hammered on. Two policemen stood stiff and officious on his doorstep. "Please come in, officers," he said politely, leading the way into the small basic family living room. He sank into a sagging old armchair as if his legs would not bear his weight.

The policemen declined to sit. "We have come for Takis. We need to interview him again," one of the men spoke up firmly.

"I don't know where he is." Petros spoke in a flat quiet voice.

"What do you mean by that?" The policeman's tone was sharp. "When did you last see him?"

"Three days ago." He looked the man straight in the eye.

"Three days? You know he is only out on bail and not supposed to go anywhere. Where is he?"

"I told you, I don't know where he is." Petros shook his head.

"In that case, I would like you to come with us now to the station."

Petros pulled himself up by the arms of the chair. "Of course. Let's go."

His wife was coming into the room with a tray of iced coffees for their visitors, and stood, dumfounded, as her husband walked out to the waiting police car.

"Don't worry, I'll see you later," Petros called over his shoulder. The policemen neither confirmed nor denied this.

Petros made a statement to the police that he had last seen Takis just after sunrise a few days before. They hadn't caught any fish and Takis had walked off saying he would see his father later.

Petros confirmed that his son had seemed upset. He had been very quiet and withdrawn since the accident. Petros said, when pressed, that he did not think his son planned to kill himself. But he did agree that, under the circumstances, suicide was a possibility.

The same policeman who had questioned Takis questioned

Petros. He remarked later that the father was as unnaturally cool as the son. "What a family," he said, wrinkling his nose with contempt.

The police let Petros leave the station after signing his statement. What, after all, could they hold the man for? Certainly not for acting indifferent in the face of his son's disappearance. But they would be watching him. Just as they would be keeping an eye out for Takis.

It remained to be seen if Takis would turn up or not. Perhaps he had just gone to stay with friends for a while, though he was supposed to let the police know about that.

But if he had run away, someone would surely have seen him.

And if he had killed himself? Well, a body would turn up sooner or later.

* * *

Off-shore the prestigious yacht, its gleaming white hull held aft and stern by anchors on thick chains, gently bucked on dark blue waves. Hired by celebrity Jake Reynolds, the great man had declared himself "bored of eating on board". The play on words could have been a line from one of his many, ever-popular, songs.

His Greek crew, and entourage, were there to keep the famous American singer happy. If Jake was happy they were happy, as they had told him often over the previous fortnight. He was notoriously temperamental. But so far things had gone quite smoothly.

Quickly the team had snapped into action to organize a good night ashore. They wouldn't stay late, though. Keen to visit as many islands as possible, Jake wanted to move on to another one tomorrow.

Just before sunset Jake got into the yacht's small motorboat.

Most of the party were already ashore. "Come on, Kim, honey." He held out a chivalrous hand to his beautiful blonde girlfriend, appreciatively ogling her long tanned legs as she stepped gracefully into the boat and sat down beside him.

Her skimpy yellow silk dress struck a cheerful counterpoint to his white jeans and T-shirt. But Jake's low-key outfit only accentuated his dark, chiselled good looks, and the aura of his star quality was unmissable. Once ashore it wouldn't be long before everyone knew who he was. Another reason for keeping the visit short, and, hopefully, sweet, as he whispered into his companion's ear. She giggled obligingly.

Kim liked to act a little simple.

Her brain was super sharp.

She played the game. She intended to make this man her husband before too long. So far he had eluded marriage but she was confident she could snag him.

Skippered by an experienced crew member the small craft zipped towards the jetty at the old harbour. Jake's personal assistant was waiting with a sleek hire car brought down from Corfu Town. "Right, Jake," he said, rubbing his hands together eagerly. "All organized."

* * *

Aeron Lehman paced the long shared balcony, ignoring the much-loved view. "What am I going to do?" he muttered over and over.

Manos had asked him to bring his guitar and sing a few songs for the early crowd. It seemed simple to Manos. "Try tonight and we see what happens." His boss had smiled encouragingly at him.

But something had held him back. "Can I think about it?" he hedged.

"Okay." Manos had shrugged his shoulders high. "You do

not want, you do not do." Diana had warned him not to put the pressure on.

"But I hear you are very good!"

"Who told you that?" He looked suspicious.

"Spiros at the minimarket." At Diana's suggestion he had asked him. "He hear you sing at wedding."

Aeron nodded. He remembered that. "Look, man, if I do it I'll be in by six. If not, I'll come at my usual time."

"Okay, Aeron." Manos nodded. "How you like."

Aeron reached the end of the balcony wall and stopped to peer thoughtfully over at the green hills.

Generally, he was feeling quite upbeat these days and enjoying the last of the summer. He knew that when he got back to New York things wouldn't be plain sailing, but he was determined to make things as simple for his kids as possible. He had promised himself that he would rise to the challenges as they came up.

"Well, here's a challenge." He laughed derisively. He just didn't know what to do about it. Take it on board or duck out? He felt foolish. What was wrong with him? He should have been jumping at this chance. Hadn't he told Bethany it was his dream to perform?

He sighed.

His dream was over, so why put himself up there again? Besides, he hadn't performed in public for ages.

No nearer to making a decision he began to pace again.

He faltered in his tracks and looked up at the sky. The sun was an orange ball heading for the horizon. He didn't have long to make his mind up. "Oh, heck, what will I do?"

"Do it," said his guardian angel.

"Do not do it," shouted his stalker demon. "You will totally mess up!"

As the demon shrieked with laughter the angel rolled his eyes. These demons always went over the top with their negativity.

"What about your new song?" the angel cajoled. "Would it not be great to sing that to an audience?"

Aeron liked the sound of that. He paused to consider it seriously.

"It's a load of rubbish," the demon yelled. "People will boo you. You will be humiliated," it snickered.

Aeron shivered involuntarily. *Just imagine being heckled in front of a full bar. Better leave it.*

* * *

Jake Reynolds's party had taken up the three best tables at the Candy Bar.

"Good evening, Mr Reynolds. I am Manos and I own this bar. I like to give you champagne from me." Manos ducked his dark head as if addressing royalty.

Jake thanked the man graciously. They ordered bottles of spirits and mixers to go with this.

Diana ferried trays back and forth bringing bowls of popcorn, nuts and crisps for each table. "Who is he?" she whispered to Manos.

"He is Jake Reynolds a big American singer." Manos looked pleased. "I see on television this afternoon that he is in Corfu."

"Ooh!" Diana looked suitably impressed. "Never heard of him, though," she said happily. She'd had a proper talk on the phone with her mother today – who admitted she'd encouraged her ex to keep phoning, in the hope of getting her home. Her mum accepted she had to live her life, and promised to sort it out with her ex.

"He has many hit records in America."

"Really?"

"Really." Manos looked at his watch. Gone six. "No Aeron." He shook his head. "He should be here to sing for this star."

Diana tutted. "Mano, get real." Her top-knot bounced as she

shook her head. "Even if Aeron had sung in front of this Jake what's-his-name what difference would it have made?"

Manos wagged his finger. "You never know." He was a great believer in fate. "What a pity Aeron he miss his chance."

Diana looked up and grinned. "Ha! Maybe not." Manos spun round. Aeron had just walked in and pulled up a barstool in front of Jake's table. The DJ pulled the plug on the record. The chatter petered out.

"Hi, everyone, as some of you know, I'm Aeron." Though his heart was hammering his smile was wide as he looked around the room. "Just want to sing you a few songs to get you in the mood for a good dinner." He ran his plectrum in a smooth arc over the strings of his guitar.

"Right on, man," Jake called out, looking pleased. The last member of his party stopped speaking and fixed his eyes on Aeron for Jake's sake.

Aeron started with an upbeat cover of a classic. An enthusiastic Jake led the clap-along. The champagne had loosened him up, but mostly he loved live music; loved to perform. Also, he knew talent when he saw it. This man, a fellow-American no less, had something which he, the seasoned star, could instantly appreciate.

Warming to the crowd Aeron swung straight into another classic. The crowd, still led by Jake, lapped it up.

An elated Aeron was clearly enjoying every minute. Diana had walked behind the seating section to watch alongside Manos. She just wished Bethany was here to see this. Then, as if her wish was granted, Bethany appeared from nowhere and together the two friends clapped and cheered as the song ended.

"Now I'd like to change the pace a little and play you one of my own songs which I wrote... only a few weeks ago," Aeron called out. After the deep talk with Bethany when he discovered his life's problem, he had poured his heart and soul into the writing of this song. "I hope you get it." He strummed the opening bars to a slow melody and the crowd was hushed.

The song spoke of broken dreams, and how you sometimes didn't even know you had given up on them. It urged the listener to do everything they could to keep their dreams alive.

Bethany knew Aeron was singing about himself. She found the song hauntingly beautiful. It was also inspirational. *You hear that and you want to make your dreams come true.* She reaffirmed her new dream of writing a bestseller. She wondered what the big man, Jake Reynolds, thought. (Word had got around.) When the last poignant notes died away Jake stood up and whistled loudly along with all the other cheers. Around the bar applauding people got to their feet.

"Seemed to like it then." Bethany grinned at Diana and Manos. Aeron looked so happy, so right doing this. She sent up a little prayer that his own dream would come true, somehow.

On a roll, Aeron upped the tempo for two more of his own songs, then bade them all goodnight.

As the DJ started up the deck again Jake's personal assistant approached Aeron. He shepherded him over to Jake who stood and shook him warmly by the hand – to the amazement of his party, especially his girlfriend, Kim. It was unprecedented for Jake to be so friendly with a no-name. Words were exchanged, business cards were pressed into Aeron's hands, and the assistant scribbled down a few details in a little notebook.

Jake pumped Aeron's hand again before making a regal exit. He signed a few autographs, shook a few hands, including Manos', and soundly kissed the cheek of the stunned Diana before sweeping off to the Paradise Hotel for dinner.

"Phew, star treatment or what?" Bethany congratulated Aeron on his performance. "I noticed his assistant passing business cards. Did they want something from you?" She held her breath and hoped.

"You'll never guess." Aeron's pale blue eyes sparkled with excitement as he shook his blonde mop of hair in disbelief. "Tell you later when I've had a chance to think about it." Bethany had never seen Aeron so upbeat. Nor so handsome.

"Gotta get on with some real work now," he quipped, "or Manos will sack me." He winked at her, walked behind the bar and started pulling pints for thirsty punters.

* * *

"I tell you this happen." Manos grinned at Diana.

"You did, Mano." Diana nodded, grinning back at him.

"Drinks all round." Manos looked at Aeron. "What will you have? Bethany? Diana?"

It was late and with the crowd gone Aeron had finally shared his good news. Jake Reynolds wanted to record the three original songs he'd sung tonight. But more than that, he wanted Aeron to work with him in New York on his new album. Aeron had answered that he had plenty more material where that came from.

"It's a dream come true." Aeron looked bemused, trying to digest the wonderful new turn his life had taken.

Bethany looked up into his eyes and it was her turn to wink.

He nodded thoughtfully. "Can't wait to tell the kids." He pulled his face into a huge smiley grin.

He hoped they would be proud of him.

But he wouldn't think about that now.

Chapter 40

Bethany couldn't believe how quiet the resort had become overnight. Just over a week ago, a few days before the end of August, the visiting Greeks had left for home in an exodus – which was apparently their custom. Many had been born in Korkyra or Hora, then migrated to Athens – like millions of others.

Jason said Athens was like a ghost town from the start of August when people flocked back to their birthplaces. Now the city would be lively again. She wanted to go and experience the buzz of Athens for herself. Diana had mentioned she fancied going there too.

Then, last night, Diana said that Manos had started making noises about closing up the Candy Bar. It depended on whether enough tourists decided to make last minute bookings hoping for a bit more sunshine before a long winter. In that case he would stay open. But they were in a "wait and see" stage at present. Aeron had already stopped working at the bar and was having a little holiday before he went home. But he still helped Manos out if the bar got a bit crowded.

On the island the days were already much shorter, and the evenings chilly enough for her to wear a light jacket when coming back from a night out. But Bethany knew it was still much warmer than in Wales.

Going to the Paradise to meet Clare and top up her tan Bethany passed a fig tree and noticed it had shed most of its leaves. They lay in a crunchy pale brown heap around its trunk, being tossed and scattered in a stiff breeze. It seemed to shout of autumn.

At the hotel the talk centred on the weather forecast. Jason had been watching it on television. "You know how usually there is rain over a wide area?" Bethany and Clare nodded. "Well, the weatherman said that by early afternoon a big cloud will sit right over Corfu, and nowhere else." He held an imaginary fat cloud in his hands over a beer mat to demonstrate this.

"And we need that rain, don't we." Clare's green eyes widened. "Sure, it hasn't rained one drop since early May."

"True," he admitted. "Our well is almost empty." He nervously drummed his fingers on the bar. "It feeds the showers and taps in the hotel and they're down to a trickle. So I'm praying the forecast is right or I'm going to have to ship in some water."

Jason explained that a small boat brought it over from the mainland and it was pumped into the hotel's water tank. "The load is so heavy that the boat is very low in the water so he only makes the journey when the sea is completely calm."

"Ah. That explains it!" Bethany nodded her head. "I saw it last year and I worried it was sinking."

"Yes, that's the one," Jason said.

Feeling decadent Bethany ordered a gin and tonic and went to sit beside the pool. Watching the sun glint on the turquoise water she breathed a deep sigh of satisfaction. What a summer it had turned into. And it wasn't quite over yet.

Clare came to sit down. "I'll take a quick break as there aren't many customers here." Jason brought orange juice complete with cocktail stick threaded with the maraschino cherries he knew she loved. She smiled her thanks. "He's so nice," she murmured.

"So I see." Bethany savoured her drink. "So, do you think you'll stay here with him for the winter?"

"He's talking about that. I could have a room at the hotel, of course. Sure, there will be plenty spare ones." She paused thoughtfully. "But I haven't decided what I want to do."

"But you love him, though?"

"Sure, of course I love him. But there's more to a relationship than just love, isn't there?"

"Oh, yes, I know exactly what you mean." Thinking about a

certain American, Bethany gave a small laugh.

Clare suddenly thought about Aeron too. She had her suspicions, never confirmed, that Bethany was smitten. *Hmm.* She asked a loaded question. "Are you going back to Plan A: New York for the winter?"

Bethany looked cagey. "Not sure."

Clare dropped the subject.

Chapter 41

By two o'clock that afternoon Aeron stood on his balcony and watched the storm unfolding. An hour ago menacing clouds had bunched together, variously hued from pearl to charcoal grey. The wind, though, sported with them, and drove them apart at every opportunity so that the sun glanced through. But now the clouds triumphed, overpowering the horizon with a quick dark assault. No sooner had they spread themselves broad and flat to the sea than they rose puffed up with their own importance and began pelting down rain.

Aeron was in awe of the spectacle. When the rain angled in heavy rods through the doorway of his apartment he scuttled inside, slid the doors closed, and watched through the glass as the storm unfolded. He thought about his kids and how much they would enjoy this sight.

He was leaving for New York at the weekend.

He had mixed feelings about that.

He was looking forward to seeing the kids. But, he was no longer welcome in his own home. He would stay in a small hotel not far from them until he could sort out an apartment for himself. He knew it wouldn't be an easy time.

Neon white veins of lightening sparked and crackled through the ominous sky and grabbed his attention back. White flashes rendered patches of sky transparent for a few seconds. Then deafening thunder rolled, crashed, and resounded from every available nook and cranny including Aeron's eardrums. It reminded him of a couple of rock concerts he'd been to where the band could afford to pull out all the stops. That reminded him of Jake Reynolds. He thought his gigs would be very grand indeed.

He still could hardly believe his luck. Back home to work with a mega rock star. The two New Yorkers had met thousands of miles from the Big Apple. How amazing was that! He felt a tingle of the excitement of finally following his dream. It had come about in such an unexpected way.

And it was all thanks to Bethany.

Diana had told him it was Bethany's idea to get Manos to ask him to perform at the Candy Bar.

He would miss Bethany.

"Oh, Bethany..."

* * *

The storm had passed, and it was now a sunny afternoon, but Petros sat on with his wife and daughter in front of the television. Though the set was blaring he did not hear it. He was a broken man.

He had the murder of a small innocent boy on his conscience. He had lost his own son. There seemed to be no sweetness left in his life. He did not even go to the *kafeneion* to see his friends, which would have brought him, at least, a little consolation. Instead he sat at home night after night with his misery.

He had told his wife what Takis had done. To protect their daughter she would not be told but she already guessed the truth anyway.

It had not yet dawned on Petros that home was more peaceful than it had been for years. Actually, since Takis came home from the army. But his daughter realized. She had always been a little afraid of him. Ten years younger than Takis, she also felt he had frightened off anyone who may have been interested in marrying her.

There was someone she liked. He had smiled at her the last time she passed him in the street in Hora. She now felt more hopeful that she would finally find some real happiness in her life.

The police had been to the house again today. They turned up each week at different times to find out if Takis had been in touch. It unsettled the family when this happened.

Petros felt his wife looking at him. "What is it?" he asked.

"I just wonder when Takis will contact us and let us know how he is."

He turned and looked at her for a long moment. "Do you really want to see him again after what he did?"

"How can you say that? He is my son, no matter what, and I just want to know that he is all right."

"I don't expect him to be in touch." He spoke decisively. It was time she stopped hoping for that.

"How can you be so sure?" She studied his face looking for clues. Her son left home to fish with his father. He took no possessions with him. To her knowledge he didn't have much money on him either. She had tried not to think it but now she had to ask. "Did something happen on the boat?" As she started to cry Petros looked stricken.

* * *

As the wind gathered strength and drove the boiling grey soup of clouds back over the sea the fresh sunshine drew Bethany out of the house. Now the season was coming to an end its rays seemed all the more precious. Passing Korkyra Minimarket, Hygeia bounded from her kennel. Bethany would miss the dog. She would soon be missing all her friends. She would miss Korkyra. She would miss Aeron.

His name separated itself from her other friends.

She would greatly miss Aeron...

She had suppressed her feelings for him since that day he was so upset. They had remained friends only.

Just good friends.

Aeron was on the path to his dreams now and Bethany was thrilled for him. And once he got back to New York he would soon forget all about the people he had shared this summer with. But she would remember him. Always.

"Bethany!"

She turned and there he was. Her stomach flipped with pleasure. "Oh, Aeron! Hiya. I was just thinking about you."

Oops, too much information.

"Good things I hope," he said rolling his eyes and pulling his lips into a smiley.

"What else?" Her tone was deliberately casual as she buttoned down her feelings.

"Going for a stroll, are you? Mind if I join you two girls?" He reached down and stroked Hygeia's head. It was a first for him. The dog gave a short bark, kicked with back legs and lifted front paws in a little happy leap.

"Hygeia seems fine with it, so who am I to argue?" They smiled at each other, falling into step while the dog nosed along the bushes at the roadside. They headed for the old harbour. Bethany broke the easy silence. "I was thinking about you working with Jake Reynolds in New York and how amazing that will be."

"Can't wait. I'm just so thrilled." He glanced sideways at her and grinned boyishly.

"Course you are, me too." She grinned back. Then her mouth dropped open as they rounded the corner. "Look, at that!" Bethany pointed to the road.

They both stopped in their tracks hardly able to believe their eyes. A huge coloured arc bent towards them from the left, always a majestic sight, but there, bouncing off the glistening road, was the very end of the rainbow. "Awesome!" breathed Aeron.

"I've never seen the end of a rainbow!" Bethany shook her head in amazement at the phenomenon. They laughed in delight.

"Where's the crock of gold?" Aeron joked.

Hygeia had been nosing in a bush close by and now walked onto the road. As she wandered through the two-foot wide striped base of the rainbow the deflected rays ran in a wash of pale green down one flank and purple down the other. The dog moved on, oblivious.

"Just have to do it," muttered Bethany, stepping right into the centre of light. With hands raised, head tipped back, she slowly revolved allowing the variegated colours to shower over her. "Special, special, special!" she intoned.

"It is," Aeron agreed. *And so are you!*

Bethany stood still and looked hard at the red, yellow and blue light spilling over her arms. She grinned in fascination while committing the precious moment to memory. Reluctantly, she moved forwards. "Your turn," she told him. "Be quick, it could vanish any second."

Obediently Aeron stepped into the rainbow. Looking down he marvelled at his white T-shirt now stained with multicoloured vertical bands.

"Wish I had camera!" Bethany clapped her hands with child-like glee. "It's a-*may*-zing!"

Aaron nodded. *You're amazing!*

He walked out of the colour shower and together they watched the rainbow begin to fade. In seconds the whole magical bow was gone and steam began to rise gently from the road surface, as rainwater evaporated in the hot sunshine.

As Bethany laughed again Aaron turned away from the smiling mouth he was longing to kiss.

Bethany felt the electricity between them but struggled to ignore it, as always.

They reached the harbour, where a few caiques bucked wildly in the foaming midnight blue waters. On the deserted apron of beach Hygeia nosed around a little heap of glistening brown seaweed. Bethany kicked at the shingle with the toe of her sandal. Beside her Aeron suddenly felt jittery. He knew it was time to speak up.

"Bethany, I wanted to thank you," he began.

"Thank me, for what?"

"For so many things, you have no idea." Gathering his thoughts he reached down and picked up a pebble. "You saved my life, for one thing." He glanced sideways at her.

"Bit dramatic, Aeron. Didn't really."

"But you did," he insisted. He overarm bowled the pebble into the sea. "You and angel Gabriella." Bethany had told him about the girl. He had believed her. "Look, I know my words are inadequate, but they are sincere." Gaining in courage, he faced her.

"Aeron—"

"No, please, let me finish. I would be so grateful if you would."

"Course. Sorry." She giggled as she clamped a penitent hand over her mouth.

This made him smile. He took a deep breath. "Anyway, on top of that you go and organize my *Big Break*!"

"Me?" She pretended ignorance. She wanted no thanks.

"Yes, you. Diana told me all."

"Hmm." Diana was usually so discreet.

"Don't be mad at her. Manos told me she had put in a good word for me so I tried to thank her. And, finally, she told me it was you who deserved the thanks. So, thanks. A million."

"Well, if you make a million don't forget your friends," she joked.

"I'll never forget you, Bethany." He caught hold of her hand. "Bethany...?" He swallowed hard. "Do you ever think of me with more than friendship?"

At his touch electricity ran up her arm and fizzed through her. *Oh no!* She did not know what to answer.

He gently squeezed her hand and raised it to his lips. She didn't pull away. His kiss had sent another even stronger electric pulse through her body. She held her breath. It would be so easy just to fall into his arms. "Before I go any further I need to tell you that Melanie and I are separated," he announced. "We're getting a divorce."

Bethany was stunned by the news. It changed everything...

285

He pierced her eyes with his and took a deep breath. "I love you," he said simply. *There, I've finally said it!* It was the truth he had been fighting.

Aeron and Bethany gazed at each other and suddenly there seemed to be absolute silence around them. They were deaf to the sounds of sea, wind, and gulls. Those three words, little but enormous at the same time, were all that there was.

The words created a wonderful intimacy.

They were the only two people on the planet.

He loves me. Bethany looked down at his hand and her hand. Their touch became a strong grip. In their clasp the whole of their love was there waiting, there for the taking. *And I love him. I can't deny it anymore. I don't want to deny it. I've only kept all these feelings locked up because he was married. Well, he's separated now. I'm not splitting up his marriage, it's already done.*

Bethany's hand holding Aeron's hand was the centre of the universe. Her breath caught in her throat. It would be so simple, so natural, so right, to just fall into his arms. She remembered the rainbow and felt they were standing inside the shower of colour together. *I love him.*

Bethany's smile spread slow and wide across her face and as it reached her eyes they sparkled like sapphires.

Aeron's mouth dropped. He had never seen her look so beautiful.

His look of awe sent Bethany's heartbeat racing. *God help me but I love him so much.*

The angel Gabriella invisibly winged in and advised her guardian angel.

Bethany's angel whispered urgently into her ear.

Like a beam of bright light on the situation, Bethany had sudden clarity. Aeron was only separated from his wife, he still wasn't free. Bethany had seen many couples part, then reconcile.

She shook her head sadly and sighed in deflation.

The magical rainbow-coloured walls of the bubble burst.

The noise of the surf hissing over the small stones came back to her, sounding to her ears like a fire being doused.

"Still married, though, Aeron," Bethany murmured almost to herself.

"She has a lover." Aeron had felt her weakening and pressed on at his stalker demon's insistence.

Bethany's stalker demon went into overdrive silently screeching at her to grab the man she wanted who was now solo. It summoned a rogue demon to help the fight.

Bethany listened to the tirade but only with half an ear. His wife had a lover. Hmm. But it was anybody's guess as to what would happen to the marriage in the end. Perhaps Melanie was just getting her own back on her husband for coming to Korkyra for the summer.

"Aeron," Bethany shook her head with regret. "I just can't. It's against everything I believe in."

He gave her hand another quick kiss then relinquished it with a sigh. "I understand."

"I hope you do. It's not that I don't like you, Aeron." *If you only knew how much!*

They turned away from each other and stared at the sea, lost in their own thoughts. Hygeia finished sniffing around the beach and shrubbery and sank down at their feet in the shade.

Eventually, Aeron spoke. "Can we still be friends? Can we keep in touch?" He wasn't giving up entirely.

"Course we can." Who knew what the future held, so why be miserable without reason? As a little flame of hope reignited in her heart she nudged him playfully. "I want to hear all about your New York adventure." She laughed. "It sounds so fantastic. I still can't get over what happened."

He laughed too. "I know! Who would have thought it?" He shook his head. "My dream came true, and at the Candy Bar of all places."

"The Candy Bar is great!"

"You said it!" he agreed. "And talking of imminent success, I want to hear all about your bestselling novel."

"Well, we live in hope." She did live in hope. She was working very hard at the text. She was also trying to make sure she had all the information she needed before she left the resort.

"So, are you coming to my leaving party tomorrow?" He had decided to host a late lunch on his balcony then move from there to the Candy Bar.

"Course I am. Wouldn't miss it for the world!"

Aeron looked around drinking it all in: the blue of the sky and sea, the warmth of the sunshine, and the freedom he had felt here. "I'm gonna miss all this," he said.

"Me too."

"And I'm gonna miss you, Bethany." He turned his head to look at her.

She looked him straight in the eye. "I'll miss you too," she softly admitted.

Chapter 42

Petros gently closed his front door with a sigh. His heart felt heavy. This morning he had walked into the kitchen and found his wife bowed over the sink, shoulders shaking with quiet sobs. "What the…" he had blustered, moving quickly to comfort her. But, feeling her body go rigid as he put his arms around her, his hands had dropped away. Powerless, he watched her blot the flow of tears with her apron.

When he tried to talk to her she insisted she was fine. "I just miss Takis, that's all," she said, averting her eyes and looking out of the window. When their daughter joined them the family had eaten breakfast in a stiff heavy silence which robbed them of their appetites.

Petros walked to the little bank of post boxes at the end of the road and opened his with a tiny key. Reaching into the box he pulled out a postcard. He looked at the photograph of Athens and as he turned it over his hands began to tremble. Shaking his head he read the few scribbled words:

This is just to let you know I am safe and well.
I have gone to start a new life which I think is the best thing for all the family.
Please remember me.
Your loving son
Takis

His knees buckled and before they gave way he hastily sat down with a plop on the narrow strip of wild grass beside the boxes. As he read the words again it was as if he heard his son speaking to him. Vividly he recalled the last communication he had had with him that fateful morning on the boat when Takis had bragged about taking the life of an innocent boy. His son's startling revelation had haunted him night and day since then.

Slowly, his thoughts returned to his wife. What would she make of this message? Surely she would be thrilled to know her son was still alive.

Then he thought of the gutting knife on the boat that last morning and the way it had glinted in the rising sun. He shuddered with revulsion at the memory of his momentary temptation.

But, no!

He could never have killed his son!

He remembered the day Takis was born. It had been one of the best days of Petros' life.

"How did it all come to this?" he asked the air. It was still unbelievable to him. He felt empty, drained. Then he looked at the postcard again. "Perhaps this is for the best, son," he murmured. If Takis had stayed he would have marched him to the police to turn himself in. Then everyone would have known that his son was a murderer.

His wife would have died of shame!

The thought of what the family had been spared galvanized him into action.

He scrambled to his feet and marched with renewed purpose straight up the lane to the police station. The sergeant on duty was the man who had come to his house. He looked at the postcard and nodded. Then he told Petros they already knew that Takis had left on a ferry from Corfu Town bound for the mainland. Petros closed his eyes and breathing hard tried desperately to remain calm. He wondered why they had not shared that valuable piece of information with him before now. It would have saved the whole family a lot of heartache.

But clearly the police had decided they were not worthy of that.

The policeman stared into Petros' obviously troubled face. "He is a man on the run," he said. Petros nodded and looked at the ground. He felt the guilt of his son weighing him down. "But the charge is one of manslaughter, not, for instance, *murder*." His pause was significant. "We have, of course, already notified the force in Athens to be on the lookout for him. But it's a big city, so..." Petros thought of the sprawling metropolis and felt a little relief. He dared to look up at the man and saw his eyes were kindly. "You know, of course, that he can never return to Corfu." Petros nodded again. He thanked the policeman and left the station.

As he walked back along the road and up the lane past the house of Ingrid and Michalis he said a prayer for them and for the repose of Panos' soul. He shook his head in sadness as he strode onwards.

A little further on by an olive grove he stopped to think things over. Beside him, the dry beige tubes of a stand of bamboo, nudged by a gentle breeze, leaned from their base and slid against each other with much creaking and clacking. Their sound reminded Petros nostalgically of the straining wet ropes on his caique. He had not been fishing for weeks. That would not do.

He looked across at the olive trees noticing that the lower boughs were already nubby with plumping green fruit. The black nets were still bunched around their bases. Any day now they would be spread out by the owner underneath each tree to catch the olives as, for many weeks, they ripened and were captured when they fell. Petros had his own olive grove to attend to. Another thing he could no longer neglect.

Nothing remained the same. Nature kept marching along.

He sighed deeply. He wished he could change the past but he knew it was a pointless thought. Like nature, he could only go forwards now, and try to make something good with the rest of his life.

He decided he would visit his priest for Confession. The priest would be bound by secrecy of the Sacrament so telling him about the murder held no risk. Then he would ask the priest's advice on making amends for his own part in the tragedy.

That thought eased him a little.

He looked up at the sky and saw with surprise that the sun was lowering. He noticed the banners of shell-pink floating over the blue dome of sky. He was suddenly aware of being in the presence of great beauty. It seemed to reach right into his soul and lifted his spirits.

Feeling very cheerful, he resumed his walk.

Nearing home he prayed his wife would now be able to look him in the eye again. He had missed her love and support.

As he reached his front door he made yet another decision. He would go to the *kafeneion* later and show the postcard around. He hoped that his friends would welcome him back, and that his life would return to some semblance of normality.

Chapter 43

"So, I just wanted to tell you how very sorry I am that I did that to you." A remorseful Jason looked at the steering wheel, while below the hilltop the blue band of sea stretched towards the grey, craggy mountains on Albania.

The girl looked at him. Her face was pale beneath the tan, mouth slack with incredulity. "Jason, what do you want me to say?"

"I think you should say whatever you want to."

"Really?" The numbness of shock was pierced by the open invitation. Anger sparked up and barbed her tongue. "Well, if you want to know, I think that you are just as *arrogant* and *self-centred* as I thought you were when you almost ran me over the first time I met you." Clare's green eyes flashed a cold hard anger. "You tell me that you planned to marry Katarina, then strung us both along for as long as you could get away with it!" He flinched at her words but knew it was true. "And the way I see it Katarina dumped you so you stuck with me."

"No, Clare, please believe me that's not how it was." Jason put his hand on her arm but she picked it off as if it was a speck of dirt. Jason's eyes were like saucers. He looked as if she had struck him.

She breathed in deeply and tried to stamp on her fury. Yes, she was hurt. Yes, she felt betrayed. Yes, she felt stupid, and a dozen other things besides, including pity for Katarina. To be engaged to Jason and then be dumped for another. Just like Patrick had done to her. *That's ironic.*

She looked at Jason. *To think I had a dream of a future with this man. But actually… I hardly know him.*

She turned her head to look out at the flat expanse of sea. Something had been extinguished in her and that was sad. She was unaware that she had been holding her breath until she sighed deeply. It brought a little relief. "I'm sorry for shouting," she said quietly.

"I don't blame you for shouting, Clare, I've hurt you. And I say again that I am sorry for that."

"Look, Jason." Clare suddenly felt as calm as the sea below them. "I didn't come to Korkyra looking for romance." She gave a little mirthless chuckle. "I came here for a break from my old routine. And to decide what to do next in my life." She stopped and examined her fingernails as if they held a clue on what to say next. She noticed the fuchsia pink polish. It was Dior. A gift from Jason when she mentioned she liked it after seeing it in a magazine. It was just one of the many nice things he had done for her this summer.

"I fell in love with you, Jason." She looked up into his eyes. The green flecks she loved so much were stationary, not dancing. He looked scared. "Really, I loved you." The past tense stabbed him in the heart.

"But?" he prompted softly.

"But, if I'm honest with myself, I have never fully trusted you." She sighed again. That was news to her as well as him. She had convinced herself of the opposite.

"Clare." He huffed, uncertainly. "You *can* trust me because I love you!" Clare looked at him then her eyes slid away towards the horizon. A sudden wave of homesickness washed over her. She had had enough of holiday-island. "I'll leave as soon as I can."

"What!" Jason was stunned.

"You sound surprised."

Understatement! She would have been shocked if she had known he had planned to propose. *This was supposed to have been my last summer of freedom.*

"What did you expect, Jason?"

His mouth twisted into a bitter smile. "I expected nothing." He suavely tried to cover his pain. "So," he became practical, "when will you leave?"

His practicality hurt. "Oh." She squeezed her lips together hard, trying to push down the tears. "Now you want to get rid of me!" She had just made a huge decision but she hadn't even begun to get over Jason. She thought it would take a long time.

"No, no, I didn't mean that at all." He didn't. "I just wondered how long I would still be able to see you." He reached for her hand and she didn't move away. "You see," he sighed, "I really do love you, Clare."

"Jason, I—"

"No, please just let me say this." She bit her lip and looked at him. "I love you and I wish you would stay for... *ever*." There, he'd said it. He had practically begged.

Clare squeezed his hand. "I'll always remember you."

Jason nodded, manfully swallowing the tears that threatened. She had turned him down. It really was over. As she gently took her hand away regret filled his breaking heart.

Clare was leaving. How would he get over her?

Chapter 44

Spiros and the family were sitting on the terrace of the shop eating a big late lunch. When customers arrived Katarina and Eleni cheerfully took turns to go in and serve them. Spiros rubbed his bulging tummy with satisfaction. "Anna that was an excellent meal." His wife smiled at the compliment.

The summer had turned out even better than Spiros had hoped for when he started extending the minimarket last winter. The whole family had pulled together and he was a happy man.

The ideas his wife and daughters had come up with had attracted many more customers. The biggest surprise for Spiros had been Katarina's sudden enthusiasm for business. She had led a family discussion on building a few rooms onto the back of their home to rent out next summer.

She had gone further than that and encouraged Spiros to have cards printed with their telephone number, and handed them out to their customers. Already some people had expressed interest in renting these rooms. "Right by the sea," they enthused. "And no hill to climb." They gave their contact details to Spiros who promised them a phone call as soon as the rooms were finished.

Much to his relief the minimarket had earned them enough money to repay the debt to Yiorgos in full. Spiros would come to a different arrangement with him about the construction of the new holiday studios.

He had not seen his brother since a few days after the death of the Welsh student. He knew from their parents that the newspaper's fee had enabled Yiorgos to take his family away from Korkyra for the rest of the summer. He was on the mainland somewhere. He would be back soon hoping that in his absence the hostile atmosphere in Korkyra and Hora against Pandora's would have cooled down.

In the light of Yiorgos' disgrace, Spiros had finally plucked up the courage to ask his mother why she favoured his elder brother over him. Her unexpected reply had shocked him.

"Oh, Spiro!" She laughed outright. "If only you knew!"

"Mama, I am asking because I *don't* know. But I tell you that I have been hurt by your attitude all of my life," he confessed, feeling like a small boy again, and ashamed of his weakness.

"Spiro, look at me." As he looked at the floor she gently brought his face upright with both her hands. "Did you never notice that I only praised up Yiorgos to you when he wasn't there?"

"No, Mama, I didn't notice that, but what of it?" He had no idea what she was getting at.

"Well, when you were not there I praised you to Yiorgos!"

"What!" He shook his head free of his mother's hands. "What are you saying to me?"

"Look, Spiro, I wanted both of you to do your best in life, and a little competition never hurt anyone, now did it?" His mother's eyes, so dark like his, were twinkling. Spiros shook his head at her and put one hand on his forehead. "Oh, Mama!" He wanted to be angry with her but he could not. Instead he saw the funny side and started to chuckle, softly at first, but this soon grew into huge guffaws which his mother joined in with. He was so relieved to hear her explanation. It boosted his happiness immensely.

When he thought about it later, though, it dawned on him that Yiorgos almost certainly had felt the underdog in their mother's eyes, just like him.

That realization had stopped him in his tracks.

Strangely, it saddened him deeply. Their relationship had been strained for years, but he loved his brother.

He made a decision. When Yiorgos came back he would get him together with their mother and ask her to explain what she had been doing between the two of them.

He didn't want to humiliate her. He just wanted the bad blood between him and Yiorgos over and done with.

Life was too short. He wanted a fresh start with his brother.

Now Spiros looked fondly at his daughter Katarina. Eleni was taking her turn in the shop. He would never play her against Eleni, it hurt too much.

Katarina caught him staring at her. "What, Baba? What is it?"

"I was just thinking what a good girl you are, Katarina." That episode with Jason, the misunderstanding which had got the community tongues wagging, was right behind them and never referred to. It had all been a terrible mistake and everyone knew that.

From what he had heard people were openly scathing about Jason. The big man was not so big anymore, it was said. It was discussed in the *kafeneion,* and on the street, that he had pushed his father aside, but now Vasilis was taking back control of the hotel. Secretly Spiros was glad about that. No matter which way you looked at it, Jason had humiliated his daughter, so he deserved it.

Katarina smiled widely. She was glad to see her father looking pleased with life again. "Can I get you some coffee, Baba?"

"No, Katarina, thank you. You just sit there and finish your lunch.

"Okay. Just give me five minutes and I'll make some for all of us." Impulsively she jumped up and kissed first her father and then her mother on the cheek.

"What was that for?" asked her mother looking pleased.

"Oh, just because I love you."

Katarina sank back into her wooden chair and ate the last of her salad pensively. She had got so caught up in the business that she didn't think of Jason nearly so often now; only every two minutes instead of every minute. But after loving him for all these years it was difficult to break her heart of the habit. Perhaps it would be impossible. There simply was no one else like Jason. Not in the community. Not on the island. Not in the country. Not in the world!

Chapter 44

From the first moment she saw him he stood, in her mind, up on a pedestal like a marble statue of a mythological god. But now she had seen his faults, and in the heat of contempt had thrown his imaginary image onto the ground, and seen it break into a hundred pieces. For days he disgusted her. She hated him with a white-hot anger. But when the heat of that anger cooled a little, she knew, even at the tender age of seventeen, that the flipside of this coin was… love.

How she would live in this small resort, so close to her lost love, she did not know.

But she would have to do it.

Deliberately she thrust her thoughts and feelings for Jason away and began to plan the interiors of the new rental rooms that would be built.

Chapter 45

In the shade of the palm tree there was the hint of a chill in the mid-October air and the blue of the sky had deepened perceptibly, though the sun still shone brightly. A relaxed Bethany sat with Diana and her friend Kevin at a table on the grass terrace of the Paradise.

There had been an influx of tourists late in the season which strung out until the second week of October. They were lured by cut-price packages, and many bars and tavernas stayed open and made a few extra drachmas to see them through the winter.

But locals and seasonal workers alike were greatly in need of rest, whether they wanted it or not, and they had struggled to cope with this little flurry of extra activity.

Diana and Kevin's friends had already left for England but they were going to Athens for a few weeks. Bethany was going with them. Diana was thinking about getting a bar job there. This would be news to her mother but Diana was determined to make her own decisions. Bethany, with Plan A mothballed, felt like continuing with Plan B. She had heard there were newspapers and magazines in English which she hoped to write for. She and Diana had discussed renting an apartment together.

Kevin had warned them not to bring too much luggage. His own bags were mainly filled with records. They would take a ferry to the port of Igoumenitsa, then a coach journey to Athens. Jason had already booked them some cheap hotel rooms in a part of the city called Omonia.

Bethany looked over at the sparkling sea then down at their bulging holdalls and something went "click" in her head. She and her travelling companions, dressed in jeans, T-shirts and trainers at one in the afternoon with luggage at their feet, took them into the realms of tourists on Departure Day.

One minute they lived here, worked here, belonged here, the next they were just visitors leaving. "It seems strange to be leaving," she muttered. Kevin and Diana nodded. "I'm starving," she added and they laughed.

"You're always starving," Diana observed.

"That's what Clare always said." They looked at each other.

"Shame she went home," said Diana. "She should have come with us." Before Bethany had time to comment Jason arrived with a waiter and set out their lunch.

The al fresco meal was delicious. Jason's mother, Margarita, had made Bethany a big vegetarian *moussaka* using brown lentils in place of the meat and they all had a portion. There were salads and dips and potatoes roasted in lemon juice, and a basket full of fresh sliced crusty village bread. When Jason came to sit down with them, he brought out a carafe of chilled white wine to wash it down with.

The meal was a bittersweet occasion. There was a lot of laughter and plenty of anecdotes about the long summer. But the undercurrent was a little melancholy.

When the meal was over they all piled into Jason's car – he was kindly taking them to the ferry port.

As they snaked up the steep hill Bethany looked back at the resort and a single tear escaped and trickled down her cheek.

"Hey, Beth, you're not crying are you!" Diana squeezed her arm. "You can come back," she added softly.

Bethany gave a self-conscious chuckle. "You're right, of course," she said. "But this summer is over and can never come again, if you see what I mean."

"Yeah, I do see what you mean. It was great wasn't it?"

"The best." *And I met an angel...!*

* * *

"Gabriella, look at me!" the angel chuckled.

Gabriella watched indulgently as Panos vigorously flapped his wings, vertically shot up ten feet into the air, then somersaulted rolling over and over in gleeful abandon.

As a boy for six years Panos had watched the butterflies carefully, envying not only their ability to fly but marvelling at their delicate manoeuvres. While in human form he had not remembered that he was, in fact, an angel.

Panos eventually stopped his gymnastics, and feet first, landed gently, not dissimilarly to a butterfly, next to Gabriella. Together they stood on the sand, side-by-side, gazing beyond a pearly sea at the crimson globe sinking towards the horizon.

Gabriella smiled up at him. A little taller than her, his colouring – with straight white blonde hair – was very similar to his human form, but his blue eyes were a little paler and larger. Though almost as old as time itself, he looked like a handsome young man in his early twenties.

When Panos was killed by Takis and passed to the other side he was delighted to learn he was angel Joshua, who had become human to prepare for special missions with children. If the murderous act had been averted he would have lived only a few more preparatory years. He had already begun his first mission. There was a little boy on the other side of the island living in an extremely dark situation at home, and he was helping him through it.

The last time Joshua had volunteered for human form was in 1789 when he had lived in Corfu Town until the ripe old age of ninety. Since then he had been helping old people with a variety of testing situations brought on by infirmity and memory loss and impatient relatives.

The angel Joshua enjoyed variety. Angels were not obliged to take human form but most of them involved with helping humans did so – some more often than others. It instilled an empathy that they may otherwise not have had.

Today, Joshua had been visiting his last earth mother. He had played a game with her – moving a bottle of chocolate sauce, his favourite ice cream topping, from the cupboard in the kitchen to his old bedroom. Ingrid had been alone in the house and when she saw the bottle on the little table beside his bed she had laughed out loud.

She couldn't see her son but he had let her know he was there. She picked up the bottle and cradled it to her heart. Huge sobs wracked her body, but she *was* comforted. The joke let her believe that Panos was happy where he had gone.

She knew she would see him again when she died.

She prayed for patience and help until that day came.

And she prayed that, when the new baby was born, she would be able to love it as much as every baby deserves.

The angel Joshua would be at hand to encourage that.

"Time for me to go," said Joshua. He and Gabriella said goodbye to each other. He had a different angel meeting to attend.

She watched as he took off from the beach at a sharp angle then with his great wings beating fast soared low over the sea. Gabriella smiled. This was Joshua's trademark take-off and preferred flight path. He said he liked to take in the view along the way.

As the fiery globe of the sun sank nearer to the horizon Gabriella, angel of Greece, stood alone and invisible to the human eye and waited.

Shortly, Jason came plodding slowly into view. His sagging shoulders reflected the gloom of his thoughts.

He had just come back from a humiliating visit to Hora. It seemed that every passer-by was covertly sniggering at him. It made his flesh crawl. It was easy to guess why, of course.

He had considered himself so clever. He had planned to enjoy a last summer of freedom then settle down and marry the girl he loved. Now he saw that he had played with fire and it had destroyed his dreams.

They had been precious dreams. *What a stupid reckless thing to do!*

His head had been turned by a pair of sparkling green eyes. A gorgeous exotic creature to be sure, but not someone who, through no fault of hers, could ever really be the life companion that he had always dreamed of. Gone from his life, he could now see that clearly. *Clare was a temptation I should have resisted.* Resisted because of his love and loyalty to Katarina. *Resisted because it would also have been the right thing to do for myself!*

His life now seemed empty and pointless. A mental picture of a pair of glistening golden eyes in a dear face sprang up. He imagined his hands gently cupping Katarina's lovely face, smoothing long thick shiny dark hair away from it and kissing sweet pink lips. He shook his head to send away the happy memory that now caused such pain.

He trudged along the rim of hard wet sand above the water's edge in the direction of the cliff at the far end. Caught up in his own misery he was hardly aware of his surroundings.

"Oh, Katarina, Katarina I was such a fool!"

"Yes, you did act foolishly."

He spun round looking for the girl who had just spoken to him. He was alone. Then it dawned on him. "Is that you, Gabriella?" His lips bunched with concentration as his eyes raked the beach.

"Yes, it is me," she said. As Gabriella suddenly made herself visible Jason jumped aside in shock. But the angel's smile reached right inside of him and calmed his fear. He found himself chuckling. "You look just like an ordinary girl again." Her own laugh was tinkling.

"Let us walk," she said, and side-by-side, they strode towards the cliff. After a few moments the angel spoke. "You feel bad and that is right." Her tone was gentle. She glanced sideways and held his gaze for a few seconds.

Jason nodded at her. He knew exactly what she meant.

Now.

Since her visit to him that night he had tried to be a better person. He thought about his father and his efforts to turn things around with him at the hotel.

"Yes." Gabriella nodded, reading his mind. "You have made a good start with your father. You have given him back his dignity and that is love in action."

Jason breathed a huge sigh of relief, feeling lighter. As they continued to walk, the wet sand turned rosy in rays of the setting sun. They had rounded the corner and were now on the far stretch of beach beside the cliff.

The sun sank to sit exactly on the rim of the horizon. Suddenly a loud sound of beaten air reached his ears. His head jerked up and he saw, to his amazement, angels winging in over the sea and cliff to congregate on the beach surrounding him and Gabriella. Then a thin towering angel with long dark hair appeared right at his side, which made him gasp and shut his eyes in momentary terror. "What the...?" he said, keeping his eyes tightly shut and even covering his face with his hands.

Then the assembled angels began to loudly clap their hands as if in applause. It soon became clear to Jason that it *was* applause.

Tentatively he dropped his hands from his face and opened his eyes.

The throng of angels continued to applaud for a little longer.

Then as one they smiled right at him. When he eventually began to smile back first one angel chuckled, then another, and another. Jason finally joined in and so did Gabriella and their combined laughter grew loud and hearty.

After enjoying this experience for some moments Gabriella thought it was time to explain it to Jason. "This is your guardian angel," she said, as the laughter petered away, pointing to the gigantic being at his side. Angel and man smiled at each other and then Jason gave him a little impromptu bow, which seemed fitting.

Gabriella continued. "And these are the guardian angels of

all those affected by your, shall we say, *poor choices*, before your change of heart."

A cowed Jason ran a self-conscious eye over them. "I'm very sorry," he muttered, toeing at the sand.

Gabriella began to point out some individual guardians. "That is your father's angel, your mother's, your grandmother's, Katarina's, Nikos' grandmother's, Gavin's... And so on."

A mortified Jason glanced at each in turn and nodded a "hello". They nodded back at him. Then they smiled at him and the laughter rose up again from the throng.

A contrite Jason bowed his head and felt forgiven.

Abruptly, the laughter ceased.

His head snapped upright.

Only Gabriella stood there. The other angels had vanished. He gasped at their disappearance which had startled him as much as their unexpected arrival.

He took a few moments to collect himself. Exhaling deeply, he looked at Gabriella. She was beaming at him. Though not every battle had been won, Jason's conversion was the triumph of her summer mission.

The angel's smile seemed like a benediction to Jason, and he basked in it.

"I have to go," she said at length.

"Before you do, I want to thank you for everything." Jason was humble. "I will be eternally grateful to you." They looked at each other meaningfully while the green flecks in his eyes danced and her grey irises shone.

She nodded and smiled. He felt there was more that she wanted to tell him. But then she simply said, "Goodbye, Jason."

"Uhh!" He gasped as the angel vanished. His heart thudded with shock. Then he chuckled and shook his head. "Goodbye, Gabriella," he muttered, wondering if he would ever see her again.

Chapter 46

Lost in reverie Jason was hardly aware of the sun finally slipping below the horizon, or the streaming crimson banners which replaced it. His mind was filled with the incredible things he had just witnessed. He shook his head in wonder before turning to walk back along the beach in the gathering gloom.

Reaching the tall cactus beside the little beach path leading to the minimarket his breath caught sharply in his chest. He stopped and stared.

Could it really be?

Yes! There was Katarina walking down the path with her dog, Hygeia. Her head was bent towards the animal talking to it.

"Katarina?" His voice was a hoarse whisper.

Her head shot up in surprise. "Jason!" Her hand flew to her throat. "Oh, you gave me a shock!"

"A nasty one or a happy one?" The question was spontaneous, yet all at once the answer was crucial.

He was the last person she had expected to meet on the deserted beach. Although her heart was racing with emotion she didn't know the answer to his question. As she studied his face his look became tender. But she was wary.

Hygeia trotted down the path, gave Jason's shoes a cursory sniff, and then bounded up the beach. Katarina automatically followed but as she passed Jason he reached out and caught her hand.

"I've missed you," he said sincerely. Her hand was limp in his. After all the heartache of the summer, all the tears she had cried, she would not hold onto him. She just would not!

"Katarina, I'm sorry." His tone was as abject as his expression. She tried to tug her hand away but he firmly held on. "Please forgive me," he pleaded.

"Forgive you!" Anger shot through her. She wrenched her hand free, stepped away and stood rigid, breathing raggedly.

"Katarina, I betrayed you. It was so wrong. And I'm so sorry."

As the words left his lips, he heard their ineffectuality echo in his ears.

Katarina's mouth twisted with bitterness.

She had wanted to hear those words.

Had waited to hear those words.

Had run over a make-believe version of this conversation in her head, time and time again.

But now her imaginings had come true, and she saw a broken Jason – as broken as the statue she had pictured – it filled her with contempt.

In the failing light he saw her contempt and it pierced him. Powerless he blurted, "I love you."

Katarina believed his words. He had asked her to marry him. They had begun to plan a life together. They had spoken of children. But after all that he had let a stranger come between them. He had made a mockery of their love! "Dear God," she screeched, "you love me, do you!"

Her stalker demon went wild with glee.

An invisible Gabriella winged in fast.

Fury snapped all self-control. Katarina struck out wildly at Jason's arms with both hands slapping and slapping until he grabbed her and pinned her against his chest.

Gabriella spoke up to Katarina's guardian angel who whispered urgent loving words to her ward.

Katarina continued to struggle in Jason's grip but he held on tight.

Finally, the girl began to listen to her angel instead of her demon.

Once that happened the fight drained away like water out of an unplugged basin. When she spoke it was with calm, curt authority. "Let me go," she insisted, and Jason instantly released her.

Jason, seriously shaken by Katarina's reaction, knew he

deserved it. He shook his head, lips pressed firmly together, nervous to say another word. But as the moments stretched out and she did not walk away he began to feel that maybe all was not lost, though he hardly dared believe it. He stared at her and couldn't hold back a smile. He was so pleased to be in her company again. His heart was full. "I love you," he murmured. Even if it made her angry again, he was powerless to stop his declaration.

But instead Katarina calmly looked upwards and watched the first stars spark into the black velvet sky. Her mind tumbled backwards over the long summer of sadness. In an attempt to overcome it she had finally thrown herself into the family business. And she had helped to make the season a success. When her family recognized her contribution, and eagerly fell in with her plans for rental rooms, she had been thrilled.

She lowered her eyes and noticed that the light of the moon was like a bolt of silver lamé unravelling over the smooth inky surface of the sea. It led like a shimmering pathway from the horizon straight towards her and Jason. Abruptly she turned away, unwilling to be influenced by the romantic setting. The unrelenting moonlight poured over them and cast a shadow, which stretched like long pointing fingers over the expanse of pale sand. A truth slipped into her mind. *I have always felt overshadowed by Jason!* He had set the rules of their relationship and she had gone along with him.

But that naïve acquiescent girl had disappeared.

She had grown up.

She took a deep strengthening breath and turned back to Jason. As she fixed her eyes on his she felt herself his equal.

When he squirmed beneath her cool gaze, she felt her power.

It was heady. She savoured it for a few moments.

But compassion for Jason's discomfort tugged at her heartstrings.

He saw the softening in her face. It gave him courage. "Do

you still love me?" His voice broke on the words.

Did she still love him? It was a question that deserved an honest answer.

A big part of her wanted *not* to love him.

But despite all the pain and despair of the summer she had to admit that she *did* still love him.

But!

She didn't trust him.

And she could not live the rest of her life walking on a sharp narrow edge waiting for the next time he betrayed her.

She shook her head.

Jason watched appalled. "Katarina! Katarina!" His face worked with emotion.

"I love you," she said, in a matter-of-fact tone. "But I can *never, ever trust* you again."

"You can!" His cry was emphatic. "You can trust me! I promise you can trust me!"

"Jason," she began, "how can I possibly trust you after what you did?"

Jason was speechless. He stared at her, his beloved. He licked his lips nervously while his mind became a maelstrom. How could he prove to her that he was now a different person? He shook his head. It seemed impossible.

Gabriella spoke to his guardian angel.

The guardian angel whispered into his ward's brain.

As the suggestion sank into his consciousness he gasped. *Yes! That is the answer.*

The three angels beamed at each other with delight.

"Katarina," Jason said gently but firmly. "I understand your mistrust but I promise you that I have changed." She noted that he now stood upright and confident. Unable to pinpoint why, she suddenly felt the despair within her transform into hope.

"Please," Jason continued, "take a walk with me now and let me tell you about something amazing and life-changing which happened to me this summer." He had been unable to confide in Clare. But this was his Katarina. He stretched out his hand and after a small hesitation Katarina held it.

Walking together slowly along the water's edge in the moonlight, Jason began to tell Katarina all about his meetings with the angel Gabriella and how it had changed him into a better person.

Gabriella and the two guardian angels grinned at each other. They all agreed it had been a good evening's work.

After a few more counselling words Gabriella announced that her mission was complete.

With crossed hands over upper torsos the trio of angels nodded farewell to each other. Then Gabriella stepped a few feet away from them, majestically unfurled her great span of wings, shot vertically into the sky, and disappeared from view.

The guardians chuckled. "I will miss working with her," they said in unison. But both knew that she would be back. Gabriella, the angel of Greece, would be working with them for as long as time itself continued.

Acknowledgements

Many thanks to Esther Griggs for camaraderie and lots of giggles in Corfu and Athens!

Deepest gratitude to Brett Syson, Renée and Robert Killian-Dawson, Janet Parkinson, Pauline Lewis, and Annie Outrim who, in that order, read the manuscript and passed along some excellent suggestions (heeded!) as well as great encouragement. And also to Noula Mouzakitis for setting up a writing workstation for me that winter in Corfu – which really helped things along.

Many thanks to friend and attorney Dimitris Zissimopoulos for encouragement with my writing as well as providing information about Greek law. The relevant law was a little complex so I did simplify procedure, and all errors (if there are any) are mine.

Big thanks for your friendship and support go to Susan Bruno, Gilly Charlemagne, Brenda Davis, Erica Evans, Joanie Gritsopoulos, Zeffie Klironomou, Dianne Microutsicos, Artemis Pappas, Sophia Periclakes, Rhian Stewart, and Mary Taylor. And to "the girls" Sandra Hill, Janet Motto, and Kath Wilks, and also Bev Lawrence – with the angels but always in our hearts.

A big thank you too to my aunty Doreen Price and cousin Rose Etta Wilkinson for your continued support and encouragement.

Many thanks also go to my highly talented singer/songwriter brother Kenny Driscoll for your support, and for simply being there.

Finally, I want to say another big thank you to my publisher, John Hunt, for your continued trust in my work, and to Dominic James at John Hunt Publishing Ltd. for your crucial part in this publication.

Author Biography

Born and raised in Cardiff, capital of Wales, Teresa spent a number of years in Athens, capital of Greece, working as a journalist and editor. She began and ended her personal Greek Odyssey on the island of Corfu. Now back in her native city she runs writing and spiritual growth workshops, as well as beavering away at her own writing.

In the Covid-19 lockdown she was kept sane by channelling the mishmash of emotions into this novel – a perfect method of escapism.

Previous titles

Non fiction

Pray Then Listen: A heart-to-heart with God, Circle Books, book and e-book.

This book was commissioned by God. "Write a book and show people how to speak to Me," He told the author. This is her work of obedience. Do you – as the author does – speak to God from your heart, listen for His reply, and do what He asks? By sharing experiences of Christ and Bible-based private prayers she shows how you too can have enlightening conversations with God.

In a spiritual journey build a close person relationship with Christ as together you explore your life-choices for a fresh start. Adapt the author's words for more intimate dialogue with God. Through simple meditations confide your troubles and listen expectantly for answers.

Overcome limiting fear and doubt by allowing Christ to guide you through the regular tests of daily life. These heart-to-hearts add greater meaning and purpose to all you do. This boosts self-confidence and resilience.

Providing foundational frameworks for prayer in the different seasons of life, this book will help us all move deeper in our relationship with God.

Andy Frost, Share Jesus International

9 Days to Heaven: How to make everlasting meaning of your life, O Books, book and e-book. Christian inspirational programme which uses nature and the senses for a back-to-basics examination of your faith in the company of God. This brings a new, life-enhancing perspective as you see yourself squarely in the context of Eternity.

This book is for people who do not yet know Christ, as well as those who want to know Him better. A simple and practical guide to joyful living.
Readers around the world have shared that it has helped them through very tough times; on occasion acting as a lifeline.
Others say it has enriched their life as it helped to deepen their relationship with Christ. Many also say that the enjoyable programme reduces stress levels considerably.
You can read more of this on Teresa's website: http://www. teresaodriscoll.co.uk

A wonderfully simple yet powerful way to reach what monks and mystics have sought for centuries: a deep, one-on-one communion with God.
John Backman, author of *Why Can't We Talk? Christian Wisdom on Dialogue as a Habit of the Heart*

A note from the author

Thank you for reading my debut novel, *Angel at the Paradise Hotel*. I hope that you enjoyed reading it as much as I enjoyed writing it!

If you have a few moments, please feel free to add your review to your favourite online sites for feedback. Also, I would really like to hear your comments on this and my other books so please do get in touch with me through my website https://www.teresaodriscoll.co.uk.

You can follow my blogs with the link on my website homepage.

With every good wish

Teresa

ROUNDFIRE BOOKS

FICTION

Put simply, we publish great stories. Whether it's literary or popular, a gentle tale or a pulsating thriller, the connecting theme in all Roundfire fiction titles is that once you pick them up you won't want to put them down.
If you have enjoyed this book, why not tell other readers by posting a review on your preferred book site.
Recent bestsellers from Roundfire are:

The Bookseller's Sonnets
Andi Rosenthal
The Bookseller's Sonnets intertwines three love stories with a tale of religious identity and mystery spanning five hundred years and three countries.
Paperback: 978-1-84694-342-3 ebook: 978-184694-626-4

Birds of the Nile
An Egyptian Adventure
N.E. David
Ex-diplomat Michael Blake wanted a quiet birding trip up the Nile
– he wasn't expecting a revolution.
Paperback: 978-1-78279-158-4 ebook: 978-1-78279-157-7

The Cause
Roderick Vincent
The second American Revolution will be a fire lit from an internal spark.
Paperback: 978-1-78279-763-0 ebook: 978-1-78279-762-3

Blood Profit$
The Lithium Conspiracy
J. Victor Tomaszek, James N. Patrick, Sr.
The blood of the many for the profits of the few… *Blood Profit$* will take you into the cigar-smoke-filled room where American policy and laws are really made.
Paperback: 978-1-78279-483-7 ebook: 978-1-78279-277-2

The Burden
A Family Saga
N.E. David
Frank will do anything to keep his mother and father apart. But he's carrying baggage – and it might just weigh him down ...
Paperback: 978-1-78279-936-8 ebook: 978-1-78279-937-5

Readers of ebooks can buy or view any of these bestsellers by clicking on the live link in the title. Most titles are published in paperback and as an ebook. Paperbacks are available in traditional bookshops. Both print and ebook formats are available online.

Find more titles and sign up to our readers' newsletter at http://www.johnhuntpublishing.com/fiction

Follow us on Facebook at https://www.facebook.com/JHPfiction and Twitter at https://twitter.com/JHPFiction